PAULINA BAKER

LOVE ME *not*

LOVE ME NOT

First edition. July 29, 2022.

Written by Paulina Baker.

Cover Design By: The Pretty Little Design Co.

Formatted by Jennifer Laslie

This book is proof that if you really want something, there is absolutely nothing that should stand in your way. (I almost gave up on writing so many times, and now look what you're about to read!)

Live your life where you'll never ask yourself
What If.

CHAPTER ONE

Brooke

She looked at him with hunger. She wouldn't back down until she got what she wanted. Ryle Anderson was the devil made by angels. How can someone so beautiful be such a douche? But Clara hoped–no, she knew she could make him go on his knees for her. She was a confident woman, not afraid of a challenge.

I stop typing on my laptop, and I take a sip of my wine. Confident? God, I wish I was confident, but it's all fiction, right? The characters in books are always confident and unafraid to speak their mind. Clara freaking Morris knows how to get men to bow to her feet, and here I am, sitting in my leggings and an oversized hoodie, writing a book about a woman who has it all. I'm not a writer, but I thought I'd give it a go. I love getting myself lost in others' realities where I can spend my days with handsome rich men and spend holidays in fucking Bora Bora. And when the book finishes, here I am again, in my tiny London apartment.

It's my love for books that pushed me into the world of editing. I finished my internship at Pandora Publishing, but it was a small company and I'm planning on going big. So I applied for a position as editor for Alstons House — The biggest publishing company in the UK.

I get up and walk to the kitchen to put the wine glass in the sink. The clock shows it is 1:30pm. They should have called by now if I got it, surely. I check my phone and I see a missed call from Aaron. Not sure how I missed that, but just when I'm about to call him back, an unknown caller rings me. Oh my god, is this it... is this them calling me, offering me a job? I quickly straighten myself and clear my throat before answering.

'Hello, Brooke Summers' speaking.' *Breathe woman, breathe.*

'Hi Brooke, this is Amanda from Alstons House. How are you?' She sounds cheerful, so surely it must be good news? The interview went ok; I think. The HR lady seemed friendly enough, and we just had a general chat about books and what I like to read, but she said they had hundreds of applicants, so as someone who has barely finished their internship, I don't see myself getting it. But, hey! A girl can dream, right? I'm only 25, so the world is my lobster... or is it oyster?

'I'm good, thank you. How are you?' My face is aching from the massive grin I'm faking to sound nice and happy. I am a cheerful person, but right now I have a large bile up my throat and I struggle to swallow.

'Also good, thank you. I'm sorry I'm calling you so late, but Mr. Alstons had a meeting I had to attend. But anyway... I am thrilled to offer you a full-time position for our editor role if you're still interested?'

Oh my god. Oh my god. Oh my god.

'Yes, of course! Thank you so much!' I scream into the phone and jump in joy.

'I've done your references from Pandora Publishing and they were sad to see you go, and only said amazing things about you. So are you ok to start tomorrow at 9am?'

'Tomorrow 9am it is.' I now have the most genuine grin on my face, teeth showing and all.

We finish the conversation and I quickly type out a message to Aaron.

Me- I GOT IT!!!

Within seconds, I get a reply.

Aaron- You go, girl! Let's celebrate at Fazzo.

Me- Sounds good!

Fazzo is this posh club where drinks are way overpriced and everyone is always overdressed, but it's also a perfect place to celebrate. Aaron has been my best friend since Uni and even though we're deep into our careers now, we still find time for each other. I just need to make sure I'm not out till late if I'm going to look presentable tomorrow morning.

'Nala girl. Come here.' I call my beautiful border collie, who comes running in with her wagging tail from my bedroom where she loves to nap. I fill her bowl and put it down for her before closing the laptop. Clara will have to wait with her story, as mine is about to begin.

I'm standing outside Fazzo, waiting for Aaron to appear, hugging myself to stay warm. Him being a journalist often means he works past his finish time and even during weekends I could find him writing, researching and watching news. I remember the first night of college. I headed to the library to check out what books they have and Aaron was already there, already doing his research for his first assignment. We got talking, and we started meeting up pretty much every day. Both of us were focused purely on our degrees instead of partying and the few parties we did attend, we left quickly as the 'getting drunk to unconsciousness' just wasn't our thing.

As for guys, I've had an occasional date or two, but males at college were pretty much about one thing only and as much as it was fun, I couldn't be bothered with the 2am booty calls. Aaron had a boyfriend in his first year, but then he ended up moving to South Africa as a nurse to help the less fortunate. Aaron tried to understand because how can you be angry with someone for deciding to help others? He was still very much heartbroken, and I was there to pick up the pieces. After uni, I got my internship with Pandora Publishing and got my little apartment outside the city centre. The neighbourhood wasn't anything amazing, but it did just fine for me.

'I'm so sorry, Brooke. My parents called again and they wouldn't stop talking.' Aaron calls as he reaches me by the entrance. His parents call often, wishing their only son would move back to Cornwall to be close to them again, but he loves London just as much as I do. The city life here is just something else. If you live in London, you've pretty much seen it all. I once saw a guy almost get hit by a bike as he was on his phone and instead of moving back to the pavement, the idiot took a step further into the road and got hit by the cab. Ouch.

'That's fine. I haven't been here long myself.'

'Love the new dress, chick.' I look at my short, black, leather dress that's tight and revealing and smile to myself as I bought it to start a new chapter in my life where I love myself and no one else.

'Thank you. It is pretty badass.' He smiles at me and we go inside. We take the last 2 seats by the bar between a group of guys in suits who are drinking and laughing about something and a group of young girls who are having a time of their lives, or at least it looks that way as they have a couple of guys chatting them up.

I order my sex on the beach cocktail and Aaron orders himself a mojito. We have a quick catch up about our day and

I tell him Nala sleeps more throughout the day now. She's a border collie I rescued from a shelter just after my recent breakup because I finally could. I always loved animals but my ex was allergic, so I had to say goodbye to my dream of owning a pet. But now that I'm a free woman, I do things I want to do without asking for permission. She's an elderly dog, and that's probably the reason she had no interest in the rescue. People prefer puppies at the end of the day, but the moment I saw her eyes, I knew she needed me and I needed her. I knew we wouldn't have much time together, but considering she's a 15-year-old dog, she still has the energy of her breed.

'So, are you excited about your new job?' Aaron asks as he takes a sip of his drink.

'Of course. You know how much I've been dreaming of working with books and now I'll be helping authors achieve their dreams. Doesn't get better than that.' I grin at him as he knows exactly how much I've been wanting this job, especially for the biggest publisher company in the UK as well.

'Maybe between time, you'll be able to work on your book too and maybe Mr. Alston will publish it too,' He winks at me and I know he's trying to be supportive but maybe I'm not cut out to be an author. Aren't you meant to be writing what people want to read? What if they don't want to read my stories? It feels way too stressful for me.

'I don't know. Maybe I'm not good enough to be published.' I shrug as I glance over Aaron's shoulder at the young women, who are giggling like little girls. I can't even remember what it was like to have a stress-free life.

'You are good enough. I read some of your work and I would definitely buy it if I saw it in the shop.' He's more serious now. He doesn't like when I doubt myself, which I do a lot, but he loves me either way.

'£100 for a book then.' I watch him with a smug on my face.

'Only if you sign it.' He puts out his hand to make the deal with me.

I sit up straight, 'Deal.' and we shake hands.

We spend the night either dancing or drinking at the bar. It's always fun to be out with Aaron, as he's such a free spirit. Journalism is a perfect job for him, but he's hoping to have a free rein soon so he can write about what he wants. By the time we're having our... 5th or is it a 6th cocktail? Aaron brings up the subject that I very much dislike.

'Ok girl, now it's time for the truth. How long has it been since your kitty cat had some serious attention?' Oh, dear lord...

'Do we really have to talk about my sex life tonight? In the public?' I think the group of men behind me must have heard us as they suddenly went rather quiet and the man sitting right behind me seemed to stiffen. Or maybe I am wrong and they're just talking about something very serious between themselves. Not that I'm paying any attention to them. I have paid no attention to men lately. Maybe that's a problem?

'Brooke. You know I love you, but it's been almost 6 months since you've had sex and I really feel you need some fun. Wouldn't it be great to shake off that douche tonight just before starting a new job?' Well, he's got a point, but after so many drinks I really don't know what I'm doing and probably shouldn't be trusted, in case I bring a serial killer home, or worse.... an accountant.

'Please, let's change the subject,' I plea as I take the last sip of my cocktail. 'Let's dance.' I grab his hand and pull him onto the dance floor. We dance for about a minute before Aaron shuffles closer to my ear and says,

'I think the guy who was sitting behind you is checking you out.'

I turn my head, but he's busy talking to others and I can't see his face. It's probably some mind games Aaron is trying to play to get me to talk to him.

I ain't falling for that, mister.

'I very much doubt it.' I look back at Aaron and shake my head. Suddenly, his eyes widen in horror as he looks just past my shoulder.

'I think we should go,' He says and so I turn around to see what's going on and right there, walking in, I see Tyler, looking right back at me. Fuck. No. I'm out of here. I turn back to Aaron and nod in agreement, but before we can start walking, someone grabs me by my wrist.

'Brooke, please talk to me,' Tyler looks down at me, pain in his eyes. What a great actor.

'Let go of me now,' I snap, trying to pull my arm free. Tyler was the love of my life, or at least that's what I thought until about 5 months ago. Been together for 2 years, and I even ended up moving in with him. All going great, I mean, who wouldn't want to date a hot musician who knew how to sing himself into your heart? I've attended all his gigs and met all of his friends. But just when I thought we might reach the engagement chapter of our lives, I found him in our bed, tongue deep in some random chick's pussy. Long story short, I moved out the same day, got my own little place, and decided to never trust another man again. What is it with them and sex? Is it in their DNA to be as horny as they can and not care who they do it with? Maybe I should switch sides. Surely women aren't as bad as men?

'Please. You can't keep ignoring me. I'll do anything, Brooke. Please give me a chance.' He steps forward, being inches away from me and I can smell his Diesel cologne, which I used to love so much. But now it makes my stomach turn in disgust. A flash of memory shows in front of my eyes, me running to our bedroom, hoping for a nice evening with my boyfriend, only to find some blonde slut spread across our bed, blindfolded while his head was between her legs and the sound of her moans filling our room. I'm going to throw up. I need to think quickly if I want to escape.

'I'm here with someone,' I snap without thinking it through. What have I done?

His eyes widen in shock and... fear, is it? Hard to say based on how many drinks I've had.

'Who?' He asks. Anxiety spurts through me when I look at Aaron and he looks as confused as I feel. He has no plan, so it's completely up to me.

Then I remember the guy sat behind me. If Aaron was right, maybe he'd be willing to help?

Oh god, no.

But I think he is my only hope.

'He's at the bar with his friends, so excuse me, but we better go back and join them.' I yank my arm free of his grip and his face reddens with anger. Using my other hand, I gesture to Aaron to follow me and as he does, I head towards nicely suited men and I pray to God this works and that they're not gonna blow my cover. I can feel Tyler's gaze burning on my back, so I put my hand on the man's shoulder, who was sitting right behind me, and he looks up.

Oh. my. God. He is a man out of a book, alright? His deep brown eyes look right at me and a line between his brows forms. I'm giving him please help me look and then I smile and sit on his lap. Fuck me. What am I doing?

'Hi baby, I'm back.' And I kiss him. Yes, I kiss a stranger. I put my hands around his neck to make it look realistic and, oddly, he kisses me back. I'll thank him later. He puts his hands on my waist and I feel what I can only describe as an electric shock shooting down my spine from his touch. The heat pulses between my legs when he pulls me closer.

I guess it has been a long time.

He is a pretty damn good kisser, too, which isn't helping. I clench my legs and I think he can tell, as I swear I can sense him smiling through the kiss. Boy, I haven't been touched in a while and now I'm here, kissing a stranger, wondering what it'd be like to have him between my legs. A scent of whisky enters my nostrils and at this moment, I realise I don't want to break this kiss that is making me melt on his lap. Hang on. Is that...? Oh my god, he's hard. I can feel his erection under my ass. Brooke, stop this. You're losing all control. Stop. This.

I pull away quickly, eyes wide open and he looks at me... disappointed? I look around and see all his friends and Aaron staring at us as if we just had sex in front of them. Tyler is gone when I look in the direction where he was. I can't see him anywhere. Snapping back to my fake date, I say, 'I'm... I'm really sorry about that.' My eyes drop to his tasty lips, wishing I could taste them again. I take him fully in now. His dark, short hair with a slight curl on top and stubble, which is so sexy. He's well built, broad shoulders, tight muscles I can see underneath his suit. I then realise I'm still sitting on his lap with my arms around his neck. I definitely had way too much to drink. He hadn't pushed me off, so I jump off quickly.

'Thank you. And I'm sorry again.' I stare into his dark brown eyes and he looks like he's about to say something, but before he does, I turn on my heel and walk away. I don't even check if Aaron is behind me, and I'm not in the mood to get into a conversation why I did what I did. As I exit the club, within seconds, Aaron is beside me. All I feel is shame, and I know the fake kiss sobered me right up.

'What the hell was that?!' Aaron shouts to me, shocked at what I've just done. I was never a woman to just hook up with anyone.

'Aaron, please don't. I... I don't know why I did that, but I couldn't speak to him. I hate him and that's the only way out I saw.' He put his hand on my shoulder as I look down, not wanting to see the judgement in his eyes.

'I don't blame you. Sorry I didn't know what to do either and to be honest,' He pauses, so my gaze lifts to meet his, and he offers me a smile. 'At least you got the hook up we talked about.' And he laughs. I slap him in the arm and join in with the laughter. It was probably one of the best kisses I've ever had, so I guess I can say it was worth it. I pull out my phone to check the time and fear shoots through my body.

'Oh, my god it is so late! I need to get home so I don't look like a zombie in the morning!' Before I can look at Aaron, he runs out to the street and stops the first taxi driving by. This man isn't afraid of anything. I laugh at him and as he opens the door for me, I quickly jump in.

CHAPTER TWO

Brooke

The alarm buzzes and at this moment I know for 100%, I had way too much to drink. Who the hell gets drunk the night before their first day at work? Oh right—I do. I cancel the alarm and push the covers off me. My head is pounding and my throat is so dry, it feels like I've spent months in a desert without a drink, but I push through it and head to the kitchen to grab some paracetamol. I down half a bottle of water and it already feels much better, but I know I'm going to regret last night's actions for the rest of the day. When I get back to my room, I look in the mirror that's hanging at the back of my door, and decide a heavier make up will be required today. I also see my bedside table through the mirror, and the flashback from the club pops up in my mind as I stare at my pink vibrator.

This guy.

This kiss.

I got back home so horny that I needed some self-love session and yet it didn't feel like it was enough. My finger trails over my bottom lip as I remember the whisky with the mint taste of his lips. The arousal is taking over once again, so I shove the memory to the back of my mind and go for a shower. I hope this day goes well.

2 hours later, I arrive at the office. A cold shower did the trick, and I am ready to conquer the world. Well, maybe not the world, but I'm ready to smash my first day at work. I come up to the reception area and a beautiful woman with blonde, curly hair and make-up on point looks up at me and offers me a warm smile.

'Good morning, welcome to Alstons Publishing. How can I help you?' She says cheerfully, and it immediately puts me at ease.

'Hi,' I reply and smile back at her, 'My name is Brooke, and it's my first day as an editor here.'

'Oh, Brooke, yes!' She stands up quickly and we shake hands.

'My name is Tess and I work here at the reception, as you probably guessed.' I like her. She's warm and friendly and absolutely stunning. I look at her grey pencil dress, which shows off her curves and suddenly my self-esteem drops as I look at my flats, grey trousers and a white shirt. Maybe I should have left my hair down, but I always found a ponytail more comfortable. Well, I'm not here to impress anyone anyway, so it really shouldn't matter how I dress.

Tess then takes me to the 6th floor where editors' offices are, and she shows me to mine. It is nice and cozy, with plenty of sunlight with a big window behind the desk, not too big and not too small.

'Amanda from HR is gonna pop over soon and talk you through things here, so just settle down while you wait. There's a break room on the left from your door which has a coffee machine.' Tess tells me and I thank her for her help. Once she leaves, I put a framed photo of Nala on my desk. When we are not together, I miss her but I know she is ok. I got an app on my phone where I can watch what she's doing, plus I got a dog walker who will take her out twice a day. Taking a glance at my phone, I see her sleeping on the sofa which makes me smile to myself.

Knock. Knock.

'Come in.' I call out, expecting to see Amanda, but a man appears at the door. Quite handsome, maybe late 20s, early 30s. Broad shoulders and tall. Blonde hair and blue eyes. Looks like the type of guy that every girl in the office would dribble over.

'Alright?' He nods with a smile. 'I'm Justin. One of the editors here.' I stand up and go to shake his hand with a smile. 'Brooke.'

'Brooke? Not a very English name.' He smirks at me.

'No. I was born in Los Angeles. My mum is English and moved to be with my dad, but after he passed away, she moved us back here to be close to her family.' I explain. My mum was born and raised in Suffolk but there are many lengths you'd go to, to be with your true love, even if you weren't a massive fan of America.

'Oh, sorry to hear that.' I hate how uncomfortable it makes people when I say my dad died.

'That's fine. It happened a long time ago, so it's ... it's ok.' I smile and try to change a subject.

'So, do you know where I can get some coffee here?' He smiles again and gestures for me to follow him.

We get ourselves coffee in the break room and grab a brownie each from the tray left by the fridge. The room is warm and welcoming, with settee and armchairs on one side with a kitchenette on the other side.

'Mr. Alstons more often than not gets us some snacks for each floor. Sometimes it's muffins, cake, or brownies.' Justin explains.

'That's very nice of him.' I know very little about the man himself other than how hard he worked to open this business and how quickly it became successful. One might say pure luck, another might say he worked his ass off.

'I think they ranked him number 1 best employer in the UK

last year.' Oh, I must have missed that. Maybe I should do some research on him, in case I ever have to speak to him.

'So, what genres do you read?' I ask, trying to get to know my new colleague.

'Sci-fi fiction, mostly. How about you? No. Let me guess.' He rubs his fingers over his chin. 'You're a romance reader.'

'Born and raised.' I say while raising my cup of coffee and we both chuckle.

I was in my office for about 20 minutes before Amanda came knocking on my door. I had it explained how they expect me to work, in what time frame I'm expected to finish each project, and just things like that. She's different from other people I met so far... Very formal. She said she was a workaholic and, in general, wasn't overly interested in socializing with other people.

'There's one more thing,' Amanda adds. 'Mr. Alstons likes to meet all his employees, so he might visit you this afternoon. Word of warning, he might be a kind employer, but make sure you look busy. You know, first impressions and that.' She smiles and my hands start to sweat. Meet Mr. Alstons on my first day? Am I dressed correctly for that? What if he doesn't like me and fires me on the spot? No, surely he wouldn't do that. Would he?

Amanda sees the photo of Nala and excitement fills her eyes.

'You've got a dog?' She asks keenly.

'Yes. This is Nala. I rescued her a couple of months ago.' I pick up the frame and pass it to her so she can take a better look.

'She's beautiful.'

'Thank you. Do you have any pets?' Amanda frowns at my question.

'I wish. My working hours don't allow me to be at home that much, so it wouldn't be fair to any animal to be left alone.' She puts the photo back on the desk.

'You know, I have a dog walker taking Nala out twice a day.

She's an elderly dog, so she spends most of her day asleep, anyway.' This seemed to get Amanda's interest. I spent about 10 minutes talking to her about different rescues and how older dogs tend to not find their last families. It's one topic I love talking about. Animals are my side passion and I'd happily follow Betty White's footsteps and volunteer at like a shelter or something.

After Amanda leaves, I take a quick peek at my phone to see what Nala is doing. She should be back from her first walk now.

Oh, there she is.

She's sitting right in front of the camera and staring right at me, her eyes looking red thanks to the flash. Creepy. It's only a view camera, so I can't talk to her, but she looks as if she knows I'm here. I smile at my phone and then Nala's eyes just slightly widen. As I start to get worried, she lets out the biggest fart I've ever heard from the dog. My eyes widen in horror as I watch her turn around and go to the sofa for her nap. I am so thankful I'm not there to smell that. I roll my eyes and laugh to myself.

It's now after lunch. My manager gave me a script for a new rom-com this morning to work on. He's a nice guy, mid-40s maybe, married with 2 kids and a labrador named Ted.

Yes, I'll probably know all about everyone's pet by the end of the week.

I start on chapter 1 and it already sounds good. A woman traveling by plane is seated next to this gorgeous man in a suit.

Man in a suit?

My thoughts go back once again to last night, remembering his smell and taste. Butterflies flutter in my stomach just at the thought of his hands on me. I clench my legs as I feel the pulsing sensation between them.

Brooke, stop it! You'll never see this guy again. This was a one-night thing and now you have to carry on with your life as if you've never met him.

I look at the clock and it's 2 pm now. Maybe I should

google Mr. Alstons quickly before he comes here so I don't look like an idiot. I type in his name and it's taking a long time to load. Someone knocks on my door.

Fuck. I'm too late.

'Come in,' I call out and my body freezes, eyes widen in horror as I look at the man I kissed so passionately just last night. I stand up quickly from my chair, my hands sweating, and my body trembling.

'What... What are you doing here?' I demand and I'm shocked as he doesn't look surprised in the slightest that it's me sitting here. Has he been looking for me?

'I came to see you.' He gives me a flirty smirk.

Oh god, the butterflies are back.

I look at his lips and wonder what they'd taste like today.

No. I straighten myself.

'Are you a stalker?' Because how else would he find me here?

'A stalker?' His eyes narrow, and he looks me up and down. 'Let's sit down.' He gestures to my chair, and he sits down on the one on the other side of my desk. Elbows now resting on armrests while he puts his hands together and holds them in front of him. My stomach drops as I glare at him, not knowing what to do. Do I call security? What does he want from me? He gestures to my chair again for me to sit down and I decide it's best to do what he asks while I figure this out. My eyes glance at the screen and now my whole body pauses and I feel I'm about to be sick as I see the google search has now fully loaded, with the top of the page showing me photos of Mr. Alstons... Mr. Alstons who is also sitting in front of me right this moment.

'Oh, my god.' An involuntarily gasp leaves my mouth. 'I'm... you're...we...' I do not know what I'm saying, but he's still just sat there, watching me, waiting for me to say or do something.

'I... I didn't know.' I shake my head. How the hell would I know that the man I kissed in that club would turn out to be my fucking boss? He doesn't stop smirking at me and it makes me anxious.

Did he know? Of course, he didn't. Did he?

'Did you know?' I choke out, and take a deep breath in, catching him looking at my lips just for a second before returning his eyes back to mine.

'No. And let's be honest, even if I did, you didn't exactly give me a chance to tell you that, did you?' I look down at the desk, feeling so embarrassed. My cheeks are burning and he can probably tell as he lets out a quiet chuckle.

'Am I... fired?' I look back at him.

'Fired? This is your first day, so why would I fire you?' His eyes narrow again, looking very confused, trying to understand my thoughts.

'Well, this was very unprofessional. You're my boss and I kissed you out of the blue so I guess...' I take a pause, not wanting to say it, but I have no choice. 'If you want to fire me, then I'll understand'

He says nothing at first, his gaze remaining on my lips and his jaws clenches. I feel like he's deep in thought—completely zoned out. His eyes snap back to mine, and then he smirks again. God, this man is absolutely gorgeous. I clench my legs because just the way he looks at me does something to my core. I think I'm gonna need a change of underwear at this point. What I'd do right now to come up to him and sit on his lap just like I did last night and push my fingers through his hair. To feel his lips on my neck and breast. To feel his erection underneath me once again and then he'd free his cock so he could slide it inside me and fuck me, right here, on the chair he's currently sitting on.

'Miss Summers?' Mr. Alstons calls and I realize what just happened.

'You seem to have zoned out.' The warmth of his smile echoes in his voice.

'Sorry. What were you saying?' I try to remain professional, but my eyes keep going from his eyes to his hair, to his chest. I know he can tell that's what I'm doing.

'I said I can keep my personal and professional life separate. That night, it happened. You weren't one of my employees then, and we didn't know each other.' He now stands up, putting his hands into his trousers pockets, and wanders to the window. 'I like the view from this side of the office.' He adds and when I turn on my chair, I see him looking at the London Bridge. It is a beautiful view from here.

'I agree.'

He turns to look at me. 'About the view or the personal life?'

'I'm... em... both?' I'm not sure what the right answer to this would be. As I'm about to stand up and join him by the window, he takes a few steps towards me. Butterflies are going crazy now, my insides twisting, my core burning as he leans forward and puts his hands on my armrests.

'I very much enjoyed that kiss. It was unexpected, but very fucking hot.' He groans out as he looks at my lips. I feel goosebumps rising all over my body, my pussy pulsing, wanting him to touch it, to touch me.

'I'm looking forward to getting to know you better, Miss Summers.' He winks at me and stands up straight. He nods in a goodbye kind of way and leaves my office.

What the hell just happened?

CHAPTER THREE

Gabriel

I sit at my desk and pull the phone out of my pocket. Scrolling down through contacts, I find the name I'm looking for, and I press the dial.

'Gabe?' Max's voice sounds through the speaker.

'Maxie boy, how are you doing, mate?' Max has been my rock throughout my adult life, and no one knows me better than him. We met at one conference in New York and we've been best buddies since. He's also the guy who was with me at the club last night.

'Alright, how can I help?'

'I found her.' I rub my hand over my face, still trying to get over what had just happened.

'You... seriously?' He's as surprised as I expected. Of course, when I told him I need to find her last night, he knew I'd get someone on the job and he wouldn't have thought that I'd have found her the next day.

'So... who is she?' His interest peaked now.

'Brooke Summers. She's the new editor in my company.' I say, amused.

'No fucking way!' He snorts out, 'So now you can't do anything or she'll accuse you of sexual harassment.' He laughs on the other side of the line and I roll my eyes.

'Let me remind you, she's the one who jumped on my lap and kissed me like there was no tomorrow.'

'No need for a reminder. I still have that scene play out in my head.'

'Perv.' We both laugh now. But truth be told, I haven't stopped thinking about her from the moment she pulled away from me, her eyes searching mine, looking me up and down, so I guessed she had no idea what I looked like. I wasn't some kind of bucket list kiss, but I'm pretty sure I know the reason. After watching her all night, listening to her voice, her addictive laugh, and how cute she sounded when she was snorting. I knew when I saw that guy come up to her and her whole body tensing, trying to pull away, that he was trouble. Her ex, maybe? Then I saw her turn and head in my direction so I stopped looking and when she jumped on my lap and said that magical 'Hey baby.' I knew she needed help to get rid of the guy. But then something else happened. What was meant to be one fake kiss to help her get rid of some guy led me to fight for control, my hard erection pushing against her ass, my lips wanting to taste more of her. I didn't even know the woman and my body was betraying me. Her sweet lips tasting of her cocktail, her long brown hair I just wanted to grip in my hand and pull on them to give me access to her neck. And when she pulled away, I wanted to pull her close again and take her to my place and fuck her all night long. It took my entire strength to stop myself from doing just that, and when I looked into her baby blue eyes, all I saw was pain. She apologized immediately and just like that, she left.

'Gabe, I've got a meeting in 5 so I'll catch you later, alright?'

'Ok. See you.' I hang up and pull out the CCTV again of this morning and watch the entrance as Brooke first came in. I couldn't believe it when I saw this footage earlier today. Lucky stars must be shining down on me today. I was going to hire a PI to find out everything about her, because when your whole body burns for a stranger, you just need to find out more about her. But there she was... coming to me. I didn't know if she knew who I was back at the club, but when I saw her expression when I walked into her office today, I knew–she had no idea who I was.

It's almost 6 pm now. I pull out Brooke's file to read through it. Brooke Summers. Age 25, which makes her 7 years younger than me. Born in LA and moved to the UK when she was 16, went to the University of London, and has two degrees in English Lit and Writing. This isn't enough. I want to know more.

I look at the CCTV cameras again and click on the 5th floor. All the lights are off, including Brooke's office. I guess it is late now. When I pick up my phone, I go to the app. I smile as I see a tail on the floor in the corner of my screen.

Time to go home.

CHAPTER FOUR

Brooke

I take a sip of my hot coffee and I glance to see Nala already napping on the sofa after her morning walk. Closing my eyes, I take a deep breath, trying to calm down my nerves. Mr. Gabriel Alstons. Unlucky stars must be shining down on me. I sigh as I look at the clock—8:15 am. It's my second day at my new job which was a dream come true but how can it be now, after I forced my tongue down my boss' throat?

Oh, the shock that came over me when I realized who the man standing in my office actually was. The embarrassment. But also the way he looked at me, amused, and when I caught him looking at my lips. Did he... want it to happen again? I, of course, remember how hard he got, but wouldn't any guy get hard just by kissing a woman? My office filled with the scent of whisky and mint, and when he came closer to me and told me that the kiss was hot, I could feel my cheeks burning. It'll probably be best for me to avoid him from now on.

My phone pings on the dining table, so I take a quick glance and see a message from Tyler.

Tyler- Please let's talk, hun. I miss you.

I don't bother replying to this. 5 months since I left him, and I spent the first month under my duvet, crying while Aaron did his best to cheer me up.

He's a dick who doesn't deserve you- he'd say. And after about a month, I truly believed that. I wanted a life that I deserved. So off I went and adopted my beautiful Nala, and found a fine apartment near to my current job now. Why the fuck did I think I'm in this life to please him and not myself? I'm the main character in my fucking story. End of. From now on, I'll only do things that make me happy.

I sit at my desk, making some more edits when my phone pings. A smile forms on my face when I see the name of my favourite person.

Aaron- Hi babe, how's your second day going?

Me- Good. I haven't seen him yet, so big success.

We had a lengthy phone call last night when I told him all about my new boss, but somehow, he just found it amusing. A shaky breath leaves my mouth. Would I want to see him? Yes. Should I want to see him? Definitely not. I don't know what it is about him that has me melting when he looks at me.

Aaron- Or maybe you should see him and have a quickie on your desk. ;)

Oh. my. God.

Me- Aaron!!

Aaron- Yeah, yeah... But I know what I saw on Saturday. That guy was totally into you.

Me- Even if he was, I am not.

Aaron- Whatever helps you sleep at night, hun. Lunch at yours this weekend?

Me- Sounds good.

I put my phone down and pull out an internet search, typing in Gabriel Alstons, as I haven't even had a chance to read anything after he left my office yesterday.

Gabriel Alston. At only age 22, he opened his own publishing company. Started only as self employed, he quickly was forced to hire more people to meet demands of his clients. He then ended up buying the building where his office currently is. At merely age 18, he started investing all the money he could earn and now, thanks to all his profits, he's the youngest self-made millionaire only at an age of 26. Now being 32, not only he owns his publishing company, he also owns multiple buildings across the country. Gabriel Alstons is still a bachelor even after being seen with multiple models and actresses. Maybe he just hasn't met his genuine match yet.

I close the tab. Don't need to know anymore. I am definitely not his type if he goes out with models and actresses, so maybe it was just a fun game he played when he came to see me. With nothing to offer him, I exhale loudly and tilt my head back, my elbows resting on armrests of my chair.

Why do I have to be attracted to womanizers?

There's a knock on my door.

'Come in.'

Tess' head pops in. 'It's lunchtime. Do you wanna come and grab something together?' She smiles and I still can't get over how gorgeous she is. She is the type of woman Mr. Alstons would date.

'Sure.' I stand up and grab my purse.

We wait for the elevator and as we enter; I turn around and stop in place when I see him. Mr. Alstons walking right toward my office. My stomach drops and I feel a shiver across my back as he knocks on my door. He's looking for me? Just as he's about to turn around, the elevator door closes, and I sigh in relief.

'What do you think he wanted?' Tess asks which means she saw the same thing I just did. I try to come up with a lie.

'Maybe he wanted to check up on how I'm settling in. You know, to see if I deserve this job.'

'I don' think so. He never checks on his employees unless they're past deadlines. Maybe...' she thinks.

'Maybe what?' I frown and hope she doesn't catch on with anything that happened between us.

'Maybe he likes you.' She grins at me like a teenage girl and I snort, shaking my head.

'Stop it. He definitely does not like me.'

'And how would you know that?'

'Well, I don't but...' To my rescue, the elevator stops and the door opens.

'Where shall we go?' I ask to change the subject.

We ended up going just across the road to the little coffee shop.

'What are you getting?' Tess asks. I carefully look at the menu and it all sounds delicious. We're next in line and my stomach begs the people in front of me to hurry.

'Three cheese panini sounds good.'

'Oh yes, it is amazing. I'll probably go for a chicken salad.' And at that moment, my self-esteem deflates again. Should I order a salad too?

'Maybe I'll get one too, then.' I think she can sense a shift in me because then she adds,

'No, definitely try the panini. You'll be in heaven.' I nod. I also order a raspberry tea and Tess gets herself a caramel frappuccino. As we get our food and drinks, we take a seat by the window, grabbing two comfy armchairs instead of stools.

'I like it here,' I comment while glancing around. The whole place feels cozy, with its warm tones and music playing in the background. Let's not forget the smell of the bakes goodies that makes your mouth water. I could sit here all day. It's not too busy, only a handful of other people here, but it's big enough that we're not right next to each other.

'It's quite a gem, isn't it? I came here on my first day, and now it's my favorite place for lunch if I don't order one for delivery.' Turning my head to the side, I look at the building and read in big shiny letters the words Alstons House. I can't believe he owns this building.

'Brooke?' I snap back and look at Tess. I must have zoned out.

'Sorry, what did you say?' I take a sip of my tea and feel the liquid warm up my insides on this chilly November day.

'What do you think about the panini?' She repeats herself as she takes a bite of her salad. I take a bite of my sandwich and my eyes widen, letting a quiet moan of pleasure escape. Tess laughs. This must be the best panini I have ever eaten.

'Food orgasm, right?' She's still chuckling.

'Hell yeah,' I look down at the panini I'm holding and Tess speaks again.

'I need to find a guy who will look at me the way you look at that panini' We both giggle now and other customers shoot their stares right at us.

'I like you.' Tess confesses with a smile.

'I like you too.' I smile back.

'Tell me more about yourself.' She asks and I guess that is a part of a conversation with a person you don't really know. I tell her everything. About me growing up in LA and the reason behind moving back here and how much I love books. I don't tell her about my night at the club with my boss, though.

'Your turn.' I exclaim, and I finish the last piece of heaven on my plate.

'Well, I was born and raised in London. My parents are both doctors, but I try to be independent. You know, without their financial help, even though they try to help me. They are very supportive, too. Doctors' daughter being a receptionist is not exactly a dream come true for them, but I've done an art designing course at uni. I hope to be a cover designer for Mr. Alstons' company one day.' She turns and frowns when she looks at our workplace building. 'I am single and have been single for a year now. I'm very picky with boyfriends. They need to be ambitious and get my motors running just right.' She winks, and I chuckle. I can think of one person who got my motor running just right, but I don't say it aloud. 'I live alone and I guess my hobbies are going to the gym and binge-watching Netflix.'

'Favourite series on Netflix?' She looks up and looks like she's thinking hard.

'You.' she answers after a brief pause.

'You?' I watch a little tv. Is she saying me?

'Yes. The series is called You. It's about a stalker trying to find his true love and oh boy, does he find her... and her name is Love.'

'Her name is Love, and she's the stalker's true love?' I frown.

That's confusing.

'You need to watch it.' She orders.

'I will.'

An hour later, I'm back at my office, watching Nala sleep on my phone. It's just a quick check-in before I go back to editing. I love this girl so much. As I watch her, a memory springs to mind.

'Hey babe,' I say to Tyler, as he sits on the sofa with his feet on the table, while I'm sitting next to him.

'Sup?' He answers coldly and takes a sip of his beer.

'What do you think about getting a dog?' I ask nicely, hoping he'll say yes and I play with his hair the way he loves it.

'Can't. I'm allergic.' I narrow my eyes at him and the anger pools in my chest.

'But your sister has a dog, and you never had a reaction.' He now turns to me, frowning.

'Are you calling me a liar?'

'Of course not!' I take my hand out of his hair. 'I just thought it'd be nice to have a dog. There are dogs with hair which are hypoallergenic.' I add, hoping to change his mind. I know he's not allergic. We've been together for two years and not once have I seen him get a reaction to a dog.

'I'm allergic to all types of dogs.' He replies blankly as he turns back to the tv and takes another sip of his beer. I give up.

I close the app and think I might get Nala a pupcake on my way home today. A sudden knock makes me jump, and I pause, hoping it's not the person I think it might be, behind this door.

'Come in.' I call out while my heart picks up the speed. Please be someone else. Please be someone else.

John, my manager, appears at the door, and I exhale with relief.

'Boy, you look like you're about to be murdered.' He snorts out.

'Har har. So funny' I roll my eyes and smile at him. 'How can I help?'

'I've just had a phone call from Mr. Alstons. He wants you

to come by his office before you leave today.' My smile slowly fades away.

Shit.

CHAPTER FIVE

Gabriel

Standing by the window, I watch people rushing places, walking with purpose, men wearing suits and carrying their briefcases, talking on their phones. Isn't it funny how we're all programmed from such a young age to believe a career is going to fulfil our lives? That we must get good grades and get into excellent schools and get high-paying jobs to be happy. I mean, I'm not complaining about my wealth, but I wouldn't thank my teachers for it. As a teenager, I did odd jobs here and there, helping neighbours with their gardens or washing their cars. I knew straight away I wanted out of my current life. I watched tv and read books on how to become rich. My foster parents always complained about expenses that involved me and how much they wish they didn't take me in. I knew then I needed more so I could help others. So the moment I started earning my money, I saved it all up, and then my neighbour, Mr. Warne, who was a financial advisor, helped me to invest it.

A knocking sound comes from the door to my office. I turn around and undo the button of my jacket as I call out,

'Come in.' I lean back on the windowsill.

A beautiful brunette with her baby blue eyes enters.

'You... wanted to see me... sir?' She asks with a shaky voice. Is she nervous?

'Yes, Miss. Summers. Please have a seat.' I gesture to the chair on the other side of my desk and I move to sit down, too. Her body is tense, and she's looking at anything else other than me, which tells me she's uncomfortable. Is she that shy around all people? As she sits down, her gaze finally meets mine and I offer her a warm smile.

'Just wanted to do a quick check-in to see how you're adjusting to my company.' I explain. 'I hope my employees have been nothing but kind to you?' Her beauty is almost unbearable, yet her shyness makes her even more desirable. I take a quick glance at her glossy lips, wishing I could kiss them again.

She clears her throat before speaking. 'Of course, yes, everyone has been so friendly so far, thank you.'

'I'm glad to hear that. And how is the workload? I hope it's not too much for you?' Her eyes widen in surprise.

'Of course not. I love books, so it doesn't even feel like work to me.' Her eyes flicker with excitement.

'Are you a reader, then?'

'Yes. I don't think you can really work in publishing if you're not a reader. Since learning how to read, I have been reading.' I nod and I can see the tension leave her as her shoulders drop ever so slightly and the corner of her lips twists upwards.

'And from what I understand in your files, you specialize in the romance genre?' She glances down at her lap and taps her fingers on her knees.

'Yes, I do. I know many people think it's a typical female read, but there's something about it where we can dream about the lives and men we wish existed.' Can't say I understand as I have never read a romance book in my entire life. I'm not into fiction at all, but she has me intrigued.

'So... you're telling me you're disappointed in real-life men?' Her glare snaps back at me, lips pulled into a thin line, clearly looking for words.

'Yes. In books, a man will do anything for a woman he loves. His priority is her. She's his life, and he's not afraid to claim her and he won't go behind her back to fuck some other slut while his girlfriend is supposed to be at work.' She says it in one breath with her voice raised, and I can see the anger in her eyes. Realising what she's just done, her eyes widen in fear, and she exhales deeply before continuing,

'I'm sorry. I .... don't know why I said that.' She stands up. 'I should probably leave.' Turning around, she walks toward the exit, but she doesn't see me stand up as well and follow her to the door. Just before she touches the handle, I put my hand on the door to keep it shut. She stops and stiffens, but slowly turns around to face me. Her eyes are glossy, as if she's trying to stop tears from falling.

'What... what are you doing?' She asks, glaring at me with her brow arched. I look her up and down slowly, taking in every detail of her beautiful body. We're so close to each other right now that I can feel her breathing change. It's deeper, but also shaky. I meet her gaze and say,

'Let me just say something before you leave.' My deep voice must be doing something to her as I see her clench her legs together and her eyes lower to my chest and then back up to my lips and I know she wants the same thing I want.

'I'm guessing your speech has something to do with the guy from the club?' She nods ever so slightly.

I put a finger under her chin and lift it up so she looks me in the eye. 'In that case, what I gather from this is that he's the biggest idiot walking around London.' Her cheeks redden and there's a brief silence between us. Not awkward, however, — It's more calming, allowing us to process everything.

'Miss. Summers?'

'Yes?' She's leaning against my door, caged in between my

arm and the wall, and I see her pulse on the side of her neck. The urge to kiss her there overwhelms me. My heartbeat syncs with hers.

'You're stunning and you're smart. Only an immature fool would let you go.' A single tear falls down her cheek, and I rub it off with my thumb. Electricity travels through my body at the touch, urging me to touch more, so I move it to stroke her lip, remembering how it felt on my mouth.

'I really should go.' She whispers and so I move away from the door and she rushes out, leaving the door open.

The entire ride home, I can't stop thinking about her. Who would be this idiotic to cheat on her? I feel anger building up inside and my fists clenching, so I take a deep breath. I turn from facing the window to my driver,

'How's your wife Mark?'

He looks at me through the rear-view mirror and smiles.

'She's very well, thank you. I finally felt the baby kick last night.'

I smile.

'Not long now. Can I ask you something?'

'Of course sir.'

'What does it feel like to be in love?' Mark sighs and takes a moment before replying.

'When you can't stop thinking about this one person... when you think about her as you're falling asleep and as you wake up. Everything you do is for her and to make her happy. And even when you're with her, you can never get enough of her. That's when you know you're in love.' Another pause... 'At least from my experience.' He shrugs, but I can see him in the mirror, smiling.

Mark has been my driver for over 2 years now and in that time he and his girlfriend got married and earlier this year she got pregnant. I wonder what it feels like to be in love. To want to spend the rest of your life with one person… It frankly feels ridiculous. Having sex with beautiful women is the highlight of my week, and they know I don't come with strings attached.

I open the door to my apartment and flick the switch on. But before I can take a step inside, the massive body forces itself onto me and knocks me down.

'Hello to you too,' I say, trying to push Bruno off me as he continues to lick my face. In moments like this, I regret choosing a German Shepherd instead of something small that wouldn't be able to jump on me.

'Sit' I command and Bruno gets off me and sits down with his tail still wagging. I stand up and straighten my jacket before going in.

'Has Lydia fed you yet?' We go in and I set my briefcase down on the kitchen island. I see a note there and pick it up.

'Bruno had another great day at daycare. Fed him last at 5 pm when I brought him home. See you tomorrow xo.' I put the note in the bin and look at Bruno sitting next to me and pat him on the head,

'What do you say? Let me get changed and we'll go for a walk.' He lets out a bark, which I know by now means he agrees.

CHAPTER SIX

Brooke

I get home and can not think straight. *'the biggest fool walking around London'* still buzzes in my head and sends a shiver down my spine. My knees feel like they're about to give up on me when I think about the way his dark eyes locked with mine. How can one person make you feel like the entire world around you just spins and you're right there in the middle of it all, locked in time? I could feel...damn, I could *hear* my heart pounding against my chest as it was about to jump out and land in his hands. I need to change my underwear.

Actually, fuck it. I'll just take a shower. But first...

I look at my bedside table, which has a special device that helps me in this sort of situation. I call him Mr. Pink.

After feeding Nala and kissing her on the head, I race to my bedroom and close the door. I do not need an audience for that. I take my clothes off, leaving me in just underwear when I lie down on my bed and pull Mr. Pink out of the drawer. He's big and... pink. I close my eyes when I turn it on and the buzzing sound fills the room. It's one of those fancy ones that also has bunny ears which make my eyes roll backward. It's a shame that no man can do this same thing, but I guess that's why it's called fiction in books. Men simply aren't capable of finding our clits. It's a lost land to them... fucking Atlantis, the lost city.

I close my eyes, and in my mind, I go back a couple of hours.

'What would you like me to do for you, Miss. Summers?' We sit in his office, a big dark brown desk between us. He's playing with a pen in his one hand while watching me intently.

I lean forward and tap my fingernails on the desk. 'How about taking me right here, right now?' I smirk. He puts the pen down and stands up, undoing his tie. The butterflies are forming a tornado inside my stomach, and the pulsing between my legs alone is close to sending me off the edge.

He walks around his desk, grabs my wrist, and pulls me up. We're inches away from each other. His one hand is resting on my lower back and I put mine on his chest. He's tense, and I see the large bulge in his trousers.

'Before I do anything, I have to warn you.' My heart pounds faster and faster. The need for him is unbearable and I can't wait any longer. 'What is it?' I whisper.

'I don't do the love-making thing. I'll fuck you so hard, you'll walk out of here sore.' He locks his eyes on my lips.

I swallow. 'Good.' and then his mouth crashes into mine, his tongue immediately slipping inside, and I throw my arms around his neck while he lifts me onto his desk. The fire burns within my core and wetness pools between my legs as he lowers me down and he moves on to kissing my neck, each kiss feels like an electric shock on my skin, and no matter how many kisses he places, it'll never be enough. I rock my hips and he groans in pleasure.

'Fuck me now' I demand in a shaky voice and his mouth moves away from my neck. He's looking right at me as he brushes my cheek with one hand while the other is working on his zipper and he pulls out his... pink cock.

No. Shit. I'm bad at imagining this.

Normal skin-colored cock. He turns me around so now I'm

bent over his desk. His leg spreads me open, and with no warning, he thrusts right in.

I push Mr. Pink in and I'm immediately glad I went for the bigger size.

Each hard thrust makes me want to scream. I grip the edge of the desk as he puts his hand between my legs and finds this sweet spot. Fucking Atlantis has been found. He leans forward close to me and whispers into my ear with his husky voice,

'Are you ready, baby?' I nod shakily, and within a few strokes on my clit, I'm thrown off the edge, pleasure exploding and I groan, clenching my legs in hope for the orgasm to not stop.

Now I'm left on my bed with Mr. Pink still inside, vibrating, and me trying to catch my breath. As Nala's snores sound from the other side of the door, I wipe the sweat off my forehead with my forearm and I chuckle to myself. I need this fucking shower now.

I walk out of my bathroom with my still wet hair. I'm planning on writing more of my book, so I throw on some comfy leggings and my favorite oversized hoodie. When I reach the kitchen, I grab my large wine glass and pour it full. I don't think you can write a good romance without even a bit of alcohol in your system. It allows you to reach your deepest fantasies and also helps your confidence. Have you ever seen a self-conscious drunk person?

Exactly.

I sit down at my small, round dining table and open my laptop. I stare at the last sentence I wrote just last night,

And now she stood in front of the decision she had been avoiding for so long. But there is no running from it now.

I stare at it for what feels like ages, my head empty. Does she give in and sleep with her colleague she's been fantasizing about, knowing it'll affect her workplace, or does she stay professional and say no?

'I wonder if there's a third option I'm missing.' Mumbling to myself, I take a sip of my rose wine. I can't think. My hands curl into fists and I let out a loud sigh as they land on the table.

'Maybe I'm not meant to be a writer' I turn to look at Nala, who is now walking towards me, and puts her head on my lap, looking up at me. I lean back in my chair and stroke her head. Tilting my head back, I take a deep breath.

BREATHE BROOKE. JUST TAKE A DEEP BREATH.

I close my eyes, trying to imagine the scene in my head, but as I'm about to think about what should happen next, my phone on the table rings. I check the caller and it's Tess.

'Hey Tess, you're ok?' I answer, while still stroking Nala's head.

'Hi, girl. I've just had the most amazing self-love session ever and now I've poured myself a glass of wine and am going to watch a film.'

'Erm... TMI Tess.' I chuckle to the phone. I probably won't tell her I've done the exact same thing. Especially since I'd be talking about our boss fucking me in his office fantasy.

'What, you don't want to hear about me watching a movie?' She says sarcastically, and I laugh.

'So, I've been thinking... What would you say about a girls' night this weekend? We can do it at my place.'

'Hmm...' I take a moment to think. It's not a bad idea. Maybe it'll do me some good instead of being at work or home. 'Yeah, sure. That sounds great. Could I invite my friend Aaron too?' I stop petting Nala and lift my glass to take another sip.

'Erm... I kind of thought we could slag off some guys and talk about their tasty sausages.' I snort and spit out my wine, that lands on top of my dog's head and on the floor. I grin at the phone.

'He'll love to join in then.' There's a long pause. She's trying to understand what I just said.

'You're saying he likes the sausage, too?' I roll my eyes with amusement.

'Yes, he likes the sausage too.' I snort out.

I like this woman.

'Then yes, of course. Bring him with you.' I get up to grab the kitchen paper to wipe the spilled wine. I am very grateful at this moment for having wooden floors and not carpet. As I go on my knees to wipe it, while still holding my phone with one hand, I catch a glance of Nala, who is sitting perfectly still, staring right at me with her eyes wide open. What the hell? It takes me a second to realize what's about to happen and when I do, I shout into the phone,

'Tess, I gotta go! I'll talk to you tomorrow!'

'Brooke, are you ...' I hang up before she can finish the question and I'm too late as the sound of the fart echoes through the walls, followed pretty immediately by the smell.

'OH, MY GOD!' I pinch my nose and I gag. Tears filling my eyes, I stand up and quickly open all the windows I can find, and then I shove my head through the living room window just to catch a breath. I try to see what Nala is doing now and I see her back on the sofa, snoring.

Nice one. Thanks for that.

CHAPTER SEVEN

Brooke

Friday comes and I'm sitting at my desk, looking at the novel I'm editing, and tears are filling my eyes.

Knock, knock.

'Come in!' I call out, and Justin walks into my office.

'How are we...' He pauses mid-sentence as he sees me crying. 'What happened?!' He takes a seat and watches me with his brows pinched together. I chuckle and wipe the tears away.

'It's the book. It's beautiful.' I minimise everything on the screen before turning back to him.

'You're... crying over a book?' The confusion on his face makes me laugh harder.

'Of course. It's not my first time and I already know this book is going to be a hit.'

'Why would you want to read something that makes you cry?' He asks. I lean back in my chair and look at him with a smirk on my face.

'Because ...' I pause for a dramatic effect. 'We love things that make us feel alive. That makes us feel things we can't feel in our normal, boring lives. And reading about true love that just fills your heart with hope reminds us of when we were little girls, watching Disney movies, dreaming about our own prince Erics.' He stares at me for a moment and then puts his arms up.

'Ok, I'll never understand.'

'No. No, you won't.' We both laugh. He's a nice guy, always friendly to everyone, and is always there to help others.

'So, did you come here for a reason?' I ask him.

'Yes. No, I mean no. I mean ... It's Friday, so I wondered if you know what that means?' I put my hands together in a Godfather style and wrinkle my forehead in thought.

'Friday usually means that it's the last day of a working week, which means tomorrow I get to have a lie in. So tonight...' I lean forward and move my finger to make Justin lean forward too, as if I want to whisper a secret to him. He leans in and I look left and right to make sure no one is listening and then I whisper, 'Tonight I can put on my cozy clothes, drink wine and read a good book that will make me cry and I can keep reading till 3 am, because I have no work tomorrow.' His head falls back and a burst of loud laughter fills the room.

'Sounds like a perfect night... for a woman.' He snorts out.

'Perfect night it is.' I grin with my teeth on show.

'However, this isn't what I was asking about.'

'What is it then?'

'Well, Mr. Alstons always finishes early on Fridays, so he tries to make it fair. Unfortunately, we have a lot to do every single day, but each week, he chooses a couple of people who get to finish early like him. He makes it fair so everyone has their go but so far no one been announced today.

'That's ... Wow, that's nice.' This takes me by surprise. I mean, he's the CEO so he can finish at any time he wants, but out of respect for his employees, he works just like them... us. Just like us. I'm his employee too.

HE. IS. MY. BOSS.

Damn it.

'Fancy a quick coffee?' He asks as he stands.

'Sure.'

We're in the break room, enjoying a small talk while Justin makes two drinks. I've been here for 5 days now and I have to say, everyone is so friendly. The environment is every employee's dream and I love it here already. Probably would be easier if my heart wasn't skipping a beat every time someone knocked on my door, but I'm sure I can move past it soon. There is no way that I'll be getting involved with my boss.

Boss.

I hate that word.

I was stupid enough to jump on the stranger's lap and kiss him.

But I felt it, and I know he felt it too. What started off as a fake kiss ended with us both wanting more. My head was telling me to run, but my neglected pussy was telling me to stay, so when I ran out of the club, I knew my head won. I wanted to turn around and go back in, but when I looked into his eyes and saw the connection forming, the chemistry that was undeniable... I had to break it. Cut it before it went further than I wanted. He helped me. He was my fake date, even if it was just for a kiss. Now, knowing I have to see him at work makes keeping that connection broken a hundred times harder. Imagine trying the best slice of cheesecake ever, but then going on a diet. Unfortunately, you live right next door to the bakery, so you see this delicious cheesecake every day you walk outside.

After we had our coffees and a croissant each, we walk out of the break room and I freeze on my heels as I see him, standing by John's desk, chatting. Thankfully, his back is facing me, so I can sneak into my office without him noticing me.

'What's wrong with you now?' Justin asks and when he sees what... who I'm looking at, he adds, 'You don't have to be afraid of him, Brooke.' He chuckles.

'I... I'm not...' Before I can finish, John spots me over Mr. Alstons' shoulder and shouts outs,

'Your lucky day Brooke! Your first week here and you get to finish early today! 1 o'clock!' The entire office looks up at me, smiling, and I can feel the blood leaving my face as mr. fake kiss slowly turns around and meets my gaze. He looks me up and down slowly, his eyes eating every inch of my body, and I feel a shiver travelling down my spine.

'Go you.' Justin bumps his fist playfully into my arm, but I don't even flinch. I keep our stare off game and then his eyes lower to my breast. He likes what he sees even though I'm wearing grey trousers and a white blouse, so nothing special compared to other employees here who wear heels and dresses that show off their cleavages... Tess being one of them. His gaze lifts to meet mine again and I see it... the hunger in them that fuels me, burning through my skin...

Fuck, Brooke! Snap out of it!

I look at John and smile wildly.

'Thank you, John!' I say a quick bye to Justin and head back to my office.

My phone pings just as I set my bag down on the coffee table. I take my shoes off and sit on my sofa next to Nala before I pull it out of my bag.

Tess- Heard you finished early, and it's only your first week. Mr. Alstons must really like you ;) x

If she only knew...

But I probably shouldn't be saying anything to her because it might put me in a poor light. I shoot her a quick reply.

Me- I guess I'm very good at my job haha. x

Tess- Remember tomorrow, at 7 pm my place. x

Me- See you then x

I set my phone down next to me and look at Nala. guilt washing over me. I have seen little of her this week while working till late, so maybe we can do something this afternoon.

Then an idea pops into my head. I rush to the wardrobe in my bedroom and pull out a box that is covered in dust. I eye it carefully and wipe it with my forearm while holding it, and a memory pops into my head.

'Let's do something fun!' I plea while Tyler is sitting, playing on his PlayStation in our living room.

'Tyler, are you even listening?' I stand on the side of the sofa with my arms crossed, waiting for his reply.

'What do you even want to do?' His gaze doesn't move from the TV, which makes my blood boil.

'I don't know...' I think for a moment. 'I bought us skates the other month so we could actually put them on and maybe head to the park.

'Skates? Are you evening hearing yourself? I'm not 10 Brooke.' I hear his words, but he's still very much focused on this bloody game.

'You don't have to be 10 to ride on skates, Tyler. People go on them or bikes. Why can't we ever do what I want?' I snatch the controller from his hands and he finally looks at me, his gaze darkening.

'Brooke, give it back!' He snaps.

'You say you're too old to go rollerblading, but here you are, sitting and playing video games!' I am not backing down on this. I then hear a shooting from the tv and we both turn our heads to see Tyler got killed.

'For fuck's sake!' He shouts, snatching the controller back. 'If you want to go rollerblading, then go fucking alone and leave me here!' It feels like a stab in my chest. The anger fills his eyes, and I

frown, trying to understand what I did wrong for him to prefer his PlayStation to spending time with me. I lift my chin up and head to our bedroom to read.

'After all that time, I still haven't used you. I was so anxious to go by myself that I refused myself from having fun.' I mutter to myself. As a kid, I loved going out rollerblading. Meeting up with my friends and racing down the road to see who was the fastest, and I won once or twice. A slight smile pulls on my mouth when I look in Nala's direction and in this moment I decide to have fun even if it means by myself.

I sit down on the bench in the park and pull my roller blades out. Nala is sitting next to me, looking around and taking in all the fresh scents.

'It'll be fine.' I say to her, not sure if I believe it myself. I change my shoes and shove them in my backpack. Putting it over my shoulders, I pick up the lead and stand up. I stumble at first, but I straighten myself quickly, taking a deep breath in and taking the first step.

You can do it, Brooke.

I go slowly, and I'm glad Nala is older now so she won't pull me. She stays at my heel the whole time while I'm looking down at my feet, praying to God I don't fall over in front of all these people. The golden leaves are now on the ground and the air feels chilly as November creeps in slowly. I'm thankful for having my layers on and my beanie hat to keep me from freezing. It's sunny today and there are plenty of people out walking their dogs or playing with their kids in the gated play area. I see a food van on the other side of the park and I'm planning on getting myself a hot drink after, as a reward for my courage.

My stomach twists in nerves when people stare at me, probably judging. What a 25-year-old woman is doing on her rollerblades. Well, if rollerblading wasn't for adults, then they wouldn't make them in adult sizes. Why do we have to stop doing things we enjoy when we stop being children? You fancy an ice cream after a long day? Have a bloody ice cream. You want to watch a new Disney movie? Watch the new Disney movie. You want to go rollerblading even though you haven't done it in like 10 odd years? Go fucking rollerblading.

I pause and straighten myself once more. No one is going to make me feel bad about it. I came here to enjoy my Friday afternoon off and that's what I'm going to do. Shooting a glance at Nala, I see her looking to her right, sniffing for something, but when I look in the same direction, I see nothing. Scratching her behind her ear, I say, 'Let's go.'

After about 10 minutes, I feel more confident and even pick up my speed. Just a little bit, but it's enough for my first time. I smile to myself as more people look at me and nod to me in acceptance. I even heard a child say to his mum that he wants his own rollerblades from Santa while pointing at me. Nala acts oddly as she's looking in every direction possible as if looking for something, and she picks up her pace.

'Slow down, please. I'll end up on my ass if you pull me.' Her tail starts wagging in excitement. I look around if I can see a squirrel or anything that might have got her attention but I still see nothing. She then picks her up pace again, this time pulling on me.

'Nala, stop.' I command, unable to stop as we're heading toward a downhill path.

Oh God. Oh God. Oh God.

I try to pull on the lead to get her to my heel again but it's not working, and she's now running, pulling me with her, and now we're on the downhill and my speed picks up so much, that I overtake Nala and I have no other choice but to let go of the lead so I don't pull her with me. A cry for help leaves my mouth, and I try to find something I can grab onto it, but the path is clear. I must look like an idiot to everyone around me as

I wave my arms around, trying to press on the brakes at the same time. But I'm not pressing hard enough. I see a tree at the bottom and I know this is my only chance. As I get closer, I put my hands in front of me so they take the hit instead of my face and I slam straight into it.

Well, one thing is certain. Sitting down is going to be painful for a while.

I sit up and rub my backside, trying to relieve the soreness.

'Are you ok?' I pause as I recognize the voice. My stomach drops when I look down and see his shadow right next to mine.

Oh no.

'Do I need to call the ambulance?' He asks, and my gaze lifts to meet his. These deep brown eyes, looking right into mine and brows pinched together in worry.

'N-no...' I mumble, and I suddenly remember about Nala. I look around when I see her playing with a german shepherd on the grass only a few feet away.

'Let me help you.' He leans forward, his hand out, but I push it away, not wanting him to touch me.

'I'm ok, thank you.' I remove the roller blades immediately and throw them to the side. His lips are now curved upwards in amusement.

'My ass doesn't think it's funny.' I snap while rubbing it with my one hand. My stomach drops with embarrassment. I don't even want to know how many people are staring at me. Mr. Alstons kneels down so we're face to face and I feel the heat reaching my face.

'Are you sure? I'm happy to check for you.' He winks at me now and I feel my chest twists in a nervous yet exciting feeling, but I refuse for him to see me that way.

'Mr. Alstons, I do not think it's appropriate for you to speak to me that way, even if we are not at work right now.' He chuckles darkly at my comment and replies while slowly leaning towards me so he's even closer,

'Then why did you just clench your legs?' My cheeks heat immediately. Before standing up, I pull my shoes out of the backpack and put them on quickly, all the while refusing to look him in the eyes. I stand up, brushing the dirt off my legs before finally looking back at him as he stands up, too.

'I guess I haven't properly apologized for the last weekend.' His smile disappears, and I look him up and down. The man looks different. He's not the man wearing a suit who I saw at the club and at work. He's wearing jeans, trainers and a black sporty-looking coat. You'd think he's just a random guy, walking through the park, all perfectly normal. But he's not normal, is he? He's my boss.

'No need to apologize.' He puts his hands in the pockets of his jacket, presumably to keep them warm as it's getting colder now with the wind picking up and the sun hiding behind the grey clouds.

'I was happy to help.'

I bite my lower lip. 'What?' And then his chuckle reaches my ears, amusement flashing in his eyes.

'I saw you that night.' He pauses for a moment. 'I saw you there with your friend. Dancing with him, and laughing at whatever conversation you were having. I could smell your perfume when you were sitting right behind me.' His gaze lowers to my lips, which makes butterflies in my stomach flutter, as he continues, 'I also saw a guy coming up to you on that dance floor, and your body language showing how uncomfortable you were. Then you looked at me and I knew straight away you needed my help.' I gape at him, unsure what to say to that. He saw me? He saw me before I even saw him. Aaron mentioned him watching me, but I didn't believe him.

'And that dress that you wore...' I stop him before he can finish that sentence,

'No need to say it. I....' I pause while I study him, his perfect face, his sharp jaw, a slight stubble and deep brown eyes and I find not a single flaw. 'I should say thank you then.' A flat tone leaves my mouth, hoping to cut this conversation short.

'But sir....'

'Call me Gabriel,' He cuts in.

'But you're my boss.' I take a step back, anxious about where this is going. I am not going there, not with him, not with anyone. That's the promise I made myself after I left Tyler. I'll never again go to that place where I could lose myself to someone else.

'A boss whose mouth you shoved your tongue into.' I freeze. With my eyes wide open, I stare at him. My heart speeds up, adrenaline kicking in, and I don't think it'd look good if I just run away from him now.

I need my job.

I love my job.

I do not want to lose my job.

'I... I didn't know you were my new boss.' He smiles at me when I finally say it. Damn his gorgeous, sexy smile.

'I never said you did. You need to learn to separate work from life, Miss. Summers.'

'I really should get going.' I turn around and call Nala, who comes and sits down at my heel. The German Shepherd follows her and comes to Mr. Alstons' heel, sitting down by him.

'Is he ...' I look between them two, surprised.

'That's Bruno. I think your dog really liked him as the moment you let go of her, she ran up straight to us.' I look down at Nala, feeling an unbearable betrayal. She betrayed me for some German Shepherd. I'll have a serious talk with her when we get home.

At that moment, I feel a drop of rain land on my cheek and I look up. Sky covered in dark grey clouds and I know I won't make it back to safety in time.

'I really should get...' And before I finish the sentence, the rain pours down on us and I shriek in displeasure. Mr. Alstons grabs my hand and pulls me with him. Running to escape the rain, we rush to the food van which has a parasol. But by the time we get to it, we're both soaked and breathless. As I go to grab my hair, he comes closer and says,

'Let me...' he takes off the hairband off my ponytail, and takes my hair in his hands to squeeze the water out of them. I watch him, and after he's done, his gaze meets mine, both of us pausing for what feels like a lifetime. The magnetic pull between us becomes stronger whenever there's contact, and it's so hard to pull away.

'You have beautiful eyes, you know that?' He murmurs, and I feel my core being set on fire.

'Thank you.' The sound of thunder breaks our moment when I reply. I look around and see people rushing around to find a hideout from this rain. I glance down at Nala, who is not impressed by this weather either, and I can truly relate to her.

'...coffees please.' I hear from behind me and see Mr. Alstons at the van now, handing money over to a teenage boy in the window. I drink up the view of him, standing there wet from the rain, looking sexier than ever. If I could just push my hand through his hair and take his drenched clothes off him...

'Like what you see?' I zone back into reality and see him staring and smirking at me while holding two coffees. I bite the inside of my cheek to hide my embarrassment and accept the coffee from him.

'Thank you, sir.'

'Call me Gabriel.' He demands while frowning.

'Sir, I'm very sorry about how we met...' The relief washes over at the sight of one couple here with us on the other end, deep in their own conversation.

'...but I love my job.' His brow raises in confusion.

'I'm happy to hear that, Brooke.' The sound of my name coming out of his mouth sends the feeling of longing to my core. I can feel the wetness between my legs that has nothing to do with the rain, but has everything to do with this gorgeous man standing in front of me, whose stare can engrave itself into my soul. He's the man that women write about in books. He's the main character's love interest. But I will not let him be the character in my story. I only recently got control of it back and I'm not giving it away, ever again.

'I don't think you understand.' It's time to put my foot down and not let my heart dictate my actions. It's got me into plenty of trouble before.

'Then explain, please.' He commands and takes a sip of his hot drink. I can tell he's not happy.

'What happened between us... It was a mistake.' There, I said it. 'And it can not happen again. You're my boss and I do not want to lose my job. Also, I'm not looking for a boyfriend.' I stare down at my coffee, unable to look at him, afraid of what I might see. I can not lose sight of my priorities right now, and I know nothing about this guy except what his mouth tastes like and how his eyes go more amber in the sun and more black when it's dark. Or how his smile does something to my stomach I can not explain, or how his scent sends off all my senses over the edge.

Stop, Brooke. Stop it!

I raise my eyes and meet his, but I can not read his face at this moment. He's watching me, as if waiting for something to happen.

'I'm sorry.' I say, hoping he will not hate me for this, but I see his lips turning upward just slightly.

'I don't believe in love.' He confesses. 'I don't think people are capable of true love, the love that they write books about. People are selfish, and I am being greedy right now, Miss. Summers. Because when I look at you ...' He takes a step toward me and I don't move. He's close... too close ... 'All I can think about is how your tongue tasted against mine. How it started as a fake kiss but finished as something we both craved and we both wanted. You can not lie to me on this, Brooke. I felt your body against mine and it wanted it as much as mine did... and it still does.' He brushes my blushed cheek with his thumb and I flinch at the contact. My whole body is on fire, burning just for him. Only him.

Nala suddenly barks out, which makes us both jump. I look down at her and I know she just saved me from making probably the biggest mistake of my life.

CHAPTER EIGHT

Brooke

I close my laptop and feel proud of myself. 5000 words written today is absolutely amazing for me and I wonder if it has anything to do with my new feelings that ignite this new inspiration. Although it is quite ironic that I am writing an office romance and here, look at me, trying to avoid one in my real life. Clara would be ashamed of me.

Sorry, girl. This is your type of thing. Not mine.

I check the time and I have only an hour till I have to leave for Tess'. Yesterday was awkward and hard... After Nala saved me from, I don't even want to think about what, I came up with some lame excuse to leave and I ran just as he was about to say something. I didn't want to hear it.

I couldn't hear it.

Because everything he said so far was true. I wanted more, and I wanted more yesterday. But last weekend was all about getting rid of my ex, and him becoming my boss made things way more complicated. It's not like I could have slept with him and then forget he ever existed. No. I'd be seeing his face, remembering every inch of his body, and this isn't something

I'm prepared for. Him confessing he doesn't believe in love helps a bit, but even though my lady area is craving him, she'll have to satisfy herself with Mr. Pink. He does a good job, compared to any of my exes, so Mr. Alstons probably wouldn't be any different.

I head for a shower to wash away all the dirty thoughts I keep having about my boss, but all I can think about as I wash my body is about how his touch would feel. I jump out, put on a pair of black leggings and my favourite oversized grey hoodie and then I hear my phone ping from the kitchen table.

Aaron- Be there in 10.

He's picking me up and we're going to see Tess together. It's been so nice to have a friend like her at work who knows how to take my mind off things, and who's so genuine. She's so beautiful inside and out and it shocked me when she told me all about her exes, either cheating or only interested in sex. I'm really losing hope in all men at this point.

I glance at Nala, who's lying down next to the window now, looking all soppy.

'Are you seriously missing Bruno that much?' She lifts her head at the sound of his name, tail wagging, and I feel guilty straight away.

'No, he's not here, Nala.' She puts her head down again.

Is my dog falling for my boss's dog now?

Un-freaking-believable. I sigh loudly, and hear a knock on my door. Thinking it's Aaron, I pick up my boots and open the door to only then freeze in place as I look into his deep blue eyes, and I feel my heart pick up the pace and my chest tighten.

'What the hell do you want?' Tyler stands there, hands in his pockets and shoulders slumped while he's looking right at me.

'We need to talk, Brooke.'

'We really don't.' I try to shut the door in his face, but he stops it with his foot.

'You need to leave now. I have nothing to say to you, Ty.' I try to force the door, but he's not budging.

'Fine. But at least listen to me.' He pleas.

I pause and open the door to face him. 'You've got 5 minutes and then I want you gone.' I storm inside and he follows me. I stop at my kitchen table and throw my hands on my hips, waiting for him to talk as he looks around my apartment.

'You've got a nice place here' He comments but I give him no reply. I fight my body from trembling at his presence as I refuse to give him the satisfaction that he still makes me react.

'Right ...' He strokes the back of his neck with his hand before he finally speaks.

'I miss you.'

'But I don't miss you.' I snap immediately.

'Brooke, please ...' He takes a step toward me and I put my hand out to stop him. My heart is beating so fast and my legs feel like they're about to give out on me. Nala now comes to stand by me and growls, making Tyler's eyes widen.

'You... you got a dog?' His voice shakes slightly, and I know it's because he's scared of dogs. I'm also surprised at Nala's reaction, as she's always friendly to people.

She knows.

My baby girl can smell his bullshit from a mile away.

'Of course I did. I can finally do everything I ever wanted since I left your cheating ass.' Nala, still growling, forces him to take a few steps back while he puts his hands up showing her he means no harm.

'Brooke, you know she meant nothing to me.'

'So?' I snort out.

'So...' He glances between me and Nala. 'So I don't understand why you can't forgive me for this one stupid accident.'

'Accident?' I raise my voice and snort again. 'You call going down on another woman in OUR bed when I was working, a fucking accident? Did you accidentally slip on the floor when she was naked on our bed and you landed face first between her legs?' I straighten my arm to the side and point my finger at the door.

'Get out!' I command.

'No.' He shakes his head. 'We belong together.'

I go to him, grab his arm, and try to pull him to the door, but he's bigger, stronger, making me only struggle.

'We do not belong together. You fucking broke me.' He's fighting back, refusing to move.

'Kiss me.' He demands.

'Get the fuck out of here, you sick son of a bitch.' He grabs my hands and pushes me against the wall, making me yelp as my back slams into it.

'Let go of me, you bastard!' Nala barks, but Tyler is now solely focused on me, and he kisses my neck.

'This...' He puts both my wrists in one of his hands and holds them above my head as his other hand travels between my legs. '...is mine. You will not be with anyone else because you belong to me.'

'What the fuck?!' We both turn our heads to see Aaron standing at the door and I take this moment to free my hands from Tyler's hold and kick him straight in the nuts. He drops to the floor, wincing in pain.

'You bitch!'

Aaron rushes to him, grabbing him by his hood, and shoves him out the door.

'This isn't the end, Brooke!' We both hear through the door.

'Burn in hell!' I shout to make sure he can hear me while massaging my wrists. Aaron quickly locks the door. I lean my head against it and take a deep breath.

I hate him. I hate him with all my heart, and I want him out of my life. He destroyed the person I used to be, and he killed all my dreams. I never want to see this motherfucker ever again.

'Are you alright?' Aaron puts his hand on my shoulder and as I immediately flinch, he pulls away.

'Shit. I'm sorry Brooke. Did he hurt you?' He looks at me with concern, and Nala also comes up to me, pushing her nose into my leg.

'No.' I say as I scratch her head. 'Thank you for being here.' I go up to Aaron and he wraps his arms around me as I rest my head on his chest.

'Thank you' I whisper and I feel a tear fall down my cheek. Aaron is my safety. My home. My person. He was there to pick up my remaining pieces after I left Tyler, and he was the one who helped me get back on my feet.

'Do you want to cancel tonight?' He asks, and I take a moment to think about it.

I could.

I could cancel tonight's plans and sob like a little girl and hide under my covers again. Or... I could truly refuse him from coming back to my life and I could start enjoying my life.

I pull away from Aaron and smile at him through my tears.

'I have a better idea...'

CHAPTER NINE

Gabriel

Music blasts through the speakers as I gaze around and see countless drunk people on the dance floor. It's a Saturday night so I guess I shouldn't be so surprised, but what I am surprised about is that Max talked me into going out. I was more than content to stay at home and enjoy a glass of whisky, while thinking about the woman who so clearly wants me, but yet she doesn't. Is it her past that scared her off men? I knew the look she gave me at the park. I've seen plenty of women looking at me like this, but yet, none of them ever refused me... until her. Brooke Summers - The pain in my ass. She said she's not looking for a boyfriend. Which is fine as I'm not looking for a girlfriend, but what's wrong with just having some fun? Is she scared of me firing her? She needs to separate her life from her job. I'm not that kind of man and so far, after only a week, I'm happy with her work. I could never fire a woman just because she slept with me, but she doesn't seem to understand it. Hell, I guess she wouldn't ... She doesn't know me at all. I've been thinking about her every day since that bloody Saturday night, and until I have more of her, I don't think I can get over it. You can't start something you can't finish.

'Are you even listening to me?' Max snaps me out of my thoughts. We're sitting at the bar and I take a drink of my favorite golden liquid and feel its burning effect as it makes its way down my throat.

'What's up?' I face him, not knowing what he just said.

'Man, you have not been the same since last weekend. Is it her?' He smirks.

'Who?' I look down at my glass. Max has been my longest friend and he can read me like a book.

'Don't play dumb on me. You've been cooped up in your apartment the whole week.'

'So? Maybe I'm playing celibate.'

'Playing my ass. How is Lydia anyway?' Oh yes, Lydia. My charming dogsitter, who I might or might have not slept with a couple of times. It's hard to refuse a woman who gives you puppy eyes every damn day, begging to jump into your bed.

'I gotta end it.' I reply before taking another sip of my golden medicine.

'What, why? You said yourself she's a great booty call.' He frowns at me and at this point, there's no point in lying to my best friend.

'My interest is elsewhere right now.' I shrug and he laughs.

'Mr. Alstons. Are you telling me you're going to chase the beautiful stranger who might not even want to sleep with you?'

'Worth a shot. I want to finish what I started.' Max's eyebrow raises as he observes me.

'Are you saying you're falling...?'

'No!' I snap out at him. 'I don't do relationships or any of that crap and you know it.'

He pauses for a moment, deep in thought, and takes another sip of his drink.

'Ok...' He shrugs in defeat. 'Good luck, man.' We clink our glasses together in cheers, and finish our drinks.

'Two more please,' Max shouts out to the bartender when I decide to look around. I'd normally find someone on weekends, who I can take home for the night, but as I gaze between crowds, I see no one who catches my attention. All these beautiful women and I could pick whoever I like and 99% chance is that they'd leave with me. It's gone down from 100% since meeting Brooke, but let's try to forget about her for now. Maybe I just need to find someone who can take my mind off her.

'Gabe, look to your right.' Max elbows me and nods in the direction just to my right where the entrance is, and the heat immediately travels to my groin when I see Brooke enter. Her hair is up in a high ponytail and she's wearing a tight-fitting red dress which gives me an amazing sight of her breasts, and knee-high black boots on high heels. I stop breathing as I take in the view of her and my cock comes to life, twitching underneath my trousers.

Fuck.

'Is that your receptionist with her?' Max asks, and I didn't even notice the people she came with. I see Tess, who works at the reception and the guy I saw her with last week. He's not her boyfriend, is he? She said she wasn't looking for one, so maybe it's just a friend. But damn, I can feel jealousy kicking in, and my fists clench tight around the glass.

'Yeah, her name is Tess.' I reply to him as I struggle to face away from her. I see them making their way to the bar and the relief washes over me when they don't notice me.

'She's fucking hot, mate...' I hear Max comment and I reply,

'Yes... yes, she fucking is...' I can't get my head straight. I want her. Right now. I want to pull her dress up high for easy access, and I want to taste her. Taste every inch of her body. This woman could stab me with her heel and I would say Thank You.

My cock is hard now, and I know I'm not going anywhere

anytime soon. I take another sip of my whisky and take a deep breath to calm down, but nothing is working.

'What do I do?' I ask Max, still watching her.

'Talk to her? Buy her a drink?' He replies from behind me.

'She's not that type.' I reply.

I now see Tess spotting me and she waves excitedly before saying something to her companions. They all turn to look at me.

She's looking at me.

Brooke's eyes lock with mine, and I raise my glass to her and smirk. Tess pulls them both and they walk in my direction. Shit. Shit. Shit.

'Pull yourself together, man.' Max says as he puts his empty glass down on the bar.

'Mr. Alstons!' Tess calls out. 'How nice to see you.'

'You too, Tess. You're all having fun?' Brooke stands just behind her, out of my sight.

'Yeah. We're having a fuck-all-men night out.' She grins widely and puts her hand on her hip. She is an attractive woman, with long blonde hair and blue eyes. Every guy's dream... except for mine.

'You are? With a guy in your group?' I look at the guy standing next to her and raise my glass to him.

'That's Aaron, Brooke's friend who always thinks men should fuck themselves.' I pause for a moment to let the information sink in.

'Are you...' I now turn my direction to Aaron.

'Gay as they come.' He smiles and raises his glass back at me.

'Sorry, I didn't mean to.' I nod once in apology to him.

'It's fine. We met last week, didn't we...'

'You did?' Tess chips in and his lips pull into a thin line now, and I understand she was not meant to know.

'Have you met my dear friend Maxie boy?' I put my hand on Max's shoulder, changing the subject quickly.

'No, I haven't.' She looks him up and down and smiles. They both shake their hands and start a small talk when I turn to Brooke.

'You look...' I start, but she stops me.

'Don't.' She doesn't look at me and I look at Aaron, who only shrugs his shoulders.

'We better get going before the dance floor gets completely full.' Aaron adds and they all say their goodbyes and walk off. I watch her every step and every movement as she moves her hips to the music and I feel like I'm going to cum just from watching her. Her hair sways from side to side as she dances with her friends and she then lowers herself on Tess' body as Tess puts her hands on her shoulders, both dancing and laughing. As Brooke slowly comes back up, still holding onto Tess, she glances at me and then away.

Fuck. Fuck. Fuck.

'You're sweating man.' Max chuckles.

'Fuck off.' I look at him and he's full-on, grinning at me.

Two young guys sit next to us and I hear them talking to each other.

'Hey, check out this chick in a red dress.' I glance at the floor and see only Brooke wearing a red dress.

'Damn, she's hot. I'm going for her.' Guy number two is about to stand up as guy number one puts his hand on his chest to stop him. I'm seeing red.

'She's mine, mate.' He barks and forces his companion to sit back down.

'Fuck. I bet she's amazing in bed, the way she moves those hips.' Man two adds and I lose it. I turn to them and speak loudly to ensure they understand me.

'You're not fucking touching her.' Their eyes widen, staring right at me.

'Or what?' Guy number 1 asks.

'Or you're fucking dead.' They both gape as I stand up, facing them. They know they wouldn't win, as I'm twice their size. Wearing t-shirts and the new generation of modern skinny jeans, I wonder how the fuck do they think they would get her? Brooke is a woman who needs a real man. Not some little fuck boy who looks like he doesn't know what he's doing.

'Alright man, chill. She's yours.' Guy number 2 lifts both his hands up in defence.

'She is.' I end the conversation.

For the next hour, me and Max spend talking about random shite as I keep watching Brooke with her friends and she's either drinking or dancing. We exchange a few looks where she either smirks or licks her lips seductively whenever she looks at me. When I realize she's had 5 drinks and is now dancing with some random guy who has his hands on her hips, I decide to screw me-staying-calm. She is not getting with this son of a bitch. I stand up,

'What are you doing?' Max tries to grab my arm to stop me, knowing I set my eyes on Brooke.

'Fuck this.' I snap and head towards Brooke.

When I'm next to her, she looks up at me with her eyes wide open.

'Fuck off.' I snap at the guy.

'What?' His eyebrows pinched together.

'I said. Fuck. Off.' I repeat myself as I stand tall and he backs off.

'What the fuck?!' Now Brooke snaps at me.

'What do you think you're doing?' I turn to her, not giving a shit if anyone is watching.

'I think what I'm doing is having a fun night out.' She replies, knives shooting from her eyes.

'Were you gonna sleep with him?' She gapes at me, then glances at him, walking away before turning back to me.

'That is none of your business.' I grab her arm and pull her off the floor and take her toward the toilets where I can speak to her. I stop by the closet for, I'm guessing, cleaners where no one can see us.

'Let go of me!' She shouts and when I do, I take a step towards her, forcing her against the wall.

'You're drunk.' I snap.

'You're drunk.' She repeats like a 5-year-old child and stumbles to the side before I catch her by her waist.

'It's not funny, Brooke. You drank too much and now you think you're carefree, but the truth is, if you sleep with him, you'll regret it in the morning.' She looks down and I lift her chin up with my finger so she looks at me.

'You're more than this, Brooke. You're not this type of person.'

'How do you know?' Her eyes are red, filled with emotion.

'Because I see it in you. And I know how much you want the thing I want. Why did you keep looking at me tonight?' I demand an answer.

'I don't know what you're talking about.' She tries to look away, but I don't let her.

'You know exactly what I'm talking about. Your smirking and sexy dancing when you looked into my eyes. Do you have any idea what you're doing to me?' Her breaths deepen as she looks at my lips and my cock comes to life once again.

'Why are you doing this to me?' I say as I rest my forehead against hers and close my eyes. She lifts her palm and cups my face, rubbing her thumb across my jaw.

'I could ask you the same question, Mr. Alstons.' She whispers back.

'I told you. Call me Gabriel.' I don't move. I don't want to let her go. Not yet.

'Ok...' She pauses before adding, '...Gabriel.' That's it. The sound of my name on her tongue pushes me over the edge. I crush my mouth into hers and she immediately kisses me back. My dick rock hard right now, tells me to take her. Right here, right now. I push my tongue inside to taste her, and it's a taste I never want to forget. I play with her tongue as she pushes her hands through my hair and I wrap my arms around her. Closer.

I want her closer. She moans in pleasure and I lift the hem of her dress higher before I lift her up, allowing her to wrap her legs around my waist. I push us against the wall. My stomach twists left and right, unable to control itself. Each kiss is more passionate than the previous one and as she rocks her hips, I can tell she is into it as much as I am. I push my hips into her and she moans again into my mouth. Moving her head to the side, she allows me access to her neck. Every inch. I want to kiss every fucking inch of her. She wraps her arms around my neck and pulls on my shirt.

She wants it.

I want it.

My tongue travels from the base of her neck to her earlobe, and I feel her body shivering under my touch. She smells of citrus and I know, as of now, it is my favourite scent. My hands grip on her ass.

'Gabriel...' she moans.

'That's right, baby girl. Call out my name.' I command, and she kisses me again. Hungry for us to connect, I check if the door to the closet is open, and it's my fucking lucky day when I find it unlocked. I smirk between our kisses when I walk us inside and close the door behind. I put her down and pull her dress down to reveal her bare breast.

'Fuck.' I growl. 'You're going to be the death of me, woman.' She smiles and I take her breast in my mouth, and she lets out a moan, tilting her head back once again. Her hands travel down my arms as I play with her nipple. Between licking it and sucking it, she shivers, clenching her legs. I know the place where she wants me. But... I pause. This... I don't want it to happen like this. I pull her dress slowly back up,

'What are you doing?' She asks with her shaky voice. I cup her face in my hands and look her in the eyes.

'We can't do it, Brooke.'

'What?' Her eyes widen.

'You're drunk.'

'Not that drunk.' She snaps, and it pains me to do this, but this is not the way I want us to happen, even though my dick says otherwise at this moment. Our breaths are both quick and deep, matching each other.

'Brooke. I do not want you to be a one-night stand.' Tears start filling her eyes and it feels like I'm stabbed right in my gut.

'I want you. I want every inch of you. I want to fuck you so hard that you'll scream my name, not just moan it.' She doesn't move, so I continue. 'Like I said, Brooke... You are so much more and you don't deserve to be quick fucked in the closet full of...' I pause and look around. 'Fucking bleach.' She snorts and I smile at her. 'I want you sober when you say yes to me. I want you sober when I give you orgasm after orgasm.' Her cheeks blush and I think about how fucking gorgeous she is.

'Let me take you home...' I take her hand in mine and notice a bruise covering her wrist. I pull up her other hand and see the same purple colour. 'What is this?' I ask her and she pulls her hands away.

'Nothing.' I snatch her hands back to me and look at them, noticing tiny finger prints and suddenly, all I see is red.

'Who the fuck did this to you?' I snap.

'No one. Let me go.' She tries to pull away, but I'm not letting her.

'Give me his name, Brooke.' I demand. I am going to break the fucker's arms and legs.

'Had a fight with my ex, alright? It's been handled, so just let it go.' I look her in the eyes and see tears fall down her cheeks. I decide to let it go—for now.

When we get back to the bar, we find Max and Tess laughing.

'Your friend here is pretty drunk, so I'm gonna take her home.' Tess' eyes glance between us and she looks at me holding Brooke's hand and my messy hair. This can't look good, but I don't care.

'Aaron brought her here in his car.' She replies and I look

around and catch him on the dance floor dancing with some guy.

'He looks rather occupied, so I'll take her. It's not a problem for me.' I look at Max, who's carefully watching me while resting his arm on the bar. His smirk tells me he has an idea about what happened. Brooke and Tess give each other a hug and I get given Brooke's purse before we walk out and get into my car.

Mark drives us to the address Brooke gave me, and I help her to the door. She can barely stand straight, so I know I'll have to help her to bed. I look around as she searches for her keys and I notice it's a pleasant area she lives in, with lots of blocks forming an O shape and a small gated playground in the middle, but it is rather far away from our office. I shiver from the cold as it is now 1am.

'Shit!' The word leaves Brooke's mouth as she slaps the entrance door to her apartment block.

'What happened?' I ask.

'I just remembered I left my keys in Aaron's car to make sure I didn't lose them.

I check the time and it'd take easily an hour to drive back to the club, and that's if Aaron is still there. I glance at my car and at her. She looks exhausted.

'Come on...' I pull her away from the door.

'Where?' She hesitates, blinking with bafflement.

'We're going to my place.'

'No. I'm not going to your place. We're not...' She shakes her head furiously ...

'We won't do anything.' I stop her before she finishes. 'You will go straight to sleep.' She stares at me for a moment before giving in, and we both get back into the car.

'Where now, sir?'

'Home.'

By the time we get to my place, she's fast asleep, her head resting on my shoulder.

CHAPTER TEN

Brooke

There's something cold and wet on my face. I open my eyes slowly and see a long, dribbling tongue licking my face.

'Nala, not now ...' I groan loudly and pull the covers over my face. When I hear a bark, I shot my eyes open because this bark does not belong to Nala. I look up from the covers, dragging them down, and realise I'm not even in my bed. The room is large, probably the size of my entire apartment, and the bed is probably twice the size of a king-size. I then see a big German Shepherd lean into my face and lick it again. I look around, confused about my whereabouts. How much did I drink? I sit up and throw my hands on my head as it's about to explode. Too much—That's how much I drunk. When I moan in pain, I realize something. I look down and I see an oversized, black t-shirt. I pull the covers over my chest to cover myself and I struggle to remember where the hell I am. There is a glass of water and a small plate with tablets on the bedside table. There's also a note. I pick it up and read it,

Two paracetamol should help with the hangover.
G.

G? I try to remember last night as I pop two tablets into my mouth and down the glass of water, feeling its soothing effect on my deserted throat. It's after I finish my drink, I see it in my mind. The club. My boss. His hands touching me. Us kissing. Then he stopped it and said. 'I want you sober when you say yes to me'. My heart's rate picks up, my breaths quicken as I remember it all.

Oh. No.

My hands are getting sweaty when I put the glass back down.

Shit. Shit. Shit.

I look at Bruno, still sitting by my side with his tail wagging.

'Hi, Bruno,' I attempt a smile, but my throbbing head wants me to hide under the covers again.

I notice my purse next to me and I pull out my phone; it's 9am. I also have unread texts.

Aaron- Girl, I need all the dets. Tess told me you left with your new boss.

Aaron- I realised I still have your keys, so I doubt you're at home. I'll sleep at yours to watch Nala. ;) Get it girl!

Tess- Brooke! I have no idea what happened last night and I need you to explain! Also, let me know you're alive and have not been murdered by our boss.

Mom- Hey honey, I'm looking forward to our lunch today. See you soon xoxo.

I throw the phone on the pillow next to mine and throw myself on my back while covering my eyes with my arm. Shoot. Me. Now.

'How are we this morning?' I remove my arm and see Mr. Alstons standing at the door. My stomach twists and I'm not sure if it's because of seeing him in dark washed jeans and a black v neck t-shirt or if it's the alcohol trying to escape my body.

'Kill me now to prevent the slow death.' I groan with a cry-faking tone as I sit up. I have no energy to shield myself from him, plus I have to appreciate him not leaving me to sleep outside my building, on the cold ground.

'That bad?' He smirks and I pick up a pillow and throw it at him. He catches it in time, unfortunately.

'I'm not going to kill you, Brooke. I'm too young and handsome to end up in jail.' He throws the pillow back at me, but it lands at my feet.

'I'm loving the confidence, Mr. Alstons.' I say sarcastically, while turning my back to him.

'Gabriel.' He says harshly. 'Surely, after last night, we can be on the first name basis.'

'Maybe...' I reply and I think about how good it felt to be in his arms and how good he tasted. I wanted more, and I was ready for more. The confidence of alcohol is truly cruel.

'Do I want to ask how I ended up wearing what I can presume is one of your t-shirts?' I ask nervously. Considering my state, I doubt I was the one who removed my clothes.

'Probably not.' Oh, dear god. He comes around and opens the blinds, which allow bright sunlight into the room, straight on my face.

'You bastard!' My head is so sensitive, I pull the duvet over it again. I hear him laugh gently.

'I'm sorry, I didn't...'

'Apologise one more time and I'll take you over my knee.' He warns, and my heart skips a beat. I stay silent.

'That's what I thought. Mark brought you some clothes to change into. They're on the chair. I'll make us some breakfast.' I hear him walking away.

'Thank you, but I don't think I can stomach anything right now.' I explain, pulling the duvet down. The entire room is still spinning around me.

'Ok, I can't argue that. I'll see you out when you're ready.' He exclaims before closing the door behind him.

I use the en-suit to freshen up. Head still pounding, I can barely stand straight, but I look in the mirror and see death. I look like death with my messy hair and bags under my eyes. And I'm currently in my boss' home. Gabriel's. Gabriel's home. And I'll have to explain it all to Aaron and Tess when I see them. The need to cut down the alcohol is strong now, because drunk Brooke thinks she can do whatever the hell she likes. After I put on the clothes Gabriel left out for me, which were a pair of jeans and an over a shoulder beige jumper, I leave the bathroom. I'm not sure how he got these clothes, but once again, probably best not to ask. I just need to get home quickly so I can make myself look like a human before meeting with my mom.

When I come out of the bedroom, I'm shocked to see the apartment he lives in. It's massive and very modern looking. He's definitely a minimalist, as I see nothing that could tell me anything about his character. I make my way to the kitchen, where I see him grabbing a bottle of water out of the fridge. Bruno comes up to me and I scratch his ear. Before I say anything, he must have heard me coming as he says,

'I think Bruno really liked your dog the other day. He hasn't been the same since.' I look down at Bruno and smile.

'Her name is Nala. And same.' I reply, and he snorts before turning to look at his dog.

'You're fussing about a girl?' His tail is wagging, and I cover my mouth to hide the amusement.

'You sure I can't make you anything to eat?' He comes up to me and offers me the bottle.

'Thank you.' I accept it. 'No, I really need to go. I'm meeting my mom later today and, well...' I point at myself, 'I look like a walking zombie.'

'A very sexy walking zombie.' He comments and I feel the heat in my cheeks. He smiles,

'Mark is waiting outside for you.'

'Who?' I exhale quickly, with brows drawn together.

'My driver. He'll take you home.'

'I- I can grab a taxi.' His eyebrow arches.

'A taxi? Don't be stupid. My driver is right outside and I'm not going anywhere today. Now before you argue, he knows where you live and you'll be home much quicker than if you were to call for a taxi and I'm pretty sure you just told me you're in a rush. So?' He crosses his arms over his chest, waiting for my reply.

Damn, I can't argue his logic here.

He smiles, as he can see on my face that he won. I sigh.

'Fine. But you're staying here, right?'

'Do you want me to come with you?' He grins at me.

'No. I think it's best you stay here.'

'Well, then.' He picks up a pair of black pumps from the floor and passes them to me. 'I'll see you at work tomorrow.' His grin remains at his face and I know I'm in trouble with this man. When I go to the front door and open it, he calls out.

'Brooke!' I turn around.

'I just want you to know that I meant every word I said last night.' I watch him for a moment and then I nod before leaving his apartment and closing the door.

'Hi, mom' I say as I come up to a table in our favorite pub.

'Hi, honey' She stands up and we share a hug.

'New jumper? It's lovely.' She comments as we sit down.

'You could say that.' I smile. When I got home, I quickly

filled Aaron in on what happened and after his 10 minutes of squealing in excitement, and me telling him that nothing was going to happen between me and Gabriel, he left. I had a cold shower, and I even put a heavier make up on today than normal to cover my death face. My head isn't hurting as bad as earlier, probably thanks to the 5 littles of water I drank before going out.

'I've ordered your usual.' my mom says as I pick up the menu.

'Oh great, thanks.' They have the best carbonara here I've ever tasted.

'And here are our drinks...' My mum nods to the waitress who sets down her glass of water and my ice tea. We thank her and turn back to each other.

'So talk to me, hon. How was your first week at work?' I take a sip of my drink and consider telling her the truth.

'It was... fine.' I avoid her eye contact.

'Just fine?' She asks with her brows lifted.

'Well, it's good, really. Everyone is friendly, and I already made a friend.' I sound like a child.

'Oh, how lovely.' My mom and I are very close. Always been, but even more since my dad's death. We moved to the UK to be close to her side of the family, but after so many years, she still feels alone and I wish I could change that. We see each other often, but a daughter would never fill that void in her heart that my dad left behind. They truly were the perfect example of marriage. Not perfect as never fighting, as no couple is that perfect, but they showed a true union. They thoroughly talked about every decision they made. Every night they went to bed together and every morning they sat at the table to eat breakfast. Even when they argued, they would put music on and forced themselves to dance to it with each other to ease off the anger.

'And how are you, mom?' I offer her a half-hearted smile, while trying to not down my drink from dehydration.

'Oh, same old, same old. Bakery is doing well, so I'm happy

about that.' My mom was always a housewife. With my dad having a well-paid job, it meant my mom could focus on our home and... me, but since we moved to UK, she had to find something, and considering all the years she spent at home, she became an amazing baker so I encouraged her to open her own bakery. The moment it opened, she'd sell out the same day, which made her very busy each day, prepping for the next one, which I think did her some good and helped her keep her mind off things. She needs to keep moving and I know it's easier said than done, but she still has so much life in her. Then again, I lost him when I was only 15 and we both struggled with it since but to her, it was her husband. The person who was meant to grow old with her but was taken away at the age of only 38.

'Met anyone yet?' I ask her, hoping for a different answer this time.

'God, Brooke.' She rolls her eyes at me. 'For the hundredth time. I am not interested.'

'Mom....' I take her hand in mine. 'You're still so young. You deserve to have someone.' I rub my thumb over the back of her hand.

'I'm not alone, you silly. I have you.' She pinches my cheek with her free hand.

'Mooom.' I lean back and chuckle. 'I'm not enough and you know it.' She sighs loudly, and the waitress brings the food to our table.

'So change of subject...' my mom says as she takes the first bite of her chicken salad. 'How's your book going?'

'Don't talk with your mouth full. That's nasty.' I point my fork at her and we both laugh.

'It's not a... it's not a book, mom ... Just a story I'm writing for fun.'

'For fun...?' She raises her brow.

'Yes. I don't think it's a good enough story to publish, to be honest.'

'Brooke Gertrude Summers...' Oh here we go. Full name

usually means telling off with her.

'Mom, please stop saying my middle name out loud.' I lift my hand to cover myself from people looking in our direction. 'When you were 8 years old. What was the most common costume on Halloween?' She continues.

'I don't know... Percy Jackson?' I roll my eyes and take another bite of this heavenly pasta and moan in satisfaction.

'Correct. Did you like Percy Jackson?'

'I loved it.' I reply with my mouth full, and she points at me with her threatening finger and I giggle.

'Yes, you did. Yet, who did you decide to dress up as?'

'Rick Riordan.' I whisper but loudly enough so she can hear me.

'And whyyyy?'

'Because I said that Rick Riordan had a more magical life than Percy Jackson because he was the one creating the world, which meant his imagination could go a hundred different directions, yet he wrote what he loved the most.' I look up and see her grinning.

'And do you remember what your dad did then?' I take a deep breath,

'He made me a mask of his face and made me a writing machine out of cardboard so I could walk around and tell everyone I'm an author.' Her lips now turn slightly downward and mine do the same.

'He was so proud of you, Brooke.' She says with her voice shaking. 'He knew you'd achieve amazing things in your life because you had an imagination for it, and he always said...'

'To predict your life, you only need your imagination. Simply believe it and it'll happen.' I finish for her and fight my tears back. Now my mom takes both my hands in hers.

'I miss your father every single day.' A tear falls down her cheek.

'Me too.' I smile through my tears, and she does the same.

'Write your book, baby. Go in a hundred directions and choose whichever one you love the most.' And all I can do is nod.

CHAPTER ELEVEN

Brooke

Tess' mouth and eyes are wide open as she gapes at me, completely frozen in place. It's Monday midday now and we're having lunch in my office, so I thought this was the time to explain everything.

'World to Tess...' I wave my hand in front of her face but get no response

'Tess...'

'What the fuck...' she mumbles. 'Brooke, that is...' She tries to find the right words.

'Unprofessional? Idiotic? Ridiculous? Plain stupid?' I offer her a few answers.

'No.' She frowns at me and leans back in her chair. 'I was going to say romantic.'

'Romantic? Have you heard a word I said?' Who in their right mind would think 'romantic' is the word to describe my situation?

'Yes. Yes Brooke. It makes total sense now, the way he looked at you at the club.' She's grinning now, teeth full on show, and I'm tempted to move away in case she explodes from excitement.

'Neither of us is looking for a relationship.' I repeat myself.

'I heard.' She's deep in thought. 'Nothing wrong with being friends with benefits thou.'

'Friends with....' I snort, 'Tess, he's my boss.'

'Yes, he's my boss too, so what's your point?'

'What's my...' I throw my hands in the air. 'You don't understand.'

'No, no, I don't. Because if the sexiest man alive wanted to be friends with benefits with me, I'd jump on the train without a second thought.' I sigh and slump in my chair.

'Brooke. There is literally nothing to lose. No strings attached.'

'Except if something goes wrong, I could lose my job.' Tess now chuckles and I roll my eyes at her.

'He's not that type of person, trust me. I can't speak about him as a person but as an employer, I doubt you have much to worry about that.'

This comment raises my interest. 'Oh, am I not the first employee to sleep with him?' Of course, I wouldn't be the first one. I roll my eyes at the thought of him sleeping with his employees.

'There was someone. It was 3 years ago, maybe.' She tries to remember. 'Yeah, they had a thing going on and as a receptionist, I get all the good gossip. She fell in love with him and wanted more from him, but he said no. He didn't fire her, but after a while, she couldn't cope with seeing him anymore, so she handed in her notice. Brooke, if you don't want a relationship but you just want some... kitty maintenance...' I snort out loud and Tess smiles at me. '...then I think he's the perfect guy.'

'It's not just that...'

'Then what is it?' She frowns and it's very hard to explain that it is not just about our hierarchy position.

'I... with my ex, I lost myself. I always ensured he was happy, and we did things he loved and I didn't even realise that by doing so, I stopped doing things I loved or I couldn't do things I wanted to do because he said no. I just disappeared and turned into this walking shell, making him happy every step of the way. When I left him, I promised myself this would never happen again.' Tess' lips turn downward. 'Don't you dare feel pity for me.' I point my finger at her.

'I'm not. It's just...' She straightens herself, 'Brooke. I get it. I've been through my amount of shitty relationships where I felt unworthy, but ...' She sighs loudly. 'You can't close yourself off from people just because you're scared they'll turn out just like Tyler. There are good men in this world, it's just finding them. Spending the rest of your life alone isn't fun at all.' She's right. I know she's right, as that's what I've been telling my mom for years, too. Maybe I'm a hypocrite, but I just feel... content with myself.

'I've got an idea.' Tess exclaims as she looks at her watch. 'I gotta go back, but after work, come with me.'

'Come with you where?'

'You'll see.' She winks at me and stands up. 'Meet me at the reception after work.' She blows me a kiss and walks out of my office.

'Have you seen him today?' Tess asks as we make our way through a busy pavement. Everyone is rushing to get to their homes after a busy Monday. My day was rather uneventful, which I'm grateful for. I got a lot done today too, which I plan on celebrating with a small glass of wine and maybe finally decide on how to carry on with my own story.

'Thankfully, not.' A guy wearing a suit and talking on his phone bumps into me and doesn't even apologize. I roll my eyes. The wind blows my hair all over the place, left to right, making my vision limited. I see Tess struggling with the same thing as she pulls her hair out of her mouth. We both struggle our way through before she stops and turns to me.

'We're here.' I look to my right at the sign on the door.

'You're joking?'

'No.' A grin appears on her face.

'You really believe that?' Big letters saying TAROT READINGS stare back at me.

'And you don't?' Another person bumps into me and they carry on walking.

'Saying sorry wouldn't hurt!' I call out in their direction, wishing I could just get to my warm home and spend the rest of the day under the blanket on my sofa.

'Trust me, Brooke.' Tess grabs my arm and hops inside, pulling me with her.

'Tess, my dear.' A woman, maybe in her 40s, comes up to us and gives Tess a hug. Her hair is black and curly, almost reaching her waist, and she's wearing a floral blouse and a long brown skirt that swings around her ankles. She's also wearing a lot of jewellery, but not the silver or gold type. They're full of colourful rocks around her neck and wrists.

'Who did you bring with you today?' She looks at me with a warm, welcoming smile.

'That's my friend from work. Brooke.'

'Hi.' I say, offering a smile back. She looks me up, and down while her hands lifted, rubbing her fingers with her thumbs.

'You need to stop worrying so much, my sweet girl.' She says.

'That's what I told her.' Tess adds before turning to me, 'This is Diane. I've been seeing her for a few years now.'

'It's nice to meet you' I say to Diane, and she smiles back. It feels cold in here, yet welcoming. The air feels heavy and my head is almost dizzy. The smell is strong too, but it's not like when you go to a cosmetic store... it's more natural, reminding me of herbs and spices.

'Your first time, Brooke?' Diane asks as she makes her way to the next room behind the curtain.

'Yes.' We both follow her and as we enter, I spot a big round table with 4 chairs around it on one side and 1 chair on the other side.

'Have a seat.' She gestures to the 4 chairs and we do as told as she goes around and sits down with us. She closes her eyes for a moment and takes a few deep breaths and I can feel my hands sweaty so I wipe them on my legs. Tess grabs onto my hand and offers me a smile and I smile back. Diane picks up a deck of cards and shuffles them as she's looking at Tess and pulls out a card after card, setting them in front her on the table. She puts the deck back to where it was and she carefully looks at the individual cards.

'You met someone.' It was more of a statement than a question.

'Maybe.' Tess' cheeks blush.

'Tall and handsome.'

'So handsome.' She sounds like a little girl with a crush.

'You'll see him again.' Tess' smile widens. 'But don't jump into it.' and just as quickly it disappears.

'What do you mean?'

'He's not looking for the same thing as you...' She picks up another card from the top of her deck. 'I see a potential, but he needs to earn it, Tess. Make him work for you. He's used to easy and if you both jump into it, you'll be just another number.' Is she talking about Max? I saw her giggling with him that night at the club, but I guess I was preoccupied with someone else.

'Show him your worth and what you're made of, and he'll worship you.' Diane smiles. 'And I also see a big change in your career life.'

'Positive or negative change?' She throws herself forward in her chair and slaps her hands on the table, which makes Diane laugh.

'Definitely positive. My advice is, accept the offer.'

'I will.' She grins while leaning back in her chair.

Diane picks up all the cards and puts them back in the deck.

'You.' She now looks at me as she shuffles them again.

'Me?' I point at myself, feeling my heart picking up the pace.

'Don't be scared.' Tess whispers to me, and Diane pulls out multiple cards again. I swallow a big gulp that was stuck in my throat. Do I believe she can read me? I'm not sure. I know there are plenty of so-called mediums who lie and deceive, but I also know there are some real deals, but I was just never interested in having a reading done. Diane looks at my cards this time and puts her hand over her chest.

'Oh, my sweet girl...' Tess grabs my hand again and squeezes it. I don't flinch. I don't move. As I look at Diane, I don't think I can breathe.

'So much loss in your life.' She sighs. 'I see you had your heart broken recently.'

'Y-yes.' I reply with my shaky voice.

'I see pain but also relief that came from it. You weren't yourself around this person.' Emotions are boiling up in my throat and I do my best to hold back my tears.

'You're shielding yourself.' She adds and looks at me with her motherly eyes, 'You feel you need to be alone to keep this person who you are from disappearing again.' I only nod. 'Loneliness isn't something that humans were made for. We seek friendships and companionships along others.' She smiles warmly. 'What happened to you was not your fault, but his. He took an advantage of you but I see you learnt your lesson. Trust your heart and your inner voice, as they only want what's best for you, and I don't mean your ego.'

'My what?' I glance between her and Tess.

'Ego is the voice in your head that says you're not good enough. It's all the negative thoughts you're thinking ... That's your ego. We all have it and most of us do believe in what it tells us but I also see...' She pauses as she looks at the wall past my shoulder, but when I turn around, I see nothing there.

'Finish the story, Brooke.'

'What do you....' I can't finish the question without feeling a shiver traveling down my spine.

'Finish the story.' She only repeats. 'Your father believes in you and loves you.' At the mention of my dad, the tears now fall freely down my cheeks.

'My dad?' Her own eyes glistening now, she replies with a smile, 'Yes. He's here, and he tells you to not live your life where one day you'll ask yourself what if. He says it's his most hated question.' I chuckle because I know that to be true. 'He also says you can't decide on something right now, but it tempts you.' Gabriel?

'He's telling you to not be afraid and that he's with you always.' Tess throws her arm around my shoulders and hugs me as my tears fall quicker. 'He misses you and your mum very much, and he's also very proud of you two.'

'I-I miss-s him too.'

'He says, no more What Ifs and to look out for a dandelion. It's a sign he's with you.' I nod and wipe the tears with my arm.

When we come out of the room, I go for the door but see Tess and Diane whispering between themselves. I give them privacy before they both come up to me and Diane gives me a hug. I hug her back and thank her for everything before me and Tess walk out of Diane's shop.

'Wanna grab a drink?' Tess asks while rubbing my arm and I cross my arms to keep myself warm.

'I am so tired Tess, I just want to go home and probably straight to sleep.' I offer her a half-hearted smile and she smiles back.

'I was like that too at first. It really tires you out, doesn't it? I'll see you tomorrow.' She kisses my cheek and we say our goodbyes before heading our own ways, and I spend the rest of the day crying.

CHAPTER TWELVE

Gabriel

I can not believe my lucky stars—I think to myself when I see Brooke's ex, Tyler Hughes, standing outside a cafe with a group of who I presume to be his friends. He's taking a drag of his cigarette while leaning back on the wall. I decide to act. I pull Bruno to my heel as we make our way towards him, and he glances at me as his brows pinched together.

'Tyler Hughes?' I ask, glaring right at him, and his companions take a step back.

'Who's asking?' He takes the last drag and throws his cigarette to the ground before putting it out with his heel. I see a glimpse of fear when he looks at Bruno. He's scared of dogs — noted.

'Doesn't matter who's asking. What matters is that you are going to stay away from Brooke from now on.'

He scoffs. 'I don't think so.' He turns to go inside, but I stop him, grabbing his shoulder. 'I don't think you understand. This is not a request.' He looks up at me and pulls himself away from my grip.

'Brooke is my girlfriend, so back off, mate.'

'One, she's not your girlfriend and two, I'm not your mate, mate.'

He turns back to me and shoves his finger into my chest. 'Brooke is mine. She might not realise that yet, but she belongs to me. I don't care if she's got you as her bodyguard from now on, but she won't be able to avoid me forever.' He looks me up and down. 'I saw you two at the club.' He scoffs. 'So I guess the slut found herself a new guy who can fuck her and pay for her? I'll give you a tip...'

He's smirking now and my hands curl into fists, trying to not lose it with him, but I know I'm right on the edge. '...she loves it when you slide your dick in very slowly so she can...' My fist meets his face before he can finish his sentence, and his companions rush further away while wooing.

Tyler is now on the ground, groaning in pain, and I gesture to Bruno to sit. 'You fucker broke my nose!' He yells out, covering his face as drops of blood fall onto the pavement.

'I'll break more than your nose if you're anywhere near her, do you understand?' He spits in my direction, but it misses. A dark laughter escapes my mouth as I step closer, placing my foot on his throat, pushing just gently, turning his face red from fighting for air. 'I'll call the police.'

He groans, and I bend down at my waist, 'Go ahead,' I smile at him, 'I'm sure my dear friend who works at the police, would love to hear about you assaulting a young woman in her own home.' His eyes widen in horror, and I take my foot off him before picking Bruno's leash. 'I believe we have an understanding?' I ask him while he's slowly going on all fours, having a coughing fit. He looks up at me, all bloody, and nods.

'Great.'

'Soon, my boy, very soon.' I smile as I speak to Bruno, who is lying down by the window, all sad once again. He's been like that every day since that day at the park.

'We'll get them' I raise my glass to him and I swallow my favourite golden liquid in one go. The doorbell rings and I set my glass on the table before I open the door.

'Mr. Alstons?' A man in his 40s appears. He's smart looking, wearing a suit and his dirty blonde hair slicked back.

'You must be Mr. Rowland.' I open the door further, inviting him in. He takes in his surroundings.

'You have a delightful place here.'

'Thank you.' I head over to my open kitchen and pull out two clean glasses. I pick up a bottle of whisky and shake it at him in question.

'Yes, please. Thank you.' He understands my question and I pour into both before heading down to my study, where we sit down at my desk.

'My dear friend Max has recommended you to me.' I start and he nods.

'I hope you understand with my publicity, I'd like to keep this private.'

'Not a single word will leave my mouth to anyone other than you, Mr. Alstons.' He takes a sip and his mouth turns downwards as he struggles to swallow.

'Not much of a drinker?' I offer him a smile and he sets his glass down.

'I find alcohol doesn't go hand in hand with my job. At all times, I have to be alert. I like this man's honesty.

'Well, here's what I have for you.' I say as I pull out a folder and slide it over to him. He opens it and skims through the pages.

'Last known address was from 5 years ago?' He asks while still looking through them.

'Yes.' His eyes narrow and he clicks his tongue.

'Ok.' He closes the folder and looks up at me. 'I can do it.' He says with certainty.

'Might take a little longer because of no recent address, but I think I have enough to go on from this.' I watch him and see no sign of reluctance. This man knows what he's doing, and he's confident. 'You've been doing this for long?' I ask him and I see a shadow of a smile on his face.

'Probably too long.' He replies and we both stand up and shake hands. I walk him to the door.

'It's been a pleasure to meet you, sir.'

'You too.' I reply and we say goodbye.

After I close the door, I head back to my study, and Bruno follows me. I sit down and finish my drink while looking through the window from my chair. I feel somehow unsettled today and I don't know what to do about it. My mind travels back to yesterday morning when Brooke was in my bed, looking all cautious and pure and I can't help but wonder, if that is what men in love see? A woman they so deeply love in their bed and get excited to have this view every day for the rest of their lives? My foster parents were completely opposite to that, I guess. They both slept separately and I don't mean separate beds. I mean, my foster mum slept in her bedroom and my foster dad slept on the sofa, both falling asleep quickly after an evening of arguing and throwing things at each other. Sometimes it'd be a pillow and sometimes it'd be an empty bottle of whisky. She loved to drink. She said it helped her forget just for a moment how wretched her life is with a husband who cheats on her and a little bastard running around. (Yes, the bastard was me). I helped her frequently to get to her to bed, and I was the one cleaning up the mess. He was barely there. Working long hours and only coming home late to eat and then go to sleep. I got slapped periodically too by her. 'He wouldn't do this to me if I didn't take you in.' she'd say and I wondered ever since, if kids are to blame for failed marriages. Would I ever be able to look at someone and say I want to spend the rest of my life with someone? I don't know, but I'm also very much open to the idea of not settling down. If I'm to have the marriage I saw growing up, I'd gladly pass on it. But then I remember, somewhere out there, there's a guy who did exactly that to Brooke and I don't understand who could cheat on her. I barely know her but there's something about her which gives off a lot of warmth and a homely feeling. I honestly can't get my head around why I'm so struck on her. A woman kissing me isn't anything new, but the way her body felt on mine, it was like a perfect match, like she was made to connect with my body and I won't stop until I explore it further. She's shielding, however, and I know she's trying to fight it. I'm not sure if it's her job she's worried about or maybe getting hurt, or maybe even a little of both. Maybe she's not the type of person who sleeps with someone without commitment, but she's still young and there's nothing to say she can't just enjoy herself. Life is to be enjoyed and explored, otherwise what is the point of living?

I turn in my chair and move back to my desk.

'I'm doing it.' I say to Bruno while scratching his ear. Opening my laptop, I sign in to my business account and the sick feeling washes over me while I'm still deciding if it's a good idea or not. I open the file with employees' information and scroll down to the letter S.

Summers, Brooke.

I click on her name and all the details pop out. I pull out my phone from the pocket of my grey track pants and start typing.

Me- Hi gorgeous.

Delete.

Me- I'm very impressed with your work so far.

Delete.

Shit, why is this so fucking difficult?! I put my phone down and rub my hand over my face as I sigh. I realise my hands are sweaty, so I rub them on my knees before picking my phone back up.

Me- How are you?

Delete. I'm pathetic. I tap my fingers on the desk while trying to come up with my opening line...

Me- Hi. It's Gabriel.

Delete. I lean back in my chair and groan in irritation. Bruno comes up to me and puts his head on my lap.

'I so wish you could tell me what to write.' I say to him and scratch his head. 'They say dogs are good women baits, you know...' I add, and his tail starts wagging. I stare at him for a moment before going back to my phone.

Me- You broke my dog.

Sent. My heart is pounding fast now and I feel like my stomach is about to empty itself.

The answer comes within seconds.

Brooke- Who's this?

We're in. Oh god.

Me- Bruno has been sulking over your dog since Friday.

Three dots appear and stop. Three dots appear again and stop again.

Oh shit.

I get up, unable to sit still, and walk around my office.

Three dots appear again...

Brooke- Gabriel?

I let out a breath I didn't realise I was holding.

Me- Who else has a dog so deeply in love with yours? ;)

I put my phone down on my desk and down the rest of the whisky from the glass. Bruno is wagging his tail while still sitting next to my chair, watching my every move.

'This is your fault.' He barks in reply when I point at him. I push my fingers through my hair and I hear my phone pings again. I pick it up to read.

Brooke- How did you get my number?

Shit. I screwed up. Will she believe if I tell her it was Bruno who messaged her? Doubt it.

My fingers hoover above the screen before typing,

Me- Am I in trouble?

I sit back down and take a few deep breaths to calm my nerves. Or maybe another glass of whisky will help. I pick my glass up and go to refill, and when I come back, I have an unread message. I take a sip before reading, my stomach twisting, and I know this whisky is about to make its way back up.

Brooke- I haven't decided yet.

Me- I'm a good boy, really. (blushing emoji)

I stare at my screen, waiting for her reply, and it comes within seconds.

Brooke- You don't look like a boy to me.

Me- Is that a compliment?

Brooke- Maybe.

I smirk to myself, and she sends another message

Brooke- Tell me something about yourself.

I take a moment to think and type

Me- I like you.

Three dots appear and disappear.

Brooke- Something real.

Me- I don't like chicken.

Brooke- As in bird or meat?

Me- Both. Meat isn't that tasty, and the texture is terrible, and birds are terrifying ... They'll chase you endlessly.

Brooke- Lol

Me- What's so funny?

Brooke- You're scared of little birds.

Me- Your turn now.

It takes a few minutes before the message pops up.

Brooke- I'm scared.

Me- Of?

Brooke- Of making a wrong decision.

Me- Regarding?

5 minutes pass, then 10 and 15. She leaves me on read and I know I'm not getting my answer tonight so I decide to shoot a quick text to Max.

Me- Met with your guy today. He seems decent. Thanks.

And I get an instant reply.

Max- You won't be disappointed, mate.

And I decide it's time to call it a night.

CHAPTER THIRTEEN

Brooke

Bark. Bark. Bark.

I pull the covers over my head.

Bark. Bark. Bark.

'Nala, go to sleep!' I mumble out from underneath my duvet.

Bark. Bark. Bark.

Knock. Knock. Knock.

'What the hell?' I groan to myself as I sit up. After rubbing the sleep off my eyes, I pick up my phone to check the time.

2am.

Knock. Knock. Knock.

I throw my dressing gown on and go towards the front door. Nala is standing with her tail wagging like crazy and whines.

Knock. Knock. Knock.

'Tyler, if that's you, I'm calling the police!' I shout out.

'It's me.' I freeze, mouth wide open now, as I'm staring at the door, unable to move.

'I'll keep knocking till you open.' Nala looks at me and whines again. I rush to open the door.

'What are you doing here?'

'Can I come in?' He asks, with Bruno at his side.

'I-em... sure.' I open the door wider to let them in, and both dogs begin to jump and lick each other.

'I told you he's in love.' He smirks as we both watch them.

'How did you even get inside?' Realising my gown is open, I pull the fabric over quickly and cross my arms. Gabriel's glance lowers to my breasts, which sends butterflies to my stomach.

'I just pulled it open. You didn't answer my question, though.' He replies. Of course, the bloody door isn't working again. The neighbourhood is pleasant and all, but for maintenance, it definitely could improve.

'What que...'

'The phone text.' He answers before I can finish.

'So you decide to drive here at 2am?' I shake my head at him and he frowns.

'I couldn't sleep.' He glances down and smirks, 'Loving your little mermaid pjs thou.' I look down and in fact I am wearing ariels pj trousers.

'What do you want, Gabriel?' I sigh, completely unready for the conversation. 'Also, how do you know where I live?'

'I brought you here after the club if you remember rightly.' I think drunk Brooke is going to take a leave for a while. 'What decision are you afraid of making, Brooke?' He takes a step closer to me and I take a step back, making the back of my legs bump into my dining table.

'Are you drunk?' I can smell the whisky on his breath and now my gut fills with fear and regret for letting him inside my home.

'I don't get drunk.' He whispers.

'I think you should leave.' I turn my head away from him.

'What are you so afraid of, Brooke?' He takes another step closer and I can feel our bodies almost touching. The tension builds between us and an electric shock shoots through my body as he places his hand on my hip, awaking every inch. I look back at him and he frowns.

'I'm not looking for a relationship, Brooke...' He open the gown, exposing me as I'm wearing a black bralette. 'God damn it woman' His eyes darken in the moonlight that comes through the blinds. 'Just because we don't want a relationship, it doesn't mean we can't enjoy ourselves.' I feel wetness between my legs, and watch as his stare eats me up and makes my legs weak. I lay my hands on his chest and he closes his eyes, allowing his breathing to deepen.

'Gabriel...' I start, but he cuts me off by grabbing me by my wrists, firmly enough for me to jump in anticipation. My stomach drops as I feel our breaths syncing, and his chest moving against mine.

'Think about it, Brooke.' He turns to dogs who are now sleeping, cuddled up to each other on the floor and calls out. 'Let's go, Bruno.' and he stands up slowly, not wanting to leave Nala behind.

'Tell me you'll think about it.' He adds, but still doesn't look at me.

'I will.' I whisper back and I swear there was a slight twitch on his mouth. After he lets go of me and makes his way back to the door, I feel like it's taking all my strength to not stop him from leaving.

'What if...' I start and he shoots me a stare that stops me.

'If you're going to ask what if about every decision in your life, then you'll never truly live.' And this statement hits me right in the heart. We stare at each other for a moment before he turns away.

'Sleep well, Brooke.' And the door closes behind him.

When the morning comes, I wake up with a smile. I'm on his mind a lot and it's driving him crazy. The ball is in my court now and it's up to me what I decide. I believe him now that he would not fire me over anything personal that happens between us, and I believe he's not interested in anything romantic. Maybe he's right... Maybe we can enjoy ourselves without ever taking it further? I know my body longs for him every day since we met, to the point where even Mr. Pink isn't helping. I dream about him every night and wake up with wet sheets. Both Tess and Aaron think I should say yes, because in their words... What could go wrong? I take a cold shower and, in the meantime, I decide to make him suffer a little more. When I open my wardrobe, I spot a black pencil skirt and a white blouse which I won't do fully up. I also pull out my black 12cm heels, and I know, even though my feet are going to hate me for it, it's going to be damn worth it. My hair gets curled today instead of putting it up as usual, and I put a lip gloss on. I feel like a sex goddess and my confidence shoots over the roof. Before I leave for work, I take a quick glance in the mirror,

'Fuck, I look hot.' I wink at myself and walk out.

'Holy fucking god, Brooke!' Tess shoots up from her seat at the reception and gasps while everyone glares at her.

'Tess, shh.' I put my finger over my lips and laugh.

'What the actual fuck...' she whispers back.

'I'm playing hard to get.'

'Yes, girl!' She jumps up twice while clapping her hands.

'It's not too much, is it?' I look down and the anxiety kicks in. Maybe I should have worn my normal clothes. Maybe it's too much.

'Too much? He's going to dribble so badly that he'll need a fresh shirt.' We both chuckle. 'I bet you, when he sees you once, you won't see him again for the rest of the day.'

'Why?' Tess gives me a toothy grin.

'Because he's going to get so hard, he won't be able to get rid of it.' And I laugh again.

'See you at lunch?' I ask while heading towards the elevator.

'You know it.' She winks, and I turn away; all eyes are on me. From men and women included. I suddenly feel like an animal at the zoo, where everyone is watching me, waiting for me to do something. My heart beats faster when I get inside the elevator and I press 5 for my floor. A man who I never seen before hops inside with me and watches me the whole time.

'Can I just say you're absolutely beautiful?'

'Erm ... thank you?' I offer a smile and I notice he's already hard, so I spin my head and I keep my gaze at the door.

'Can I take you out maybe...?'

'I'm sorry, but I'm not interested.' I turn to him and smile again. When the door opens, I rush out.

On my floor, everyone is staring at me too. John stands at his desk with his mouth open and Justin gives me two thumbs up from his office. I chuckle before I disappear into my office and close the door.

Well, this was... awkward. I take a few deep breaths and I swear I can hear my heart pounding against my chest. When I turn towards my desk, I see a bouquet of a dozen red roses. I walk up to it and notice a note which I pick up and read,

'Think about it. There's nothing to lose. G' My cheeks warm. I smile to myself before setting the note down. A knock now sounds on my door.

'Come in.' I call out and move the flowers onto the windowsill. When I turn around, I see Gabriel standing there with an impressive bulge in his crotch, and his jaw ticking.

Mission accomplished.

'Oh good morning, Mr. Alstons. How can I help you today?' I smile warmly, yet he still doesn't move.

'Thank you for the flowers.' I look at them and then back at him. He shuts the door, locking it behind him, and walks up to me.

Oh, *shit*.

'What is this?' He's barely inches away now.

'What's what?' I smile innocently, and the sound of his heavy breathing reaches my ears.

'You realise everyone is looking at you, right?'

'Are they?' I make puppy eyes and lean back on the end of the desk. 'Are you looking at me?' He grabs my hand and puts it over his very hard cock. My core twists at the feeling of him, and I can tell he's big. Bigger than I've ever had before.

'What do you think?' He asks.

I clear my throat. 'I take it you like what you see?'

The corner of his mouth twitches. 'I think I'd love to take you over your desk right here, right now.' My clit awakens, pulsing between my legs.

'I think there's something else you should know, Mr. Alstons.' I say seductively.

'And what is that Miss. Summers?' I bite my lower lip and then say,

'You wouldn't find doing that too difficult, as I'm not wearing any panties.' His whole body tenses and I feel his cock twitch underneath my touch. I remove my hand and look him up and down. He groans and I turn away, walking toward my chair.

'If that's all, sir,' I gesture to the door. 'I really need to work.' He clenches his fists while I stand tall. 'I don't think my boss would be happy to see me flirt with men during my working hours.' I wink at him and his mouth turns upwards.

'No, he definitely would not like that and would fire any man trying to flirt with you.' He warns and walks out of my office.

CHAPTER FOURTEEN

Brooke

Isn't it funny how one day can change your entire perspective? I'm not a spiritual person, at least not the way Tess is, but I believe there's something more out there and I believe there are genuine psychics and that one afternoon I got my proof. My dad is with me. I smile to myself as I stand in my kitchen and pour myself a glass of wine.

One won't hurt.

I still haven't made my decision about Gabriel, but that doesn't mean I can't make him suffer while he waits. I never saw myself as a friend with benefits type of girl, but when thinking about it... what is there to lose? We can't deny our chemistry, no matter how hard we try, and it's only sex, so I don't need to think about getting to know him. He could sleep with his socks on for all I know and it won't affect me because sleeping together would not happen. I would not be spending the rest of my life with him and considering I have no plans on finding a boyfriend, then why not have some fun while I'm still young?

I stare at the screen of my laptop. I haven't been able to

carry on with my story because of the writer's block. Should they get together or maybe I should throw in a surprise new love interest? I rub my chin with my finger and think. Seconds turn into minutes and minutes turn into an hour before I realise I've got nothing. I sip on my wine when my phone pings. A gasp leaves my mouth when I see a photo of Tyler that Aaron sent me. I stare at my ex's black eyes for a good minute before my phone rings.

'Tess?'

'Why are men such douchebags?!' she chokes out her question.

'Are you ok? What happened?' I set my glass down and turn my laptop off. I can get back to it later.

'Oh, just once again, I'm interested in a guy who doesn't look past my looks.' I know plenty of women who'd kill to look like Tess. A walking barbie. Every little girl's dream. But as I'm getting to know her better, I see everything comes with a price and sometimes beauty can be a curse, just like a blessing.

'Do you want to come over and get drunk?' I glance at my freshly opened bottle of wine and I know I have one more hidden somewhere.

'Be there in 20.' I hear her mood shift through the speaker.

'Is this what I think it is?' Tess grins as she's looking at the board hanging on the wall.

'What do you think it is?' I ask, while pouring two glasses of wine. It's my second one in the evening.

'I think it's your vision board.' She crosses her arms over her chest and turns to me. 'Tell me more.' I sigh and come towards her, passing her a full glass, and glance at my board.

'Postcard from Greece. I've never actually been but my dad promised to take me one day as that's where he knew he loved my mum and proposed to her...'

'Awww...'

'Obviously he never got to take me.'

'I'm sorry.'

I smile at a memory of him. He would have loved Tess. 'It's ok. I will go there one day.'

'Yes, you will.' We clank our glasses in cheers and take a sip. 'The picture of the book is me, dreaming of having my book published. I've wanted to be an author for as long as I remember.' I sigh before adding, 'Well, I need to finish writing it first.'

'You can do it, Brooke.' She puts her hand on my shoulder.

'The picture of the house...' I look at the photo I found online, a beautiful free standing farm house, made of red brick, with a black roof and double front door with plenty of land around it. 'It's my dream home. I hope to have enough land so I can rescue more dogs and have my writing study with a floor-to-ceiling window and a view of the garden. And...' I chuckle to myself. 'The study has to be so big, so it can fit multiple of bookcases. Call it my little library.'

'I definitely see this life for you.' Tess comments, and it warms my heart just thinking about the type of life I desire for myself.

'So tell me what happened?' I ask. Tess' smile turns into a frown as we go to sit on my sofa. She sits cross-legged and I pull my leg under me while resting my head in my hand.

'So Saturday night, me and Max exchanged numbers.' She starts and I already know this will not end well.

'He messaged me this afternoon, asking if I fancy popping over his place tonight.'

I watch her and reply, 'Well, maybe he meant to get to know you?' Anything I'll say is going to be useless due to my lack of knowledge about this type of thing.

'I replied saying, oh what you have in mind. And his reply was...' She pulls out her phone from the back pocket of her skinny jeans and opens the message. 'What I have in mind is the colour of your panties.' I pretend to gag, which makes her smile. It doesn't, however, match her eyes.

'Have you replied to him after that?' She puts her phone down on my coffee table and takes another sip of her wine. 'Nope.' Her tone is flat. 'Diane said to make him sweat, and that's what I'm going to do. It's up to him to decide if I'm worth it.' I nod, unsure of what to say.

'And you... has Mr. Alstons seen you today?' She winks at me.

'Yes, he has.' I snort out and look down at my glass, swirling the wine inside it.

'Once?'

I confirm with a nod, and her smile spreads from ear to ear.

'I told you.'

'He told me he wanted to fuck me over my desk.' She chokes on her wine, and I quickly take the glass of her, laughing. I slap her on her back.

'A-and... wh-what did you tell him?' She asks while trying to catch her breath.

'That I'm not wearing any underwear.' I shrug and her eyes look like they're about to pop out of her eye sockets.

'You savage. I love it!' She smiles again, and our laughter echoes from the walls. I still very much remember the feeling when he said those things and how much I wanted him to follow through. After I sigh, I notice Tess is completely zoned out, so I come up with a distraction.

'Let's dance.' I put my glass down and call out to Alexa, that is standing next to my tv to play 10 things I hate about you by Leah Kate. I turn the volume up. The music plays and we both get up, holding hands and moving to the tune.

'Do you know the words?' I ask.

'Of course!' And we join in as the lyrics start.

'Ten, you're selfish,

Nine, you're jaded,

Eight, the dumbest guy I dated!' We sing out loud, almost shouting, while jumping up and down, throwing our hair in the air.

'Only 6 seconds and I had to fake it.' And we both burst out laughing.

'Well, well...' We both almost jump out of our bodies before turning to see Aaron standing in my kitchen and pouring himself a glass of wine.

'Someone care to explain why I wasn't invited to the party?' We both laugh and race to Aaron, throwing our arms around him from each side.

'Can't. Breathe.' We let go, and we're all laughing now.

'It was very short notice Tess needed to unwind.' I explain, but I know Aaron isn't upset about it and is just joking around.

'You saw the photo I sent you?' He asks before taking a sip of his wine.

'What photo?' Tess adds.

'I saw Tyler walking to the bar today, and he looked well beaten up...' Tess' eyes widen and she looks at me. 'Do you think it was Mr. Alstons?'

'What?!' This question takes me by surprise. 'Why would you think that?'

'He saw your bruises on Saturday, did he not? And you told him it was your ex.'

'Yeah, but he doesn't know who my ex is.' Tess chuckles.

'You really think a rich CEO like Gabriel isn't capable of finding out such little details like the name of you ex?' I don't reply to that. I ... didn't think about that but... would he... no ... surely not.

Maybe.

'Anyway...' Aaron puts his arm over my shoulder and speaks to Tess.

'I need some catching up if I'm going to be calling someone a twat.'

She starts to explain when I glance at my closed laptop, sitting on my dining table, and I know exactly what I'm going to write.

'Brooke, what's wrong with Nala?' I turn back and look at my dog, who's staring at us with her eyes wide open, her body completely still. My eyes widen in horror before I shout,

'RUN!' And I rush to my bedroom, Tess and Aaron matching my energy and running with me. I shut the door and turn around to see them both standing there with brows raised and lips pulled into thin lines.

'What the hell was that...' Tess starts but stops as the sound of fart comes from my living area and both Aaron's and Tess' eyes widen in shock.

'She started doing it last week and trust me... they're actual killers.' I choke out while laughing.

'What are we going to do?' Aaron asks,

'Party in my bedroom?' I shrug and Aaron lifts his brow at me.

'I love you Brooke, but I'm not attracted to women, let alone two at once.' Tess playfully punches him in the shoulder. 'You'd be lucky to have a threesome with us.' I cover my mouth to hide my laughter.

'Maybe. I'd rather not find out, thou.' Aaron adds, and I point at him with my finger and very serious face.

'You're locked inside here with us while insulting us. Say one more thing and I'll push you through that door and lock it behind you.' Now Tess is giggling and Aaron puts his hands up in surrender.

'I'm sorry.' At this moment, I feel thrilled with my life for having two of the best people in it. I know for a fact, if I was to call them to say I killed someone, these two would help me hide the body.

'What's up with your face?' Tess frowns at me and I snap out of my thoughts.

'What?'

'You were looking all... dopey.' She adds and Aaron nods in agreement.

'I just love you guys so much.' I smile warmly and they both aww at me before going in for a group hug.

CHAPTER FIFTEEN

Gabriel

I stare at the empty glass in my hand, wondering what happened to me. Seeing Brooke the way she dressed today did something to me, and I'm not talking about the boner I've had all fucking day. I didn't leave my office in fear of bumping into her and not being able to control myself. It's taking more strength than I expected when it comes to Brooke, and I don't know how much longer I can last. I'm only hoping she'll say yes soon enough and I can punish her hard for making me suffer. I can't believe I ended up going over to her place last night, either. 2 o'clock in the bloody morning. I'm surprised she didn't kick me out, but I think Bruno was a big help. I wanted to see her—I needed to see her. Seeing her apartment for the first time gave me an extra insight into her character. It was warm and homely, unlike my apartment, which just breathes emptiness and coldness. But that's me. Cold and empty inside.

I hear a knock on my door and Bruno jumps out of his bed and lets out a bark. One bark always means one person.

'It's open, dickhead!' I call out and then I heard the door

open and shut before Max appears in my view, grinning like an idiot.

'Just checking Bruno's senses.' He says before he heads to the kitchen and pours himself a glass of whisky.

'It's rare to see you this late in the day?' I lift my arm up to look at my watch. '11 o'clock. Shitty date?' He takes a seat on the sofa and glares at me, his eyes burning a hole in the side of my face. I tilt my head and laugh. 'What did you do?'

'I did nothing.' He snaps at me, which only makes me laugh harder. 'You know your receptionist?'

'Tess?' I eye him, hoping he's not screwing one of my best employees.

'Yeah, well, we exchanged numbers Saturday night and so I messaged her today to see if she wanted to come over.'

'Come over?' I raise my eyebrow at him, not liking this one bit.

'Yeah, but she shot me down.' He takes a big gulp of his drink and stares at my turned off tv on the wall.

'I don't blame her.' I shrug and scratch Bruno's head as he sits down next to me. 'Ive known her for a while and she won't go for a one-night stand, mate.' I explain to him. 'She's looking for her soulmate.' Max scoffs, before finishing his drink and setting the glass on the table.

'Soulmates.' He chuckles. 'Should I just propose to her, then?'

'If you want in, invite her on a date. She likes romantic gestures, you know, flowers and dinner with candles.' He rolls his eyes at me and throws his leg over the other one. 'Get to know the woman.'

'What happened to you, man? You were all for one-night stands before you met Brooke.'

I shoot him a death glare. 'I still am. But if you want Tess for a one-night stand, you have no hope.' Max sighs and leans back onto the backrest and lets his head fall back. 'She's so fucking hot, Gabe.' His stare remains at the ceiling, and I stand up to refill my glass.

'Then the decision is yours.' He says nothing until I'm back with my drink and I take the sip.

'How's the situation with Brooke?' He finally asks, and honestly, I don't think I have an answer for him. My cock is suffering here, thinking about her day and night, about her lips on mine, about her curvy body that makes me almost cum just at the thought of it. 'I have no idea. She knows what I want, but it's up to her to decide.' I shrug and I hope she'll decide soon. Another set of knocking comes from the door and Bruno barks once and then twice, which throws me off. I have no idea who'd come to my home at 11 o'clock at night.

'Waiting for someone?' Max glances in the same direction, watching me go to get the door. 'No.' I reply.

My stomach twists when I see Brooke standing in the doorframe, wearing a long winter coat and black boots, her hair soaked from the rain.

'Brooke?'

'The answer is yes.' She says and rushes towards me, crushing her mouth to mine while cupping my face in her hands. I'm taken by surprise and now my cock pulses, ready to experience Brooke Summers. I wrap my arms around her waist, pulling her closer while kissing her back. She said yes. I close the door without breaking the kiss and as I'm about to reach for her zipper of her coat, Max fake coughs. We both freeze and Brooke withdrawers fast, her face red like a tomato. I turn to see my best friend, raising his glass at us and smiling.

Shit.

Of course, she made me forget he was here.

'Goodbye, Max' I call out to him.

'No, I-I'll go. I'm sorry, I shouldn't have ...' she says, but I put my finger over her mouth to stop her from talking. She is not going anywhere now. She's mine. My cock twitches when I think of the things I'm going to do to her once my best friend leaves.

'Out.' I bark at Max once again and he stands up, laughing. As he gets near us, he places his hand on my shoulder.

'Have fun, kids. Lovely to see you again, Brooke.' He nods and smiles at her. She smiles back, but the redness on her face remains.

'You too.' She replies, and Max leaves, shutting the door behind him.

'Where were we?' I ask and Brooke chuckles.

'I'm sorry.' She repeats and I cup her face in my hands.

'Never, ever say sorry for coming to my home. I'll kick any sucker out of here just to be alone with you.' She smiles.

The smell of alcohol registers in my head. 'Did you drink?'

'I did.' She nods, 'But I'm fine now.'

'Brooke, I told you I want you sober....' And now she puts her finger across my lips to stop me from talking. 'I'm fine. I had a few drinks, but I sobered up before coming here. And anyway, even if I didn't, the rain outside would have done the job, anyway.' She smiles.

'You want a towel?' I look at her wet hair, but she shakes her head. 'I'm here for one thing only.' She smirks and I ask, 'And what is that?' I grin at her and she takes a step back and slowly unzips her coat, dropping it to the floor, revealing her completely naked body.

The air leaves my lungs as I gape at her beautiful curves. I rush over to her and lift her up as she wraps her legs around my waist. She quickly kicks off her boots while I walk us to my bedroom and we stare into each other's eyes, me smiling and her laughing. I kick the door open and walk inside just to then kick it back to close on Bruno's face.

'That was rude.' She frowns.

'Right now, I don't care.' I lie her down on my bed and she pushes herself up so her head rests on the pillows. I take off my black, long-sleeved top and throw it to the side, before joining her on the bed, hovering just above her.

'Are you sure?' I ask to confirm my green light.

'More than sure.' She cups my face, and my mouth connects with hers. The electricity between us matching, as we were born to do this, I lift her leg and rub my hand over her outer thigh towards her ass as she puts her hands on my pecks and squeezes, making me go wilder. I break the kiss to then reach her neck and I feel her body shiver at this spot and I mentally note to always kiss her there. I make my way down slowly, starting at the neck, then collar bone, then I stop at her breast. Her nipples are hard, and she lets out a moan as I take one into my mouth. She pushes her hands through my hair as I suck on it, and I can feel her hips thrust forward. I flip my tongue up and down, left to right, feeling her back arch towards me. Both our breaths are now quick and I lift my head up to look at her.

'You're ok?' I ask, not really knowing what she's comfortable with.

'More than ok.' she says through her deep breathing.

'Is this...' I move my fingers down her side and then they slowly travel between her legs where my thumb touches her most sensitive part of the body. She lets out another moan as I stroke it, '... ok too?' I finish my question and she closes her eyes, only nodding, so I lower myself between her legs and drag my tongue against her inner thigh. Her whole body shivers and her moans reach my ears, encouraging me to go in. Her moans become louder when I replace my thumb with my tongue. I use my index finger to stroke her pussy up and down before sliding it inside, making her gasp. Her back fully arches, making me push on her stomach to get back down. I now push the second finger in and curl them so I hit her g-spot while my tongue still plays with her clit. I flick it with my tongue up and down before Brooke groans out, 'Oh my god, I'm close.' And I smile against her beautiful, wet pussy. I keep doing what I'm doing, feeling her pulsing on my fingers. Grabbing my hair in her fists, she arches her back again before shouting out,

'Oh my god, the Atlantis!' And we both stop. Her body tenses while I have a million things going through my head right now. Did she just say Atlantis? What the fuck is Atlantis? Does she mean the lost city? Is she thinking about some historic place while I'm going down on her? I slowly lift myself up and see a pure horror on her face. She's covering her mouth with both her hands while looking up at the ceiling.

'Wh-what is Atlantis, Brooke?' She closes her eyes and just doesn't look at me.

'Brooke, are you ok?' I move to lie down next her and move her hands away.

She then finally looks at me. 'I'm not a freak.'

'I never said you were.' My brows draw together, trying to understand what had just happened. 'I'm just confused.' She takes a deep breath and turns her head to look at the ceiling again. 'I... I might have previously compared the...' She stops. 'You know what? It's stupid.' She tries to stand up, but I stop her and turn her face towards me. 'Tell me.' I demand and she takes a deep breath in.

'Not that long ago, I compared clitoris to Atlantis, the lost city, as it's pretty much impossible to find for men.' She said in one breath, and I stare at her for a moment, seeing fear in her eyes as to what I'm about to do. Clitoris is Atlantis... I let it sink in before I tilt my head back and let out the loudest laugh. I drop myself back on the bed, still laughing, and Brooke now sits up and punches me playfully on my shoulder.

'I told you it was stupid.' She snaps and I manage to control my laughter when I push myself up on my elbow and look at her. 'Do I get a prize for finding the lost city?' And she's the one chuckling away now.

'What would you like?' She asks,

'I'd like to finish what we started.' I put my hand over her waist and pull her closer, putting my lips on hers, and we're back to our moment.

'You are something else, woman.' I say against her mouth and she smiles. I place myself over her again and put my hand on the back of her head and pull her closer. When I push my tongue inside to play with hers, I enjoy the sweet taste, and I know I'd happily live off the menu of Brooke Summers. Raw, beautiful and sweet.

'Is there anything you don't want me to do?' I ask before I completely lose myself to this woman. She looks up at me, a smile that warms my icy heart, and says, 'Do your best.' Challenge accepted.

I place my hand between her legs again, and I'm happy to learn her pussy is still very much wet for me.

'That's a good girl.' I groan before slipping two fingers back inside, forcing her to gasp. And I kiss her again. Her arms wrap around my neck and I slide my fingers in and out slowly, picking up the speed of pushes as she moans against my mouth. Moan after moan flips my world upside down and my whole body tells me I'm here to please this woman. I curl my fingers just slightly again and rub them against her G-spot. Her hips roll forward and our gazes lock, and her mouth opens in the shape of a small o.

'Come for me, baby girl.' I command at her and feel her pussy pulsing on my fingers before she tilts her head back, gasping, her whole body tensing. She grips onto the sheets beneath us and lets the orgasm take over.

Brooke takes a moment to catch her breath before glancing at our sweaty bodies. I'm pushed into the sitting position and she follows. She looks down as she undoes my belt and then the zipper, pulling my jeans down and then boxers, freeing my hard cock. Her eyes and mouth open wide, and I smirk.

'Like what you see?' I ask and she looks up at me. 'Fuck me now, Gabriel.' She replies and I don't wait for any further instructions before I flip her over on her all fours and her head rests on the pillow, while her ass is high in the air, waiting for me. I pull a condom out of my bedside table drawer and put it on as quickly as I can. Grabbing my cock, I position it against her sweet entrance. She flinches as the tip touches her, and I wrap her long hair in my fist and pull on it so her head is tilted back. In one hard thrust, I'm inside her and she cries out loudly,

'Oh god!'

'No, baby girl.' I say while moving slowly, in and out, in and out. 'God will not help you here.' And I thrust hard again, and again, letting her moans fill the room. I'm fighting internally to stop my dick from coming, as I'm not ready to be finished with her just yet. Still, it's so hard as I stare at her sexy ass. This woman has officially got me by my balls. I raise my hand that was resting on her hip and I slap her ass, hard, and she tilts her head back even more.

'Again.' She demands and I listen. I slap her again before moving my hand over her thigh, landing between her legs again, rubbing her Atlantis and within seconds, she's tensing, and groans while her orgasm takes over once again.

'Oh, Gabriel!' And that has me following her, my cock emptying itself inside her. Both our breaths quick, I lean forward and kiss her on the head. Heading into my en-suit, I get the condom disposed of and to freshen up. I rinse my face with cold water and dry it off, not wanting to remove her scent from me. I think I'm in love with her sweet, tight pussy and I've only had it once. Fucking love at first sight. When I go back, I find Brooke, under my covers, fast asleep. I go to join her and as she has her back to me, I pull her in close to me, my hand wrapped around her waist, and go to sleep myself.

The next day, when I wake up, I find her gone.

CHAPTER SIXTEEN

Brooke

I am the worst person ever—fact. But when I woke up next to him in the early hours this morning, it felt too... intimate, and this is what I'm trying to avoid. My body still shivers when I think about what we did, when I fully gave myself to him, and oh boy did he not disappoint. I'll try to forget the little Atlantis mishap and I hope he can forget it, too. But I know I'm now facing a serious conversation with him, after I left his apartment without saying a word. My toes curl in as I think about his lips on me and his hands touching me, and there's no way Mr. Pink can now compete with that. I only wonder how we're going to make this work. Last night, when I thought it was even a chance that Tyler's face was Gabriel's doing, I felt something shift within me and before I knew it; I was on my way to him. I don't regret it, but I know we have to talk about it and set some boundaries. Tess and Aaron are due an update, as I didn't leave my place till after they left first. It can wait, though.

A knock sounds from the door of my office.

'Come in.' I call out and straighten up in my chair.

Gabriel's face appears and my stomach drops as he closes the door behind him. He locks it.

Oh shit.

We stare at each other for a moment, and just the sight of him makes my panties wet. Take me, I want to say to him, but I swallow it hard.

'How can I...'

'Cut the bullshit, Brooke.' He snaps.

I deserved it.

'You walked out on me.' His tone is bitter and goosebumps raise on my skin. I decide to stand up and walk toward him.

'I'm sorry.'

'You're sorry?'

'I am.' I look up at him and see his jaw clenched, so I put my hands on his chest, immediately seeing a shift in him. 'I got scared. Sleeping with you wasn't in my plan... it was... a step too far.' I see his jaw unclench and his facial features soften.

'We need to sit down and talk.' He places his hands on my hips and nods in agreement.

'Let's meet at my place tonight?' I ask, and I see a twitch in the corner of his mouth.

'We can leave together if you'd like?' He offers, but I shake my head. 'That's one thing I want to talk about. I don't want people to know.' He nods in compliance.

'8 o'clock good for you?' A smirk pulls on his lips now.

'Give me any time and I'll be there.'

'Good.' We let go of each other and I smile back at him. 'I should get back to work now. My boss is very strict.' I wink at him before sitting back in my chair.

'I'm good friends with him. I'm sure he'll understand.' He turns and opens the door, but I call out to him.

'Gabriel?'

'Yes?'

'Was Tyler's face your doing?' He stares at me for a moment and I see mischief in his eyes before a smirk appears on his face.

'Who's Tyler?' My eyes narrow and I scoff at him. He leaves the office, closing the door behind him, and even though I'm pretty sure I have my answer, I decide not to push the subject.

I stare at my screen where a draft is sitting with my comments on the side of it and wonder if it'll ever be me, having my draft sent to an editor, being prepared to be published. I'm now more determined than ever, knowing my dad is watching and cheering me on, but also at this moment, a memory comes to my mind.

'What the hell are you talking about?' Tyler asks while he's shaving above the sink in our bathroom.

'A book.' I reply while standing in the door with my arms crossed over my chest. It's Saturday morning and we're going away for a weekend as Tyler has a gig in Bournemouth.

'You want to write a book?' He shoots me a stare through the mirror on the wall.

'Yes.'

'An actual book?'

'What other books do you have? Yes, an actual book, Tyler.' I roll my eyes.

'I don't think that's a good idea.' He shakes his shaver and taps in on the sink to remove the rest of the hair and rinses his face with water.

'Why not?' I raise my brow at him.

'You read books, Brooke, not write them.'

'That's why I'm saying I want to give writing a go. I've always dreamt of being a writer.' He dries his face with a towel and turns to me. 'You're an editor. Editors don't write books.' My stomach drops as this insult and self-doubt kicks in. Is he right? 'But maybe I could...'

Before I can finish, he comes up to me and cups my face in his hands. I look at him and think about him being in a self-made band; he knows how hard the work is and maybe he knows with my lifestyle, writing would be too difficult.

'Maybe you're right.' I look down, and he kisses my

forehead before walking out of the bathroom. 'I'm always right, baby.'

My phone pings and I see a text from my mum.

Mom- Come see me at the bakery tomorrow.

I'm lucky enough my mum's bakery is only a 10-minute walk from my office, but I always spent my lunch breaks with Tess. I reply immediately.

Me- Everything ok?

Mom- Of course. I just wish to see my daughter.
I'll give you the triple chocolate cupcake. ;)

Me- And coffee.

Mom- Deal.

Me- See you tomorrow. Xoxo.

I set my phone down and start reading the draft on my screen.

One day it'll be my turn.

It's now 7 o'clock and I'm sitting at my laptop, words pouring out of me, which is surprising as I've had writer's block for days now. Nala is fast asleep on the sofa and I have a radio on for some background noise. The twists in my stomach make me nauseous with each tick of the clock, knowing 8 o'clock is getting closer. My throat feels dry and my stomach is telling me it'd happily empty itself, so I go to the fridge and pull out a bottle of water, taking a big gulp of it. I lean on the worktop and take a deep breath.

This is insane.

The knocking sound comes from my door, which makes me jump and spill the water over the floor. Nala jumps off the sofa and rushes to it with her tail wagging. My hands tremble as I open the door and see Gabriel standing with Bruno at his side. I look at his perfect face, stubble more of a beard now, which somehow makes him even sexier. His hair perfectly styled as always and I remember pushing my hands through them. I swallow hard when Gabriel asks, 'Can I come in?' I notice he's also holding a bottle of wine and my nerves ease a bit. Yes, a drink will definitely help.

'Of course, sorry.' I open the door wider and Bruno runs in to Nala, both jumping, running around each other, sniffing each other's butts. I chuckle.

'Wasn't sure if I could bring him, but I think he sensed where I was going as he wouldn't let me leave without him.' Gabriel comments as he steps inside.

'You can always bring him. Nala loves him.' I still watch them, feeling too nervous to look up at him.

'Does that mean there'll be more times?' I now turn to see him smirking.

'Is that for me?' I glance down at the bottle he's still holding, and he passes it to me.

'Yes.' He replies and I nod. I take it to the kitchen where I grab some kitchen paper and go to wipe the floor, but before I can kneel down,

'Let me do it.' Gabriel takes the paper from my hand and wipes the water I spilled. In the meantime, I pour two wine glasses full and when I turn around, I see him reading what's on my laptop.

'I ...sorry... It's private.' I mumble as I race over and put the glasses down before turning off the laptop.

'Sorry.' He says and I awkwardly smile at him. 'Is that your book?' I snort.

'I wouldn't call it a book.' I explain, and he frowns.

'Is it a story you are writing?'

'Yes.'

'Would you like it published one day?'

'Yes.'

'So it's a book.' My cheeks feel warm and I pass him his glass of wine.

'Maybe one day.'

'Are you hoping for us to publish it?' This surprises me. I haven't thought about it but ... 'I think our situation makes me not want to go with Alstons House.'

'Why?' He crosses his arms over his chest and narrows his eyes. Even his confused face makes me want to kiss him. I take a big sip of my wine before answering, 'I feel like my story wouldn't be taken fairly if people knew I wrote it.'

'Ah. Employee privilege.' He chuckles.

'Exactly.'

'Well, I'm sure the story is amazing and will get published straight away.' He raises his glass 'To the unwritten stories that deserve to be read.' I smile widely now and lift my glass back to him as we clink them together. I glance over his body and I can't decide if I prefer him in the suit or the dark-washed jeans and the knitted blue sweater he's currently wearing. Actually, scratch that. I prefer him naked.

I feel a tingle between my legs and I look away before it becomes anything else. He's now studying my vision board, as Tess called it, and he's looking at each picture carefully before turning back to me.

'Shall we?' I gesture to the sofa and we both go to sit down. Nala and Bruno are now curled up to each other, asleep, and Nala rests her head on top of his; I smile at the sight of them.

'What's this?' Gabriel nods to the pen and paper on my coffee table and I take a deep breath.

'I'd like to talk about rules.'

'Rules?' His eyes narrow.

'Think of them as boundaries. We're not interested in a relationship, correct?' He nods. 'So I thought to make this easier, we could come up with some rules that would allow us to keep feelings out of this...' I pause and take a moment to think. 'What exactly is it that we're doing?' I ask him. He looks at me and I feel like something is stuck in my throat. I tap my fingers on the glass, waiting for him to reply.

'You've never done this before, have you?'

'No' I answer sharply and he smiles at me.

'Think of it as friends with benefits.'

'Would we be exclusive?' I ask again, wanting as much information as I need.

'Do you want us to be?'

'Yes,' I say immediately.

'Ok.' He nods down and takes another sip of his wine. 'So let's talk about rules.'

'Rule 1. No staying over.' I demand, and he narrows his eyes before grabbing the pen and paper and writing it down.

After we finish the list that pretty much only I came up with, as Gabriel had nothing to say, we look down at it.

1. No staying over.
2. No romantic gestures
3. No showing up as a couple in public
4. No checking each other on social media.

'Remind me again, why can't I look you up on Facebook or Instagram?' He asks while staring at the paper.

'Because it will only allow us to get to know each other more and that way I don't have to think OMG IM SLEEPING WITH A GUY WHO ADDS MILK IN BEFORE CEREAL.' He looks up at me with his nose wrinkled.

'Who would put milk in the bowl before cereal?' I raise my

arms up and arch both my brows. 'A psycho, that's who.' I reply, and a laugh escapes from his throat.

'I'd like to add a rule.' He picks the pen up again and writes something down before pushing the paper closer to me. I lean forward and read.

5. No talk of work out of hours.

'I can live with that.' We both sign it in turns. When I go to stand up, I realise a second too late that I'm about to step on Bruno's tail. So I end up tripping, falling right onto Gabriel's lap, of course. His arms wrap around my waist immediately and the heat builds up around my core as our eyes lock.

'You're ok?' He smirks, but his words don't register with me, as my gaze lingers on his lips, making me want to kiss them.

'Eyes up here, baby girl.' He chuckles and the words baby girl coming out of his mouth, sends a warm shiver down my spine. I go to stand up, but he's gripping me. My heart skips a beat when I feel his hand move up and down my back.

'I have to admit; The leggings and hoodie look really does suit you.' I look down and realise I never had the chance to get changed as he arrived early.

'So...' we both say at the same time.

'Do we ... like... arrange set days?' I ask, heart beating fast at his proximity.

'We just go day by day. You can message me or just pop into my place and or I can come here.' His hand travels underneath my hoodie, now touching my bare back, and I can feel goosebumps appear on my skin. Our lips are so close, it'd be easy to just lean in and...

Before I can finish my thought, as if he read my thoughts, his lips connect with mine. He puts his hand on my leg and pulls me closer to him as I wrap my arms around his neck. He slowly lies us down on my sofa and I move my legs to wrap around his waist. I pull him closer to me and feel his cock already hard. My core bursts into flames as his hand travels up my hoodie to my breast and when he puts his hand under my bra, I realise it's undone. I move away and look at him.

'How did you...?'

'I know a couple of tricks.' He smirks and kisses me again. He grabs my nipple between his finger and thumb and pinches it, making me gasp against his mouth.

'You're fucking beautiful, Brooke.' He whispers as he strokes his thumb over my breast. My panties are now completely soaked, and I feel the need for friction between my legs. He thrusts his hips forward slightly, and it has me urging for more.

'Please.' I whisper into his ear as he's now kissing my neck, sending shivers through my whole body. A sexy smirk appears on his face when he stops and lifts his head up to look at me. He sits up and leaves me breathless. Pulling me up, I straddle him as he returns his hands on my back and hooks my bra. I narrow my eyes at him and frown.

'What are you doing?'

'This...' He places a kiss on my lips '... is a punishment for your outfit yesterday.' My eyes widen at this confession.

'See, you left me wanting all day and I couldn't stop thinking about you.' He rubs his thumb over my lower lip. 'So now you can feel what I felt. Maybe you'll learn to be a good girl next time.' He grabs my ass as he finishes the sentence and pinches it. I don't move. I just stare at him, unsure if it's cruel or hot, but I know there's no point in fighting this today.

'Well played, Mr. Alstons.' A smile forms on my face.

I'll get you back. I think to myself as I push myself off him and straighten my hoodie. Gabriel also stands up and calls for Bruno, who gets up quickly and is now at his side.

'I shall leave you now, Miss Summers, but we'll be in touch.' He leans in and kisses me on the cheek. My whole body swears at him and begs him to stay, but I don't voice it. That was his plan all along. He glances back at my board on his way and I hear him make a hmm sound before he goes for the door.

'See you tomorrow, Brooke.' He looks at me, and I only nod before he leaves and closes the door behind him. I'm now standing in the middle of my living room, all alone and horny.

It's now the next day, lunchtime, and I'm sitting at my mom's bakery. I still can't wrap my head around the whole idea of friends with benefits with my boss, and I'm still due to tell Tess and Aaron. They're going to go crazy and probably angry that I didn't tell them sooner, but we're all meeting up on Friday after work for dinner, so I'll tell them then. I pick a piece of my cupcake and put it in my mouth.

De-fucking-licious.

'There you go, sweetie.' My mom places a cup of caramel mocha in front of me.

'Thank you.' The hot beverage warms me up immediately as I take a sip. It is getting colder and colder now, and the wind always makes it even worse. I keep my hands on the cup to warm them up, too.

'How's work?' She asks as she sits down opposite to me. Her bakery is doing well enough, she could hire help. Just now I see 7 people in the queue and lunchtime only just started for many offices.

'Good.' I swallow another piece of my triple chocolate cupcake.

'And your book?' She smirks and I sigh. 'I'll be emailing some agents this weekend to see if I can get the ball rolling.' She claps her hands in excitement and I chuckle. 'Don't celebrate yet. It could take months or even years to find the publisher.'

'Well, good thing that you're working for one of the biggest publishers in the country then.' She winks at me, and I pause. I can't tell her about Gabriel. She wouldn't understand and she'd probably tell me it's a bad idea. Maybe it is, but it was my decision. Mine and no one else's, which I can finally say for myself.

'I'd prefer not to use my employee privileges, mom.' She rolls her eyes at me.

'Anyway, is there something you wanted to talk about?' I change the subject, and she straightens herself before speaking up.

'We haven't talked about Kate's wedding yet.'

Oh crap!

Of course, after my breakup with Tyler, I didn't exactly want to talk about weddings, and then I had to find a new place and I was applying for jobs and then Gabriel happened so I completely forgot about my cousin's wedding that is happening next month.

'By looking at your face, I'm guessing you forgot?'

'Yeah.' I murmur as I lean back in my chair. 'Do I have to go?' I was never close to Kate. Both parents are lawyers, so she grew up quite spoilt, always making comments about my looks or my job or even my relationship status. 'You could do so much better than editing books.', 'If you could do your makeup I'm sure you'd find a boyfriend.', 'He will not propose to you hun if you don't look good for him.' She'd said on multiple occasions. She, herself is in marketing and her fiancé is an accountant and she makes sure she goes to the hairdresser once a month at least. Nails and lashes are always done and even recently I saw a post on her Facebook that she got her lips done. I'm happy where I am, and I'm working towards getting published and as for love ... Like I said, I'm happy where I am.

'Brooke, honey.' She looks at me with her worried look. 'I know things changed, but you can still bring a plus 1 and I'll be there too. We can do it.' Her warm smile always helps me feel at ease.

'I'll ask Aaron. He loves a good party.' I return her smile and deep inside pray I can get him to come with me.

CHAPTER SEVENTEEN

Gabriel

'We know you were born in the Alexandra hospital.' Mr. Rowland, the PI I hired, tells me as we make our way through the park with Bruno on his leash at my side. I spot only a few people with their dogs, as the cold seems to keep people indoors these days. I inhale the cool air and its refreshing effect.

'And her name?' I ask, and Mr. Rowland pulls out another paper from his folder.

'Piper Wood. Age 17, parents Mary Wood and George Wood.' I nod, and the sound of my mother's name makes my stomach drop and my heart race. We stop at the food truck and order two coffees. Once we receive our order, we sit down on the bench nearby. It wasn't even that long ago I couldn't care less about finding out where I came from but it was when Max told me his father was diagnosed with diabetes and he got checked out himself, I started thinking if there might be anything I should be wary of. As the social worker who was on my case passed away years ago, I spoke to Max and he told me about Mr. Rowland. So I contacted him to see what he could find. However, with each day waiting for him to contact me with any information, I found myself more intrigued by the people who made me and then abandoned me. Am I incapable of love because of them? Because the moment I was born, I was unloved and unwanted? My heart aches at the thought, but I shake it off before speaking again.

'Do you have her medical profile?'

'Yes. She was a drug user, but medically, there was nothing noted. No heart diseases, no cancer, no diabetes. She was medically fit.' So drugs were more important than her own baby. Noted. I sip on my coffee and stroke Bruno's head with my free hand.

'Anything on my father?' I ask him, but he shakes his head.

'Not yet, but I'm looking into it.' I nod in acceptance. I don't know how long it'll take him to gather up all the information, but so far what he found, I wasn't able to find myself over months of looking. We say our goodbyes and he leaves while I stay on the bench, enjoying the view of the park and my hot beverage. I never thought I'd find myself searching for answers at the age of 32. It wasn't an interest to me when I was 18 and moved out of my foster parents, so I didn't think it'd ever come to haunt me. I imagine if life would have been different if I grew up in a loving home, where both parents love you and love each other. The type of shit you see on the TV. Would I be different then? Would I possibly be married with children by now? But I snap out of imagining the what if life that never happened. I will not cry over spilt milk, so I'm just going to focus on my now and believe that I'm where I'm meant to be. My business is a massive success and I have a great friend who I can always count on. I also have...

'Gabriel.' I turn my head to see Lydia coming in my direction, smiling while holding her own drink. 'Hi, Bruno.' She rubs his head and kisses me on the cheek. 'Hi, Lydia.'

She sits down next to me. 'So what is so urgent that you wanted to talk about?' Her short brown hair sways in the air as she keeps trying to keep them off her face. I texted her this morning to meet me here, thinking it's best to do it in public, knowing what women can be like.

'You're a wonderful woman Lydia, you know that, right?' Her smile immediately disappears from her face and I swallow hard. I place my hand on her knee before continuing.

'And you're great with Bruno.' Her eyes are now glistening. 'Lydia, I like you. I do but...'

'Don't.' She snaps. 'It's not you, it's me, right?' She shoves my hand off her and looks away.

'We were never serious, Lydia. It was always just a fling and you know it.' I bark back because she knew from the beginning I don't do relationships. She knew what she was signing up for and at least I had the decency to tell her we were over instead of just goating her or whatever people call it these days... Actually, it's ghosting, I think.

'Is there someone else?' She asks, and a tear falls down her cheek. I hate I hurt her, but we would never last.

'No. You know I don't do relationships.' She's staring at me, hurt in her eyes as more tears start falling. I rub them off her cheek with my thumb. 'Our time is simply over. We knew it was going to happen.'

'But I thought we were getting serious. I thought things we changing between us.' She says with her breaking voice. Before standing up, I add. 'I'm sorry if you caught feelings, Lydia. I really am. But it's not going to change my mind now. I wish you all the best and I hope we can keep our professional relationship and you can still look after Bruno.' She stands up too and faces me with her chin lifted as she wipes away her tears. 'I knew something changed considering it's been 2 weeks since you last called me. I think you just got bored with playing with me and it's time to find someone new, is that right?'

'No, Lydia. We both knew what we had was just fun.' I snap, tired of explaining this to her when she knew from the beginning.

'Well, then...' she adds and pours the rest of her drink over my head before turning on her heel and walking away. I watch her leave and feel the weight being lifted off my shoulders.

'I've had better.' I say to Bruno as I lick my lips. 'Let's go home, boy.' And we head towards the exit.

When we get home, I fill Bruno's water bowl and set it on the floor. Before heading for the shower, I slap him playfully on his side.

I look in the mirror in my bathroom and I see my hair all sticky. I didn't tell her about Brooke, because it wouldn't change anything, plus I'm not in a relationship. The end of us was inevitable, even if Brooke said no. I turn the shower and strip my clothes off, throwing them in the laundry basket. I step in, feeling the cool water washing the day's stresses away. I close my eyes and stand there for a while, just letting the water pour down on me while I take deep breaths. My intent is never to hurt anyone, but women seem to think that if they say yes to me, I'll magically fall in love with them over time. Which happened... never. At least with Brooke, she's also trying to avoid feelings and wants to keep it as sex. Maybe that's what got me interested in her. That and her walking out on me after our first kiss, of course. I know our time will also end one day, but for now, I want to enjoy every moment. Just thinking about her makes me hard and I look down and smile, as now I know she's mine. I take my hard cock in my hand and imagine her sweet pussy surrounding it. With my grip tight, I pump slowly, my mind going back to our night together, remembering her citrus scent and the fruity taste of her tongue. When I was looking at her ass while thrusting into her and listening to her moans filling the room. My cock is now pulsing in my hand, and I know I'm close. My heart is racing, wanting—needing her touch again and when I remember how she moaned my name, it sends me over; the orgasm exploding as I tilt my head back and groan.

Bruno lies down next to me on my bed after I call him up and stroke his head on my stomach. I pick up my phone and write out a message.

Me- How are you?

A reply comes within seconds, and my heart picks up at seeing her name appear on my screen.

Brooke- Good. You? :)

Me- Could be better, could be worse.

I watch the three dots on the screen before the message comes through.

Brooke- How could it be better?

I smirk before lifting my other hand from Bruno's head to type faster.

Me- It'd be so much better if you were here. ;)

Three dots appear. Three dots disappear. Three dots appear again.

Brooke- I'm sure it would be ;)

I chuckle to myself. This woman is going to be the death of me, I swear.

Me- Wanna meet?

Brooke- Can't. A bit busy at the moment.

Me- What you're doing?

Brooke- Binge watching Netflix. Tess recommended me this series to watch.

Me- What series?

Brooke- You

Me- Me?

Brooke- No, you silly billy! You is the name of the series.

Me- I wanna watch it too.

Three dots appear. Three dots disappear. Three dots appear again. My heart skips a beat.

Brooke- Bring snacks.

I grin widely to myself…

Me- On my way.

I knock on the door and Brooke swings it open a moment later.

'That was fast.' She comments as I walk inside and set the bags of shopping on her dining table.

'My car is fast.' I offer her a smile and she rubs her arm with her other hand. I love how shy she appears to be around me.

'No Bruno tonight?'

'No, not tonight.' I reply and look at Nala, who appears to be very unsatisfied with her tail between her legs. I call her and she comes up to me.

'I'll bring him next time, I promise.' I stroke her behind the ear, which she seems to enjoy. Brooke, in the meantime, unpacks the bag.

'Two types of popcorn?' She arches a brow.

'I didn't know if you prefer sweet or salted.' I shrug and she stares at me with her nose wrinkled up.

'Salty forever.' She opens it and pulls out a bag before placing it in the microwave. Reaching into the carry bag again, she gasps loudly when she pulls out a large bag of M&M's. 'How did you know?' She pulls the bag into her chest.

'Know what?' I chuckle, and she offers me a warm smile.

'They're my favorite.'

'Noted.' We both smile before she unpacks the rest of some random chocolate bars. When the microwave pings to let us know the popcorn is ready, Brooke pulls out a plastic bowl and pours the popcorn into it.

'Do you want a drink?' She asks, while holding all the snacks in her arms. She looks fucking adorable with her another oversize hoodie, pjs bottoms and pink fluffy socks. Her hair is also done up in one of those messy buns or whatever women call them and I think she's probably the most beautiful woman I've ever seen.

'Why are you staring at me?' She asks and I realise I haven't answered her question yet.

'A water will be fine.' I nod.

'There are some drinks in the fridge, so just grab what you fancy.' She makes her way to the sofa and sets everything down on the coffee table. Quickly grabbing a bottle of water from the fridge, I sit down next to her.

'I like your look today.' I'm wearing grey joggers and a black hoodie myself. 'We're matching.' I wink at her and her cheeks redden just slightly as she glances down.

'So catch me up. What is You about?' I ask as I grab a few pieces of popcorn and pop them in my mouth. She's right. Salty beats sweet.

'So it's about this guy, Joe. He meets a woman named Beck at the bookstore and falls in love with her, but he's a real stalker. He even kidnaps her ex and keeps him in this glass made box to keep him away from Beck and then he kills him.'

'Sounds... romantic.' I comment, frowning, at which Brooke chuckles. 'I don't think it's meant to be romance. I only watched 2 episodes.'

'Let's watch it then.' I nod toward the tv, and she picks up the remote, finding You on Netflix.

'Before we watch...' She turns to me. 'I hope you don't think it's Netflix and chill because ...'

'What's Netflix and chill?' I ask with my brows pinched together.

'It's er.... It's when you watch something but you never actually... finish it.' She makes a shape of a circle with her thumb and finger and pushes her other finger inside it.

'What are you doing?' And she stops immediately. 'Sorry I just ...' I laugh loudly and her eyes widen at me.

'Did you seriously make a sex hand gesture like a 10-year-old at me?' She jabs me in the side, laughing at herself now.

'Don't laugh at me.' I grab her hand and kiss her on the back of it.

'I'm happy to just watch.'

She looks me in the eye and nods. 'Good.' She straightens herself on the sofa, pulling her hand away from me. 'It's my time of the month, so no tricks.' I put my hands over my chest and bow slightly to her. 'I'll behave. Promise.' She chuckles once more before pressing play on the remote.

About 2 hours later, we're onto episode 5. During the last episode, we somehow went from sitting on the other ends of the sofa to now, me having my arm stretched out on the back cushions and Brooke sitting much closer to me, with our legs almost touching. Nala remains asleep on the floor in front of us.

'That Beck isn't very smart, is she?' I comment.

'Give her a benefit of the doubt. She probably wants to believe he's good.' She shrugs. 'And what about that Peach? Do you think she's in love with Beck, too?' I snort and pop another m&m into my mouth.

'Maybe.' At this point, Peach had faked trying to commit suicide and is now gone for a run, but what she doesn't know is that Joe is right behind her.

'Do you think he's going to kill her?' She asks and sits up, fidgeting in anticipation of seeing what happens next.

'I think so.' I reply but instead of looking at the Tv, I'm looking at her. My heart skips a beat when I think about how much I want to kiss her.

Snap out of it!

I think to myself and then Brooke jumps up and shouts.

'Oh, my god he hit her with the rock!' She points at the tv where I see Peach lying on the ground with blood dripping from her head.

'Well, she's dead.' I snort out and she turns to me. 'Why are you laughing?'

'I'm not laughing.' I grab her hand and pull her onto me, in a straddling position, I see her eyes widen in shock and her hands resting on my pecks.

'I told you, not tonight.' She warns, and I smile.

'Who said anything about sex?' Her mouth opens slightly, then closes again. The raindrops are hitting the window and the episode is still playing on the tv but right now, we're just looking at each other. I sit up and kiss her. Her kisses are unsure, almost afraid, and her body tensed, but then I whisper.

'No sex, I promise.' Her shoulders drop and her kisses become more passionate. My arms wrap around her and my hands are placed on her back. I pull in closer as my tongue enters to meet hers. She now tastes like the chocolate she's been eating this evening and her hands cup my face, her thumb stroking my beard. My cock twitches underneath my zipper, but I keep it at bay. Suddenly, a ringtone from Brooke's photon fills the room, and she pulls away from me.

'I have to check it.' She whispers and I nod. She stands up and picks up her phone from the coffee table. 'It's Aaron. He was meant to call me tonight.'

I get up too and grab her hand. 'I should get going, anyway.' She smiles, but it doesn't quite reach her eyes.

'Are you sure?' I nod and place a kiss on her cheek.

'I'll see you soon. Thank you for the lovely evening.' A sparkle appears in her eye as she answers the phone.

'Hi! Let me just pause the tv.' She looks at me and I turn to leave.

CHAPTER EIGHTEEN

Brooke

It's Friday afternoon now, and me and Tess are heading to the restaurant where we're meeting Aaron for dinner. I haven't spoken much to Gabriel since Tuesday night, except for the occasional glances we'd thrown each other's way at work. My body reacts every time I see him and I still can't believe we're in this no string sex agreement or that we haven't actually had sex since signing the agreement. My aunt Flo couldn't find a worse time to appear. I look up at the grey sky and I'm wishing for the warmer days again. After living in LA all my childhood, I don't think the English weather is something I can ever get used to. The dull and cold autumns and winters and even Summer doesn't last very long. I clutch my bag closer to me as the breeze hits me in the face. My brown scarf helps, but I wish I had something to cover my face—something that wouldn't make me look like a professional thief. Tonight, I'm also telling Tess and Aaron about Gabriel. Tess has been asking every day if I made my decision, but I've been changing the subject or just saying, not yet. It's time to tell my friends I'm sleeping with my boss.

As I reach the entrance to the restaurant, a man bumps into me and I swear to God, the next person to bump into me, will be thrown onto the road.

I look up and completely freeze when I see Tyler. His eyes widen as if he has just seen a ghost. 'Shit. Sorry.' And he rushes away.

Another proof that Gabriel must have had something to do with his face. The involuntary feeling of satisfaction fills me as I watch him disappear from my sight, and a smile tugs on the corner of my mouth.

'Was that your ex?' Tess appears next to me, and I nod, still looking in his direction. I don't feel sad when I see him anymore. My heart doesn't even flinch, it just remains at its normal speed and I know I'm so over him. I smile to myself and we head inside. Aaron waves at us from the booth on our right, so we make our way and join him. We all hug in turns and sit down, picking up menus from the table.

'Had a good day, ladies?' He takes a sip of his blue cocktail.

'It's been quite busy, actually. Mr. Alstons had so many meetings, it has rushed me off my feet today.' Tess adds, and it makes sense now that I haven't seen him today.

'Oh, Mr. Alstons.' He rolls his eyes in pleasure and I snort. 'Brooke, please just say yes to him already!' Thankfully, a waitress appears and takes our order for drinks. We both order the same cocktail as Aaron's, but I'm mentally noting to not have more than two.

'So ...' I change the subject with them, already forgetting what Aaron was saying. 'Any plans for the second date?' I ask him. Tuesday night he called me after his first date, which in his words 'was fucking amazing.' Aaron is looking for a soulmate. Someone who he can make his famous scrambled eggs for, and someone who can put up with his work chatting. Max hasn't messaged or called Tess since she shot him down, so we try to avoid the sensitive subject for now.

'Tomorrow night we're going out bowling.' Aaron grins with his teeth on show.

'What is he like?' Tess rests her face in her hands, elbows resting on the table.

'He's...' Aaron pauses for the dramatic effect and he puts his drink down. '... perfect.'

Both me and Tess awww him. 'He's a lawyer. He loves travelling just like me, he loves good food just like me, he listens to everything I have to say and he kissed me on the cheek at the end of our date.' I am so happy for him as he has had little luck with guys in the past. I'm keeping my fingers crossed that this time, the luck is turning for him.

We get our order, which is pepperoni pizza for Aaron, grilled chicken salad for Tess and spaghetti Bolognese for me, adding a big side of fries to share as well, because of course, who doesn't love fries? We dive into our meals when I speak up. 'I actually have some news I wanted to share with you tonight.' They both freeze with their forks halfway in the air, filled with food on them before they look up at me.

'You slept with him.' Tess more of announces rather than asks, a smirk slowly appearing on her face. I nod and hear both forks being dropped back on their plates.

'I knew it!' She shouts out and I shush her.

'When?' they both ask at the same time.

'Saturday night.' I answer and they both glance at each other, frowning.

'But we were at yours on Saturday night.' Tess mutters.

'After you left, I mean.' They're both smirking at me now and I roll my eyes at them.

I've spent maybe half an hour explaining to them what actually is happening, about our rules, and that we don't want anyone to know. Both Tess and Aaron are excited for me and demanded I give them all the details with a hint of a 'how big is it' question, to which I only smiled and they accepted that as an answer. My phone pings on the table and we all shoot a glance at it.

'Is that him?' Aaron calls out excitedly.

'Maybe let me check first.' I chuckle as I pick up my phone and, in fact, see the name Gabriel appear on the screen.

'It is him, isn't it?' Tess asks, and Aaron answers for me, 'Of course it is. Look at her grinning like a child. A smile that reaches both ears definitely means a hottie is texting her.' He knocks on the table. 'Tell us what he's saying.' I scoff at them before I open the text.

Gabriel- Spend tomorrow afternoon with me.

I read out loud and they both gasp.

'Do it!' Tess tells me. They're both grinning like children now.

Me- Is this a question or a demand?

I reply and both Tess and Aaron now schooch closer to me, watching my phone.

'Are we in high school now?' I ask, while laughing at their silliness.

'No, but this is exciting.' Tess exclaims.

'Look, he's replying!' Aaron points at my phone where three dots appear.

Gabriel- Bit of both. I need a top up of that pussy of yours before I get withdrawals.

I cover my screen a second too late and they both gasp out loud.

'Go, you girl!' Tess calls out and I receive taps on my back for a job well done.

'Can I have some privacy, please?' I mutter politely, but all I see are two shaking heads.

Great.

Me- 7 o'clock at yours?

I type and hit send. Aaron is jumping up in his seat.

'My girl is getting laid.'

'Well, someone out of our group should.' Tess snorts out.

'Hey, it might be my turn tomorrow.' Aaron barks in defence.

'We'll keep our fingers crossed for you.' I tell him as I let my head rest on his shoulder.

'Thank you.' He replies sarcastically and my phone pings again.

Gabriel- Make it 4. I'm cooking.

The sounds of awing hit my ears and I frown.

'Why don't you look happy?' Tess looks at me, eyes filled with concern.

'I'm just not sure if this isn't too... intimate. We agreed to sex only and no romantic gestures.'

'Listen to me.' I look at her. 'Dinner means nothing. It's probably a good warm up to get the feel of each other.' Maybe she's right. Dinner doesn't mean feelings, and I'm probably reading too much into it. My hands are now sweaty when I hover my thumbs over the screen, but then another text comes through.

Gabriel- Bring Nala with you, of course.

Another round of awww comes my way. He is thoughtful and the fact that both our dogs get along so well makes me like him even more. Like. Nothing romantic. Just like. As I'm deciding on what to reply, Aaron snatches my phone away and types something.

'Hey! No!' I snap, trying to get it back, but I'm too late. He gives the phone back and I read the message.

Me- Sounds good to me. Just gotta decide what to wear ;)

I roll my eyes. 'You guys are so immature!' I groan out and they're both grinning again. The excitement hits me as I think about seeing him tomorrow but also nerves. Yes, we had sex already, but it was ... Sudden ... Unplanned. This is... premeditated, and I need to prepare myself.

Another text comes through, and I feel my cheeks burning.

Gabriel- Why not come naked like the last time?

'What the hell?!' Both Tess and Aaron gasp and cover their mouth, so I quickly put the phone away. 'Change of subject... I need your help.'

'What is it?' Aaron asks this time, looking slightly concerned.

'I need some... tips.'

'Tips regarding what?' Tess asks, and I swallow the hard lump before glancing between them two.

'You two have more experience and I... Well, I don't....' I mumble, and Aaron cuts in. 'Out with it, girl.'

'Blowjob.' I announce slightly too loudly where the eyes of other customers turn our way. I slouch in my seat and they both laugh at me. Tess reaches for my hands and turns me towards her. 'Listen now to your bj guru, Tess.' She smirks, and I know I'm in for a lecture.

CHAPTER NINETEEN

Brooke

Green sweater? No. Yellow tank top? No. My grey hoodie? Hell no! Why is it so hard to choose an outfit?! I stand in front of my wardrobe in just a towel, hair still dripping wet and I'm ready for a Britney Spears breakdown. Maybe a dress? I look through my clothes and see nothing that is appropriate for dinner with my fling. Yes, he's my fling. I wonder how long are we going to do this for and then I remember it barely even started.

'This is useless.' I mutter under my nose and throw myself on the bed. I still have an hour till I have to leave and I'm not in the slightest part ready. My stomach twists with anxiety and I'd happily text him now to cancel the dinner but knowing him, he'd come here and drag me out, even if I was fully naked.

Suddenly, a purchase I made about a year ago comes to mind. I jump off the bed and rush back to the wardrobe where, at the bottom, there's a box sitting, covered in dust. I pull it out and open it. A wine red fabric is smiling at me.

'Hello, my old friend.' The dress still has tags on it as Tyler didn't like it and in his words '*made me look bigger than I actually was.*'

I drop the towel to the floor and put it on. I pull the straps over my shoulders and look at myself in the mirror. It's a beautiful dress with a V neck, which makes my boobs look amazing. It's down to my mid-thigh and it sits nicely tight around my waist with a skater dress type bottom. I look fucking good in this dress and I regret ever listening to my ex.

I straighten my hair and apply light make up so I don't make a mess on Gabriel's sheets. I put on my 12inch black stilettos, which always help to boost my confidence. After gathering everything I need; my phone, keys, lipgloss, and Nala, I decide to sit down at my laptop. With 20mins left until I have to leave, I get a text message.

Gabriel- My driver will be outside in 10.

He's sending his driver to pick me up? Butterflies flutter in my stomach when I think about seeing him soon, and my heart pounds against my chest.

Deep breath in. Deep breath out. Deep breath in. Deep breath out.

I type,

Me- Thank you.

I feel my core twist and wonder if I'm going to make it to his place without being sick. Another text comes through, followed by another. I smile when I read them.

Aaron- Have fun riding his massive cock. Not at all jealous.

Tess- Make him work for it, girl! Remember, you come first. ;)

My body relaxes and my intercom buzzes.

'Coming now.' I answer and take a quick peek at myself in the mirror before throwing on my coat.

You've got this, Brooke.

I take Nala and we leave.

Gabriel's driver is right outside, waiting with the door open.

'Hi, Mark.' I smile warmly.

'Hello, Miss. Summers.' He nods his head.

'Brooke.' I correct him and he smiles. 'Brooke.' He says. I get in the car and Nala takes the seat next to me. The entire drive I've felt my stomach twist left and right, so I was focusing on taking deep breaths. Even Mark ended up getting me a bottle of water from the mini fridge. Yes, Gabriel has a freaking mini fridge in this car. I gulped the entire bottle in one go and felt immediately better.

I'm now standing in front of his door and I can feel my hands getting sweaty. I take a deep breath in and knock. He takes mere seconds before opening the door.

Was he just standing and waiting there?

He offers me a warm smile, which I return and walk in. Nala immediately pulls to go to Bruno who is now standing by the sofa with his tail wagging like crazy. I let her free and they're both just happy to be together, which makes my heart melt.

'Puppy love.' Gabriel comments.

'Excuse me?' I turn to him, and he gestures at the dogs. 'Oh yes.' I chuckle and exhale quietly. I've got this.

He helps me take my coat off and pauses mid-way. I turn to catch him with his eyes wide open, staring at my dress.

'What?' No response.

'Is it... not good?' I ask and swallow the lump in my throat.

'You look...' He starts and pauses. '...absolutely gorgeous.' Heat reaches my cheeks and I glance down. 'Thank you.' He puts my coat on the hanger and comes toward me. Putting his hand on my lower back, he whispers into my ear.

'If it wasn't for the food in the oven, I'd rip this dress off you, and fuck you right now.' Goosebumps appear on my skin and my pussy pulses at his confession. Do I tell him I have no underwear on tonight?

No. I'll wait.

He's wearing dark jeans and a white shirt with sleeves rolled up to his elbows and a couple of top buttons undone, which reveals his chest hair. The rich outlines of his shoulders also strain against the fabric. I'll be kissing this chest later tonight. My heart skips a beat again, and I feel the wetness pool between my legs.

'You look very handsome today, too.' He smiles and we walk further into his home. While he's checking on the food, I notice his glass dining table is covered in candles and it's set for two. I come up to the large, floor-to-ceiling window, and I look down where people remind me of little ants that you could just step on. The view forces me to take a step back as the dizziness creeps in.

'What's wrong?' Gabriel comes up and passes me a glass of wine.

'I'm scared of heights.' The best red wine I have ever tasted is what I take a sip of. I'm not even going to ask how much the bottle cost him.

'You're not going to fall through the glass.' He's smirking and I chuckle sarcastically.

'It's the looking down that makes me feel dizzy.' I glance at Bruno and Nala playing with a squeaky duck next to us and smile. 'They're so good together, aren't they?' I say without looking at him and feel his hand once again on my back as he places a kiss on my cheek.

Oh dear lord, just take me now.

'So are we.' He replies and I lift my eyes to him to find him watching me. His eyes are hungry and his gaze is stripping me to my raw core. I feel the hair on my arms stand up at the tension coming from his gaze.

'Come sit. Dinner's ready.' We walk towards the table and a dish with steam coming out of it is sitting in the middle. We sit on opposite ends, but we're still close to each other. Gabriel lifts the lid to reveal a pasta dish, and the scent hits my nose, making my mouth water.

'It smells delicious.' I comment.

'It's the only thing I can cook. I hope you like tuna?' He picks up my plate before putting the food down on it.

'Love it.' I smile at him as he returns it. There's a bowl filled with salad too, which I pick up and help myself to.

'It looks amazing, thank you.' I add hesitantly.

'But ...?'

'I'm just worried this is... it feels like a date.' I explain and he searches my eyes before speaking up.

'Would you prefer to come in, fuck, and leave?' He asks but calmly. I take a moment to think about it.

'No, of course not. I'm just...'

'Don't worry.' He chips in. 'There are no feelings, no relationship. I will not fall in love with you.' I chuckle. 'Well, that's something to say to a woman on a date.'

'Well, it's not a date.' He smirks, and we both raise our glasses.

'To a good not date.' He says.

'To a good not date.' I repeat.

We talked. We laughed. We joked. The dinner was amazing, and I mentally noted that I need to ask him for the recipe.

'That was amazing.' I say as I grab the napkin and wipe my mouth.

'Glad you liked it.' He leans back in his seat and studies me carefully. 'You missed something.' Leaning forward, he rubs the corner of my mouth with his thumb slowly and I feel the sudden pull to him. I don't know if it's because we drank two bottles of wine or if it's him looking so damn good that I'd happily have eaten this dinner off his abs. Maybe it's a mixture of both. Yes, let's go with both.

'It's taking all my self-control to not crawl under this table and taste your fucking pussy right now.' He confesses and I open my mouth in shock. His lips are turned upwards, and I'd be lying if this didn't sound like heaven right now. I clench my legs as the pulsing sensation takes over and I can't think clearly. 'And it's becoming even harder now as I see your breathing deepen.' This man can see right through me.

'Come with me.' He takes my hand in his and pulls me off my seat. We go toward his bedroom, but the corridor is long and there are plenty of doors that I don't know where they lead. My heart skips a beat with every step we take, my clit begging for attention now, but I'm doing my best to stay calm. He stops by the last door and pushes it open. We now make our way downstairs and meet another set of doors. When I step in, my mouth drops to the floor. A fully equipped gym with bars and bike and other machines that I don't know the names of, because well, I don't go to the gym. He pulls me again to another door and my heart jumps in excitement when I see a room with a jacuzzi in one corner and a sauna in the other corner.

'How big is this place?' I ask. I swear my apartment would fit in here 10 times, if not more.

'It's big enough.' He smiles. 'I want you to know that you have access to all this.' My eyes widen in surprise. 'What?'

He nods in confirmation. 'Yes. Everytime you're here, feel free to use anything you like.' I glance around and all I want is to jump in the jacuzzi.

'Wanna give it a go?' He clearly sees me eyeing the tub before going up to it and turning it on. The machine comes to life and bubbles start to foam on the surface just as Gabriel unbuttons his shirt.

'I- I didn't bring any costume with me.' He puts out his hand to me, so I walk toward him and take it. 'Who said you need the costume?' He drags the strap off my shoulder and replaces it with a kiss. I tilt my head to the side as he makes his way higher to my neck, and then to my ear. 'I've been waiting too fucking long for this.' The other strap is now pulled down too. I'm now wetter than I've ever been before and I want to dig my nails into his back as he pushes into me.

I was never a foreplay type of girl till I met him and realised just how much he does for me compared to any other men I've been with. A real man knows, lady's always first. The fabric is thin enough that when his thumb rubs over my nipple, I feel every bit and I let out a moan as my nipples harden under his touch. He grabs the hem of my dress and pulls it up off me completely and this time, his eyes darken like a night sky when he realises I'm completely naked.

I smirk at him as I remove my stilettos, then turn to step into the jacuzzi. The water is warm and welcoming and my feet feel like they died and woke up in heaven as the ache from the heels gets washed away. I sit down and the foam from the bubbles covers my breast, at which I see Gabriel frowning.

He removes his shoes and then his jeans and now he's standing in front of me in just his boxers and I see he's already hard. I'm aching to touch his beautiful muscles, but I don't move from my place. The water washes away all the stress I had, since most likely last night, when I agreed to today. He pulls his boxers down and I stare. Yes, I stare at his big, hard cock and I pull my lips together to hide the smile. The sound of Gabriel laughing reaches my ears, but I don't look up.

'Like what you see?' He asks and I can only manage a nod. He laughs again, before stepping in to join me. However, instead of sitting down, he makes his way to me. Both hands on each side of me, helping him to stay up, his mouth literally inches away from mine and I realise I'm holding in my breath.

'You're so damn beautiful.' He lifts his hand and strokes my face gently before putting it back underwater. The pulsing between my legs is now unbearable and I'm close to begging him to touch me. 'Gabriel ...' Before I can say anything more, he thrusts a finger inside me and I tilt my head back, allowing a loud moan to escape my mouth.

He smirks. 'You were saying something?' I shake my head and crush my mouth into his. My whole body is aching for him and I can not wait any longer. A second finger enters now and I breathe deeply against his mouth. He pushes them in hard, finger fucking me before his thumb joins in, rubbing my clit.

'Oh, fuck yes.' I groan and rest my head on the headrest cushion behind me as my vision becomes blurry and all I can do is moan. I arch my back which pushes my breast above the water, and Gabriel takes the advantage of it, taking my hard nipple in his mouth, sucking hard, and within moments I feel the pleasure explode within me and my toes curl as I hold firmly onto his hair.

He lifts his head up to face me, with a smile spread across his face. 'I missed those moans.' He gives my sensitive area one last stroke and I tremble under his touch as I try to catch my breath. It takes a moment for my vision to come back and to think straight and before I know it, he lifts me up and lies me down on the floor, leaving my legs still in the water. While lowering himself on me, I feel his touch on my thighs and the arousal comes back within seconds. I don't know how I'm going to walk out of here. He places kisses on my inner thighs before feeling his lips reach my clit. He kisses it gently, and it sends shivers through my whole body. The inside of me burns with anticipation and excitement.

'So fucking perfect.' He growls, before reaching for his jeans and pulling out a condom. 'Don't you dare to move.' I lay with my arms above my head and watch him put it on his wet cock and giving it a few pumps. The wetness fills my pussy once more and my stomach drops in excitement as I watch him come closer, ready to fill me up. He takes hold of my wrists. 'Don't move an inch.' He commands and I smile, 'Yes, sir.' His eyes sparkle at the sir comment and I know I've hit the jackpot. He positions himself between my legs, and I feel the tip of his cock stroke against my entrance. He's not letting my wrists go as he thrusts inside hard, making me cry out. My back arches, and my moans fill the echoey room.

'Yes. Yes. Yes.' I groan as he pushes in aggressively. I try to move to touch him, but his grip remains strong and I don't know if it's torture or even a bigger turn on.

'Don't. Move.' He commands. Each thrust sends me closer to orgasm. He's dominant, aggressive, merciless, and I fucking love it. Making love is fun, but getting fucked by this man is just another level. He puts both my hands in his one while his free hand travels under my ass, slightly lifting it, and I swear it feels even better as his cock hits the very specific spot with every thrust. My moans get louder and I tilt my head back before he says.

'Look at me.' Another command and I open my eyes, looking into his, with my mouth in a shape of an O while moans and groans leave it.

'I want you to look at me when you come.' He adds.

'Let go of my hands.' I plea with my breaking voice.

But he only growls back, 'No.'

His mouth crashes into mine and his tongue immediately enters and finds mine as they tangle, tasting each other. I fear I'm becoming addicted to this man. Unable to move, my arousal rises and I'm ready to explode.

'Come for me, baby girl.' His free hand now travels to my front and his thumb strokes my clit again, which sends fireworks of pleasure between my legs and I cry out his name. My brain is left fogged and I'm breathless when he whispers in my ear with his husky voice, 'We're not done yet.' He picks up the speed as he takes my nipple in his mouth again and sucks so hard, I moan again and within the moment, I feel his cock pulsing inside me, and then his whole body tenses as the orgasm take him over the edge and he groans in pleasure.

So. Fucking. Hot.

We're both breathless now and I don't know how we're planning on getting off the floor. He rests his face in the curve where my shoulder meets my neck and he places a kiss there.

'I don't think I can move now.' I exclaim. A smile spreads across my face and I feel his shoulders move up and down before the sound of a laughter reaches my ears.

'Then my job here is done.' He moves away to look at me and kisses me hard, leaving me once again, wanting more. What is wrong with me? Am I becoming a sexoholic? Is that how they feel? Because I could have his mouth on me and his cock inside me 24 fucking 7.

CHAPTER TWENTY

Brooke

I stare at my hot cup of coffee, thinking about last night. I went there, all nervous and doubtful, and ended up leaving barely able to walk. It was nice of Gabriel to drive me home in his freaking Jaguar. My mascara was all smeared by the time I got home, and I was thankful for not putting much of it on. It was hard to get Nala out, but I said from the beginning—no staying overnight. Gabriel didn't argue when I said it was getting late and I needed to get home and he even offered me his shoes, so I didn't have to wear my heels. God, I felt like I was fucked to the moon and back. This morning I woke up with panties soaked, but Mr. Pink just wasn't the same anymore. Maybe I need to upgrade it.

'Earth to Brooke.' I look up and see Aaron staring right at me, frowning. 'What did I say?' He crosses his arms over his chest, waiting for my reply.

'Erm ... Your coffee is too hot?' I shrug. Of course, I'd zone out while we were out at the shopping centre, having a drink. People rushing around us, all preparing slowly for Christmas. The smell of cinnamon is almost overbearing. I wish I loved

Christmas like the rest of normal people, but since my dad's passing, it just hasn't been the same.

'No!' Aaron snaps.

'Sorry.' I smile in apology. 'So talk to me. I'm all ears.' I lean forward and rest my arms on the small, rounded table.

'He. Is. Perfect.' He kisses his fingers in a French chef gesture and I chuckle. 'And yes, we ended up having sex.' I gasp in excitement and clap my hands.

'Tell me more.' I demand, and now it's his turn to laugh.

'He went over to my place and well, I invited him over... One thing lead to another, and his amazing ass has christened my sofa, bed and armchair. He was so...' He thinks of the word, '...sensitive and gentle. I could have just melted into his arms, Brooke.' His eyes glisten with happiness and I'm so excited for him. He deserves someone who will love him for who he is. And who he is, is the most romantic and funny and also stubborn person in the world. He will always put you first before thinking about himself, and if you ever need him, you can rest assured that he'll drop everything, just to be there for you. I love this man with all my heart.

'Are you crying?' Aaron frowns at me and I feel a single tear falling down my cheek. I quickly rub it off with the side of my hand before answering.

'I'm just thinking about how much I love you and how much you deserve all the happiness in the world.' He takes my hands in his and now his eyes are glistening.

'You are going to make me cry, so stop it. I'm an ugly crier and you know it.' We both laugh and inhale deeply at the same time.

'Well, anyway...' He takes a sip of his hot chocolate, 'He called me this morning saying he had a lot of fun last night and he wants to see me again.'

'Of course he wants to see you again.' I squeal. 'You're the best guy there ever will be.' I wink at him and his cheeks blush. I wish he saw himself the way I do. He always finds himself self doubting and he shouldn't.

'And the date with Gabriel?' He smirks, waiting for me to give him all my details from last night.

Had the best sex ever. I'm now addicted to Gabriel Alstons' dick, and I want to live in his home just so I can use his fucking jacuzzi.

'It wasn't a date.' I say defensively.

'Ok, yes. How was the sex date? Is that better?' I nod while sipping on my hot drink before setting it back on the table.

'It was great.' I answer and he frowns, not satisfied with it.

'How good?'

'Really. Really. Good.' I lift my brows with each really, and I grin at him. 'This man has a freaking jacuzzi in his flat. Yes, an indoor jacuzzi.'

Aaron gasps, 'No fucking way.'

'Yes, way.' I nod my head in confirmation. He leans forward to whisper to me. 'Please tell me you had sex in it.' I tilt my head to the side, biting on my lower lip, and that's an answer enough to him as he covers his open mouth with his hands. 'You slut!' He slaps my hand, and we both burst out laughing.

'I also wanted to ask you something. Remember Kate's wedding I was invited to?'

'Oh, my god yes! You were meant to go with...' He stops himself before saying his name, but honestly, I don't care anymore.

'Tyler. It's fine now. I am so over him.' I offer him a smile and this time he knows I'm telling the truth. 'Anyway... yes, but now I have no one to go with, so I was wondering if you'd be my plus one.' He's staring over my shoulder at something, so I wave my hand in front of his face. 'Who's the one not listening now?' I cross my arms, slightly annoyed now.

A grin appears on his face, and he finally looks at me. 'I have a better idea.' He stands up and starts waving. I turn around and my mouth drops when I see Gabriel and Max make their way toward us. My stomach twists at the memory of his naked body, but now he's fully clothed, which makes me somewhat disappointed.

'Are you crazy?' I turn to Aaron, who has a diabolical plan face planted. 'Oh, you just wait.' He replies before turning to them. 'Hi, guys. Doing a bit of shopping?'

'Hi. Yeah, my sister will kill me if she finds me doing last minute Christmas shopping again.' Max replies and turns to me, bowing his head. 'Brooke, nice to see you again.'

'You too. How are you?' I smile and mentally note to kill Aaron when they leave.

'All good. Work is keeping me busy a lot.' I glance at Gabriel, who is watching me and smirking, making butterflies appear in my stomach.

'And how are you, Aaron? I heard you had a date last night? Hope it went well.' Gabriel finally speaks up and my eyes widen in shock as he basically tells Aaron that he knows about his whereabouts. Aaron, however, doesn't seem to mind at all as he smiles at Gabriel.

'It was perfect, thank you. Same goes for your.... Not date?' He asks, making air quotes, while I take a sip of my drink and start choking on it. Gabriel slaps me on my back.

'I'm fine.' I say, while raising my hand up. Aaron watches me grab a napkin to wipe my mouth when Gabriel turns to him. 'It's been very fun. Thank you for asking.'

'See Gabriel, we've just been talking and Brooke has been invited to her cousin's wedding. I was meant to be her plus one, but unfortunately I can't make it....'

Oh dear God. No. No. I shoot a stare at Aaron that tells him to stop talking, but he only smiles before turning back to Gabriel. 'So maybe you'd be willing to replace me to ensure her safety and entertainment.' I slouch in my seat and don't look at any of them.

'Well, when it comes to safety, surely I can't say no.' I look up at him quickly and say,

'I can always find someone else ...' But he lifts his hand to stop me from talking. 'That's ok. I'll be happy to be your plus one.'

Aaron claps his hands. 'Well, it's a date then!' He calls out and then stops to realise what he said. 'A not date then.' He corrects himself and I shake my head at him. Gabriel puts his hand on my shoulder. 'We can talk about the details later.'

I offer him a smile and nod. After we say our goodbyes and they disappear from our view, I turn to Aaron. 'What the hell was that?!'

But he only shrugs. 'I solved your problem.'

'No.' I shake my head furiously. 'You just caused a problem.' But I only get eye rolling in return.

'Do you really prefer a gay friend over a handsome, rich man in who, Kate, won't be able to find a single flaw?' I pause to think. He is right. Kate finds anything and everything to judge me on, and there is absolutely nothing she can say about Gabriel. He's rich. Richer than Kate and her fiance put together. He's handsome, with not a single hair out of place. And it's only for one night. I can tell my mum he's just a colleague from work. But it also means he'll get to meet my family and it could scare him off. I swallow a hard lump in my throat. We're only a fling, so it doesn't matter what he thinks about my family, and I'll have a saviour at my side for the night.

I sigh loudly, 'Fine.'

'See...' Aaron leans back in his seat, arms resting behind his head and one leg put on top of the other. 'I'm a problem solver.' I roll my eyes at him, but he might have just saved me from the night of embarrassment.

I sit at my dining table in the kitchen, writing out emails to agents regarding my book. Dear Mr/Mrs ... Blah blah blah. My book is about blah. Blah. blah. I drop my head back and groan.

Emailing 20 different agents is certainly time-consuming. I only need one. One agent to believe in my story. Clara is my spirit animal, someone who I aspire to be like. Strong, independent, and not taking any shit from anyone – especially men. I glance at my vision board, seeing the picture of a book with the name and the cover. I want my story to be this. A book. I spent an hour on the phone with my mom today and I told her I have my plus one. I'm not sure she believed the 'colleague from work' , but I'm not focusing on it right now. She wanted the name, and I refused to give it to her. She'll see him once and that'll be it, so there's no point in getting her hopes up. My tv is on for the background noise and some random nature programme is playing. I glance at it as they talk about butterflies and how they transform into these beautiful, colourful creatures and I smile to myself. That's how I feel now, since breaking up with Tyler. My life is more than content. I love what I'm doing, chasing my dreams, having sex with the most gorgeous man alive, and I have my best friends who truly are the best. I'm more than happy with my life. An idea pops into my head so I grab my phone and write it down in the notes so I don't forget to organise it tomorrow. As I'm about to put my phone back, a text comes.

Gabriel- I'm still thinking about last night.

A smile forces itself onto my mouth. Clearly must have left an impression, the way he did on me.

Me- Same.

He replies straight away.

Gabriel- Want a do over? ;)

Oh, how badly I'd want to. My panties are getting wet just

at the thought, but no, I am not getting sucked in into this addiction.

Me- Sorry. Busy tonight.

Gabriel- You're not watching You without me, are you?

I laugh out loud and type the reply.

Me- No. I don't even know how the episode ended, thanks to you. I'm sending out emails.

Gabriel- You're working?

Me- Emailing agents about my book.

Gabriel- They'll fight over you ;)

Me- I wish. Lol

Gabriel- Listen to Hall of Fame for me, please.

I ask Alexa to put the song on, and it starts playing. A smile spreads across my face as I lean back in my chair and listen to it. I pick up my phone to text him.

Me- Cheeky.

Gabriel- ;)

Me- Thank you though.

Gabriel- You're welcome.

Gabriel- When's the wedding?

Me- 15th of December. You really don't have to come with me... Aaron was just being sneaky.

Gabriel- It's fine, don't worry about it. I'll take any chance to see you in a dress and heels.

Heat rises in my cheeks.

Me- Seeing you in a suit won't be so bad either. ;)

Gabriel- Control yourself, woman. We'll be in front of your family.

I snort, and press send on my last email.
Now let's pray to the god of authors.

CHAPTER TWENTY-ONE

Gabriel

I study the empty land in front of me.

'What are you thinking?' Max asks, while typing something on his phone.

'I think it's time to start doing something here.'

I bought a large land, just outside of London, thinking one day I'd build a home. Years later, I still didn't feel like the time was right for such a big move. I love my flat in central, but I think with age, longing for some peace and quiet kicks in. My life has been hectic for as long as I can remember and I'm still not sure if the peace and quiet I'm starting to desire won't just bore me to death. But something is nudging me to do it.

'What changed your mind?' Another question flies my way and I don't actually have an answer to that, so I just shrug. I walk around the land and try to picture the house, the garden. Bruno would have plenty of space and I wouldn't need a dogsitter then.

'He'd love it here.' I murmur to myself.

'Who?' Max looks at me with his brow arched.

'Bruno.' I exclaim, and he nods in understanding. 'He would.'

'I hope this has nothing to do with Brooke, though?' I shoot a glance at him and frown.

'Why would you even think that?'

'I don't know. You've been... different since meeting her. Calmer.'

'Maybe it's my age.'

He scoffs. 'You're 32 like me, mate. Just remember, nothing will happen between you two. She wants nothing past sex.' Of course, I know that. I want nothing past sex myself. But why is wanting a change in life such a bad thing? We've had our fun partying and sleeping around every weekend, but I feel ready for the next step. Maybe once I build, I'll try to travel more. My business is doing well enough that I'm not always needed at the office, so my days become... a little boring.

'Good thing I'm not looking to settle down then.' I bark and he understands it's time to change the subject.

'Have you heard from Rowlands?' He asks as we take a walk around the land and I mentally try to imagine what I want this place to be. The air smells so different here to London. It's weird. I think I can actually smell grass and trees and I have to be honest, I'm loving it. No petrol smell, no greasy food stands... just nature. It's quiet too, with no noise of cars and people, just the sound of birds. I inhale the fresh air and feel my lungs thanking me.

'Yeah, we've got a meeting next weekend. He's got something, I think. He sounded quite enthusiastic, if you can call it that.'

'He's not a man of many emotions, is he...' Max snorts out and we slowly make our way back to my jag.

The drive is quiet, and as we're in the middle of nowhere, even the radio decides to not work. I have been absent, and I can feel our friendship being affected.

'Listen, I'm sorry I've been quiet lately.' I start and Max scoffs,

'Let's not do this ladies' chat shit. I can see you're losing interest in the party life, mate, and there's nothing wrong with that.' I keep my grip on the steering wheel tight. Is he right? Am I losing interest? My phone starts ringing and Max glances at it.

'Lydia.' He informs me and I simply shrug.

'Ignore it.'

'Does she call often?' I keep looking at the road and uneasiness washes over me. My palms sweat and I can't exactly say why.

'Too often.' I scoff. 'I was polite. She thought I was in love with her and I apologized for it. She knew I had no interest in a relationship and that was it for me. I have nothing else to say to her.'

'I'd block her number. This chick sounds craaazy.' He says crazy with a singing tone. I respond with another snort. 'I might have to.'

'And what about the wedding?' My eyes shoot to look at him, brows pinched together and my body tenses. 'What fucking wedding?'

Max tilts his head back up in laughter. 'Brooke's cousin's wedding that you agreed to go to.' The tension leaves my body as I slouch my shoulders back and exhale heavily. 'What about it?'

'Well...' He pauses for a moment, '...From what I understand, wedding dates are usually a big thing. You know, meeting her whole family?' I can feel his gaze on the side of my face.

I clear my throat. 'It's no big deal. It's one night and she'll probably tell her family I'm a friend. She was going to take her gay friend, so I doubt the wedding is for 'romantic dates only.' I shrug my shoulders in dismissal. Sure, I wondered if it's taking it a bit too far, but I'm sure Brooke would say something if she thought that too.

'We'll have some drinks and dance, and then have sex somewhere in the closet.'

'True. Just be careful, you don't want to catch any feelings.'

'I won't.' I say coldly. 'What's going on with Tess?' I ask to once again change the subject of Brooke. It's enough that I can't stop thinking about her. I don't need added conversations. I'm already counting down the hours' until I see her again. This woman has me by my balls so hard that if she asked me to bark, I'd fucking bark for her.

'I don't know. I fucked a chick last night, but kept thinking about your bloody receptionist.'

'Yet, you still don't wanna ask her out.' I sigh loudly. A simple rule: you want something, go and fucking get it.

'I don't do dating, though. She sounds like she'd drive me crazy. Maybe she's one of those that will tell me how many babies she'd want on the first date and second date, she'd ask for my spare house keys.' I laugh out loud.

'Only one way to find out.'

The next day at the office, I'm sitting in another boring meeting where everyone is updating me on how the business is doing. 'Marketing great. Finances great. New author signed. Multiple books getting published. Authors are satisfied.' Of course, everyone is happy. All my employees are paid well above the average salary and they're treated with respect and in return, they put their 100% into their job roles.

'And how's the timeline for our editors?' I ask John, who quickly opens his folder and skims through the papers. 'Not one book is delayed. Everything is being done on time and a couple of them are even looking at being done early.' I nod in satisfaction and he adds, 'Our new employee, Brooke, is proving to be valuable. She has a great contact with the authors and I'm receiving only positive feedback about her.'

I nod once more while I play with a pen in my hand. Through the glass window, I see her walk by and she glances at me. I give her a flirty smirk, to which she smiles and shakes her head. A flutter appears in my stomach as I watch her and I wish I could take her away from here and keep her hostage somewhere high in the mountain where she wouldn't be able to escape. I'm struggling to understand the change. Whereas normally I'd go about my day as normal, and just see whoever I'm seeing in evenings, I find myself thinking about Brooke all the time. What is it about her that calls to me so much? Pussy, of course, is fucking perfect. Her moans imprint onto my skin every time we have sex, but it's also her laugh, and how she goes about herself is different to my normal dates. She doesn't need to try to impress others. She doesn't need to dress up to make me hard. Within minutes, my phone pings on the table in front of me. I pick it up and smile when I see her name.

Brooke- When are you going to be back in your office? Wanna see you.

My heart skips a beat, and my cock stiffens underneath the zipper. I shoot her the reply.

Me- Should be done by 1.

Brooke- I'll come by after lunch.

Amanda from HR now speaks up, 'Also, our receptionist, Tess, once again mentioned to me her interest in moving up.'

'What's her degree in?' I ask.

'She has a degree in design.'

'So we'd be looking for a cover designer role for her.' She nods. 'Have a look at our quotes and deadlines for our designers and email me the report.'

'Will do, sir.' Tess has been my employee for years now, but unfortunately, because of a lack of roles, she ended up applying for a receptionist job. She's been amazing so far, but I know this isn't the role where she'll truly thrive in.

I'm sitting at my office, reading the stats for designers and I see they don't have any delays, everything is met to authors' satisfactions and so I e-mail Tess.

From: Gabriel Alstons.
To: Tess Philips.
Tess, please come see me tomorrow at 10am.

A reply comes straight away,

From: Tess Philips.
To: Gabriel Alstons.
Of course, sir.

Someone knocks on my door when I close my laptop,

'Come in.' I call out and see Brooke come in and lock the door behind her.

Oh yes.

I get up, straightening my suit jacket with one hand. She comes up to me and kisses me immediately.

'I missed you.' She whispers into my mouth and my cock comes to life. I wrap my arms around her waist to pull her closer.

'Miss. Summers, shouldn't you be working?' I smirk as I stroke my hand on her back.

'I should. Don't tell my boss.' She warns and pushes me against the wall. My balls harden as she rubs the bulge between my legs.

'You missed me too?' She asks, and I chuckle.

'Too fucking much.' I growl before she unzips my trousers.

Once my cock is free from the containment, she strokes it ever so gently, and I groan in pleasure. I kiss her again, more passionately this time. Our tongues connect and I taste her sweetness. Meanwhile, she gives my cock a few pumps which make me weak in the legs. She suddenly breaks the kiss and smirks at me.

'What are you...?' She puts a finger across my mouth and lowers herself to her knees.

Holy fucking fuck.

She kisses the tip of my rock hard cock. Her tongue trails around it, making me tremble.

'Fuck.' I growl and my cock twitches.

She now licks along the length, and my hand wraps her hair around it. I watch her as she takes my shaft in her hand and slowly wraps her mouth around the tip, slowly sucking while pumping me with her hand, too. She takes more in and I shiver. Pleasure taking me in as she sucks harder and husky moans leave my mouth.

'That's it, baby girl. Take it all.' The sound of gagging reaches my ears and I smile.

So fucking hot.

She sucks in a perfect sync as her hand pumps me too and then she takes a break where she pulls away and her tongue plays with the tip and that's where I tremble the most as she focuses on the most sensitive part.

I can feel I'm close and as she takes me in fully again, I push her head, encouraging her to take more in. Her other hand cups my balls now and gently strokes them. I immediately explode inside her mouth, pleasure vibrating through me as I empty myself inside her. I put my finger on her chin and make her raise up to face me.

'That's my good girl.' I groan, still breathless, and she swallows. I smile and place a gentle kiss on her lips.

'I'll better get back to work.' She smirks and turns on her

heel to head out of my office. I widened my eyes in shock. She's leaving? What the actual...

Before she leaves, I grab her wrist and jerk her back to me before crushing my mouth into hers. Kissing her passionately, I lift the hem of her grey skirt. I pick her up by her legs and she wraps them around my waist. Her hands mess my hair up as I lower her on my desk. My hard cock pressed against her entrance. I feel heat rising in my core. I'm still free, so I just reach with my hand and I move her panties to the side before stroking her clit. She moans loudly, so I kiss her quickly to quiet her.

'You ain't leaving till I get to fuck you.' I groan against her mouth.

I put on the condom I had in my desk drawer, just in case.

While positioning into her entrance, I smirk at her and then, with one hard push, I'm inside. She gasps, dropping her head back. My one hand is on the back of her head and the other one is on the table, helping me stay up. I inhale the citrus scent that comes from her and I feel overwhelmed as I thrust into her again and again, hard and quick, without letting her catch a breath. Her tight pussy grabs onto my cock and I know I'm home. Before I know it, we both come together. She tilts her head back with her teeth, grinned together to not be too loud and I spill once again inside her. Once she catches her breath, she rests her forehead on mine.

'You ain't playing games with me, sweetheart.' I say with my breathy voice.

'It was worth a try.' She chuckles and I smile. I kiss her once more before pulling out. I dispose of the condom and do my zipper up as she straightens her clothes and hair.

'Goodbye, Mr. Alstons.' She smiles.

'Goodbye, Miss. Summers.'

CHAPTER TWENTY-TWO

Brooke

Fish eating your skin is probably the weirdest thing the beauty industry came up with. I stare at my feet in the bowl, while a ton of little fish nibble on my 'dead skin'. It feels... weird. It tickles, but I manage to hold back laughter as I glance at other women who remain calm while the little sea creatures eat their feet.

'What do you think?' Tess asks me and I glance at her. She isn't bothered by it either, so maybe I can try to enjoy it? No—it's weird.

'It's... different.' I reply and glance down at my feet again. You poor things, companies buy you from god knows where and they put you in these little bowls, forcing you to feed on human skin.

'Max messaged me.' She says out of nowhere, which snaps me out of staring at my legs.

'What did he say?!'

Tess pulls out her phone from the bag on the floor and reads the message.

'Hey Tess, wanna grab a bite?' She rolls her eyes.

'That's...' I'm trying to find a word for it, but it's hard. Has he ever been on a date before?

'It's pathetic.' She says for me. 'He stops texting after I tell him I don't want a hook up and now, after almost two weeks, he asks me if I wanna grab a bite. It's pathetic.' I can't argue with her about that. I don't know Max, but I know he's definitely not scoring points with Tess right now and if he wants her, he'll have to try much harder.

It's been over a week since I blew my boss in his office and we met two more times since. Sex with Gabriel is fun and freeing—and wild. And I mean eye rolling, toe curling, shouting his name out wild. I haven't seen him since Wednesday, so I'm going to need to top up on my addiction soon, but today I'm having a girls' day with Tess. We got very close since I started and I don't know if it has anything to do with me, but the day after the bj, Tess went to see him and he informed her about his plans on moving her to cover design role but there's some paperwork that needs to be filled out first so it can take a few weeks. Of course, we had a celebratory dinner and drinks. I am so happy for her, I've known it's what she wanted to do.

'What did you reply to him?' I ask her after she shoves her phone away.

She shrugs, 'Nothing. This type of message doesn't deserve a reply. He'll have to try harder.' And I totally agree with her.

'It just feels so lonely sometimes, you know? It's not just about the sex but it's about...' she pauses to think, '...not being alone all the time. I get home every day and it's always empty.' she's frowning hard and I take her hand in mine and squeeze. She smiles, but the smile doesn't reach her eyes.

'Have you ever considered a pet?' I know Nala been there for me through thick and thin. I can probably call her one of my best friends. And it definitely doesn't feel lonely when I get home and she greets me at the door.

'I have, but... I don't think id have the time for a dog,

Brooke. They need walking and with my schedule, it wouldn't be fair.' I take a moment to think and sigh loudly.

'Well, there are more animals than just dogs, you know?' This sparks her interest. 'For example, cats,' I smirk and she looks up, considering it.

'I didn't think about cats.'

'How about this?' I straighten in my seat and move my feet slightly, which scares off the little fish before they return to their feed.

Gross.

'I can take you to the rescue where I got Nala. They're amazing people and they can talk you through the process and show you what animals they have.'

She's thinking... 'I don't know... I don't wanna jump into anything so quickly.'

'You don't have to. Just ask questions, take in the answers, and you can think about it. A lot of the animals in rescue have been abandoned and maybe they're not kittens or puppies, but they still are looking for their forever homes where they can snuggle up to someone on the sofa instead of spending their days in cages.'

'Ok!' she yells out. 'Sold. Take me there after the pedi.' I smile. If I can help my friend, and an animal in need, I'll consider my day an enormous success. I pull up my phone and see no emails. It's been two weeks since I emailed different agents and still haven't heard from any of them. How long are they supposed to take? I sigh to myself.

'Still no words from agents?' Tess asks and I shake my head.

'I'm sure you'll hear from them soon.' She offers me a smile and I return it with a half smile.

Hopefully.

'Ok ladies, let's get your feet out.' The lady who's doing my pedicure comes over and I pull out my feet immediately, relief washing over me, I won't get fed on again. Tess, noticing my relief, chuckles.

We pull in front of the rescue. It's on the edge of London and has a big land surrounding it. The sounds of whimpering and barking reach us the moment we get out of the car.

'That's so sad.' Tess frowns.

'You'll have that with any rescue. Nala was the same.' I still remember when I walked into it the first time and I walked through the kennels and each dog and cat looked so sad, it broke my heart. I needed a full day of crying at home after visiting this place, even with knowing I was getting nala out of there. She was just sat by the door to her kennel when I walked by and she pushed her paw out, trying to grab my leg. I looked at her and she sat up, and her tail wagged. I kneeled down to her and stroked her head. The employee informed me she was an older dog and the man who owned her passed away, and unfortunately, no one from his family could take her in. Her eyes gleamed with hope as I looked at them. I asked her if she wanted to come with me and she barked once and got up, standing tall. I turned to the employee and smiled. It was her.

Now I stand in front of this building once again and I fight back the tears threatening to fall.

We go in and get greeted by a man in his early 20s, I'm guessing. His name tag says Sean.

'So what are you looking for, ladies?' He asks us politely and Tess answers,

'I'm just wondering if I could just learn about the process and maybe have a look at what animals you have. I'm still considering if a pet is the right idea for me.'

'Of course.' He nods and offers us a smile. He spends maybe 15 minutes explaining how they do a home visit and how they bring the animals or they can be collected from here, depending on a person's preferences. They do charge a fee of £300 for adoption to help support the organisation, but I remember throwing an extra £200 as a donation. Once they finish their Q&A, Sean takes us over to the kennels. The whimpering and barking noises now are much louder. When we go in, Tess gasps loudly and when I turn to her, I see a tear fall down her cheek. I take her hand in mine and squeeze as we walk forward slowly. She looks at every dog, all different breeds, Staffies, cross breeds, Dalmatians, Yorkshire Terriers, elderly, younger, some not even a year old. Completely heart breaking. I can tell Tess is trying her best to keep it together. She has a huge heart and I know this is all very difficult for her. We make it out of the first kennel when she speaks up.

'This is horrible.' Her voice almost breaking.

'We do our best to look after them,' Sean says, 'But unfortunately with so many animals, we can not provide what an adoptive family can.' He's doesn't smile. I don't think anyone could smile while in here.

'Here's our cat kennel.' He gestures to the next building. This one is much quieter as we enter, just some meowing here and there. First kennel on the left reads.

Name: Felix
Gender: Male
Age: 16

'He's an oldie.' I comment and kneel to stroke his cute ginger head. He's gorgeous. I look up at Tess and see her looking around.

'I wanna take them all.' She says and Sean chuckles. 'We all do.'

We make our way further in when Tess suddenly stops and looks down on her right. I step back to join her and see a beautiful tabby cat, fast asleep on her pink blanket.

Name: Cece
Gender: Female
Age: 3

'Who's that?' She points at the cat and Sean joins us. Cece lifts her head up and slowly stands up, stretching her front and back legs, and then we notice a little black kitten underneath her.

'That's Cece. She hasn't been long with us. We received her pregnant because the owner couldn't look after the kittens. She had 3 kittens here, 2 of them are already adopted. Just this little princess is left. She's 4 months old.' She's staring at them with her eyes wide open. Cece comes up to us and Tess slowly kneels down and strokes her head before saying, 'My nana's name was Cece. She was the best grandma anyone could have asked for.' Her voice is shaky.

'Are you thinking about Cece or the little one?' I kneel next to her and gesture toward the little black kitten, who's still sitting on the blanket. There's silence for a moment before Tess looks up at Sean with tears spilling from her eyes.

'I'll take them both.'

We're back at the reception and Tess is filling out all the paperwork required to book the home visit and once everything is done, she can collect her two princesses. She's grinning like a child on Christmas morning who found out Santa brought her the best barbie doll that ever existed.

Sean asks. 'When are you available for the home visit?'

'Tomorrow.' She replies so quickly, I'm not even sure Sean finished his question. We all laugh.

'We don't normally do home visits on Sundays but I see you don't live far away from me, so maybe I can make an exception, seeing how excited you are.' He smiles warmly.

'Yes, yes, please.' She claps her hands together.

The doorbell rings, alarming us of someone entering the rescue and when I turn, my eyes open wide when I see Gabriel carrying a large box inside. We both stop in place and glare at each other.

'You're stalking me?' I ask, crossing my arms over my chest, and he chuckles.

'Yes. My name is Joe and I'm here to kill your friend.'

'Who, me?!' Tess quickly turns around and notices Gabriel standing in the entrance.

'Oh Mr. Alstons, hello.'

'Hi Tess.' He sets the box down.

'Mr. Alstons, I'll be with you in just a minute.' Sean calls out,

'No problem, Sean.'

'What, what are you doing here?' I ask him.

'I can ask you the same thing. Maybe you're my Joe.'

I scoff, 'If anyone's Joe, it's you.' He laughs.

'I'm adopting two cats.' Tess explains.

'Good for you, Tess. Congratulations on your new additions.'

'Just need to do the home visit tomorrow so hopefully I'll pass that.' She glances at Sean, who smiles at her before turning back to typing something on the computer.

'Sean.' Gabriel calls out to him.

'Yes, sir?' He looks up from the screen.

'Scratch the home visit. I'm vouching for her.' Both my and Tess' eyes widen and our mouths gape at him.

'Yes, sir.'

'Do...does that...mean...?' She says with her breathy voice, glancing between us all.

'You can take them home now if you want.' Gabriel explains and tears start falling down her cheeks once again as she rushes towards Gabriel and throws her arms around his neck. He hugs her back, chuckling away. I smile at the sight of them and warmth fills my heart.

'Wait, I need to buy everything.' She shouts out as she pulls away from our boss and she turns to me.

'What time do you close?' I turn to Sean.

'6pm.' He says and I turn to Tess grinning. 'Let's go shopping now then.'

Tess jumps out and calls out back to Sean. 'I'll be back soon. Give me 2 hours.' He nods in confirmation before Tess speeds outside to the car. I laugh as she doesn't even say bye.

'So...' I start as I walk toward Gabriel. 'What are you doing here?' He crosses his arms across his chest now and smiles.

'I sponsor this place and do donations once a month. I got Bruno from here.'

'You're joking?'

'No, why?'

'I got Nala from here.' I tell him and he smiles widely.

'Small world.' He exclaims and I whisper, 'Small world indeed.'

I go to leave and when I open the door, Gabriel calls out.

'Would you ...' I turn around to him and he looks unsure.

'Yes?' His eyes narrow and his body looks tensed.

'Would you like to go to the Christmas fayre with me tomorrow?'

'Christmas fayre?' I think about it. It could be fun, but isn't that breaking the rule?

'Public rule.' I reply and he nods. 'How about we pretend we bump into each other?'

'I'll think about it.' I wink at him and leave. Going out in a public place like that is definitely breaking the rule, so why did I almost say yes?

CHAPTER TWENTY-THREE

Brooke

I wake up to the pinging of my phone. It feels too early, so I pull the covers over my head and let out a groan.

Another ping.

Another ping.

I sigh loudly and push the covers off. 10 unread messages. 9 of them from Tess, sending me photos of Cece and Dede as they're sleeping, cuddled up together on her bed. I smile and reply,

Me- You're one proud mummy.

A reply comes immediately,

Tess- Indeed I am.

I can't explain how happy I am for her. And how Gabriel helped still lingers in my mind. He was amazing, and he clearly is a big deal there, if one of his words can make them scratch the home visit. We all knew she didn't need one, though. Her home is always clean, always filled with food and there's enough space for two cats. A mother and daughter. She told me she couldn't decide. She simply couldn't say, 'Ill take this one and leave that one.' I snort when I think how full her hands are gonna be now.

It's 7:30am now, so I'm definitely not getting up yet. It's just about getting light and the sky looks clear for now, which is good news as I'm really sick of the rain. The last message is from no one else other than the man himself.

Gabriel- I'll pick you up at 3pm.

I rub the sleep off my eyes with my free hand before replying.

Me- Pick me up for what?

Gabriel- Christmas fayre.

Shit. I forgot about his invitation.

Me- I don't think it's a good idea. It's breaking the rule.

I stare at my phone, waiting for the reply. He takes a good minute to answer.

Gabriel- It's something to take your mind off things while you wait to hear from agents. Plus, I'm not going to fall in love with you because we spent the afternoon together and I'm sure you won't either. Plus, there'll be no public affection. I promise to keep my hands to myself unless you beg me to make you come again.

My clit pulses at the thought.

It's way too early for this.

Me- Fine. But your place after.

Gabriel- I'm planning on using the gym after, but you can join me.

I don't even want to think when was the last time I've been to the gym. But seeing Gabriel sweat... that's tempting.

Me- I'll try but under one condition.

Gabriel-What's that?

Me- You go topless.

Gabriel- Deal ;)

I set the phone down and take a deep breath. Now I'm very much looking forward to this afternoon.

3 o'clock comes and I have my travel bag ready with some gym clothes, shower stuff, hair band and other bits I might need while I'm at Gabriel's. I'm wrapped warm in multiple layers and thick socks to ensure I don't get cold at the fayre. My stomach fills with butterflies when the sound of intercom rings.

I push the button and call out, 'On my way.' I quickly put my brown boots on, my thick winter coat and a black beanie. My neighbour's daughter Allie will come and sit with Nala while she does her homework.

When I get out of the building, I spot Gabriel, waiting by the car, with Mark behind the wheel. He smiles warmly and opens the door for me. I get in and he goes around to get in on his side.

'Hi Mark,' I call out

'Hello Miss...' He stops himself when he sees me frowning in the mirror. 'Brooke.'

I smirk, 'Better.'

'What's better?' Gabriel asks as he shuts his door.

'Your driver struggles to remember my name.' I chuckle and Mark smiles.

'I'm sorry, Brooke. I'll do better next time.'

Mark drops us off at the fayre and tells Gabriel to call him when we're ready to be picked up. The cold air hits my face and I shiver. I'm thankful for my layers now, even if I look like a muscular grinch. Gabriel lifts his arm so I can hook mine on it, but I shake my head.

'Sorry, I forgot.'

We make our way in and the place is already pretty crowded. Stools have long queues of people and I can smell a mix of cinnamon and mulled wine. The sound of oil sizzling, people laughing, and Christmas music playing through speakers hit my ears as we make our way through the stands.

'How's Tess today? Did she pick up her new companions?' I chuckle and pull my phone out of the pocket and show him the picture she sent me earlier today. She's sitting in her snoopy pyjamas, cross-legged on the cream leather sofa and has her arms wrapped around the cats who are sitting on her legs. She has the biggest smile plastered on her face, too. Gabriel laughs at the sight.

'I guess that answers my question.' Before putting the phone away, I press on the email icon just to check it quickly, but I have no new emails. I make a face to myself and put it back in my pocket.

'Still nothing?'

I shake my head.

'I know how we can cheer you up.' He grins and when I look in the direction of his glance, I smile wildly myself.

'Let's do this.'

In the changing area now, we're sitting on the bench. A bit too close to each other as our legs bump when we lift them up to put the skates on. The current slot finishes in 5 minutes, so we need to be ready by then so we can get on ice.

'Are you a good skater?' I ask him and he snorts out, 'Better than you.' My eyes widen at this comment.

'Excuse me, how do you know what kind of skater I am?' I jab him in the side and he flinches, laughing it away. 'If we go by the way you roller blade...' I laugh at his very... accurate insult. 'When was the last time you skated?' I ask him and he shrugs. 'Never skated in my life.'

'What?!' I shout a tad too loud and people look up at us. 'Then how can you be better than me?' He's finished putting his skates on and watches people still on the ice.

'It just doesn't look that difficult.' He shrugs again and I swallow the laughter that threatens to leave my mouth because... Boy, he's in for a treat.

We stand up off the bench and he stumbles. As I try to reach out to him, he puts his hand up between us. 'I'm fine.' My wide grin must be obvious as he then adds, 'Don't do that. I bet you I'll stay up the whole time.' He straightens himself up, and a giggle leaves my mouth. I like the challenge.

'Bet me what?'

His brow arches, 'What what?'

'What's the bet for?' He looks away and rubs his index finger and thumb over his beard, and then he leans closer to me so he can whisper into my ear. 'I fall on my ass, I go down on you so hard that you won't even have the energy for sex after.' My body trembles and this time, it's not from the cold.

'And if you stay up on ice?' I mumble back to him in my breathy voice.

'If I stay up on ice, then you do the thing you did in my office last week.' I smile at the memory of his moans when I took him in my mouth. 'Deal' I turn to him and realise our lips are way too close to each other. I quickly pull away and start walking toward the ice. He's much slower, trying to follow me, and I snort when I see him almost lose his balance twice, and we're not even on the ice yet.

This is going to be fun.

We watch as people leave the ring, couples, parents with children, friends, all are laughing, having a great time. I glance at Gabriel, whose lips are now pulled into a thin line.

'Doubting yourself?' I elbow him in his arm.

'Dream on woman.' He looks at me, his expression deadly serious. 'I'm about to win our bet.' I scoff and one of the employee makes his way toward us to open the barrier and let us on. We're first in line and my stomach twists in excitement to see how long he can last.

'I give you less than 2 minutes till you're on your ass.' I mutter to him, and he scoffs.

As the barrier opens, we take our step onto the ring and I was right. Not even two steps in, Gabriel stumbles and his feet go up in the air, landing straight on his ass with a thud.

I burst out laughing while others get around him to skate away. People glance his way and my stomach hurts from the laughter, tears falling down my face. Seeing a grown, confident man slipping on ice and going up in the air like that? That's sticking in my head for life. He lifts himself up on the elbows, shaking his head in utter disbelief. The next second, I feel his foot push into my legs, making me stumble, and my ass joining him on the ice.

'Smartass.' He barks and starts laughing himself.

We lasted all 10 minutes on the ice rink instead of the hour Gabriel paid for. After his fall number 15, we decided it's best to not risk any broken bones—or egos. I still giggle to myself as we walk away from the rink.

'It wasn't funny.' He snaps, and it only makes me laugh harder. I'm suddenly halted by the iron grip on my wrist. Pulling me in closer, he says in a broken whisper, 'Stop or I'll pay my debt right now.' I stop immediately, feeling the flutter between my legs, and he lets me go. 'That's what I thought.' It's him that chuckles now.

It's getting dark now so families with kids are slowly leaving the fayre and the place gets filled with more adults who came here for food and drink. I straighten my scarf as also the wind picks up.

'Are you hungry?' He asks, and I look around. There's not much of an interesting choice, either a deep fried sausage or a plain burger... We make our way further on when I spot a churro stand and I grin widely, shooting my glance to him.

'You want churros?' I nod. We join the queue which is massive but the smell of the cinammony goodness from the stand, makes the wait worth it.

'Brooke?' a voice from behind me calls out and when I turn around, I see Aaron making his way to me.

'Hi!' I smile and we hug. He and Gabriel shake hands before he turns to me.

'Having fun?'

I smirk playfully. 'It's definitely a lot of fun watching your boss,' I glance at Gabriel, ' who was so confident he can skate, falling on his ass the moment we stepped onto the ice.' Aaron laughs out loud and Gabriel snaps, 'Hey!'

'Sorry.' I wave my hand and we both continue laughing.

'And who are you with?' I ask Aaron as I look around him and then a man appears at his side, who places a kiss on Aaron's cheek.

'This is Dean.' He smiles at me and I return it.

'And this is Brooke, my best friend.'

We shake hands. 'Nice to meet you. Heard a lot about you.'

'You too.'

Aaron gestures then to Gabriel. 'And this is Mr. Alstons, Brooke's…' He pauses and I finish, 'Friend.'

They said their hi's nice to meet you's.

'So, where are you off to?' I ask them and they both look at each other, grinning.

'We're going to the Ferris wheel.' They both say together and I smirk.

'The best spot for make-out session?' They both glance at each other, which gives me my answer.

'Well, have fun then.' I add, and Aaron hugs me one more time.

'You too. We'll talk tomorrow.' I nod and they both walk away.

When I check the queue, we still have 5 people in front of us. I tap my foot on the ground and put my hand on my hip.

'That hungry now?' Gabriel asks and I scoff,

'The smell alone makes my mouth water.'

'Wow, you're hangry.' He puts his hands up in defence and I look at him with my eyes narrowed.

'Didn't think you'd know the word, considering your age.'

'My age?' He startles. 'I know you're hangry but there's no need to be insulting.'

'Sorry. I just looove churros.'

We're finally next.

'What can I get you?' Before I can answer, Gabriel steps in front of me and speaks up.

'Triple portion of churros, please.'

'Chocolate sauce with them?' He looks down at me, and I nod with a massive smile on my face.

'Yes, please.' He takes out his card and pays for the food. Within a minute, I'm holding the tray of the Christmas heavenly sticks and a cup filled with hot chocolate. We move to the side of the stand and I lift one up, dip it on the chocolate and take a bite. I moan loudly while rolling my eyes back.

'Seriously?'

'What?' I glance at his annoyed face.

'You're gonna make me hard if you carry on with these moans.' I laugh. I take another bite, but the wind blows my hair on my face so it's hard trying to rub them away with the back of my hand or trying to blow them away.

'Damn hair. Should have put them up.' I snap and Gabriel comes closer, pulling my hair off my face and tucking them behind my ear.

'Thank you.' I stuff the rest of the churro in my mouth and moan again before remembering myself.

'Sorry.' I mumble with my mouth full, and he groans in disappointment, shooting me a penetrating look. I put the tray out so he can help himself. He picks one up and studies it.

'You've never had churros before?' I pinch my eyebrows together.

'No.' He says simply. He dips his churro in the chocolate and takes a bite. A moan leaves his mouth.

'Oi!' I call out laughing and his eyes widen at the realisation at what he's just done.

He winks at me, 'Payback.' I take another bite of my churro and feel the chocolate leak at the side of my mouth.

'Crap!' I cry out.

'Hang on.' Gabriel slowly rubs the chocolate from the corner of my mouth and chin with his thumb while looking me in the eye. I feel something shift in my stomach and butterflies flutter at the touch. My body urges me to kiss him, but then I snap out of it and to loosen the situation, I rub my chocolate-covered churro all over his face. His cheeks and nose are now covered in chocolate. I laugh loudly as he inhales a deep breath and lifts his finger to rub some of the chocolate off his face and licks it.

'I think it'd taste better from the cup, not my face.' His gaze snaps back to me.

'Cheer up, baby.' I demand and then I notice a cheeky smirk appear on his face as he takes a step toward me.

'Oh no …' I take a step back and realise I'm against the stand, with nowhere to go, while I'm holding a tray full of my beautiful churros. He takes another step forward, slowly closing the distance between us.

'Gabriel, no!' My laughing stops as he grabs my face and rubs his chocolate face onto mine, spreading it all over my cheeks and mouth.

'No!' I cry out, laughing again. 'I'm gonna drop my churros.' He stops and his entire face is completely smudged now.

'I look like you now, don't I?' I ask and Gabriel pulls out his phone. 'Let's check.' He now stands next to me and lifts the phone one with his front camera on. His other arm is across my shoulders and I lean into him while we're both smiling.

Click.

We glance at the screen and we look like cavemen covered in dirt and mud, trying to hide from predators. We both burst out laughing and Gabriel makes his way to the stand to grab a couple of napkins.

'Shall I call Mark?' He asks and I nod, while chewing on another churro.

'Hamster cheeks.' He chuckles and I wrinkle my nose at him.

I remove my shoes and set them on the side while Gabriel makes his way to the kitchen.

'Fancy a cup of hot chocolate?' He calls out.

'Yes, please.' I answer before going further in. Bruno comes to greet me, so I say hi and stroke him behind his ear. I put my bag on the marble island and watch Gabriel pull out the milk from the fridge.

'Good man.' I say, and he looks up at me, confused.

'The milk.' I gesture at his hand.

'The milk what?'

'Hot chocolate should be made with milk, never with water.' I explain.

He snorts, 'Well, obviously,' and turns away.

I rub my hands together as they still feel frozen. Silly me for not bringing my gloves and thinking that keeping my hands in my pockets will be enough. It's the middle of November now and it's freaking freezing. Gabriel notices what I'm doing, so he turns around and comes up to me, grabbing both my hands between his. I'm caught off guard when he pulls my hands closer to his mouth, blowing into them to warm them up. I watch him as the feeling of my fingers comes back. My breathing becomes heavy as I acknowledge our proximity and I know we're not about to have sex—he's just helping me. The blood circulation come back into my hands. I also feel a flutter in my stomach, which I push away.

'Tyler would never have done that.' I mumble under my breath, but Gabriel catches it.

'What did you say?'

'Sorry I just...' I pull my hands away and he straightens up, '...Tyler would never do that for me. He'd have a go at me for not wearing gloves and he'd say it was my fault I was cold.'

Gabriel's forehead wrinkles. 'Well, I'm not Tyler, am I?' He turns around and goes back to making our drinks.

'No, you're not.' I murmur and this time he doesn't hear me.

I sit on the island and Gabriel leans against the worktop as we're drinking our hot chocolates. The hot liquid warms up every inch of my body and I feel myself relaxing.

'I love your socks.' He chuckles and I look down at my pink, fluffy socks that have individual toes. I lift my feet up and wriggle my toes at him. He snorts at me, and I smirk. Gabriel let me put some music on his Alexa, so Zombie by Bad Wolves is quietly playing in the background.

I take another sip of my hot drink and make a mmm sound. 'This feels good.'

He smiles.

'I believe…' He sets his mug down and takes a step toward me, 'That I lost a certain bet to you.'

'Did you?' I say in my flirty voice and he nods slowly in reply, placing both his hands on each side of me, caging me in. After setting my own empty mug on the side, I throw my arms around his neck.

'Remind me what I won.' I look up, pretending to think, as his gaze slides downwards. My pussy throbs in anticipation.

He puts his mouth on my neck, kissing it slowly and tenderly, making all the hair on my body rise. I tilt my head to the side to allow him easier access. Under by Alex Hepburn plays now but I'm fully focused on Gabriel's touch as he now strokes my thighs. My clit pulses at his touch and I know I need more.

Right now.

I cup his face and kiss him hard. His arms wrap around my waist and pull me closer, allowing me to feel his already hard cock against my pussy, with only our clothes separating us. Our breaths, both heavy, match each other as I lean slightly back. I rub his cock with my hand and he groans against my mouth. He starts to unzip my jeans when…

PING.

I stop what I'm doing and freeze in place. Gabriel stops as well, and he pulls away just slightly.

'Is this an email notification?' He asks and I nod. My heart is now pounding against my chest and my palms sweat.

CHAPTER TWENTY-FOUR

Gabriel

'Are you going to read it? I ask her, and she slowly turns her head to side and picks up the phone with her shaky hands. I take a step back to give her space and I see her whole body tensing up.

'It'll be ok.' I add, and she tries to smile but fails. She presses something on her phone and reads. I hold my breath in, waiting, and a moment later I see her lip turn and tears appear in her eyes.

'It's a rejection.' She whispers and my heart aches for her.

'It's ok ...' I take a step toward her, but she stops me with her hand. She looks up, blinking fast before adding. 'My book doesn't sound original enough and they don't think there's enough target audience for it.'

'That's bullshit and we know it.' I throw my hands in the air before cupping her face in them. 'Brooke, let my proof readers have a look...'

She snaps, 'No!' and jumps off the island.

'Where are you going?' I watch her grab her coat.

'Home. I can't do this tonight Gabriel, I'm sorry.' I go up to her and take her shoes off her before setting them on the side.

'What are you...' she starts, but I pull her back inside. I sit her down on the sofa, where Bruno comes over and lies his head on her lap. She pets him behind his ear when I speak up.

'All authors have plenty of rejection emails behind them and you know it. There is no author who got successful with their first try. This agent was simply not meant to be working with you because he most likely was an idiot if he doubted you. You want someone who wants to see you succeed.' She doesn't look at me as she keeps petting Bruno. I can almost feel how this email shattered her confidence.

'Maybe I'm not meant for this. Maybe writing is, in fact, too much for me and I should stick to my job.' My eyes widen in shock,

'Why? Because of one rejection letter?' She nods.

'Look at me.' I demand, and she slowly raises her eyes to meet mine.

'Do you want to write?' I ask her, my lips pulled into a thin line. She takes a moment to think and takes a deep breath. 'I've wanted to write my whole life.'

'Then let me help. There's nothing wrong with getting help to achieve your dreams, Brooke.'

She shakes her head furiously. 'I don't want anything from you.' Her eyes are red. 'We're not together, Gabriel, we're not even friends. We're a fling. We meet up for sex and say bye. This...' She gestures between me and her, 'It's nothing.' I flinch at the sting of her words.

She stands up and adds, 'I have to go.' and leaves.

After I've used my gym to work out the stress and take my minds off things, I jump into the shower. I let the cold water hit my sweaty body, and I put my hands on the wall, dropping my head down and taking deep breaths. I want to help her. She is being too stubborn and I can help. Plenty of people get help to achieve their goals. I know I've used Max's help sometimes, even if it was stupid as watching Bruno so I could go and meet a potential author. We all rely on each other in some way. But she told me I'm no one to her. That we mean nothing. I know we're not together. I'm fully aware of that. It was my idea in the first place, but to call me – us – nothing? That stung. Even after a heavy workout, my heart is still aching. It never ached like that before, so I'm not sure what could have caused it. Maybe it's the fucking churros. I wash myself quickly before stepping out and looking in the mirror. I see myself yet I don't recognise my expression, my eyes look dropped, as if the life was sucked out of me.

Who are you? I rub my eyes and wonder if Brooke is becoming too much for me, like Max said. The idea of her hurt hurts me even though I don't love her. I shake my head and head to my bedroom and reach out for the phone I left on the bed.

I shoot out a quick e-mail before calling Max.

'Gabie boy! How are you?' His voice puts a smile on my face immediately.

'Drinks in an hour?' I search for a top in my drawer while holding the phone between my ear and my shoulder.

'Usual place?' I can hear his grin through the speaker.

'Sounds good.'

This evening, I decide to not think about Brooke. She made herself perfectly clear when she said we're just a fling and we only have sex. So tonight I'm going to ignore my thoughts and focus on myself. I sit at the bar with a glass full of whisky. I much prefer pubs to clubs. It's quieter and you can have an actual conversation.

Shit. Am I getting old?

'Gabie boy ...' A hand lands on my shoulder before I turn to see Max taking the seat next to me.

'What are we sulking about tonight?'

I shrug, 'Nothing.'

'Oh no, I see it on your face. What is it?'

I sigh, 'Brooke...'

'Man.' He stops me, 'I told you, you're going too far with her. Break it off while it's not too late.' He orders a pint of beer. And the waitress winks at him.

'What are the chances I'll be sleeping with her?'

I roll my eyes, '95%'

'Why 95?' He snaps in my direction.

'You're still thinking about Tess.'

He pulls his lips into a thin line and doesn't reply. He takes a big gulp of his beer before speaking up again. 'Seriously, mate. Break. It. Off.' I stare at my glass and wonder if he's right. I've never sulked over a woman before. Am I sulking? Is that what sulking feels like? We had such a good afternoon until that bloody email came through.

'I just wanted to help her.' I mutter.

He exhales loudly. 'You're not here to help her. You're here to fuck her and that's it.' He shrugs and I know he's right. That was the deal, but I can't help wonder how her life could change if she'd only listened to me. Yes, I worked my ass off myself, but I was a kid, and I had no one watching my back till I met Max. He believed in me and it gave me all the strength I needed to carry on. Oh well.

I pick up my glass to Max.

'To being single and happy.'

'I'll cheer to that.'

Few hours and an unknown number of drinks later, I'm much more cheerful. It's the funny feeling where you're still aware of what's going on, but yet, your brain is too far gone to think about anything serious. I stare at Max, who's flirting with the waitress, while he was meant to order more drinks. She's a beautiful woman, with curly black hair, dark-skinned, perfect curves. I'm not surprised Max is drooling all over her.

'What are you thinking Gabie boy?'

'I'm thinking that no matter who I look at, they're not Brooke.' I can feel my head move side to side involuntarily. Max grabs me by my shoulders and shakes me.

'Then go and kiss her and confess your undying love.' He laughs. We're both very much drunk right now.

'Why won't you invite Tess for dinner?'

His body tenses at the question, but he still moves slightly from left to right. 'I'm scared.'

My eyes widen. 'Of what?'

'Of acting like a dick in front of her. I know how to pick up women at clubs or pubs but dinners... that's a prince charming fucking story, and I'm no prince charming. Plus, I tried.'

'You tried?'

'I asked her if she wanted to grab a bite.' He shrugs and I tilt my head back, laughing out loud and almost losing my balance on the stool. I grab on to the bar quickly enough that I don't make a fool out of myself.

'Let me guess, she didn't reply.' He shakes his head way too many times.

'Do you want a tip?' He leans forward and tilts his head to the side as if I'm about to tell him the biggest secret.

'Send her flowers with a note.' I mutter.

'What should I say on the note?'

I choke out, 'Definitely nothing about grabbing a bite.' He punches me in the arm.

'Women ...' He sighs.

'Women ...' I repeat.

I barely make it back to my apartment when my phone pings.

Max- Gt hme k?

I laugh and try to type back, but it takes me way longer than expected.

Me- Hmevm

Delete.

Me- I mkvniv

Delete.

Me- Nocnjkd

Fucking. Delete.

I press and hold the microphone symbol and speak.

'I'm home, Maxie boy. Speak morrow.' and I let go, while the voice message gets sent to Max.

I sit down on the floor against the island while my whole world spins around me. Bruno comes up to me and licks my face.

'Bruno, since when are there two of you?' I laugh to myself.

Ping.

I tilt my head to look at the phone on the floor. I lift it up and can only make out the word **Brooke**. For fuck's sake, he's not giving up. I press the microphone icon again and speak.

'Mate, stop naggin' me about Brooke. It's already enough I can't stop thinking about her. I'll be fine once I get some sleep.' The message gets sent, and I set the phone back on the floor. My head drops to the side and I close my eyes.

A loud knocking on the door wakes me up. Knocking? How can I hear knocking from my...

I open my eyes and realise that, in fact, I'm not in my bed but on my kitchen floor. My head throbs with every knock, so I put my hands up to massage my temples.

Fucking hell, what happened last night?

Another set of knocking makes me flinch in pain, and I groan

'One second!' I shout out and I glance at my phone. 7am. I drag myself off the floor and make my way to the fridge, where I pull out a bottle of water and down it all in one go. I sigh loudly as my head pounds like it's going to explode.

Another knock.

Shit, I forgot there's someone outside. I put the bottle down and make my way to the door. My eyes widen when I see Brooke standing in the threshold.

'We need to talk.' Words leave her mouth before she storms inside my home.

'Come in.' I say sarcastically. She turns around and looks at me. 'Are you drunk?'

'I was.' I mumble out, as every sound feels like a stab in my brain.

She scoffs, 'I know.'

'How do you know?' She sets her bag on the island and pulls out two mugs out of the top cabinet.

'I could tell in your voice last night.' She exclaims as she turns on the coffee machine. I sit on the stool, resting my head in my hands on the island. 'We talked last night?'

'Well, you sent me a voice message.' I pause now and try to remember when I sent her a message. I pull my phone out of the pocket and check messages.

Brooke- I'm sorry about earlier. Can we please talk?

Me- Voice message.

I press on it and the message plays back. 'Mate, stop nagging me about Brooke. It's already enough I can't stop thinking...' I turn my phone off before the rest of the message plays out.

Shit. It wasn't Brooke, as in Max saying Brooke. It was Brooke, as in the message from Brooke, to which I replied. I stare at the black screen when she sets a mug of hot coffee in front of me and takes a sip of hers.

'I guess it wasn't meant for me.' She leans on the worktop. She's already dressed for work, looking beautiful as ever, in her black knee-length skirt, white blouse and black jacket, with her hair braided to the side.

'Shit. I'm sorry.' I mutter, 'I went out with Max and just lost the time.' She only nods back.

'It's not ... It's not what you think.'

'And what do I think?' She frowns.

'I don't love you.' I shake my head, but she doesn't reply.

'Gabriel...' I look up at her from my seat as she now stands on the other side of the island, leaning her arms on it. 'I think it's going too far.'

'What is?

'We. This... fling.' She looks down, refusing to meet my eyes.

'Yesterday felt too... personal. And then I said some harsh words to you and I'm sorry about that. But I can't let myself feel anything right now... for anyone.' I nod in understanding. 'I think it's best we stop now.' Something stabs me in my chest, probably fucking heartburn from the alcohol. It feels so heavy and my stomach twists itself. I feel like I'm going to be sick. 'I understand' I say with shaky voice.

'Are you ... ok?' She tilts her head to look at me, but I only push off the stool and take a step away.

'Brooke. I already said, I don't love you. We both knew flings come to an end, so it is what it is. I need to go for a shower. I'll see you at work.' I turn on my heel and walk away, leaving her behind.

CHAPTER TWENTY-FIVE

Brooke

You regret breaking it off with him.

No, no, I don't.

I take a deep breath and enter the building. Tess stands up when she sees me, a smile spreading from ear to ear.

'Hi hun!' she calls out and comes over to give me a hug.

Stay strong. Don't think about him. You don't care about him.

'How's the babies?' I ask her and she quickly pulls out her phone and shows me the hundred and one photos of Cece and Dede: sleeping, eating, playing, drinking, etc. I chuckle.

'You do look happy.' I look at her and offer her a warm smile.

'I am.' She's still looking at the phone. 'Thank you.'

'No reason to thank me, silly. You saved them.'

'I love them so much.'

'I know.'

'Miss. Philips?' We turn around to see a man holding the largest bouquet of red roses I've ever seen.

'Er, yes?' She puts her hand up to tell him it's her.

'I've got a delivery for you, miss.' She gapes at the flowers and glances at me. I shrug my shoulders to tell her I have no idea what's happening. The man sets the flowers down on the reception desk and asks her to sign the document to say she received them.

'Who sent them?' She asks the man, but he shrugs. 'No idea. But there's a note if you can find it.' He gestures at the roses.

After he leaves, Tess tucks into the flowers, searching, when she finally pulls the note out.

'Aha!' she calls out in triumph, waving it up in the air.

'Read it.' I tell her and she opens it. As she reads it first to herself, her mouth flies wide open.

'What?' I frown at her and she passes me the note to read for myself.

I'm sorry for being... me. I guess you make me very nervous, but I would really love a second chance to get to know you. Please have dinner with me soon.

M xxx

'M as in...' I start but she finishes, '...Max.' Her lips are pulled into a thin line.

'What are you going to do?' She looks up at what probably is like 50 red roses and she shrugs. 'I guess he deserves a chance now, doesn't he?'

'Well, it's better than a hook up or grabbing a bite.' We both laugh. I then kiss her on the cheek and head to my floor.

When I get to my office, I power on the computer and log into my email. New message pops up and when I open it, my stomach drops and my mouth turns into a frown.

Another rejection.

I close my eyes and take a deep breath in. I've spent all last night thinking about how I overreacted. I mean… I knew I'd get plenty of rejections, but I guess it suddenly became very real when I actually got it. Hearing from someone that my book isn't good enough isn't something a writer wants to hear. Even Stephen King's Carrie had thirty rejections and look at it now. I know I can do it. I believe in my book and I know someone will believe in it too.

I take a deep breath and shake my shoulders. I still have more agents to hear from.

Knock. Knock.

I jump in my seat and my stomach twists when I think it could be Gabriel standing behind my door.

'Come in,' I call out, and I exhale when Justin comes in.

'You're alright?' He takes the seat on the other side of the desk and I lean back in my chair.

'Yeah, all good. You?' He shrugs.

'What's up?'

'Just running behind my deadline, you know? This guy has so many fucking mistakes in his script, I wonder if he even reread what he wrote in his first draft.'

I chuckle, but he shakes his head. 'Not funny. There is literally no world building, but he says it's an adult fantasy.'

'Maybe I can try to help you. I'm not great with fantasy, but I can see what I can do.' I offer, but he shakes his head again. 'I'll be fine. I better get going though, I have a call organised with the author soon.' He gets up, and as he opens the door, he turns back to me.

'Brooke?'

'Yes?' I look up at him.

'Would you like to grab lunch… together… sometime?' This startles me.

'As … friends?' I murmur, and he looks down at his shoes.

'As… date.' He replies, and suddenly I feel sick in my stomach.

'Justin, I'm not looking for a relationship right now. I'm sorry.' I say sincerely. And even if I was ready to date, I'd definitely need time to get over Gabriel because knowing I'll never see him again out of work makes my heart ache. We got too close and there's no denying that. I should have said no to dinner. I should have said no to the Christmas fayre. If we stuck to the rules, then maybe we could have carried on for longer. There's no point sulking over it now, though. Done and dusted.

'As friends then?' His smile doesn't quite reach his eyes. 'I could do with talking through part of the book with someone who has a fresh set of eyes.'

I smile at him, 'Of course.'

'Great. I'll come and get you later.' And he leaves.

I spend the morning staring at my screen, unable to focus on the draft. I read a sentence and then I realise I didn't take anything in, so I reread it. My comments are clumsy, not detailed enough. I feel frustration building up in my chest and I slap my hands on the desk before pushing myself away and standing up. I look through the window and watch people rush to wherever they're going. I hate this feeling – ungrounded. My thoughts are all over the place and I can't focus on a single thing. I take a few deep breaths and close my eyes.

Ground yourself, Brooke. You're ok.

I leave the office and head to John's desk, where he's busy on his computer.

'John,' I call out and he looks up at me. 'Brooke. Can I help you?'

'Can I please finish my day from home?'

His brow arches. 'What happened?'

'Just having a terrible day. I don't know, I just can't focus.'

He takes a moment to think, 'Mr. Alstons has to approve working from home, I'm afraid.' My heart skips a beat when he says his name. 'Could you ask him for me, please?'

'He called in sick today, actually.' Sick? I know he was

hungover, but I know a shower and big bottle of water would make him feel good enough to come to work. Did he not come because of me? If so, it's another proof that we did the right thing by breaking things off.

I sigh, 'So there's nothing else you can do?' He shakes his head. 'Unless you wanna call him and ask, but I wouldn't recommend it.' I scoff and go back to the office.

I sit at my desk and pull out my phone to check on Nala. She's not in, so her dog sitter must have taken her out. My breathing becomes heavy and I start to feel a hot flush hit me. I get up and tilt the window open to allow the cold air inside. I want to call him. I want to see if he's ok. My thumb is above the call as I press on his name on my phone.

Call him. You want to hear his voice.

A knock comes from behind my door.

'Come in!' I shout out quickly, putting my phone away.

'Ready?' Justin pops his head through.

'Sure.' I smile. I completely forgot about our lunch and now I regret to agreeing it. Why do I feel like something is wrong?

We're sitting at the cafeteria on the other side of the road from our building. Justin tells me about this author and how it's his debut novel, so he's quite stressed out about the process. So Justin tried to assure him and help him when he can but also he can't hold his hand. At the end of the day, the book belongs to the author. I order myself a cup of green tea, hoping it'll ease my unreasonable nerves.

'Are you not feeling well?' I look up from my cup and see Justin frowning.

'Yeah, I think I might have caught something,' I offer him a half-hearted smile. The place is crowded, filled with the noise of people chattering and laughing. Doorbell constantly ringing with new people coming and going. I glance through the window at our building, not even sure why.

'You look pale, Brooke.' My heart is now pounding against my chest, and I feel like my lungs are shutting down.

I'm going to be sick.

Justin grabs my hand on the table and holds it in his while rubbing the back of it with his thumb.

'Is there anything I can do?' I stare at our hands connected and my vision becomes blurry, the sounds become muffy. I swallow the hard lump in my throat before pulling my hand away.

'I, I gotta go. Please tell John I went home sick.' I pick up my purse and rush out the door without looking back.

When I get home, I drop my bag to the side before sliding down to the floor against the door. I hug my knees and rest my head on them.

Breathe, breathe.

Nala comes up to me, whimpering and trying to shove her nose in my face.

'Nala, not now.' I murmur. My vision is back to normal but my heart is still yet to slow down. I take off my jacket and throw it to the side, along with my shoes. Then I jump at the sound of my door knocking.

That's definitely not a way to slow down my heart rate.

'Who is it?' I call out, lacking the energy to stand up.

'Open up, Brooke.' A familiar voice sounds through the door. I shuffle slightly to the side and unlock the door. It swings open, hitting me, and then Aaron appears crouching down next to me.

'What happened?!' His face, full of worry.

'What are you doing here?'

'Tess called me, saying you were fine this morning and you pretty much ran out on Justin all pale.' So I tell him everything that happened, last night and today, as he helps me up and walks me to the sofa where I tilt my head back and close my eyes.

'Oh hun. That sounds like a panic attack.'

'A what?' I look at him with only one eye open, and he chuckles.

'It's when you're really stressed. Sometimes it can bring on an attack. It's your body telling you, it's feeling too much.'

I snort out, 'Too much.'

He tilts his head at me and twists his mouth. 'You've got your first rejection last night, you got stressed out and said things to Gabriel you didn't mean, then you stormed home and when you were ready to apologise, he basically said he can't stop thinking about you, so you freaked out and told him it's over, then you're the one who can't stop thinking about him and when you find out he didn't turn up at work, you freaked out once again.'

I snap my head up straight and frown at him. 'I can stop thinking about him.'

He scoffs, 'Can you?'

I stare at him for a moment before laying my head back down. 'Another proof I did the right thing by breaking things off.' I say. Aaron doesn't reply, but I hear him sigh.

'Come here.' He moves to the end of the sofa, pulling me with him, so I lie down between his legs and he starts to massage my temples.

'That feels good.' I close my eyes and enjoy the feeling.

'I know.' He says joyfully. He stays like that for maybe 10 minutes, in utter silence, and I feel my body return back to relaxed and heart now beating at normal speed.

'What would I do without you?' I snort and I can see him smirking when he replies, 'Struggle.'

When I sit up once again, Aaron gets up and goes to the kitchen.

'I don't think you did the right thing.' He comments as he pulls out two mugs.

'With what?'

'With breaking things off with Gabriel.' I frown, but he doesn't see it as he puts the kettle on.

'I think you're great together.' He adds, and I throw my cushion at him, which hits him in the back. He turns around and gives me a finger.

'I'm not doing it again!' I snap.

'Doing what?' He puts sugar in both mugs and throws in a tea bag each. English people and their tea. Worried? Have some tea. Sad? Have some tea. Happy? Have some tea. Aaron's lucky I like his tea.

'Loosing myself again.' I pull my legs to my chest and rest my chin on my knees.

'And who says you'd lose yourself with him? Have you ever had to pretend to be someone else around him?'

'No...' I murmur.

'What did you say? Can't hear you from here.' He calls out as he pours boiling water into the mugs.

'I said no!' I shout out.

'And has he ever been unhappy about how you acted or what you did?'

I look to the side, not wanting to answer him anymore.

'Answer me, woman!' He turns around and walks back to the sofa with both mugs, and he puts them down on the table as he sits down.

'No.' I poke my tongue out at him.

'So why do you think you'd lose yourself with him?'

'Because...' Because I don't know. Because I'm scared of things changing. Because I was so truly happy once with Tyler. Because... 'It doesn't matter, it's over.' I shrug and he sighs loudly at me.

'Don't you sigh at me!' I bark back. 'I'm happy you believe in love, but Gabriel told me himself, he doesn't.'

He scoffs. 'Just because he doesn't believe in love doesn't

mean he doesn't feel it. You can't just not feel. We're human. We feel.'

'Well, I'm focusing on myself now and I don't need a man in my life.' I shrug and pick up my mug to take a sip.

'Ahh. Hot.' I set it back down and Aaron laughs. 'I forgot to add cold water, sorry.'

He now takes my hands in his. 'Listen Brooke, sometimes we're not ready for certain things, but it doesn't mean they won't be thrown our way, and it definitely doesn't mean they're there to hurt us. Sometimes the universe knows what we need better than we do.'

I make a farting noise with my mouth at him and he lets go of me, 'So stubborn.' And I laugh. My phone rings in my bag, which is still on the floor. I get up to fetch it quickly and see an unknown number.

'Hello?' Aaron mouths who is it to me and I shrug to him.

'Hello, is this Miss. Summers?' A male voice sounds through the speaker.

'Yes, this is she.'

'My name is Ben Maxwell. I'm a publishing agent.'

My heart skips a beat when I hear who he is and I mouth oh my god to Aaron.

'Oh hi, how are you?' I ask him.

'I'm good, thank you. You see, my friend reached out to me and told me I might be interested in your book. I wanted to see if you'd be up for a meeting so we can chat?'

A friend? I frown and struggle to speak when I ask him, 'A friend? Can I know the name?'

And just like that, my excitement turns into pure rage when he replies,

'Gabriel Alstons.' My smile disappears and my free hand curls into a fist. Aaron frowns when he looks at me, and I shake my head.

'Erm ... I'm a little busy right now, but could I get back to you, please?'

'Of course. You can just call this number and then we can arrange something.'

'Great. Thank you.' We say our byes and I hang up the phone.

'What happened?' Aaron asks immediately and I snap, 'Don't' while dialling Gabriel's phone number.

First ring, second ring, third ring, fourth ring... and voicemail. I hang up and turn to Aaron.

'I'm going to kill him.'

CHAPTER TWENTY-SIX

Gabriel

The ringtone of my phone fills the car quickly and the name Brooke appears on the screen. I reach out and press decline before putting my hand back on the steering wheel. She made her decision, so be it. Yesterday I felt like a truck hit me. My whole body ached and couldn't even focus at the gym, so I gave up and spent the day chilling with Bruno. Today, I have a different task in mind and that's what I'm focusing on. I stop at the red light and look around. There're bottles from beer on the ground, blankets and pillows by one of the door and right in the corner of a closed bank, there's an old mattress and some boxes on top of it. A child runs by and stops, mere metres away from me. He slowly turns around and his eyes widen as he studies my Jag. His yellow hoodie is covered in dirt and he has a big hole in his jeans – and no, I don't mean these fashion holes where companies ruin jeans on purpose. I roll down the window,

'You like it?' I call out and he nods. When the light turns green, I decide to pull on the side and kill the engine. I jump out and gesture for him to come over. He makes his way slowly, unsure if he can trust me, I assume.

'What's your name?'

'Theo.'

I nod, 'That's a manly name.' He must be 6 or 7... or maybe he's just tiny. I know nothing about kids other than that they love balloons.

'My dad chose it for me.'

I crouch down to his eye level. 'And where is your dad?'

'He went to see my aunt to see if we can borrow some money.'

I study him and notice his dirty, overgrown nails and I can almost see his cheekbones as his face looks droopy.

'Are you hungry, Theo?' He looks down and nods slowly. I study the surroundings and spot a co-op shop.

'Let's go then.' I take his hand and at first he's not too sure, but once he sees where we're going, his shoulders relax and he grips my hand back.

'So, what do you like?' I ask him and he smiles widely.

'Chocolate.'

'Of course, that'd be your answer.' I chuckle and throw some chocolate bars into the basket.

'But let's also get you some proper food.'

We make our way through aisles and pick up some bread, milk, eggs and some ready meals for him and his parents. He frowns when he sees the full basket on my arm.

'What is it?' I ask him and he looks up at me.

'I don't have any money and...'

'Theo. I guess that's a good thing you're not paying for it.' I reply, and he narrows his eyes.

'Come on.' I gesture to the self check out.

Once we're out of the shop, we walk towards my car again. I glance down at him and ask, 'So, where do you live?'

He points to our left. 'At the end of this road on the right.'

'Ok then. Jump in....' I press my key to unlock the car, '... and I'll take you home.' But then he suddenly frowns.

'What is it?'

'My dad told me to never get in the car with a stranger.' We're now by the car so I crouch down to him again. 'And your dad is a very smart man, Theo. But I mean you no harm and I only want to make sure you get home safely with your shopping. Plus, you get to have a ride in my car.' He studies my face for a moment before saying, 'I like you.' and I chuckle. We jump in the car and I start the engine. Theo is swaying his legs in turns as he studies the inside of the car, a smile stretching from ear to ear.

When we park outside Theo's building, my phone rings again.

'Who's Brooke? Your wife?'

'No.' I snort out. 'She's a friend,' and I press decline.

'If she's your friend, why don't you want to talk to her?'

'Long story, mate. Let's get you home.'

I carry the shopping bags to the third floor when Theo just pushes the door open.

Do they not lock their home?

We go inside and he shows me to the kitchen. The stench of mould hits me as we make our way through this flat. Kitchen might be a bit of a stretch as it's two cupboards on the floor and two cupboards above, with a small fridge next to it. In the same room, there's a brown coffee table with cans of beer on it and newspapers. I see no sofa but a few camp chairs around.

Theo helps me put the food away, and I make him a sandwich and pour him a glass of juice. He sits down in one of the camp chairs and puts a show on with a weird yellow square person who lives underwater and makes burgers. I pull out my wallet and pull out a handful of £20 notes and set them on the side in their kitchen area.

Theo watches me, and I point my finger at him. 'That's for your parents, not you.'

He then gets off the chair and sets his plate on the coffee table before rushing toward me and wrapping his hands around my waist. 'Thank you.'

I swallow a hard lump in my throat and close my eyes to calm my nerves. I don't like the idea of leaving him here. No child should live like this—ever. My childhood wasn't happy, but I had food, bed and clothes. This... this is unimaginable. I say my goodbye and leave Theo with a large ache in my heart.

I park my car two streets later and I look up at a tall building. It's like Theo's. I see sheets covering some windows, a few other windows have cracks in them. I sigh deeply before going in. The smell of urine is so strong, it makes my eyes water, but I make my way to the top floor. The sounds of baby crying reach my ears on the third floor and on the fifth I hear people arguing. Once I'm on the six floor, I stare at the door with number 14. My heart rate speeds up and my breathing deepens as I try to force myself to knock but feel frozen in place. I lift my hand slowly, curling it into a fist, and finally knock on the door three times. I hear movement behind it and steps that are getting louder and louder. A young woman appears in front of me while swaying her baby from side to side.

'Can I help you?' She whispers, as her baby sleeps in her arms.

'Erm...I...' She narrows her eyes, waiting for me to say something.

I clear my throat before speaking up quietly. 'Does Piper Wood live here?'

She eyes me up suspiciously and maybe it's because of my suit, so I offer her a smile to show her I mean no harm.

'No, sorry. It's just me and my baby.' She glances at her tiny human and smiles. 'Did she live here before me, maybe? I've been here for two years now.'

Two years... Mr Rowland could only trace this address from three years ago.

'Maybe. Thank you for your time and I'm sorry for

bothering you.' She nods politely and closes the door.

I stand there for a moment; the tension leaving my body. I can't tell if I feel relieved or disappointed. When I turn to make my way downstairs, someone speaks up, 'Excuse me.' I turn around and see a man in a flat 15 door. He looks to be in his 50s, wearing black joggers and a white vest.

'Yes?'

'You're looking for Piper Wood?'

'Yes, I am, but I got the wrong address.' I offer him a smile and take a step on the stairs when the man adds, 'I knew her.' I pause and turn back to him.

'Who are you?'

The words struggle to form in my mouth, but I mumble out. 'She's my biological mother.' His mouth opens wide and stares at me for a moment, then nods. 'I can see it now. Come in.' He opens his door wider and I go in without a hesitation.

We sit down in his kitchen at the dining table. This place is nicer than Theo's, but still not a condition that a person should live in.

'Can I get you a drink?' He asks as he turns on the kettle.

I shake my head. 'No, thank you. I'm not here for long.'

'Of course, of course. So, what made you look for her now?'

'I don't know, really. I guess I just wanted to know my story, to find out why a woman who should have loved me left me.' I shrug and I swear this man's blue eyes just got darker. He's frowning at me when he joins me at the table with his cup of tea.

'Piper was my friend.' He says.

'Was...' I arch my brow, and he lifts his gaze to mine and I see his eyes glisten with tears.

'She passed away three years ago.' He says and just like that, I feel as if someone stabbed me right in the gut. 'How?' I ask with my breathy voice.

'Ovarian cancer.' I look down and nod slightly as I process

in the information.

'She was...' He starts again, 'The funniest person I've ever met. She was kind to everyone she met. I first met her when she was 16 and she was pregnant.' I look at him and he's trembling. 'She was a drug addict. And so was your father.' He takes a sip of his hot drink. 'Your father died of OD while she was still pregnant. I know little about him unfortunately, but your mother took it very hard. She cried for months and refused to speak about him, so I can only presume they had something real. Your mother quit the drugs the moment she found out about you...' I feel my heart pounding against my chest, ready to leap out. '... She was excited at first, but after your father's death, she said she couldn't do it alone. We all tried talking to her, tell her we'd all help to look after the baby – you...' He gestures to me, 'but she kept saying this wasn't the life she wanted for you. That you deserved so much better.' He waits for my reaction, but all I do is watch him.

'So once you were born, she told the hospital that you weren't coming home with her. She signed all her rights away and when she came back, she wasn't the same person. She stayed in her flat for months, refusing to see anyone. At one point, we were worried she killed herself.'

Stab in the heart.

'She cried, wailed every day for you. We all heard it, but we couldn't help her.'

Another stab in the heart.

'After months, she finally came out and spoke to us, but never mentioned you again. We still heard her cry, but when she was with us, there was never a mention of you. And she managed to get her life straight... as much as she could, I guess. She stayed clean, though, so that's the most important part. After her 40th birthday, we knew something wasn't right. She was losing weight, and she never felt ok anymore. After going to doctors and having tests done, it was...'

'Cancer.' I finish for him.

He nods, 'Cancer... She decided to not fight. She said her life wasn't worth living, that she lost so many loved ones, she was ready to go early herself.'

Another stab in the heart, and now I'm fighting the burning sensation behind my eyes.

'She loved you very much and by the end of her time, she finally talked about you. She said she prayed to god every day to look after you and that she imagined you grow up and being so handsome like your father. She thought you'd go to college and then university and be successful, and she hoped you'd find the love of your life soon after so you have someone to share your amazing life with.' A tear escapes my eye and falls down my cheek. I rub it quickly, but the man doesn't seem to notice – or at least pretends to not notice.

'I might have some photos of her if you'd like to see?' He asks and I nod. He walks out of the kitchen and then comes back within a few minutes, carrying a small box. Setting it on the table, he lifts the lid and passes the box to me. I lift the photo and see a couple on it.

'That's your parents.'

I definitely look like my father. Dark, slightly curly hair, dark eyes, tall and good looking. Still a teenager. My mother was stunning. Long, straight hair, also dark eyes, a smile that could light up any room she enters.

'They look happy.' I comment.

'They do.'

I lift another photo and see my mother, but this time pregnant. She's holding her bump and smiles at the camera, but the smile doesn't reach her eyes. She's skinnier than in the last photo, assumingly because of drugs or lack of food. The bump is small.

'That was after your father's death. She tried her best to keep it together... for you.' I nod.

'You can keep them, if you'd like.' He offers and I smile to him, 'I'd love to. Thank you.'

CHAPTER TWENTY-SEVEN

Brooke

Second day he's not been at work, and he keeps declining my calls. I make my way downstairs and see Tess gathering her things up.

'You're ok, hun?' She asks, and I shrug. 'Been better and been worse.'

'He's still not answering?'

'Nope.'

'Are you going to see him?' I nod and glance toward the exit.

'I forgot to ask about Max.' I turn back to her, changing the subject. We're both walk to leave.

'I'm seeing him Saturday night.'

'Is he...?'

'Yes, he's picking me up.' She lifts her chin up proudly.

'Make sure you don't sleep with him.'

'I won't.' She snorts out, 'I'm going to wear my granni's underwear so I'm not even tempted.' We both burst out laughing.

'I'll see you tomorrow.' She places a kiss on my cheek and

hops into her car. I make my way toward Gabriel's place. Aaron was a big help last night with my panic attack, as he called it. After he left, I looked it up, and he was right. I promised myself to not get so worked up again and take it day by day. I'll allow myself to feel what I need to feel and right now it's anger at Gabriel for trying to help me with my book. He knew I didn't want his help. If he thinks I'm not capable of doing it, then he can say it to my face. Also, I'd much rather not do it at all than use my privileges to get what I want. I certainly do not need Gabriel in my life. It's a funny thought considering I barely slept last night, after he didn't answer when I called. I sigh loudly and straighten my scarf. I blow into my hands to keep them warm and the memory of his touch and breath on them makes me flinch.

Think straight, Brooke!

It's dark now, so I'm glad the streets are crowded and that he lives in the busy centre. It's crazy how we women can feel so vulnerable the moment the sun disappears from the sky.

I stand in front of his door and question my decision to come here. Maybe I should have left it alone and move on, but my anger is nudging me, encouraging me to do this.

I knock.

Bruno barks twice but no answer. I saw his car outside, so I doubt he'd be out.

I knock again.

Bark bark.

Nothing.

I put my ear to the door and listen intently, but I hear nothing. His place is massive so unless he was on the other side, then I wouldn't hear him. I sigh loudly and think. I pull out my phone and dial his number but of course, after 4 rings, it goes straight to voicemail. He can't ignore me forever... I'm not giving up.

It's suddenly now that I remember him telling me about his spare key. I feel sick at using it and to be honest, I shouldn't be using it, but... I reach out under the doormat and pull out a single key. I put it in the lock and twist. The door opens. Bruno runs up to me with his tail wagging, so I give him a scratch behind his ear.

'Gabriel?' I come in and close the door behind me. I hear a weird thudding from across the hallway.

'Where's daddy?' I ask Bruno and he runs away toward the bedroom, stopping by the door that leads to the stairwell to the gym. The thudding is louder now, so I open the door and stroll downstairs. When I open the door to the gym, I see Gabriel, wearing shorts and... topless, giving his all on his punch bag.

'Gabriel?' I call out, but he doesn't acknowledge me.

His punches are angry, ruthless, as if he's trying to calm himself down.

I make my way toward him before calling out again, 'Gabriel!'

Nothing. I'm almost scared to get near him as I can smell pure fury off him. I place my hand on his back and we both almost jump out of our bodies, and of course I scream like a little girl.

Gabriel pulls out his ear buds out.—of course he had them in. I roll my eyes.

'What the fuck are you doing here?' He puts his hand on his chest while the other hand resting on his knee as he tries to catch his breath. The sweat covers his body. Fuck, I feel my clit pulsing.

No, I'm angry at him.

'You're avoiding me.' I snap.

'I'm not.'

'Then why aren't you answering your phone?'

'Why would I answer it? You were clear when you said we're done.' He stands up straight and punches the bag again.

'I had a phone call from the agent.'

'Good for you. I'm not in the mood for this now, Brooke.' Another punch.

'Well, tough because he said his friend Gabriel Alstons called him to say he might be interested in my book and he wants to meet.'

'So?' Another punch.

'I told you to stay out of it. I'm much rather not get published at all than doing it with someone's help.' Another punch.

'You're too stubborn. Meet him, don't meet him. Don't care.' Another punch, this one even angrier.

'Are you going to look at me?' I demand.

'Are you going to leave?' Another punch.

'No.' He stops now, grabbing onto the bag with both his hands.

'What do you want from me?'

'I want you to understand what you did was wrong.' I snap and he turns, looking at me with his cold eyes.

'I did nothing wrong.' He stands up straight and let's go of the bag. 'It's you that is so stubborn that you can't admit what you want.'

'What I want is to do this on my own.'

'And does it feel good doing everything alone?' He takes a step toward me and I take a step back. The smell of his sweat body hits my nostrils and the surrounding air thickens.

'Do you really prefer to be all by yourself and do everything on your own?' He takes another step, backing me into the wall. He's so close now, I can feel his breaths on my skin.

'Are we still talking about my book?' I murmur and his eyes suddenly darken. 'You tell me.' I've never seen this... darkness in him before. Sure, he was intimidating, but this is something else. I feel pressure building up in my core as I watch his chest move.

'You're scared. You're not being independent as you think you are. Sure, you are a strong woman who can manage anything by herself. But you're also scared of losing that control.' He pulls out his phone and press something, disconnecting his earbuds and allowing the song Control by Zoe Wees to play through the speakers.

'That's ironic.' He snorts.

'What is?'

'This song that matches your cowardness.'

'I'm not a coward.' I snap, 'I just made myself promises which I intend to keep.'

Gabriel tilts his head back and laughs darkly.

'Admit it. You're a coward who runs away when things become more than you wanted.' He snaps, and his lips are mere inches away from mine.

'I didn't run away. I decided I had enough.' I try to stand straight, but my legs are weaker by the second and I don't know how long I can last.

'You had enough?' His brow arches.

'Yes.'

'Your clenched legs tell me otherwise.' He tilts his head just slightly and touches my lips with his without actually kissing me. My body trembles and I can't think clearly.

'I don't even have to touch you to know how wet you are right now.' He growls.

Before I know it, my body moves involuntarily, and my mouth crushes into his. He kisses me back immediately, with one of his hands going on my lower back and the other behind my neck, jolting me closer to him. I drag my nails across his bare back. He pushes us back against the wall after I jump up. I wrap my legs around his waist, pulling him even closer, and feeling his hard cock against my pussy. He groans at the connection and his tongue enters to meet mine. I taste him, realising just how much I missed him. A moan escapes me as he thrusts his hips into me, making me want to beg him to fuck me.

I'm losing it.

He pulls away slightly and whispers, 'I believe I owe you debt.' and my stomach drops. He walks us now to a pressing bench, and he puts me down right next to it.

'I always pay my debt.' He murmurs as he grabs my hem of my skirt and lifts it up.

'Lie down.' He demands and I do as he says, my heart filled with excitement. He kneels in front of me, removing my soaked panties, and throwing them to the side.

'Always ready for me like a good girl.' He growls.

'I thought I was a coward.'

'You are.' He snaps before spreading my legs wide open with his hands. His touch is light and painfully teasing as he places kisses on my inner thigh. Making his way higher and higher, before the last kiss lands on my clit. A shaky gasp escapes me as he ignites the fire in my core.

'Fucking perfect.' He says with his husky voice, before stroking my clit with his thumb. A moan of ecstasy slips through my lips.

'Gabriel, please.'

He smirks at me. 'You have no control here, baby. Right here, right now, you belong to me.' Something in my heart twitches, but I push it aside as his thumb presses harder, making my breaths deeper and my moans louder. It's then I feel his two fingers rubbing my entrance.

'Gabriel.' I groan, and he thrusts them inside, making me gasp. They curl up while inside, rubbing my spot perfectly, and I feel the pressure building up.

I'm close.

'One.' He groans and I shudder as the orgasm reaches me, exploding within, making my toes curl. He doesn't stop, though. As I try to catch my breath, he carries on. He's not allowing me to breathe. He's punishing me. I try to sit up but he pushes me back down and before I know it, he focuses on rubbing my clit, putting just enough pressure on it so the next orgasm follows within seconds and I shatter again, arching my back and grabbing onto the sides of the bench.

'Two.'

Is he fucking counting the orgasms he's giving me? My

body is half ice and half fire, feeling all the shivers from his touch, yet also feeling the burns, his skin leaves on mine. He groans and this time, he allows me to catch my breath. He lifts himself up and undoes my blouse, revealing my lace white bra and he growls at the view. I glance at his large bulge in his joggers and feel arousal rising again. He puts his hands behind me, undoing my bra within one movement. He lifts it up to free my breasts. My hard nipples pointing in his direction and he smiles before kneeling next to me again and taking one of them in his mouth. Another moan leaves my mouth and my pussy starts pulsing again.

I can't.

I can't do it again.

He sucks hard, making me arch my back and needing friction on my clit as it pulses wildly. I put my hand on his back and dig my nails into his skin. His groan tells me he likes it. His other hand plays with my other nipple, rubbing his thumb along it, making me want to scream. He moves his hand between my legs. Stroking my clit once again. As I feel close again, he stops and pulls away.

'God dammit.' I snap, and Gabriel chuckles darkly as he lowers himself between my legs. He looks at my pussy for a moment, a smirk appears on his face before he takes my clit into his mouth. He's not patient anymore as he also thrusts two fingers inside me, curling them to reach my g spot and sucking hard on my clit. Dizziness hits me like a thunder, and I roll my eyes up in pleasure. He gives his 100% and within moments, the most intense orgasm I've ever experienced hits me and I cry out, gripping hard onto the sides of the bench, but Gabriel doesn't stop as I call out his name. My whole body shakes when he finally slows down and I swear, I'm having an out-of-body experience, as I can not move a single muscle.

'Three.' He chokes out and it barely registers in my brain.

Three.

Three orgasms in a space of... 10... 15 minutes, maybe? I can't move. I can't think.

Gabriel stands up and walks up to where my head is, grabbing my face in his hand before saying through his gritted teeth, 'Coward.'

CHAPTER TWENTY-EIGHT

Brooke

I come out of the bathroom, wearing one of Gabriel's t-shirts that is so big, it easily covers my ass, and a pair of his boxers. I'm still trying to unfog my brain, and the cold shower helped a lot. Now Gabriel is waiting for me in the kitchen to talk. But there is nothing to talk about. What just happened between us changes nothing. This – fling – is over. We're getting too emotionally attached, so it's best to stop before one of us gets hurt. But if it's not too late yet, then why am I frozen in place, unable to leave his bedroom to go and face him?

I shake my head to snap out of it and open the door.

Once I reach the living area, I notice Gabriel in the kitchen, cooking something and talking on the phone.

'Yes, of course.' He chuckles. 'Uhum.'

I take a seat at the island and watch him make pancakes.

'Miranda, it's going to be fine.'

Miranda?

I reach for my bag and search for my phone, but it's not there.

My mom's name is Miranda. I glance back at him with my

eyes narrowed, trying to see whose phone he's holding.

'Yes, I'll see you at the wedding.'

Wedding?

'Ok. Nice chatting to you, bye.' He hangs up the phone and passes it to me. I gape at him.

'What did you do?!' I check the calls and he, in fact, has just spoken to my mom.

'Your phone kept ringing, and it was driving me insane.' He flips the pancake on the plate and pours more butter onto the pan.

'What did you say to her?' I snap.

'She wanted to let you know that your cousin, Kate, is very excited to meet me, so I said I'm looking forward to meeting them all.'

'Gabriel. We... you can't be my plus one.' He turns and sets the plate full of pancakes in front of me.

'Pancakes for dinner?' I frown.

'Why not?'

He turns away again, and I sigh loudly. Kate knows he's coming, so if I turn up without him, I can just imagine the comments that'll be thrown my way.

Couldn't you keep him for longer?

Oh hunnie what did you do?

Did he find someone else?

I roll my eyes and take a bite of the covered in syrup pancakes. A mmmm sound escapes my mouth and Gabriel shoots me a look.

'I'm not even sorry.' I shrug at him.

He's now wearing a fresh pair of joggers and a loose vest which still shows off his muscled arms.

'About the wedding...' I start, but I struggle to find the right words.

'Kate is the kind of cousin that judges you at every corner, so your mum understood that you'll be bringing a friend from work, but Kate is to believe I'm in fact your date?'

'How did you...?'

'Your mum told me.'

Of course she did.

'Well...' He turns around and watches me.

'I don't know what to do.'

'How about this? I help you survive your cousin, pretend to be your date and once the wedding is off, we can go our separate ways.'

Something twists in my chest when he says to go our separate ways. That is what we want, isn't it?

'Are you sure?'

He shrugs, 'I'm happy to help.' And he turns back to the pancakes. Once he's done, he stands on the other side of the island and starts eating his meal. I watch his mouth move and remember the feeling of it on my body.

I'm finding a man who is eating pancakes sexy. That's different.

'I really should get going.' I murmur and he looks up at me. He nods. 'Very well. Let me go and get your clothes.' He walks away and I stare at his behind. A girl can look, there's nothing harmful in it. We all have needs and fantasies. Why are only men praised for being pervy but they condoned us women for a similar behaviour?

I stand up and place the dishes in the dishwasher. I also wipe the worktops before making my way to the sofa where Bruno is resting.

'Hi, big boy.' I smile and sit next to him.

'What a big mess, hey?' He lifts his head up to look at me.

A small box sits at the coffee table. I shouldn't look; I know I shouldn't. But he pulled out my phone out of my bag and everyone knows – You don't go into ladies' bags. So I sit up and pull the box closer. I pick the lid off and pull out a photo. It's a pregnant, teenage girl, holding her bump. She's smiling, but somehow her eyes look like they're begging for help. She's so pretty. I set the photo on the side and pull out the next one. It's the same girl, but not pregnant this time. She's sat on boy's lap as he has his arms around her waist. Both are laughing, like the full, belly hurting laughs. The boy looks...

I pause as I study the boy's face. He really reminds me of Gabriel. The same dark eyes and jaw line...

'What are you doing?' Gabriel stands in my view and jerks the photo out of my hand.

'I'm sorry, I was...' He shoves the photos back in the box and puts the lid back on.

'Are they your...?'

'Biological parents.' He answers and my eyes widen in shock. He passes me my folded clothes.

'You can get changed and go.' He says and I don't miss the stab in his words.

'I didn't know you were adopted.' I whisper as I take my clothes off him.

'Because I wasn't. I lived with my foster parents till I was 18.' He drops onto the sofa next to me.

After all that research on him, I knew how much he was worth and what buildings he owned, but I never found anything about his family. Maybe he's refusing to talk about it.

'How did you...'

'Brooke.' He snaps, 'You told me I mean absolutely nothing to you, so why are you trying to talk to me now?' I put my hand on his and shake my head. 'You don't mean nothing to me, Gabriel. I, I overreacted on the whole rejection thing. It hit me harder than I expected, but I do consider you a friend.'

He scoffs, 'A friend.' I swallow the hard lamp in my throat. I'm not admitting to anything else. A friend is where I draw the line.

'Talk to me.' I plea. I see it on his face that he's fighting it inside, but it'll be a matter of time where he won't be able to keep it to himself. It'll eat him alive.

He exhales loudly before speaking. 'Decided to find her.' He gestures to the box. 'But today I found out that my father died of OD and my mother knew, no matter how much she loved me, it wasn't the life she wanted for me.' He pauses and takes another deep breath. 'So she gave me up, hoping that I'd have a happy and fulfilling life without her. She also passed away three years ago because of cancer.' His lips are now pulled into a thin line when he looks at me and I'm fighting back the tears. This is so sad. I struggled so badly when I lost my dad, but Gabriel lost both his parents before he even got the chance to meet them. He's tapping his foot onto the floor and I see his shoulders tensed. I now understand the angry punches I witnessed earlier.

'Is there anything I can do?' I ask, but only get a shake of his head in return.

'I'm fine. I'll be fine.' I know he'll be fine, but that doesn't mean he's ok right now.

'There's something I learnt yesterday.'

His brow arches. 'What is it?'

I smile half heartedly, 'It's ok to feel whatever you need to feel. Trying to ignore them or push them away will only make it worse, so...' I cup his face with my hand and stroke his jaw with my thumb. 'Allow it all to process and allow yourself to mourn your parents.' I see his jaw clench and eyes redden. I know he's fighting it back, maybe because of me, because men are always taught that only women are allowed to feel vulnerable and they should never show their emotions. But this whole idea is bullshit. I move to straddle him and he leans back on the cushions, putting his hands on my hips.

'It's ok.' I whisper and wrap my arms around him. It takes him a moment, but then he puts his arms around my waist and pulls me in. His head rests on my chest as I stroke his hair. He doesn't cry, but I can tell this is good for him, as I sense his shoulders deflate from the tension. A single tear escapes my eyes and I wish I could take all his pain away. It's what we do, isn't it? We nurture the ones we... care for.

Knowing Gabriel quite well now, I know he'll end up

drinking tonight to try not to feel so I make a swift decision I hope I won't regret. I pull away from him slowly. 'I'll be right back.' And I race to the island. Grabbing my phone, I send the text. Thankfully, I get a reply immediately and I exhale in relief. I put it back in my bag and return to where Gabriel is sitting. I take his hand. 'Come on.'

'Where?'

'To bed.' I offer him a warm smile. He stands up and follows me.

Once we're in his bedroom, I pull the covers down. 'Get in.'

His forehead wrinkles, but he does as I say.

I get in on the other side and lie down next to him. His one arm is behind his head while the other rests on his stomach. I prop myself up on my elbow and he turns his head to look at me. 'What?'

'You really are a great guy.' I smile and push myself closer to him. His arm that rested on his stomach now goes around my waist and pulls me in. I rest my head on his chest and start drawing circles with my finger on his peck.

'What about your rule?' He asks,

'I don't really care about my rules right now.'

We spent all evening talking about our childhoods. I told him about losing my dad and my mom not coping, moving to UK and trying to adjust to the new life here, my mom running her amazing bakery and me going to university. Then Gabriel gave me glimpses into his past, and unfortunately, even though his mom wanted a better life for him, that didn't seem to happen. He had it tough. How can a child flourish when he spent every day feeling unwanted and unloved?

Yes, I cried once or twice and it was Gabriel consoling me where it should have been the other way around. He did well, tough with moving out as soon as he turned 18 and working hard for his career, but I can also tell that he feels lonely. I know he said he doesn't believe in love, but what if it's more about fearing it like me? What if he fears of becoming what his foster parents were? That kind of marriage would leave a big imprint on him, and it probably haunted him if he ever thought about settling down. I witnessed an amazing marriage. My parents were always madly in love, but it was my own experiences that put me off. It's crazy how different traumas can lead people into the same beliefs. Love sucks. End of.

I watch Gabriel's chest fall and rise and I bite my lower lip as arousal hits me.

Addict. I'm addicted.

'You're making it worse, woman.' My eyes snap to his, realising he's awake.

'What?' He shoves the covers off him, revealing a large bulge between his legs.

I chuckle.

'Is it that funny?' I shake my head, but a smirk remains on my face.

He lifts himself on his elbow, and his free hand touches my thigh. I can't figure out why my body goes numb whenever I'm around him. Just the sound of his voice makes my body come alive, as if he's its master, listening to each of his commands, wanting to obey. I beg my brain to speak up, to help me fight this, but it stays shut. I now realise just how hard it's going to be to stay away after the wedding.

But you can enjoy yourself till then.

Damn it, brain. Help me.

But my heart rate picks up, muting my pleas. Goosebumps cover my body as his hand slowly makes its way higher, trying to reach its destination.

'We shouldn't.' I whisper.

'I know.' He removes his hand and a frown forces itself on my face.

I hop into a shower, turning the temperature down, as I can still feel his touch on my skin. Closing my eyes, I let the water fall on my face, taking deep breaths as I shiver from the coldness. I'm trying to gather my thoughts, but no matter what I do, they go back to him.

I can't feel anything; I can't.

My heart is beating fast and a single tear escapes.

I can't...

The water suddenly starts warming up, so I open my eyes and glance at the thermostat to see it's been turned up. I'm then turned around and Gabriel crushes his mouth into mine, pushing me against the cold tiles of the shower. I hiss as it sends the icy shiver down my spine and he smiles against my mouth. Kiss after kiss, I taste hunger coming from him as his hands explore my body and I wrap my arms around his neck, pulling him closer, warm water falling on us now.

'What are you doing to me, woman?' He murmurs, and he digs his fingers into my ass, which makes me groan. My clit is now pulsating, and I know there's no going back from this. My body is his. It can be his until I say so, but he's not having my heart. He pushes his erection into me and I feel weak in my legs. His hand travels to my front, grabbing my breast and giving it a firm squeeze. My moan breaks our kiss and our eyes lock as it escapes my mouth. I watch as drips of water travel down his face, and he rubs his nose against mine. I decide to take whatever control I have and I turn us around, pushing him to the wall now, my hands landing on his pecks and digging my nails into his skin as he kisses me deeply. My stomach drops, my core burns with his every touch.

I feel – alive.

I feel – powerful.

I break the kiss and look him in the eyes, feeling our deep breaths. His mouth is slightly open and I want to taste his lips again, but before, I go on my knees, my hands pressing on his stomach and I look at his hard cock, pointing at me — asking me to take it in my mouth. I bite on my lower lip as he pushes my hair away from my face. My lips part as I move my head forward, taking just the tip of him in, and the sound of his groan echoes off the walls. I feel like I'd come with a single touch. I suck slowly as he grabs my hair in his fist and thrusts his hips, pushing more of him inside. I gag, tears forming in my eyes as he fills my mouth and I struggle to take all of him in.

'That's my good girl.' He growls and the vibration of his voice hits my core. I suck hard as he continues to thrust himself in. His cock pulses and I know he's close, so I cup his balls in my hand, gently massaging them and he tilts his head back, allowing moans to escape his mouth as he shutters apart, filling my mouth with his release. I swallow it all and carry on sucking as his whole body trembles. When I move away, I give the tip a lick before he jerks me upright by my shoulders and rubs the rest of his release from the corner of my mouth. We look into each other's eyes for a moment before his hand grips the back of my neck and forces me forward, pushing my mouth into his. With one arm, he lifts me up, allowing me to wrap my legs around his waist, and pushing his tongue inside. I shiver under his touch and dig my nails into his back. A groan leaves his mouth as he turns us around, placing me back on the wall and this time it's warmer thanks to the hot water. His new erection is pushing against my clit and I moan against his mouth. He grabs his cock and positions it against my entrance.

'Condom.' He murmurs, with pure annoyance on his face.

'I'm on the pill.' I say.

'Are you sure?'

'Oh, my god, Gabriel. Yes.' I snap, losing my patience. I need him inside. Now.

He kisses me again, pushing his tongue in to meet mine, making my body melt underneath him. His cock once again is positioned against my entrance, ready to go in.

'Call out my name, baby girl.' With one, hard push, he's inside me and I call out his name per his demand.

'That's my girl.' My heart skips a beat at the sound of his words. He picks a strand of hair from my face and tucks it behind my ear. Another thrust forces a groan out of me. I move my hips, syncing our movements together. His kisses are possessive – messy; his tongue claiming mine. He thrusts slowly but hard, making me tilt my head back, allowing moans to flow freely. Our eyes connect, causing the electricity to form between our bodies. Like a magnet, I'm pulled to him.

'Say you're mine.' He growls and thrusts even harder. I bite my lower lip, making a hissing sound. 'Say it.' He demands again. The room is now filled with steam, which makes it hard to see anything other than his deep brown eyes looking right at me. He turns his head and places a gentle kiss on my neck as he slows down. Each kiss higher than the previous one and then he grabs my earlobe between his teeth and pulls on it, making me tremble. My whole body shakes and I forget what my name is. When he lets go, a whisper tickles my ear, 'Say it.'

'I'm yours.' I moan out, and his thrusts pick up speed and return to hard possessive pushes. My eyes close and I allow him to do what he wishes; then I feel his thumb rubbing over my hard nipple. Loud moans leave my mouth as I draw blood from his shoulders, at which he growls 'Fuck.'

The pressure builds up in my core, and I see a smirk on his face.

I'm close.

Within the next thrust, I shudder, allowing the orgasm to explode within me. I cry out as my whole body tenses and my back arches forward. It takes me a moment to come to and I feel numb – breathless. If it wasn't for the shower still running, I'd think we're frozen in time. Gabriel's also trying to catch his breath while he's looking at me with hooded eyes.

He then opens his mouth to speak. 'Do you want breakfast?'

CHAPTER TWENTY-NINE

Gabriel

Knock. Knock.

'Come in.' I call out, and Tess appears in the door.

'You called for me, sir?'

'Tess, hi, come in.' I gesture to the seat on the other side of my desk.

'How are you?' She sits down, her shoulders looking tense.

'I'm good, thank you.'

'And the cats?' Her expression changes, like a flick of a light, from nervous to excited.

'They're the best. I love them so much.'

I chuckle, 'I'm glad'

'Thank you for what you did at the rescue.'

'You're welcome. I've known you long enough, so it wasn't a problem to vouch for you.' She smiles widely, and she spends the next 10 minutes showing me photos and videos of her cats, Cece and Dede. I pretend to be interested out of politeness, but one photo does make me chuckle where both cats, including Tess, are wearing matching pyjamas.

'Sorry.' She puts her phone away. 'You wanted to speak to me?'

'Yes.' I smile and look through my papers on the desk before pulling out one and sliding it to her. She gasps as she reads it. 'No way! Really?' She calls out in disbelief.

'Yes.'

'Are you sure? Oh my God!'

I laugh, 'Yes Tess, I'm sure. I'm offering you the position as a cover designer.' She stares at me with her mouth wide open. 'The pay is pretty much doubled. Hours are the same, and you'll have your own office like Brooke. All you have to do is sign the contract and you can start from the New Year.'

She jumps up in her seat, clapping her hands together. 'Where's the pen?' She's searching the desk and I hand my pen over to her. She snatches it off me and signs at the bottom of her new contract.

'I'm so excited, thank you so much.'

As she opens the door to leave, she turns around to me, 'Sir?'

'Yes?'

'I know it's not my place but... Brooke seems very happy with you.'

I nod, and then she leaves.

After Tess leaves my office, I stare at my blank screen. The whole last 24 hours take over my mind today. So many emotions filled in one day, I'm surprised I didn't have a breakdown. Finding out the truth about my biological parents felt like a stab in the chest. Everything I was, where I came from, was gone.

If I searched for her earlier, I would have met her; maybe even convince her to get treatment. She was alone for all those years, after losing my father and then me. Sure, she had friends, but... she was alone – truly alone. My heart twists uncomfortably at the thought of her spending the nights crying to herself.

She loved him, and she loved me, but she chose to give me a better life over her own wants. That is what true love is, isn't it? Wanting the best for the other person. Maybe I'm starting to understand it more now and the idea of spending all my life alone somehow feels unappealing. She wanted me to live a successful and fulfilling life and I hate it did not happen. Sure, at first I was satisfied with my career and wealth but somewhere along the way, it became less and less important and now, there's something missing and I can't pinpoint what exactly. There must be something more for me; something more meaningful. I know there's a new chapter of my life waiting somewhere for me.

And then back at home, when it all seemed too much, Brooke appeared and just like that, the feeling of emptiness disappeared. Whenever she's around, I don't feel like I'm lacking. It's a comfort feeling, being just near her. I'm used to bossing people around, being in charge – a leader – always came easily to me. But with her? When I'm with her, all I want is to pour my heart into my hands and give it to her. She's afraid of losing control, because her ex broke her, and I'll happily let her rule me. I'll do anything to make her happy because that's what you do when you...

My eyes widen in shock at what I was about to say.

It can't be.

I can't be.

No.

I power on the computer and go on the shifts of all my employees. Brooke has today off. She booked it a while ago now and she didn't want to tell me why. I put my face in my hands and take a deep breath.

Fuck.

What have I done?

The wedding is this weekend, and after that, it's over for us.

I open google and type in Mindy's bakery, memorise the directions and rush out of my office.

I push the door open and notice a big queue in front of me. A young man stands at the till, so I very much doubt that's Brooke's mother. I look around and notice an older woman with the same brown but short hair as Brooke, so I decide to try my luck.

'Excuse me.' The woman turns around and I see familiar baby blue eyes.

'I'm looking for Miranda Summers.'

'That's me.' She throws the cloth over her shoulder and wipes her hands onto the towel hanging from her apron.

'My name is Gabriel Alstons.' I offer her my hand and she narrows her eyes before taking it. 'So that's you.'

'Yes,' I offer her a warm smile, but she doesn't return it. She makes her way behind the counter and pulls out a muffin before placing it on the plate and puts it down before me. I take the seat and thank her.

'How much do I owe you?'

'On the house.'

I take the bite and make a mmm sound as the chocolate flavour hits my taste buds. The muffin is perfectly moist, literally melting away in my mouth. 'It's amazing.'

'I know.' She winks at me, and I feel the tension between us lifting slightly.

'How can I help you?' She asks, and I try to find the right words. 'I wanted to talk about Brooke.'

'Stay away.' She says immediately.

'I'm sorry?'

She glances around to make sure no one is listening before speaking up. 'I love my daughter with all my heart. She's my everything since I lost my husband years ago. But if you're looking at anything serious with her, I'm warning you now. Since her ex broke her heart, she put up a wall bigger than the wall of China around it. She only recently started to become herself again. She's going to say no to you and she'll only hurt you.' I allow the words to process, even though I've known all of it already.

'I know... the truth it... I don't know what she told you about us but we have been... seeing each other.'

Her brow arches, 'As in...'

'No commitments thou, no dating... But yeah.' Now she takes a moment to understand what I'm telling her.

She shakes her head. 'She's stubborn, just like her father.'

'I've never met a more stubborn person than her.' A chuckle leaves her mouth.

'I don't know what you want me to tell you, Gabriel. Do you care about her?'

'Yes.' An easy answer to an easy question. Something I haven't seen coming, but it happened.

'Then all you can do is try. But it won't be easy.' I nod.

'Can I have your support?'

She chuckles again, 'I don't know you, but if what you say is true that you've been seeing each other, then I can tell the last few weeks she seemed... happier. She's worth the fight, and she's got the biggest heart, hence the big heartache, when something happens.' I nod in understanding. 'You hurt her, though, and I won't be held accountable for my actions.' She points her finger at me and I put my hands up in defence. 'Of course.'

I stand outside her block of flats. My heart is pounding against my chest as I pull out my phone and text her.

Me- Are you home?

Three dots appear. She's always quick to reply.

Brooke- Yes, why?

Me- It's cold. Care to let me in?

Brooke- Where are you?!

Me- Outside.

The door buzzes, and I pull it open. Each step to her apartment makes my stomach twist, and when I'm standing right outside her front door, I lift my hand to knock, but... I can't. I'm frozen in place.

Knock, damn it.

My stomach twists when Brooke opens the door and stares at me.

'What are you doing?'

'I...' I lift the carry bag to show her. 'I brought salty popcorn.'

She studies me before opening the door wider to let me in.

'Shouldn't you be at work?' She asks as she pops the bag in the microwave and turns it on. I sit down on the sofa and stroke Nala's head.

'I've had a few meetings this afternoon, so I'm finished for today.' She pulls out two bottles of water out of the fridge and throws one to me; I, of course, catch it with one hand.

'Show off.' She scoffs, and I laugh awkwardly.

'Do you want to find the show? The remote is on the tv?' I told her I've been wanting to watch the next episode of You as I don't have the Netflix thing on my tv. I don't watch tv so never bothered with getting it even thou Max tried to get me into it.

'What are you reading?' I notice a book on the coffee table as I pick up the remote.

'Julia's letters. It's a rom com but has good spice in it.'

'Spice?'

She chuckles, 'You know... lots of good sex scenes.'

'So you're reading porn?'

'Call it what you wish.' I press on Netflix icon and try to

find continue watching. I press on You and then pause it. Brooke grabs the bowl filled with popcorn now and comes to sit down on the other side of the sofa. Nala goes over and sits by her legs, pushing her head onto her lap.

'She's a needy one.' She smirks as her hand strokes the dog's head. 'By the way, I had a text from Tess. That's amazing news.'

'She deserved the job. I only made it happen.'

'I know, but you didn't have to. She didn't apply for it.'

'I know. You also just broke the Rule 5.'

'Rule 5?' Her eyebrows pinch together.

'Don't talk about work out of hours.'

She chuckles, 'Sorry.'

A drink of water clears my throat. 'I-Ive just came here to talk to you about something.' I wipe my clammy hands on my legs.

'Yes?' She watches me, waiting for me to speak. The words struggle to form in my throat, so I clear it again and finally say,

'Look, I know you set the rules...'

'Run.' she whispers.

'I'm sorry, what?'

'Run!' she now shouts, jumping off the sofa, and racing to her bedroom, closing the door behind.

What the fuck?

I then see Nala, sitting perfectly still, staring right at me with her eyes wide open.

'You're ok?' And a second later, the sound of the loudest fart I've ever heard reaches me. I gape at the small creature who's still sitting perfectly still.

'What the...' And then the smell hits me right in the face. The worst smell I've ever smelt; it's pure death. I cover my mouth and nose with my hand and gag, tears filling my eyes as I gag again. I rush to Brooke's bedroom and bang on the door,

'Let me in!' I call out.

'I'm sorry, you were too slow!' She replies, and I can't believe it.

'What the fuck, Brooke? Open...' Gagging again, '...the fucking door!'

'I'm sorry!' I hear her laughing on the other side.

'You'll pay for this!'

'Only if you survive this!' I rush around and open all the windows I can see, while trying my best not to gag again. The stench isn't disappearing and when I glance at Nala, she's fast asleep on the sofa. I gag once more before racing to the kitchen and opening the fridge to stick my face in it. The cold is refreshing, clearing my skin from the smell, which likely made my face green.

Pure death. This dog must have expired years ago because that smell isn't normal. I'm pretty sure a bathroom after an explosive diarrhoea smells better than this.

I keep my head in the fridge for a while before hearing Brooke's bedroom door open.

'Is it safe?' I hear her ask.

'I don't know! You tell me!' I snap, and she chuckles. 'It's safe.' I jump at her touch on my back. She bursts out laughing.

'You think this is funny? You almost killed me!' I bark, but she only laughs harder.

'Collateral damage, sorry.'

My eyes widen in shock. 'Did you just call me collateral damage?'

'I had to protect myself, ok?' She looks at me with her puppy eyes.

'You're paying for this right now.' I lift her up and throw her over my shoulder and start walking toward her bed. The sound of her laughter is like music to my ears, but she's not being forgiven any time soon.

CHAPTER THIRTY

Brooke

'I've got an invitation to Kate's wedding.' I wave the letter in front of Tyler, who just stepped through the door with shopping bags.

'Awesome.' He replies coldly. 'I'm sure you're going to have lots of fun.'

'Tyler, it's for me, plus one.'

'What does that mean?' He pulls a beer out of the fridge.

'It means you get to go with me. Have you never been to a wedding?' I frown at his lack of reaction.

'Sure, to play... not to attend.' He sighs loudly as he takes the seat next to me on our sofa and picks up the remote. 'Do I have to go?'

'Excuse me? Why wouldn't you go?' I feel the tension building up between us and it's guaranteed to cause a fight.

'I don't like weddings, Brooke. And your cousin doesn't even like me.'

'She doesn't like anyone deep inside, but we can show her how happy we are.'

He snorts, 'Sure.'

'What does that mean?' I snap, and he rolls his eyes at me while clicking through the channels.

'Kate pisses me off, alright? Last Christmas dinner she kept asking if I was going to find an actual job.' That's true. Kate is very intimidating, and she doesn't have a sensitivity limit on her tongue.

'Well, you wouldn't be spending the evening with her, but with me.' He settles to watch some documentary about a rock band from the 80s.

'Tyler, can you look at me?' I throw the invitation on the table, burning now with anger at him. He slowly turns his head to me and I see very little interest in his eyes for what I want to say.

'We're a couple and the invitation is for both of us. I don't wanna go by myself, but she's my family so...'

'For fuck's sake, Brooke.' He takes a drink of his beer. 'Find someone else to go with you. Maybe that mate you have, what's his name... Alex, Alan ...?'

'It's Aaron! And I shouldn't have to ask him, considering I have a boyfriend!' My hands clench into fists and my stomach drops. He doesn't care – I know he doesn't.

'Whatever. Just ask him. It's not that big of a deal.' His gaze returns to the screen.

'You're such a dick.' I shout and storm out of the room.

'You're alive?'

'Yes, sorry. Zoned out.' I offer Gabriel, who's currently driving, a smile. We're on our way to Bournemouth for Kate's wedding, but it's early. Mark took some time off, plus Gabriel said he'd like to drive. He picked me up at 7 o'clock, we grabbed some breakfast and we hit the motorway. Aaron was kind enough to stay at my place with Nala and Gabriel said Bruno has gone to his dog sitter. I stare through the window and watch cars drive by. I asked him not to go fast, so he sticks to the middle lane. It's not so much that I don't trust his driving abilities, because he is an excellent driver, but I don't trust the others. Every time we get close to a car in front, my heart speeds up and I grab onto a handle, pressing the imaginary brake with my foot. You hear horror stories about cars just suddenly braking for no reason or pulling out right in front of you. Plus, you also get drunk drivers and it is Saturday morning. The worst thing about drunk drivers? They're usually the only ones that survive. My heart clenches at the thought of people who died, but they did nothing wrong. Gabriel can see the anxiety in my expression, so he adjusts his driving for me, which I'm very thankful for.

'I'm sorry again about the other day. If I let you in, we'd both suffocate from the smell.' I rest my head on the headrest while watching him and I notice a frown on his face.

'I did not appreciate that.'

I chuckle. 'Surely the blowjob apology was worth it?'

'Debatable.' I see the corner of his mouth twitch, so I know he's over it by now. He was over it the moment the first groan left his mouth when I sucked on his cock and then he was over it again when I got on top and rode him and made him come.

I observe him and wonder what it is about men driving with only one hand. The longer I stare at his hand, the most my core twists. Women as species are odd... What else am I gonna find attractive? Oh, I know! Wait till he puts his hand on the back of my seat when he reverses the car.

'You're clenching your legs again.' He exclaims, and I snap once again out of my thought and relax my body. I see a smirk appear. 'Shut up.' Now he chuckles at me.

'We're not far away from services. Wanna grab a coffee?' He asks and I immediately call out, 'Yes!'

We park right outside the entrance.

'I'll be right back.' Gabriel throws his coat on and steps out of the car, allowing the cold air to enter, making me shiver.

I rub my arms to warm up before pulling out my phone and dialling Aaron's number.

'Hey, how's Nala?'

'She's good. Stop worrying. We're currently watching Love is blind. Do you think you can fall in love with someone without actually seeing them?'

I snort, 'I'm not sure. I mean, love is more than looks, isn't it?'

'Of course, but how do you know if the sexual attraction is there? Can you be with someone if they don't turn you on?'

'Aaron, it's way too early for this type of questions.' I laugh. 'I mean, sure, the physical attraction is important, but I'm pretty sure they put pretty people on the programme anyway so, the point of it is probably moo.'

'Moo?'

'You know, not important? I don't know...'

'Well, anyway. How's the drive going?'

'It's alright. We're about an hour away now.'

'Oh, by the way, I finally got the dets out of Tess. She did, in fact, sleep with Max.'

I gasp, 'Oh my god.'

'I know. And she was wearing the granny panties so ... We can just imagine.'

I burst out laughing. Yes. How that went down is something I can imagine. 'I'll call her tomorrow when I get home.' I see Gabriel walk out of the building, carrying two cups.

'Gabriel is coming back, so gotta go.'

'Ok, love you and have fun,'

'Will do. Love you too.'

The door to the car opens again and the cold air hits me – again.

'Oh, come on!' I snap while my body shivers.

'I had to get inside somehow. Here.' He passes me my drink and the warmth of it makes me smile. 'What did you get me?'

'Hot chocolate.'

I smile, 'Perfect choice.'

'Let me guess, you called Aaron to check on Nala?'

'Yeah.'

'How is she?' He takes a sip of what I'm guessing is black coffee.

'Good. They're watching Love is blind.'

'Love is what?' His brow arches.

'Programme where people talk to each other without ever actually meeting in person to see if they can fall in love.' He snorts at me.

'Don't you believe in love without physical attraction?' I take a sip of my drink and the hot liquid immediately warms up my insides.

'I mean, sure, you can care deeply about someone, but physical attraction and sexual compatibility are just as important. Imagine spending the rest of your life with someone who loves vanilla and you fantasize about being tied to the bed.'

I almost snort my drink out. 'Do you like being tied to bed?'

He gives me a sexy smirk. 'I'd much rather tie you up to the bed.' I feel the heat reach my cheeks and he chuckles. 'Let's go.' He puts the car in gear and reverses out of the space, with his hand on my seat, of course. I'm not going to lie; I like the idea of him tying me up.

We reach our destination.

'Where the fuck are we?' He snaps as he drives his jag over a very bumpy road, throwing us up and down, left to right.

'It's like a B&B farm thing.'

'Farm?' He shoots me a death stare. 'Like in, they own farm animals?'

'Well, yes, I imagine they...' I pause when the realisation hits me. 'Oh, my god. You're afraid of the chickens!' I cover my mouth with my hand.

'I'm not afraid. I just don't like them. And you could have told me.'

'I forgot! Plus anyway, you are the one that offered to come without asking where it takes place.' He sighs loudly just as the car hits another bump and Gabriel's head hits the roof.

'Fuck!' He barks out and I laugh. 'I'm sorry. I didn't think it'd be this bad.'

'I'm going to need another apology blowjob.' I laugh even harder.

I go in to the reception. The lady takes my name and passes me the key.

'Erm, could we maybe have two separate rooms?' I ask and the lady looks through her book, shaking her head. 'I'm sorry, but we're booked up for the wedding.' I nod and thank her, my stomach dropping at the idea of spending the night with him again. It's the last night we spend together and I don't know how I feel about it. Happy… nervous… excited…dreading? I sigh loudly and I turn around to exit. My eyes widen in shock when I see Gabriel sitting on the hood with his legs lifted high up, while a single chicken runs around the car.

'I told you I hate chickens!' He calls out, steam pouring out of his ears, and all I can do is laugh. I shoo the chicken away, but he's still unsure if it's safe to get back on the ground.

'Get down, you big baby.'

'Shut up.' He slowly puts his leg down.

'Help me with the bags?' I open the trunk and he grabs my arm to stop me.

'I'll handle the bags.' I roll my eyes at his 'I'm the man' gesture, even though it warms my heart deep inside.

My make up is done – I even did smokey eyes which turned out much better than I expected. My hair is done; nicely slicked back and hair sprayed to keep it that way all day. I bought a beautiful navy flare, knee-length cocktail dress that covers my chest but leaves my back bare; which means – no bra tonight. Gabriel is getting dressed in the bathroom. We're trying to put the chicken incident behind us so we can try to enjoy ourselves tonight, but I'm pretty sure he'll remain on the edge for the rest of the visit. I smile to myself when I remember him sitting on that hood, truly scared for his life.

'What're you laughing about?' I see him in the mirror, standing right behind me, more handsome than ever in his black shirt and black suit. No tie and the shirt isn't fully done up. His one hand is in the pocket while the other one is on the button of the jacket. My heart skips a beat and I feel my core burning up.

'You look amazing.' I choke out, and he gives me his flirty smirk. I feel as if the room temperature suddenly shot up to 100 degrees and my body begs to go to him.

'I'm going to wait with my compliment until you get dressed yourself.' I chuckle as I reach for my dress and head to the bathroom. After closing the door, I lean myself on it, trying to steady my breathing. Great, I'm wet now.

Shit. This is going to be hard.

CHAPTER THIRTY-ONE

Gabriel

The time stops, and my heart races when Brooke walks out of that bathroom. My cock twitches underneath my suit pants and I suddenly feel like I'm overheating. I undo another button of my shirt and twist the collar to allow air in that's been knocked out of my lungs.

She bites her lip. 'Are you going to say something now?' There are no words to describe her beauty. This woman right in front of me looks absolutely stunning when she's dressed up and also when she's wearing her leggings and hoodie, but damn, right now I want to fuck her till we're both unable to breathe.

I clear my throat. 'You look gorgeous.' I offer her a smile and her cheeks redden at my compliment. She turns around, and I notice something on her lower back. 'What is that?'

She chuckles, 'Oh. I got it when I had my day off.' I study the black ink on her skin.

'It represents becoming a better version of yourself.'

'I love it.' I reply, rubbing my thumb over the black butterfly.

'Shall we?' I pull out my elbow, and she links her arm around it.

'We shall.' She smiles and we walk out of our room.

The ceremony was nice. On top of the hill, with a sea view behind the happy couple. Brooke's cousin, Kate, looks pretty and very much in love with her fiancé. We haven't had a chance of saying hello yet, but she shot us a glance a couple of times. I saw Brooke tensing up, so I grabbed her hand and held it, rubbing my thumb over the back of it every now and again, and it seemed to calm her down. I'll lie if I say I didn't look around us, in fear of the freaking bird coming back, but so far, so good. She looked at me a couple of times during the ceremony and shared her warm smiles with me. Did I picture us getting married? Yes. Is this some kind of mental awakening? No. Feels more like a mental breakdown. But for some reason, it feels right. She fits in my heart and it's now that I feel fulfilled. She also fills my emptiness with her light and makes me happier than I've ever been. I never want to let her go but just the thought of telling her fills me with dread and makes my hands sweat.

'Are you ok?' she whispers and glances down at our linked hands so I pull it away.

'Yes, just really hot in here.'

'It's December and we're sitting outside.' Her brow arches and my chest tightens.

'Probably just because we're crowded in.'

Now we're standing in the queue to congratulate the happy couple, and I feel her tensing up again.

'Remember to not take anything she says personally.' she whispers to me.

'I'll be fine.' I assure her, and she nods.

We're next.

'Brooke!' the bride calls out and pulls Brooke in for a hug. 'I'm so happy to see you. You look amazing.'

'Thank you.'

'It's amazing how just a little practise can affect your make up skills, right?' She smiles widely and I see Brooke's hand clenching into a fist, so I take one in my hand and squeeze. Kate's eyes now turn to me.

'And who is your plus one?'

'This is Gabriel.' She looks up at me and smiles but it's not her genuine smile, it's the 'I don't wanna be here' smile.

'Congratulations on your happy day.' I bow to both of them. Her fiancé remains quiet as Kate does all the talking and he only nods along. I pull out an envelope from my jacket and pass it to them. 'This is just a little something to help you start your new life.' Kate takes it and thanks me. I pull Brooke away to allow the other guests to speak to them and we head straight inside for the bar.

'Large glass of wine, please.' She orders from the bartender and sighs loudly.

'One glass of whisky, no ice please.' I add. 'How are you holding up?'

'Well, it has been worse, but the night is young.' She chuckles as she glances around and spots her mum walking towards us. She gives me the look before turning to Brooke.

'Hi, honey.' They hug each other. 'I didn't catch you before the ceremony'

'No, we haven't been here long ourselves. This is Gabriel.' Brooke gestures to me and we're pretending it's the first time we're meeting.

'Nice to meet you, Ms. Summers.' I take her hand and kiss the back of it.

'What a charmer you are!' she smiles. 'Just like when we spoke on the phone.'

'Here are your drinks.' The bartender calls out. We turn around and thank him. I give him a handful of £20 notes and say, 'For our future drinks.' He nods and walks away. I turn to Brooke. 'I have a feeling we're going to need more.'

She takes a big sip of her wine. 'Definitely more.'

Brooke's mum chats to other family members as we make our way around, Brooke just nodding at people.

'Aren't they your family?'

'They are, but we've never been close. I never met most of them until I moved here.' She shrugs and we see Kate making her way back to us.

We both take big gulps of our drinks before she reaches us.

'Brooke, hun. Are you two having fun?'

'Of course, yes. The party is great.' And she's not lying. People are dancing, chatting and drinking. A typical wedding, in my opinion.

'So, Gabriel. Is my sweet cousin treating you well?' She asks politely, but the between-lines words hit Brooke as she rolls her eyes.

'Treating me well? I can only hope it's me that treats her the way she deserves to be treated.' Kate doesn't seem satisfied with the answer, but she only nods. 'Yes, Brooke always struggled to find a good man for her.' I feel anger building up inside me, but I have been warned, so I stay polite while listening to her insults.

'What do you do for work? I was told you work with Brooke?' She smiles at both of us.

'Something like that. I'm between different projects, really.' I squeeze Brooke's hand to comfort her.

'Oh, so you don't have a stable job?' Her brow arches, and I see the amusement in her eyes.

'No, I definitely have a stable job. You see, other than owning my own publishing company, at which Brooke works, I also owe a few other buildings around the country, and I invest a lot as well. I feel like I do well for myself financially. Someone has to earn the money to spoil my little monkey.' I pop my index finger on the tip of Brooke's nose, and she chuckles in amusement.

If we were in a cartoon right now, I'm pretty sure Kate's mouth would drop to the floor. 'Oh... oh that's, that's amazing. I'm very happy for you both.' She chokes out.

'And you, Brooke, do you still have that hobby of yours to write a book? Oh Gabriel, since she was little, she always wanted to pretend to be a writer.' She snorts out, and I remind myself that it is very illegal to hit another person, especially a woman – on her wedding day. Before Brooke can answer, I quickly jump in. 'Oh yes, Brooke is an amazing writer. I want to give her own writing study in my home I'm currently building. She already has agents wanting to speak to her about her latest book and I'm not surprised as she's so freaking talented, just like she is fucking gorgeous.' I lock my eyes with Brooke's and see her mouth slightly open.

'Oh well, good for you, Brooke.' Kate mumbles out. 'I'm gonna go and find my husband, I think.' She glances around and rushes away from us. Brooke bursts out laughing and I shortly follow after.

'That just made my day. No! Made my year!' She calls out as she grabs onto my arm.

After having our meal and making small talk with some of Brooke's family members, the dj plays music and people hop onto the dance floor. I excuse myself from the table and go onto the patio for some fresh air. However, as I step outside, I'm hit with smoke from people's lit cigarettes. I glance around and notice the beautiful view of fields and further down the beach. I take a step off the patio to avoid all the smoke and inhale the cold, fresh air.

'Want one?' My head snaps to the side where a man is standing, offering me one of his cigarettes. I think about it for a moment and nod, taking one out of the pack and putting it in my mouth. He lets me use his lighter and I inhale, which sends me into a choking fit.

'Non smoker?' The man chuckles.

'Yeah.' I choke out. 'But felt like maybe I needed it today.'

He nods in agreement. 'Weddings can do that to you. I'm Mike.'

'Gabriel.' We shake hands and I take another drag, this time smaller, and I manage to keep in it before exhaling.

'My wife is inside, making small talks with everyone. I hate small talks.' He says, breaking the awkward silence.

'I don't mind them, but I see how they can be awkward.'

'You're here with your wife?'

I shake my head, feeling an ache in my heart as I remember after today, she'll return to being just my employee. 'Just a date.'

He nods. 'You looked serious when I saw you two inside.' I watch him, my eyes narrow and he immediately puts his hand up. 'I'm not a creep. Just like to observe as my wife talks to people.' I look forward to the sea line and he adds, 'You just looked really in love, so I said to my wife you'll probably be next to get married.' I sigh as I let the sting of his words hit me. Married. Would I want that? I think so.

'Gabriel.' A familiar voice calls from behind me, and Brooke joins us. 'I was looking for you.' Just the way she looks at me sends my head spinning. My heart whispers the words I never thought I'd say.

'You're smoking?' She gasps as she notices a cigarette in my hand.

'Yeah, but I think it was a mis...' Before I finish, she snatches it off my hand and takes a drag, inhaling like a pro. 'That feels good.' She says as the smoke leaves her mouth at the same time.

I arch my brow. 'You're a smoker?'

'No. I used to be, though.' She shrugs. 'But today ...' She takes another drag 'It feels good.' I watch her as she stomps the cigarette into the bin that has an ashtray on top of it.

'Fancy a walk?' I ask her and a smile appears on her face. After I say my goodbye to Mike, we make our way to the beach, where the sound of waves echoes in my ears. My heart races as it tries to decide if I should tell her how I feel before it's too late, but the words struggle to form. I'm not good at this.

'My mom seems to like you.'

'Oh yeah?'

'Yeah. She loves how you protected me from Kate. She knows normally I just take her insults.'

'I would never allow anyone to talk to you like this.' I look straight on, as we step onto sand and my feet sink in. The sun is setting now, making the sky orangey-pink.

'It's beautiful here.' She comments.

'It is.'

'But I think I'll break my leg if I carry on further.' She glances at her heels, so I scoop her up, allowing the sound of her laughter to reach my ears. I want to hear this laugh every day. I walk us further onto the beach before setting her down and sitting on the cold sand. Brooke joins next to me and links her arm around mine.

'Are you really building a house?' She asks as we watch the sun lower itself behind the horizon.

'I will be. I have the land and the project is ready but the building will start after new year.'

'How exciting! You need a reading nook by a large window, with cushions and blankets.'

'I do.' I swallow hard, imagining the little nook with her on it, with a book in hand.

The breeze from the sea ruins Brooke's hair and they fly around, landing on her face and sticking to her lips.

'Damn it. It's always windy by the sea, isn't it?'

'Let me ...' I turn to her and pull the hair off and tuck it behind her ear. Our eyes lock and my heart speeds up.

She bites on her lower lip and smiles, but there's something else in her eyes. When she looks at me, I feel happy. I feel like it's only us and no one else matters. I lean toward her and her eyes lower to my lips.

'Gabriel...' she whispers against my mouth.

'Shhh.' And I kiss her gently. No tongue, no claiming, no lust. Just pure emotions that flow into our kiss. She kisses me back, placing her hand on my cheek. It's slow and raw. I'm allowing her inside my heart now. My body was hers for a while, but now I'm giving her my heart. The taste of her lips is imprinted on mine and I don't want anyone else other than her ever kissing me. She pulls away and rests her forehead on mine.

'We... we should go.' Her breathing is deep, just like mine.

'Ok.'

We spent the evening mingling with the crowd. Brooke danced with people and even I was stolen to the dance floor by different women. Kate, however, avoided us since our last conversation, which we didn't mind at all. We drank, we laughed, we ate, and we talked. It felt nice being away from home, even if it was just for a day. All the rules seemed not important here, but I had to think of a way to talk to her when we're alone. I stand with a group of gentlemen, chatting about the market while watching Brooke being swooped around by her uncle. Her eyes meet mine and she smiles. Then the song finishes,

'Excuse me, gentlemen.' I set my empty glass down on the bar and make my way to her. Next song, I Won't Give Up by Jason Mraz plays when I extend my hand to her.

'Can I have this dance?' She looks unsure but in the end, takes it. I put my hand on her lower back as the other one links with hers and I pull her in closer. I watch her as we start slowly dancing and see her glancing around.

'I'm right here.'

'I know.' She finally looks at me and smiles. 'Sorry.'

'It's ok.' I pull her in even closer and feel my heart pounding at the closeness between us. Everyone could disappear right now and I wouldn't even notice, as my eyes are on her and her only.

'Did I say you look absolutely stunning this evening?' I whisper in her ear.

'You might have mentioned it earlier.'

'Well, I'm saying it again then.'

'The wind ruined my hair, though.' She snorts out.

'Still fucking perfect.' I see goosebumps form on her neck. The lyrics of the song are hitting the right places in my heart as he sings exactly what I feel right at this moment. I decide to not give up on the idea of us. I'm going to tell her – soon and her heart will be mine just like mine is hers. I'll make all of her dreams come true and I'll do everything in my power to make her happy. Because that's what you do for the person you love. Our eyes lock and we carry on looking at each other till the song finishes.

We decide to finish our night early so we can leave in the morning, so we say our goodbyes to everyone and even Kate looks relieved when we say we're leaving. Brooke appears tense as we walk out of the hall, and I'm not sure if I did something wrong. As we enter our room, I help her remove her coat and hang it on the side, along with my jacket.

'I'm exhausted.' She murmurs as she sits on the bed to remove her heels.

'Let me.' I kneel in front of her and take off the first shoe. She leans back on her hands and breathes deeply.

'Brooke.' I start, but she stops me. 'Not tonight, Gabriel, please.' Does she know what I want to say? Looking at the hem of her dress makes my cock twitch as I imagine running my hand up her leg, making her body shatter under my touch like I did it many times before. I lift her leg up and remove the other heel before putting my lips on her calf. A deep exhale leaves her mouth as I place another kiss higher up.

'Gabriel, we can't.' She sits up and looks down at me, but when I look her in the eyes, I see our emotions synced. 'This is too hard.' She says in a flat speech tone. I cup her face in my hands as she tries to look away, but I don't let her. Her eyes glisten with tears as I place a kiss on her cheek.

'I wish we could stay here forever.' I whisper as I pull her forehead to mine.

'But we can't.' She chokes out with her voice breaking. Her eyes close as I kiss her again at the corner of her mouth and she tilts her head slightly to the side.

Then our mouths crush and I give in fully. Her hands cup my face, and I lift her leg over my waist while stroking her outer thigh. She moans against my mouth when I grip her ass and I push her further onto the bed with me on all fours above her. Our kisses are slow, passionate, similar to the one on the beach, yet so very different from any other time back in London. She's undoing the buttons of my shirt without breaking the kiss and I push my hand behind her head to pull her even closer. We're as close as we can be, yet it's still too far for me. My hand travels up her body, slowly reaching between her legs, and a groan leaves her mouth. She's already wet.

'That's my girl. Always ready.' I whisper and kiss her again. My thumb strokes over her clit, forcing a moan to escape, as she tilts her head back.

'Mine.' I growl into her neck before kissing her there.

'Yours.' She whispers in return.

I push two fingers inside her soaked entrance and she cries out, so I quiet her with my mouth, allowing her moans to vibrate throughout my body. I push my fingers hard while stimulating her clit at the same time, and her whole body shakes underneath me. Digging of her nails into my skin makes me groan in pleasure and I push my fingers harder, making her whole body react. I curl my fingers to hit her g spot and her body falls apart as orgasm hits her and her back arches out. She cries out into my mouth and I feel every vibration of her on my skin. After a moment of her catching her breath, I push my trousers and my boxers down, freeing my very hard cock. While kneeling on the bed, I remove her wet panties and pull her up so she sits on me. Her legs are wrapped around me as I lift her up slightly so I can position my cock into her and then slowly let her slide right into it, making her gasp.

'Fuck' I growl and push her head towards me as I crush my mouth into hers, kissing her passionately. She rotates her hips, making my eyes roll back in my head. My other hand is on her back and I jerk her even closer to me, making every inch of our bodies connect. I pull on her hair, making her head go back to give me an easier access to her neck. I lick from the bottom up to her ear, making her body tremble before lying us back on the bed. After I lift myself up, I rip the material that touches her perfect, smooth skin. She gasps as the dress lets go and now I have a view of her perfect breasts. I lean forward and flick her hard nipple with my tongue, which makes her hiss. I lick around it while she grabs my hair into her hands and tries to push me lower, pleading for me to suck on it, but I take my time with it. The sounds of her moans play in my ears. My cock leaks now as the need to be inside her overwhelms me.

'Gabriel.' The sound of my name rolling off her tongue sends a shiver down my spine and I take her nipple in my mouth to suck it hard. Making her back arch forward, I take the advantage and I throw my arm behind her and keep her in that position.

'Oh, my god.' She cries out.

When I let go and look down at her, I see her breathless, looking right at me, waiting for me to fill her. She grabs my face and pulls me in, kissing me instantly. I groan as I position myself against her entrance. Both our bodies are set in flames, burning with the need for each other, but yet we can't get enough.

'Hard.' She demands and her wish is my command. I cover her mouth with my hand and thrust in hard, only hearing the muffled scream. I keep my thrusts slow and hard, my cock celebrating every push as if it's the last one. I allow her moans and cries to echo in my mouth as I continue kissing her, not wanting to let go of her.

I'm yours. My heart whispers, but I don't allow those words out. I lift her ass up to get a better angle, and her whole body shakes as I thrust again. I groan as I feel my cock pulsing, letting me know I'm close.

'I need you to come with me, baby.' I command, and she nods. She clenches, trapping my cock inside, making it even tighter, and with one more push, we both come, the orgasm taking over as I spill into her and she cries out, digging her nails into my ass. I collapse on top of her, the air completely knocked out of my lungs. She's breathless like me and she makes me face her, before placing a gentle kiss on my lips.

We both collapse on the bed after having a drink and without saying a word to each other. Something shifted between us today, I can feel it but I think as we went onto a more emotional level, somehow she seems even further away. Her back is turned to me, so I push myself closer and wrap my arms around her, kissing the side of her head. I lay there still for a while, thinking about her – about us and how terrified I am of losing her. Her breathing became deeper, letting me know she's fallen asleep. I lift my head up to look at her and I place another kiss on her ear before whispering,

'I love you.'

CHAPTER THIRTY-TWO

Brooke

I'm avoiding him and I know it's cruel. But yesterday, things... changed. It was then, on the beach, when I kissed him. Not a kiss where you want to fuck them, but a kiss when you truly care about them. Maybe I have imagined things, and it was my heart playing tricks on me, but when he asked me to dance, and the damn song played, I felt his eyes on me. I felt like I was the only person who existed right then for him, and it scared the shit out of me. My heart talks – screams even at me while my brain remains mute, so I tried, I tried to not let it go further. Of course, he then had to kiss me when we were in the room. Of course, he had to make my heart flutter and take over my body completely. An addict's withdrawal is hard, not because adjusting to life without your drug is hard, but because when you get another hit, it feels so much better again. We didn't fuck last night. No. It was as if our souls were merging, meeting for the first time and saying, 'That's me.' and accepting each other. After last night, I felt like a piece of him has truly imprinted itself onto my very being and I can't shake it off. Every time his mouth opens, I'm terrified of the words that might come out. I don't want to hurt him, but we're not meant to be. I have plans – goals for my life that I have to achieve on my own, so I can not let another person stop me from reaching for my dreams.

We spend the morning in silence, packing our things, taking showers in turns. I'm wearing comfy grey joggers and a long sleeve jade colour top. Nothing fancy, but I wanted to be comfortable on our drive back. The moment I get home, I'm planning on hopping on my sofa and reading a book while Nala lies on my legs. Yes, a book where I can focus on a fictional man will definitely take my minds off all my problems. That's what they were written for in the end, right?

'I've got everything now, so ready when you are.' Gabriel zips up his travel suitcase and stands up straight, throwing his hands on his hips.

'I should be done in 5 minutes.' I keep my gaze down. I'm a horrible person, yes, I know. But the shield around my heart is shattering and I need to put it back together before it's too late.

'Ok. I need to make a phone call quickly, anyway.' The door to our room opens and closes. I exhale deeply, relieved he left the room. My eyes move onto the bed and my heart skips a beat when I remember how his skin felt on mine, how he claimed me and showed me his true self. I swallow a hard lump in my throat and look in the mirror. It's nothing special, yet a man as gorgeous as him looks at me as if I'm the only woman on this planet. I try to snap out of the thoughts and put my make-up bag in my suitcase before zipping it up. Gabriel walks back in and I tell him I'm ready. We put our coats on and he takes both our suitcases.

Breathe, Brooke. Just breathe.

I pop quickly to the reception to check out, say thanks for a nice room and meet Gabriel, who's putting the bags in the boot.

'You sure you have everything?' He asks with his voice resigned.

'Erm, yes. Pretty sure.' He closes the boot and then looks up at me, but his body tenses as his gaze follows just past my shoulder.

'What?' I turn around and see a chicken standing maybe 5 metres away from us, staring right in our direction. I chuckle.

'It's him again.' I glance back at his set face, his clamped mouth and fixed eyes.

'One, it's a her. Two, I very much doubt that one specific chicken wants to kill you.' I snort out, but he is not finding it funny.

'Brooke, this blood thirsty beast is staring right at me. He– She did the same thing yesterday when you weren't here.'

Amusement fills me as I glance between them two. A tiny little chicken scares a big man like Gabriel. A man who bosses people around for a living.

'Brooke, get in the car.' His commands with cool authority.

'What?'

'Get. in. the. Car. I don't want you getting hurt.'

'Gabriel, I'm not afraid of a little chicken.' I scoff at him, but his expression remains dead serious. In a split second, an odd sound comes from the animal before it charges for Gabriel. I gasp as I watch Gabriel jump and run to the front of the car and scream.

'Fuck off. I'll make a fucking dinner out of you.' and they both run in circles. I burst out laughing as I make my way to the driver's door and open it, allowing Gabriel to slide in quickly and I shut it behind him, before the chicken reaches us. Once Gabriel is out of reach, the hen slows down and walks back to where she came from. My stomach hurts from laughing as I get in the passenger seat and put on my belt.

'I told you she wanted to kill me.' He snaps, but I'm unable to control my laughter. Tears are flowing down my cheeks as he glares at me, his expression becoming softer until he laughs with me. Once we both calm down, I turn my head to look at him and we both smile. For a second, it feels good, it feels... like it's meant to be. I look at his eyes that are filled with emotions and my heart thumps, pushing me out of my thoughts and making me clear my throat.

'Let's go then.'

'Did you want to see your mum before we go?' He asks before starting the engine.

'No, I'll see her tomorrow, anyway.' He nods and we begin the drive home.

We arrive outside my place, and I glance at it through the window. This is it. That's where we say our goodbye and go back to being boss and employee. Just thinking about him not touching me shatters me. I turn to look at him and he's still holding onto the steering wheel, looking straight in front of him. The air between us thickens, and it's hard to breathe.

I inhale deeply as I fight back the tears. My body stops me from opening the door and walking away. I beg my brain to help me through this, but I get no response. As I open my mouth to speak, Gabriel speaks first. 'Let me get your bag.' He opens the door and gets out without putting on his coat.

The cold air fills the car, making me shiver. I don't move. I can't. Then the shut of the boot snaps me out of it and I open my door and get out, pushing it closed behind me. I put on my coat as he makes his way to me, standing right in front of me now. We gaze into each other's eyes and my heart is breaking.

This is it.

This. Is. It.

My body trembles and I'm unable to speak. A drop of rain falls on my face, which makes me flinch.

'Brooke...' He starts, his expression tight with strain.

'Please, whatever you're going to say... don't.' I warn with my voice breaking, tears filling up my eyes.

'But I...'

'We had a lot of fun.' A cold knot forms in my stomach, and I feel it... the acute sense of loss.

Please, don't say it.

Another drop falls, followed by another. I glance up at the dark grey sky as it starts to shower, and neither of us moves.

'Do we really have to end this?' His husky voice reaches not just my ears, but my heart – my soul. I close my eyes, allowing the cold rain to touch my face, hoping it's covering up the tear that escape.

No, we don't. I want to say but I don't. Another piece of my heart shatters as he takes a step toward me and cup my face in his hands. Fear, stark and vivid, glitter in his eyes.

'Brooke.' He whispers and I watch the rain fall on his face. The sky cries with me, knowing the pain that lingers between us.

'I...'

I shake my head furiously. 'Gabriel, don't.' My chin shakes as I fight with myself to not break down. I see his eyes redden, which only breaks my heart more.

'Please.' I choke out, 'Don't say it.'

He pulls my forehead to his, allowing me to hear his heavy breathing.

Don't. Say. It.

Please.

Don't.

'I love you.' The three cruel words leave his mouth and I give in, allowing tears to fall freely, unable to fight, unable to think. They're out and they can not be taken back. A chuckle of pain leaves me.

'Please, say something.' He lifts my face to look at him.

'Gabriel...' I groan out with my breaking voice.

'I know you feel it too. Tell me you want this as much as I do. I know you do. I feel it between us. Brooke...' I shake my head again.

'I can't give you what you want.' I reply and his eyes widen in surprise. 'Gabriel, you deserve someone who is ready for your love, but...' He shakes his head, letting go of me and taking a step back. 'I can't do this. It wasn't meant to... You weren't meant to...' I struggle to find the words. My whole body trembles and it's not because of the rain.

'I made a promise to myself and I must keep it. I need to follow my goals before I can...'

'I'll wait.' He snaps.

'I don't want you to wait. Please... Gabriel, please. Let me go. We were never meant to be.' I see him flinch at the stab of my words and it kills me to see him like this.

'Brooke, let's try, let's...' I put my finger to his mouth and offer him half a smile.

'Find someone who will make you happy. A person who deserves your love. Someone who will teach you to ice skate...' We both snort through the tears. 'Someone who will make you laugh. Someone who will whisper the three words to you every day for the rest of your life. You deserve it.' His body shakes as I touch his arms. He leans in slowly and places a kiss on my mouth, which I return. It's gentle, it's slow, it's beautiful.

It's a goodbye.

'I love you.' He whispers against my mouth before rushing away and getting into his car, and driving off. Leaving me on the pavement, ready to break down as I watch him disappear from my view. Leaving me with an inexplicable feeling of emptiness.

I open my door and Nala immediately runs up to me, taking a sniff and letting a whimper sound out.

'Gosh, girl, why are you soaked?! Did you walk back to London?' Aaron calls out as he stands up from the sofa. I close the door and lean my back against it. Tears start falling again and I let a scream leave my body.

It's over.

It's done.

We're done.

I start to wail, allowing the pain to leave through my mouth. My body slides down to the floor as I burst into tears, crying, screaming. The agony takes over my body, fogging my brain.

'Brooke!' He runs up to me and pulls me into a hug. I'm not even strong enough to hug him back now, so I just let my head rest on him and allow my heart to scream and beg for relief which doesn't come.

I broke his heart.

I broke my heart.

I broke us.

'What happened?' He asks, but I can't speak. I shake my head as his hands tighten around me. I cry into his shoulder, feeling every sharp, broken piece of my heart stabbing my soul.

'He's... he's gone.' I choke out. 'We're over.' Words that make me break all over again as my tears soak through Aaron's top. This time I wrap my hands around him, grabbing onto his t-shirt, trying to grab onto something good, but I'm too weak; my body is too weak. He makes a shhh sound, trying to comfort me, but my ears allow nothing in. All I hear is his voice whispering, I love you. It hurts, it hurts so badly I can't breathe. Air was forced out of my lungs and they were made to breathe without it, but how can you breathe without air? That's how it feels without him in my life now.

CHAPTER THIRTY-THREE

Gabriel

'Gabe, what the fuck happened, man?' I see him gape as he takes in the damage. My suitcase lying in the middle of the room, broken glass shattered in almost every corner and whisky spilled over counters, sofa, and front door. He steps carefully around the glass with pure panic on his face, and then he sees me sitting on the floor, leaning against the window. My body is slouching, completely given up. I'm still catching my breath after the recent breakdown. The moment I walked inside and closed the door, everything came crushing down. I threw the suitcase and tried to pour myself a glass of whisky with my shaky hands, but spilt most of it. So I threw the damn glass and the sound of it breaking was so satisfying, I grabbed more glasses, filled them full, and threw them too. I wanted my surroundings to match my insides.

Shattered.

Broken.

Unfixable.

I screamed to allow at least some of the pain to escape, but as my voice left, the heartbreak didn't follow. Everything in this damn house reminds me of her and I'm tempted to set this shithole on fire. The only relief I feel is that Bruno isn't here. I don't feel like I'm in control of my own body and fighting it back is useless. My eyes are red and puffy from anger and I'm pretty sure I have a cut on my hand from the glass as it stings, but I don't bother to check.

'It's over.' I say blankly, while staring at the floor with my head tilted.

'What's over?' He crouches and studies me for... injuries is my guess.

'I told her I love her.' A deep exhale of his breath reaches me.

'By the condition of this place, I won't bother asking how it went.'

'It's over.' I repeat, feeling my voice breaking, and he takes a seat next to me.

We sit in silence for a while and I feel my heart finally slow down. Maybe it's dead – turned into a rock. I feel nothing – empty. My gaze remains on the floor as it hurts to even try to move them. My whole body gave up on me, but I manage to open my mouth.

'Why did you come?' I murmur out.

'Tess messaged me, saying you might need me.'

'I'm glad things are working out for you.' I say with an exhale.

I feel Max's body move and hear his footsteps as he makes his way to the kitchen. I finally manage to turn my head, and I see him pull out a dustpan and starting to clear up the glass off the floor.

'Leave it.' I groan and I close my eyes as my head trembles at any loud sound.

'You're my best friend, Gabe. I'm here to help, so shut up and let me clear it all up before Bruno gets back.' I watch him pick up every single piece of the glass, and I find it ridiculously poetic how the pieces of the glass remind me of my heart.

Chuck it in the bin.

It's no longer needed.

He follows by wiping the countertops and mopping the floor.

'Not sure what to do about your sofa, mate.'

'Throw it out.' He frowns at my response.

'I'll just call a cleaner.'

It's been two days since I last saw Brooke. I haven't been in the office as I allowed myself to break down completely, but today it is changing. I've put my navy suit on and I'm planning on checking how things are going at work before going to my meeting with the realtor. Making my way to the kitchen, I look at the brand new sofa. This is now the only piece of furniture Brooke's naked body didn't touch. I clench my hands into fists at the thought but quickly snap out of it at the sound of my phone pinging. My heart rate picks up as I quickly pull it out and is slows right back down when I see the name.

Max- Ready for today? This is a big day.

Me- If all goes to plan.

Max- Honestly, I'm so fucking proud of you, mate.

Me- Drinks after?

Max- Call me when you're ready.

Me- Will do.

It is a big day and if it all goes well, I'll be an owner of an apartment building, and that's just a start. I glance around and my head must be playing tricks on me, as I swear I can hear Brooke's laugh echoing off these empty, cold walls. I take a deep breath in to steady myself and refocus on my plans for the day.

'Morning sir,' Tess calls when she sees me enter the building. I simply nod and make my way to the elevator, pressing for the 6th floor. Inside, I'm followed by John from editing who also just arrived.

'Mr. Alstons.' He gives me a slight bow of his head.

'John, how are you?' I try to make small talk, which today seems challenging.

'Very good, sir.'

'All good on your floor?'

'Miss. Summers been off this week, so there are few delays, but we're working on it.' The sound of her name makes my insides twist.

'Why has she been off?'

'Some family emergency.'

'Very well, I believe there's enough staff to cover her absence?'

'Yes, of course.'

'Very well then.' He exits the elevator on his floor and I stay in to go to mine.

Once I'm in my office, I power the computer and check all the logs. Everything seems good in here and I wonder how I'm going to juggle everything in my life soon.

Hard work.

It's always hard work and I know how time-consuming it's all going to be. But it'll be worth it.

My stomach drops as I pick up the phone and dial the reception.

'Tess, hi. Could you please come to my office?'

'Yes, sir. Coming now.'

I wait no longer than 2 minutes before knocking comes to my door and Tess comes in.

'Please have a seat.' She's clearly uncomfortable.

'Can I ask you something?'

'Of course.'

I lean forward in my chair and rest my arms on my desk. 'Why has Brooke been off this week?'

She sighs deeply and takes a moment before answering, 'Do you really need to ask?' Her mouth turns into a frown.

'So there is no family emergency?' She shakes her head in response, and then I nod in understanding.

'Please don't give up on her.' Her plea surprises me.

'I've tried, but Brooke made herself perfectly clear.'

'But...' she snaps, pushing herself up in the chair, 'You're so good together. She's just too stubborn to admit it. She's scared.'

'Tess, I appreciate your concern. I really do. But it was Brooke's decision, and she made it. I tried to persuade her, but it didn't work.' I inhale deeply. 'She asked me to move on, so I'll grant her the wish.' Now she slams her hands onto my desk.

'You men are so clueless!' I widen my eyes at her outburst and she immediately apologises.

'It's just... Do you love her?'

'Tess...' I roll my head. I definitely do not need this conversation today.

'Do. You. Love. Her?' Her demands for an answer are serious. Her eyes shooting fire arrows into me.

'Yes.' I snap. 'Of course, I fucking love her.'

A smile appears on her face. 'Then fucking fight for her.' She immediately apologises again for swearing in front of me, which makes me chuckle.

'Got any advice?' She thinks and thinks and thinks ...

'Romantic gesture won't do it for her. She's too stubborn and too stuck in her misbelief.'

'You don't say...' I roll my eyes in amusement.

'You need to simply tell her you two are getting married.' She shrugs, and I burst out laughing. 'If it was only that simple.'

She sighs, 'I don't know. But Gabriel– Mr. Alstons...

'Gabriel.'

'Gabriel... She is hurting. And I mean a box of tissues and a large tub of ben & jerry hurting. The spoon and a jar of Nutella hurting. I saw it.'

'You women are a very odd species indeed.' I arch my brow and she shrugs. 'We love too deeply; that's our issue.'

'And ice cream and chocolate makes you happy?'

'Oh yes.' She snorts out.

Odd species indeed.

CHAPTER THIRTY-FOUR

Brooke

'Thank you for meeting my today.' I shake Mr. Maxwell's hand and we sit at the table.

'I'm not going to lie, the place you chose for our meeting quite surprised me.'

'It's my mom's bakery.'

'Oh.' He glances around, taking the atmosphere in. 'It's lovely.' I nod and smile. The waitress brings our order, which is two coffees and a piece of my mom's red velvet cake each. My stomach has been twisting since the moment I opened my eyes today.

Yes, this meeting is truly nerve wrecking.

I decided on simple skinny jeans and a smart navy blouse, smart but yet casual.

'So ...' He starts and I swallow hard. 'How many rejections have you had so far?' He pulls out my draft and sets it on the table between us.

'9.' I admit. And each one hurt like hell.

'Well, you can consider yourself an author now then.' His

chuckle helps me relax my shoulders. 'Can I though?' I sip on my coffee, trying to warm up my stiff body.

'Of course. Now, I have read your chapters, but I would really like to hear it in your own words, what your book is truly about.' I spend the next 10 minutes explaining about my inspiration and idea, and what lesson I hope for this book to bring to women. A true love story doesn't always happen with the prince saving your life and you giving yourself to him. Sometimes more work is involved where people have to realise their flaws and misbeliefs before they can learn the meaning of true love. Or sometimes you get the right people at the wrong time and there's nothing you can do about it, other than learn to live with the fact you'll never be with the person you love.

'See, when Mr. Alstons...'

Heartache.

'...called me. He said he didn't read the book, but one of the most amazing people he knows wrote it.' The surrounding temperature suddenly rises and I feel my cheeks heat. He notices it and offers me a smile. 'I normally wouldn't believe in that as there's plenty of amazing authors.' I nod.

'But Mr. Alstons runs a very successful publishing business and I know he has a good eye for new talents.' I swallow a hard lump in my throat and feel my hands tremble. 'I went in totally blind into your draft and normally, as a man, it's not a book I'd enjoy.' We both chuckle and I understand he might to not be a good match for me. What man enjoys a good spicy book?

'So I gave it to my wife.' My hands start to sweat as I wait for him to continue, but he annoyingly takes a bite of his cake and then sips on his coffee some more.

'And...?' I finally ask, while remaining polite.

'She loved it.' My heart sings.

'However, I have a very interesting idea.'

My eyes narrow. 'What is it?'

'How would you feel about traveling to America?'

'You're doing what?!' Tess snaps, slamming her hands onto the reception desk. Everyone turns to look at us now.

'Quieter please.' I murmur, thankful when they notice there's nothing to look at, so they turn back to whatever they're doing.

'Brooke, no, please.' She pleas and I understand. I do. If it was the other way around, I'd probably beg her on my knees.

'I'm not moving...' I try to explain, but all she does is shake her head. 'I don't understand why you're handing in your notice.'

'Because...' Yes, that's not very easy to explain. Many reasons really... 1. Gabriel (that's why I refused to do the whole fling thing. I fucking predicted this happening.) 2. I might be going writing full time (yes, I might be jumping the gun too early) and 3. Gabriel (yes, again).

'Because of Gabriel.' She finishes for me.

'I have to do this. Please, understand.' I take her hand in mine, begging her to see my reasoning. She slowly nods.

I pack up my office, taking everything I own, which is... not a lot. A framed photo of Nala, a photo of me with mum and dad, another photo of me, Tess and Aaron at the club. Yep, couple of photos. I grab my notebooks too, in which I've written book ideas and my pens.

Like I said – not a lot.

A knock sounds from my door, which makes me jump, but relief hits me when it's Justin's head that appears. I'm holding my hand over my chest. 'Jeez, you're giving me a heart attack.'

'I just heard the news. Is it true?'

'Yep.' I continue to push the photos down in my bag.

'Wow, I thought you liked it here.'

I sigh, 'I did, Justin. Just, I guess it's time for a new chapter in my life.'

His brow arches. 'But you've only been here for like a month.'

I look up and him and start laughing. 'It is ridiculous, isn't it? But I'm getting a deal for my book...' which I still can't freaking believe, '... and I guess it happened sooner than I expected.'

'Well, I'm happy for you. We'll miss you here.'

'I'll miss you too.' I offer him a half-hearted smile. Not even two months... it's crazy how such a short period of time can turn your entire world upside down. I grab my filled to full bag and open the door to leave, when I suddenly freeze in place and shut it back.

'What happened? Changed your mind?' Justin jokes, but I am not laughing.

'Do you know how long Mr. Alstons is down here for?'

'Erm, he had a meeting scheduled with John and he wasn't there when I came here, so I'd say a while.' I exhale deeply as my heart pounds against my chest.

I can't see him. I can't.

'Can you distract him so I can get into the elevator?'

His forehead wrinkles. 'Why?'

'I...' Come up with a reason, Brooke. 'I just don't want to explain why I'm leaving again and I just want to go home.' He thinks about it for a moment and I'm not sure he believes me, but then he shrugs, 'Ok.'

He makes his way to John's desk and starts talking to them both, but he's standing so both John and Gabriel have to face away from me. This is my cue. I don't bother closing the door behind me as I rush to the elevator and press the button, tapping my foot on the floor as if it's going to make it faster.

'Yeah, she handed in her notice today.' Mumbled voices reach me.

No!

'Where is she?' Gabriel's angry voice echoes through the office.

Oh, my god.

Hurry up, you stupid elevator.

'There she is.' John now speaks up, but I'm turned away from them. The elevator door opens and I rush inside, pressing the button for the bottom floor, and stand still, facing the back.

Close. Close. Close.

I keep my eyes closed as my heart races, trying to jump out of my body. I hear footsteps.

Please, just close!

The door closes, but...

'You're not fucking quitting.' Gabriel's voice reaches my ears and my stomach drops. I open my eyes to see him in the mirror, standing right behind me.

'Well, I did.' I reply with my shaky voice while keeping my gaze on my feet. He grabs my arm and jerks me around. 'Look at me.' He snaps and my body trembles at his touch and heart flutters at our proximity.

'What do you want?'

'You're not quitting. Why did you quit? I told you this is work, not our private life.'

'I'm not quitting because of you.'

Liar, liar, pants on fire.

'Then what?'

'Gabriel. I told you this would happen, why this whole fling wasn't a good idea, and now everything I was afraid of happened.' I snap at him and he takes a step toward me, so I take a step back. He's inches away now – way too close. My body comes to life just as it always does around him, and I feel the electricity between us.

'And what exactly happened that you were afraid of?' He asks with his husky voice.

'Feelings...' I murmur, 'You have caught feelings, and it was meant to be just sex.'

'I caught feelings? I alone?' He rubs his chin and my

stomach drops as I take in his scent, so familiar to my heart. 'I…'

'Don't lie, Brooke. I wasn't the only one who started to feel…'

'Don't.' I snap, pointing my finger at him. He pushes me to the back wall, his lips mere inches away from mine. I can hear my own heartbeat in my ears and my breathing deepens.

'Admit it, you coward.' He groans. I look him in the eyes and feel the magnetic pull, his piece imprinted onto me, begs to connect with him but all I do is whisper, 'I can't.'

The elevator door opens, and I run out, leaving him behind.

CHAPTER THIRTY-FIVE

Gabriel

Christmas was depressing.

New Year was depressing.

Did I try to forget? *Yes.*

Did I succeed? ***No.***

I spent Christmas Day with little Theo and his parents, as I was invited over for dinner, after I told them what my plans were.

So, yes. I bought their apartment building. They couldn't turn down my offer, which was more than double to what the building was worth. So now here I am, an owner of the building and I'll be remodelling the whole thing, plus furnishing each apartment, ensuring all residents' needs are met. Theo's dad cried when we met the first time and he found out I was the 'angel in a suit' who bought them food and left money, which was just what they needed to pay for hot water.

Meeting Theo was a true eye opener for me and I couldn't sleep for many nights, while trying to figure out what I could do to help them. I spent the Christmas Day meeting all the residents and chatting to them about how they'd like to see their building change. The rent was overpriced for what it was so they were relieved to hear I'll be reducing it once everything was signed. I also brought presents for all the kids, thanks to Theo's tip on how many kids live there and what are their interests.

I've made my money and then I had nothing to do with it. As a child, I believed I needed money to be happy, but with age you learn a true purpose of finances, and it's not to own but it's to help. I've invested, I bought buildings and opened my company which made me a millionaire and now it's time to give it back to people who need it most. Along with having my house built, I'll also have the company renovate the building and each apartment, free of charge for the residents. My mother wanted to provide a better life for me by giving me away from all this, and now I've returned, wanting to provide for people who couldn't leave.

New Year I spent with Max and Tess, watching them dance, kiss and snuggle like a pair of teenagers. I'm happy for them – I really am. But I felt a stab in the heart every time I looked at them. Max worked his ass off for her, improving himself every step of the way and there was a mention of some new kink for granny pants or whatever it means.

Bruno seems to have caught my depressive episodes as all he does now is whimper and mope about. He's missing Nala as much as I'm missing Brooke. Two broken hearts. I take him out whenever I can, but he always pulls in the very well known direction and I'm tired of the constant battle of wills. The quicker we move, the better.

Now I pull the door open and enter. Glancing around, I spot Brooke's mum sitting at one of the tables, having her lunch.

'Ms. Summers.' I bow my head as I stand by her table.

'Have a seat, Gabriel.' She gestures to the chair on the other side, which I take. She called me two days ago, saying we needed to meet – so here I am.

'Ryan, one black coffee please, no sugar.' I smirk. 'It's my job to remember. Don't be so happy.' And a smirk disappears.

'So, how can I help?'

'Help?' she snorts out, 'I think you did enough.'

'Excuse me?' I draw my brows together.

'Brooke has been a shell of a person again. Just like after she left Tyler... But she's also refusing to talk, so do you care to explain to me why she's not happy about receiving a deal for her book and why her eyes are always puffy when I see her?'

Shit, these words sting. She made me believe she was truly moving on and wanted nothing to do with me.

'I'm sorry, miss, but I made you aware of my feelings toward her. After we came back from the wedding, I confessed and she rejected me, like I was nothing to her.' I bark because I won't allow someone to talk to me like I did something wrong here. 'I tried talking to her but she point blank refused to even look at me. All I wanted was an actual relationship with her.'

Brooke's mother tilts her head back and laughs. 'I warned you. I told you her shield is put high, high up. You simply didn't reach high enough.' She takes a sip of her steamy drink.

'Or maybe she doesn't love me.' I shrug and thank the waiter as he puts a cup of coffee in front of me before walking away.

'You silly boy. My daughter loves you and it was very clear to see at the wedding.' My heart stills at these words, my chest expanding, ready to burst. I only wish they came from Brooke's mouth, not her mother's. 'I watched you two, you know... After you told me about how you felt, I wanted to see it. But what I saw was not a guy in love with a girl, but a man and a woman, both having deep feelings for each other and both burning with positive energy when they were near each other. I know my daughter better than anyone, and I know when she's truly happy.' As I stare at my coffee, I swallow a hard lump.

'I tried.' I murmur out.

'Not. hard. enough.' she puts her hands on the table. 'She's going to America.' My eyes widen in shock and feel my head spiralling. 'What?!'

'Not moving, but the deal she got on her book... They want to meet her in person, so she's going tomorrow for a few days.' I sigh in relief. 'But...'

'But what?'

'But she said it'd be easier if she lived there.'

My stomach twists and I feel like my lunch is about to reappear in front of me any minute. 'She wouldn't move....' I say to myself.

'Unless...' she starts, but waits for me to continue.

'Unless she's running away.' I see her head nod in confirmation that I guessed it right.

'She's too scared to admit her feelings because she's terrified of losing herself. Tyler never agreed with her, never wanted to do things she wanted to do and whatever idea she had was never good enough.' The anger boils through my veins and I wish I did more than just broke this guy's nose.

'She is enough.' I snap.

'Then show it to her.'

CHAPTER THIRTY-SIX

Brooke

The flight was fine. I was sitting with a woman and her baby in the middle aisle and in fairness; the baby cried only half the flight. I tried to help but I don't think I'm as maternal as some women are, which is ironic as all women should love and want kids, right? Maybe it's not something I'm meant to do in my life. My mum sent me another text to remind me this was only a few day trip and to not under any condition, look at any rentals. I scoff at it because, well, if I decide to move, then no one is going to stop me. Aaron is trying to be supportive but I see it in his eyes – the worry. The constant asking if I'm ok and if I need to say I'm fine, one more time, I'm going to throw up. I've got a meeting with the publisher tomorrow at 2 o'clock and it's only 11am now. Jet leg can wait as I'm going to force myself to stay up and see a bit of New York before having an early night. I've never been to the city before, but I mean, who would want to leave LA, the beaches, the people ...

I dropped off my bags at the hotel and raced out to do some

shopping. Of course, I messaged everyone, saying I survived the flight and landed safely. It's a basic rule for travelling, isn't it?

Make sure to let us know when you arrive.

The streets are crowded, so I push my way through. Everyone rushing around like headless chickens to wherever they need to be. I guess people in London appear more ... I want to say chilled even though both places seem rushed, but New York is just another level. As I wait for the lights to turn green, I gasp when I see a man with a chicken on a lead on the other side of the road.

Oh. My. God.

I snap a quick photo and start typing a message.

Me- Check this out! Maybe you'd want to have a pet chi ...

What the hell am I doing? I delete the message and put my phone back in my bag. I cross the road and nod at the guy with the animal who only glares at me as if I wanted to eat his pet. So freaking rude. I roll my eyes and continue walking, in a search of a place where I can have dinner.

I found a quiet spot on the edge of the centre and thankfully, they had free tables. I sit awkwardly on my own and I play with my hands as I wait for someone to take my order.

'Hello, my name is Josh and I'll be your waiter tonight.' A man in his early 20s stands next to me.

'Oh hi. Nice to meet you.' I smile warmly. 'Can I have a glass of whisky, no ice and...' I glance through the menu, 'Hunter's chicken, please.'

'Of course, anything else?' He asks as he writes down everything I said.

'No, thank you.' He takes the menu off me and walks away. I pull out a book I started reading on the flight and open it to the most recent page. This one is good. It's about a man who is a total slut until he meets this female character and the best part? She's still a virgin... and they end up sleeping together and at first it's all gentle and he's trying not to hurt her but by the time you reach the middle of the novel, she's tying him up and riding him like a cowgirl rides a bull. I'll ignore the fact that spicy books now remind me of Gabriel and how it felt, being in his arms, how his body claimed mine with every touch, every kiss. He made me feel special, beautiful and like nothing else mattered as long as he had me. And at the same time, nothing mattered as long as I had him. But I didn't have him, no. I had his body for the time being, but that was all it was... a quick fling that finished earlier than I expected. I knew we were going too far, when he invited me for dinner and when we went to the Christmas fayre, when he made me laugh until my belly hurt... Flings don't work like that. You're in and out. You don't talk about your families. You don't joke around and get to know each other. We fucked up and now we're paying for it. I can't be with him. My book is what I need to focus on. I'm finally where I wanted to be. My dreams are coming true and I'm finally happy.

Ok, content, maybe...

I will be happy once I forget Gabriel Alstons existed and maybe New York can be my new start where I can move on and just write. My phone pings on the table and my stomach twists when I see the name.

Gabriel- (A photo of us from Christmas fayre attached.) You were the most beautiful woman I've ever seen, even with chocolate smothered around your face.

I snort out at the message and smile to myself. It really was a fun day, and winning our bet felt even better as I watched his feet go up in the air and his ass lands on the ice.

My heart flutters at the memory of him touching me and making me laugh. Tyler was always serious in any situation, unless he was out with his band having drinks. I couldn't laugh with him when he was busy on his PlayStation or having a nap in a day because he had a gig. I sigh as I put the phone away without replying and start reading my book.

'Miss. Summers, thank you so much for travelling all the way here.' I shake hands with a stunning woman. She doesn't look older than 30 and you know, when a woman can wear a 12cm heels for work, she's there to rule. She pushes her long, fire-red hair over her shoulders and smiles widely.

'Hi, thank you for meeting me. It really means so much.' I offer her a smile in return.

'Let's go to my office and we can have a chat.' Her hand is placed on my back as she directs me to the office to our right with Miss. Brown label on the door. 'Carla, can we have two coffees, please?' She calls out to her receptionist, who nods and rushes away. Miss. Brown gestures to the sofa in the corner as she takes a seat in the armchair on the other side of the little glass coffee table.

'Did you have a pleasant flight?' She asks as she gathers some paperwork and a pen. The office is full of natural light, and it's minimalist, with her desk in the corner and only a desktop screen on it. There is a small bookcase with some books on it but not many, and I wonder if she has a bigger collection somewhere else.

'Yes, it was good. I spent most of it just reading.'

A quiet chuckle leaves her mouth. 'I wish I had time to read. I can't remember the last time I held a proper book for leisure purposes.'

My lips pull into a grin. 'Books are my life.'

'They used to be my life, too. You know, I was one of those girls at school who wore glasses, didn't have many friends, and just read on every break. Add the colour of my hair to the mix and I was bullied a lot.' She doesn't seem bothered by her story, at least not anymore.

'I'm so sorry.' I frown, but she waves her hand. 'It's in the past now.'

Carla comes in and sets the tray down with two cups of coffee, sugar, and milk.

'Thank you' We both say in sync before she leaves.

'Yeah, I loved books. I thought to myself that one day I'll make a living from my passion for them and as you can tell...' She lifts her hands up, gesturing to our surroundings, '... I did.'

'It is really impressive.' I say excitedly as I put a spoon of sugar and add some milk to my coffee.

'But there's something I didn't predict.' She leans forward as to say her secret, 'It gets very damn lonely when all you focus on is your career.' I swallow hard.

'Don't get me wrong... I love my job. But I'm now 32 and I don't even have a boyfriend as time simply doesn't allow it.'

'Don't you feel fulfilled with your work? I mean, to achieve what you did, doing something you absolutely love, must be very rewarding.'

She snorts out, 'In its own way, yes. But then after a long day of hard work, I go to my empty home and I have no one to talk to, no one to help me relieve the stress. I have a cat, of course, but a cat won't have a glass of wine with you or play with your hair as you watch a film together.' We both sigh and stare at our drinks for a moment.

'Anyway...' Miss. Brown clears her throat, '...Sorry, I know I'm mumbling.' She chuckles and I shake my head, 'No, it's ok really.' I offer her a smile to show it is really ok. But in my opinion, it's down to the person as to what they want from their lives. I'll be very content with Nala and my laptop and occasionally Tess and Aaron.

'So I have actually read your draft personally.'

'What did you think?'

'Loooved it. But I quickly realised I needed to read it when I was at home, if you know what I mean.' She gives me a wink and we both laugh. I feel more at ease now and I believe we could have a superb working relationship in the future. My biggest dream is about to come true, and my heart flutters as I think about it. We then carry on talking about my book and what it could mean for me, about the deadlines and my plans for my second book. It's all so exciting I could burst from all that happiness.

'There's only one thing I'd love for you to consider.'

'What is it?'

'I'd really love for you to consider moving here. It'd be easier to arrange meetings and to work through your current and any future projects. I just think it'll be an enormous investment from your side, but it'll be worth it.'

I already knew this, Mr. Maxwell said it'd definitely be easier if I was closer but… to leave everyone behind… but it is my dream… but I'll miss my mom… but it's what I've been working for, for such a long time. So many thoughts are crawling through my head now, I almost feel dizzy.

'Listen,' She pulls out a piece of paper from her folder, 'I understand it's a big decision, so take this…' She pushes the documents over to me, '…have a read, then take some time to consider it. I don't mean a month, but if you need a week to decide to talk to your loved ones, that's fine. We'd pay for your move and help you find a place to settle down.' I look down and notice the amount it says on the advance. 'If you decide to go ahead with us, simply sign the contract and then we'll go from there.'

I don't smile anymore. My heart is pounding against my chest as I now stand in front of this massive decision and I have a week to choose. Do I stay in London and be with people I love or do I move to New York to start fresh, with no Gabriel and a deal for my book? I inhale deeply. 'Thank you. I'll think about it.'

CHAPTER THIRTY-SEVEN

Brooke

I haven't slept at all that night after the meeting and then I had my flight back to England. Trying to decide has never been harder and my head feels like it's about to explode. I know what everyone is going to say… I know, but I also know they truly want what's best for me. A fresh start sounds amazing, considering I've been unable to get into my own bed without Gabriel's scent hitting my nose. I could just buy a new bedding, but I feel like I'm punishing myself for what I did to us and if it means I get to cry every night, so be it. I deserve it.

When I got home, Aaron was waiting for me with Nala. My beautiful girl has slowed down a lot in the last month and it kills me knowing her time might be coming. Last time I saw her happy and playful was when she was with Bruno, but as cruel as I might be to her, I can not allow myself to see him again. Every time I saw him since the wedding, my heart was calling to him and it took all my strength to fight it back, but I don't know how long I could remain strong for, so giving in my notice was the smartest decision.

'There's a package for you on the table.' Aaron calls out as I hang my coat up. I see a brown cardboard box with a note attached to it. I pick it up to study it.

'It's not a bomb, trust me.' A scent of cinnamon escapes the box and makes my mouth water. I pick up the note and read it out loud.

My first time trying. Let me know if they're good.
G. xxx

My heart stops beating and my stomach twists.

'Who brought this here?' I glance at Aaron, who is sitting on my worktop and is eating a sandwich. 'Guess.'

'He was here?' My eyes widen in shock, and he nods in confirmation. I glance back at the box and feel my hands sweat when I consider opening the box. Or I could just throw it out.

'Don't you dare to throw it away. Open it.' Aaron snaps. I roll my eyes at how well he knows me. I open the box and my heart flutters at the sight of churros and a small plastic tub filled with chocolate dip.

Great.

I'm now fighting the tears that threaten to emerge. I'm not going to cry in front of Aaron again. He had to pick me up way too many times, and I need to show him I can hold myself together.

'You can cry, you know?' He says with his mouth full and I turn my head to face him, 'Shut up.'

A groan of annoyance leaves his body as he jumps off the counter.

'Do you miss him?' I stare at him for a moment, a feeling of sickness forming in my stomach. He widens his eyes at me, waiting for me to reply, but I don't give him the satisfaction.

'Grrh, you will never admit it, will you?' He walks to my bedroom to pick up his suitcase, bringing it to the hallway.

'They want me to move there.' I announce and see him halt in place. My heart aches at the thought of leaving him. Maybe he could move with me and we could still see each other often and he could bring Dean with him, even.

'Are you going to move?' He asks, but still doesn't move.

'I have a week to decide.'

'So you're deciding if you wanna run away?'

I exhale loudly, 'Aaron, I wouldn't be running awa...'

'Bullshit, Brooke. I get it you want the deal and it's been your dream and I am more than proud of you, but the book isn't the reason you're considering moving and you know it.'

I gape at him as he glances down at the box of churros I'm still holding.

'Give it here.' He snatches the box and sets it on the table. I watch him open the container with chocolate, before picking up a churro, dipping it in and taking a big bite of it. Then he gestures to it and shouts, 'If a man making those just for you doesn't tell you he loves you, then I don't know what does.' He rolls his eyes in pleasure as he swallows the bite. 'It's so freaking good.' He takes another bite and I let out a chuckle. 'Don't laugh, woman. Eat them while they're warm.' He snaps, so I join him. Taking a bite of it tastes like cinnamon heaven and I wonder if he, in fact, made them himself, considering how good they are.

After we finish, we decide to take Nala for a walk but we ended up stopping at the cafe, as Nala struggled to go any further. Aaron brings out two coffees and we take our seats outside. It's cold, but it's sunny, so I'm thankful I dressed up warm. I sip on my drink when I see Aaron staring at me.

'What now?' I tilt my head to the side with amusement on my face.

'You really don't think you can have your dreams come true and have true love at the same time? He asks, and my mouth turns into a frown. 'Aaron...'

'Brooke. This man would walk through hell for you. I know it. I saw it in his eyes, the way he looked at you.'

'Tyler used to look at me the same way.' I scoff out.

'Nope. He didn't.' Now Aaron looks amused at calling me out.

'What do you mean?' I pinch my brows together as I take another sip of my coffee.

'Tyler looked at you like... Like you were his prize. Like he owned you and he was happy about it. Gabriel, on the other hand, looked at you as if you owned him. You could say jump off the bridge and he would, knowing he was making you happy.' Aaron's words burn on my skin, trying to enter inside but I don't allow them. I don't allow myself to think about what could have been if I told him how I felt on that nasty day we got back to London.

A single tear escapes and makes its way down my cheek.

'Brooke...' His lips turn downwards.

'Can we please stop talking about him? Please.' I beg him and he slowly nods. It's too much for me and I'm struggling to see the light on the other end. I'm now understanding that a fresh start might be the only way out for me.

The relief hits me when I feel a vibration in my pocket. I pull out the phone to see Mr. Maxwell's name on the screen and I press accept.

'Hi.' I call out, pretending to sound happy.

'Hi, Brooke. How are you? How was New York?'

'It was great, yes, Miss. Brown is an amazing woman.'

'I know, yeah, so did you get the deal?'

'Yes, yes, I did, but she wants me to move there.' I notice Aaron frowning and my heart aches at the sight of him.

'Well, I'm actually calling you with some news.'

'Oh?' There's a pause for a moment and a shuffling of paper sound comes through before he speaks again. 'I've got you another offer.' My stomach drops. 'It's probably the same you got in New York, if not less, but it is in the UK.'

'Oh.' is all I manage to say.

'Have you signed the contract yet?'

'No, I have a week to decide.'

An exhale of relief comes from his mouth.

'Ok, they're happy to give you a week too, so have a think and let me know, ok?'

'Ok.' I hang up the phone and see Aaron glaring at me. 'What was it?'

I shrug, 'Nothing important.'

CHAPTER THIRTY-EIGHT

Gabriel

I sit in my car when my phone pings. Picking up, I see the name I didn't think I'd see again.

Brooke- Churros (thumbs up emoji) Thank you.

My thumbs hover above the screen as I stare, struggling to think of the reply. My heart races and my hands are sweaty.

Don't screw this up.

I bite on my lower lip as I type.

Me- Do they taste as good as me?

Delete.

Me- They remind me of you.

Delete.

Me- You're welcome.

Delete.

I groan in annoyance, tilting my head back. Why is this shit so hard? I feel like I was better off before, when I thought I wasn't capable of love and now this woman is slowly killing me, like a poison that is kept being added to your food and every day, you just feel slightly worse than the day before, until you're unable to move, to speak, to breathe but then it's too late because you're on your deathbed. That's how the last month felt. Every day gets worse and my heart's aches are becoming stronger, keeping me awake at night.

Me- I miss you.

Delete.

'Fuck.' I shout as I slam my hand into the steering wheel and take a deep breath in. I drop my head, trying to come up with something – anything, just to get her to reply. I push my hand through my hair before the last attempt.

Me- I know how much you love them. Did you have a good flight back?

Sent.

I exhale loudly and close my eyes, waiting for her to reply or not. But to my surprise, a reply comes straight away, which makes me jump in my seat.

Brooke- It was good. No babies on board, so got some sleep.

I smile to myself as I read her response.

Tread carefully now.

Me- Oh, that's good news. And the meeting go ok?

I stare at the screen as three dots appear. The wait feels like a lifetime and when the reply comes; I exhale deeply when the reply comes.

Brooke- Yes, all good.

When I'm about to type again, I see another trio of dots appear, and my stomach drops. I have a bad feeling about this one. And then it comes...

Brooke- Gabriel, please stay away. You can't keep showing up.

I grip my phone so hard, I'm surprised it didn't bend. Frustration builds up in my chest as I type out another message.

Me- I miss you.

But this time, three dots never appear. I sigh and close my eyes to settle the burn that floods them before shoving the phone in my pocket and stepping out of the car. As I close the door and turn, I bump into someone.

'Hey!' a female voice said . I look up and see Lydia staring at me with her eyes wide open. 'Gabriel...'

'Lydia, hi.' I offer her a smile, but she doesn't smile back. 'How are you?'

She straightens her coat and clears her throat. 'What, you suddenly care?'

Now that I think about everything that happened between us, I start to understand how she felt. It basically happened to me too, after Brooke broke it off and I thought we had something. The twisting of the gut makes me nauseous when I think about how I hurt her or any other woman before her. I am ending this womaniser life for good.

'Lydia, I'd like to say I'm sorry.'

Her eyes narrow, and I continue to speak, 'I didn't understand it before and I now realise how badly I hurt you. That was never my intention, I promise.' She's watching me intently, waiting for me to go on. 'I hope you can forgive me one day and I hope you find the happiness you're looking for.'

Her facial expression softens when she starts to speak. 'You've had your heart broken, haven't you?'

'Is it that obvious?' I play with the car keys in my pocket, feeling uneasiness, and Lydia only nods. 'Yes, it is.'

'How do you get over it?'

'I'll tell you when I find out.' She shrugs and puts her hand on my shoulder. 'It's fine, Gabriel. If you love someone, make sure you fight for them until the very last breath.' She offers the tiniest smile before walking away.

'Gabriel!' Theo calls out and races toward me, wrapping his hands around me.

'Alright buddy?' I chuckle out.

'Yeah, dad got a new job yesterday, so we ordered pizza to celebrate.'

'That's' great.' I grin widely.

'Mr. Alstons, hello.' Theo's mum, Christine, appears in the hallway. 'Please, come in.'

We make our way into the living room. The apartment still has the same mouldy smell and I can not wait to change the living conditions for everyone here.

'I'm only here for a moment, I was wondering if I could have a look at Theo's room so we could start designing what he'd like it to look like.' Theo's eyes light up and he turns swiftly to his mother, jumping up and down. 'Oh, my god.'

She laughs at his reaction. 'Of course, go ahead.'

As we enter the room, I feel as if the air been knocked out of my lungs. Grey walls, dark brown curtains, beige carpet and a single bed with white sheets. This is not a room for a 10-year-old boy. I only spot a couple of cars and a school backpack in the corner.

'Where do you do your homework?'

He shrugs and points to the bed.

'Tell me what you like.' I say as I take in this small room and plan in my head what I'll do to it.

'Football. I'm going to be a football star.' He says excitedly.

'And your favourite colour?'

'Erm... green!'

Noted.

'Well, I've got some ideas for your room but I'm going to keep it as a surprise if that's ok.' A wide grin appears on his face as he nods.

I now park on the side of a sandy road and notice Max making his way to me.

'How you doing, mate?' I step out of the car and we do the bro hug.

'Just been to Theo's and god man... You would not want to see his room.'

'That bad?' We talk as we make our way onto the building site. The foundation is done which I'm thrilled about and they're starting to build the columns.

'Me and Tess are going to Mexico next week.' He announces, which takes me by surprise.

'What for?'

'A holiday.' He shrugs and kicks dirt with his foot.

'Max is taking a girl on a holiday? That's new.'

'Don't be rude. I'm a new man.' He pulls on the collar of his shirt and lifts his chin up.

'Well, good for you, man.' I slap him on the shoulder. Even if I don't always seem it, I'm happy for them. I won't lie, it has taken me by surprise at first as Max was an even bigger womanizer than me and he wasn't even sure he liked Tess at that level, but within one dinner, he started singing a different song. I can't exactly question him, as isn't it similar to my situation? Being kissed by a stranger lead me to falling in love for the first time in my life. No one prepares you for that. You think love is just full of butterflies and laughs and sex, but no one tells you about the heartache that also comes with it, when the person you love doesn't want you.

'Tess tells me Brooke got the deal in New York.' He adds, and of course he had to bring her up.

'Yes, I heard that too.'

'Do you think she'll take it?'

'I doubt it. She won't leave her friends or her mum behind.' He nods slowly in response.

The architect is already waiting for me, with the plans lay down on a camp table. We say our hello and general chitchat about how things are going and so far, everything is ahead of the time, which makes me very happy. I'm not building a villa, but it'll be spacious enough to have some gatherings indoors. I will fence the land with an electric gate, so I know Bruno won't escape.

'So, Mr. Alstons, how are you today?'

'I'm good, Ellie. How are you?'

'All well, sir.' She makes a slight accent on the word sir. I've been aware of her secret hints since we signed the contract, but I also have been uninterested. She doesn't seem to get my hints, and that's my guess, because how can someone be standing out in this cold, in a coat that barely covers her ass with the zip undone so her tits pop up? I'm not that man anymore and I'd prefer Brooke in her oversized hoodie than a stranger who dresses provocatively.

'So, I've got the plans here for the layout of the room, but I just wanted to check with you what it's all going to be.' She leans on the table, shoving her ass out, looking like she's about to be taken from the back. Max gives me the look and I shrug, quietly snorting, before coming up to the table and studying the layout.

'So this is the living room area, correct?' She points her pen in the biggest section of downstairs.

'Yes.'

'And to the right there's going to be an open-plan kitchen.'

'Yep.'

'Now, we have this area on the left. Is it going to be your office?'

'No.'

Her brow arches. 'Can I ask what is it going to be?'

'It'll be a private little library, but with a big desk by the window. Call it a writer's office.' I smile to myself.

CHAPTER THIRTY-NINE

Brooke

I type in on my laptop Apartments for rent New York, and I press the first link which takes me to zillow.com. I scroll down, looking at different prices, neighbourhoods, sizes and trying to decide which would suit me best. Name Gabriel still appears on my phone when I glance at it, reading his last message.

Gabriel- I miss you.

That was yesterday and I still haven't replied, and I'm not going to. I realise now that the only way we can move on is for me to disappear and take a chance at the fresh start. The entire city of London is now tainted for me. The air is hard to breathe and in every corner I take, I'm terrified of seeing him. But then Miss. Brown's words sound in my mind, about how lonely it gets. Well, if it means I get to be alone but never get hurt again, so be it. I'll do my best to be happy with my work and my books.

Tyler also loved me at first, I believe. There was also the

chemistry and electricity and our bond when we were inseparable. He kissed me, he made me laugh, and he cared... until he didn't. Everyone feels happy at the beginning until real life kicks in and you realise it's not all butterflies anymore. It's putting up with each other's anger, feeling of boredom, shifts in moods and more. Gabriel has never been in a relationship, yet he expects me to jump into his arms so we can ride into a sunset together.

I am ready to get on with my life, though, to start a new chapter where no one else will make my decisions other than me. My heart healed once already so I know it can do it again. The worst part is that I know Gabriel owns a piece of it, and I'll never be able to get it back. So the best way to avoid him is to get as far away as possible.

Knock. Knock.

I jump at the sudden sound. I'm not expecting anyone, but I get up and open the door to find my mom standing there with a tray of cakes.

'I love you.' I say with a smile.

'I love you too, honey.' She comes in, setting the tray on the table.

'Oh, I love you too, mom but I was talking to the cakes.' She rolls her eyes, and we both burst out laughing. But the moment she glances at the screen of my laptop, her lips turn into a frown.

'You decided.' It's a statement, not a question.

I put my hands into the pockets of my jeans and lower my gaze. 'Well...'

'Brooke, hun ... I am so proud of you.' My gaze snaps to her, my eyes wide open in surprise at her words.

'You're what?' I ask to confirm I didn't mishear it. She chuckles and then comes up to me, pulling me into a hug. 'I'm proud of you. Your dream is coming true.' Tears fill my eyes as she pulls away and I see her eyes glistening, too. 'You've always wanted this and I know dad would be proud of you too.' She offers me a smile.

'Thanks, mom.'

'Let me make us some tea.' She rushes over to the kettle and pushes the button down. I pull out two mugs and two green tea bags to throw in. I open the tray, but as I reach for a slice of cake, a hand slaps mine away.

'Ouch.' I pull it away, rubbing it with my other hand.

'Have some control, young lady.'

I scoff jokingly, and she returns to making us tea.

'I just hope it has nothing to do with Mr. Alstons?' She speaks without looking at me.

'Mom...' I plea her to stop as I jump up to sit on the worktop.

'Honey, I understand the deal, ok? But I'd hate for you to accept it simply based on escaping him. He loves you, you know?' She picks up the two mugs and passes me one.

'How do you know that?' I arch my brow and she laughs.

'Brooke, I wasn't sure who was more in love at that wedding, Kate and her husband, or you two. Trust me when I say everybody saw it.' The air leaves my lungs, making it difficult to breathe.

'I saw it in you, too.'

I scoff, 'We're outstanding actors.'

'You're a terrible actress.'

'Mom, I'm about to sign the contract and the deal will be done, ok?' She pulls her lips into a thin line and I see her shoulders move up and down slowly.

'Where is this contract?'

'It's over...' I gesture to the coffee table but freeze when I see Nala holding the contract in her mouth. 'Nala, what are you doing?' I set my mug on the table and take slow steps towards her. 'Hey baby, come here...give it back, please.' I pull out my hand, pretending I have a treat for her, but she doesn't even flinch. 'Nala...' She then shakes her head swiftly and with a help of her paws shreds the paper into pieces, 'No!' I shout and run, unable to save it. I shoo Nala away before realising I have a lot of small pieces of the contract instead of one. I drop on the sofa as I exhale with annoyance.

'Well, I'm guessing that's going to be a problem?' My mom picks up my mug and brings it over to the coffee table. Nala stares at me with her tail wagging.

Traitor.

'I'll need to get another copy.' I rush to the table and pick up my phone, dialling Miss. Brown's number.

'Brooke, hi, how are you?' She answers on the second ring.

'Hi, Miss. Brown, I've got a slight problem. My dog chewed the contract as I was about to sign it. Is there anyway I could get a new copy?'

'You know what? How about we fly you over and we can sign everything here? We'll start the apartment search right away.'

'Excuse me, what?!' Aaron shouts as I throw another top in my suitcase. 5 days ago, I made my decision and now I'm flying back to New York to make it a reality.

'I told you, I'm going to New York.' I study the clothes that lie on my bed before folding them and organising them into piles.

'You're going today and you're just telling me?' His arms are crossed over his chest as he watches me from the doorframe.

'I knew you'd try to stop me.' I reply in a flat tone. There is no turning back.

'Of course I would. I think you're making a mistake.'

'It's done now, anyway.'

'Not until you sign the contract, it isn't.'

I tilt my head back and exhale loudly, 'Aaron, please. I've decided.'

'To be stubborn and run away from happiness.' I turn to face him now.

'To start fresh, to be able to finally live my dream, to be happy.'

'Call it whatever you want, Brooke, but you're running away because you're so scared of getting hurt, even though Gabriel was ready to give you the world.'

I scoff. 'And how do you know that?'

He inhales deeply before speaking again. 'Because I have spoken to him occasionally.' My eyes shot wide open. 'What?'

He takes a seat on my bed and starts taking out my clothes of the suitcase. 'He called me a few times, wanting advice on what to do about you?'

'And what did you tell him?' I take the clothes he got out and put them back in.

'Well, the day after the wedding I told him to tread carefully as he might scare you if he just tells you he loves you.'

My mind travels back to the morning, where he told me he had to make a phone call before leaving back for London.

'It doesn't matter anymore.'

He takes another pile of clothes out.

'Stop it!' I bark and put them back inside.

'Brooke, did you know he's building your dream home?' I freeze in place as my gaze meets his. 'Wh-what?'

'Tess told me. Max saw the plans and from the description she recognised the home you have the photo of on your board.' My heart races and my stomach twists. He looked at that board when he was here; he saw the photo. Is he really building my dream home?

I shrug, 'I don't care.'

A snort leaves his mouth. 'Yes, you do.' A sting of his words hit me and I close my eyes, feeling them burning.

It hurts, because I know he's right.

CHAPTER FORTY

Gabriel

The phone rings just as I lift the stick with weights on above me. I slowly lower it before picking it up off the floor.

'Aaron?' I answer.

'She's doing it! Gab...she.... ed...now...' I hear the urgency in his voice, but the signal is bad, so I make my way to the door and go upstairs.

'Mate, I can't hear you. Are you driving?'

'Yeah. I...ooke.... ica....' Well, this is useless. I race upstairs now, taking two steps at the time.

'Say it again, Aaron!' I call out as I reach the top floor and head to the kitchen to get a bottle of water.

'Brooke is moving to America!' I freeze. 'She decided to take on the deal and move and now she's on her way to sign the contract and look for the apartment! Gabriel, she's not listening to me, she's too freaking stubborn! Do something!' He shouts into his speaker.

'Which airport?!' I demand while searching furiously for my car keys.

'Heathrow! She's on her way there now!' I hang up and run out, leaving the fridge door open behind. I ignore the elevator and jump down the stairs as quickly as I can, rushing to the underground garage. When lifting my hand up to unlock the car, I drop the keys.

'Fuck!' I turn around and try to pick them up just to drop them again. The anger builds up inside, and I feel like I'm going to explode. She's not moving to America. She's not going anywhere, even if I have to force her to let me publish her book.

Once in the car, I put the phone on the stand and start the engine. Pulling out of my space, I'm making the wheels spin before I drive out. I dial her name, but it goes straight to the voicemail.

'Brooke! God damn it! I'm on my way to the airport! You're not going anywhere, do you hear me?! Please, wait for me! I fucking beg you, Brooke! I love you, ok? I want to spend the rest of my life proving it to you, but I can't do it when you are halfway across the fucking globe. Brooke, please, I will never ever hurt you! Call me when you get this message! And do not get on the fucking plane!' I finish the call and inhale deeply. My hands are shaky as I hold onto the steering wheel, overtaking any car that's in my way. I dial Max's number.

'What's up, mate?'

'Brooke is moving to America!' I shout out.

'What?!'

'I'm on my way to the airport now to stop her!'

'Shit. Do you need me to do anything?'

'I don't know... I need you to talk to me.'

'Ok. Listen, you'll make it in time, ok? I know you will and she'll finally change her mind.' I exhale with my shaky breath. My chest tightens and my brain fogs.

'What if I'm too late?'

'Mate, only one way to find out.' There are some whispers coming through the speaker before Tess' voice comes through.

'Remember, she loves you!' I nod to myself. Burning of my

eyes makes it harder to see ahead. I move to overtake another car without noticing a car coming from the other direction. I press on the gas even harder and I just about make it back into my lane. An exhale of relief leaves my mouth.

'I gotta go.'

'Keep us updated ... It'll be ok.' Tess answers.

I fucking hope so.

I dial Brooke's number again, but it goes straight to voicemail again.

'For fuck's sake, Brooke! Turn your bloody phone on and call me. Do you understand me? I don't know if I'll make it in time or if you will listen to my messages before getting on the plane but...' I take a deep breath in and my voice calms before I speak again, '... if I don't make it and I don't see you again... promise me one thing. Be happy, ok? All I want for you is to be happy and be yourself. Spread your wings like the butterfly on your back and live your life to the fullest. I'll be the first person to buy your book... I am so proud of you, baby. I knew you could do it... I just hate that your happiness doesn't include me... I love you...' I exhale deeply and hang up.

CHAPTER FORTY-ONE

PART 1

Brooke

I thank the taxi driver and hand him the money. Pulling my suitcase behind me, I make my way to the security check out. When I pull my phone out, I notice it's dead, so I quickly pull out my charger from the suitcase and put it in my bag so I can charge it soon. Once the bag has been checked in, I go through the security, but with each step, my body feels heavier, as if it's trying to stop me. Unfortunately, I've made my decision so... that's that. I go through without buzzing, which is a first for me, and I search for a place where I can get a drink while I wait. I order a hot chocolate from Starbucks and sit down at the table that has a plug for my charger. After plugging the phone in, I take a sip of my drink and glance around at all people who wait for their flights. A couple sit down at the table next to mine and I can't help but to overhear them talking.

'I'm so excited, baby.' A young woman calls out excitedly.

'I'm so happy to call you my fiancé now.' A sound of a kiss reaches my ears and I flinch.

'I love you, baby.' The woman says.

'I love you too.'

I close my eyes, trying to clear my mind. Why do I want to leave this airport and drive to him? I don't understand why I'm still so... stuck in the place and I can't get out of it. My body burns at the mere thought of him. My eyes burn when I imagine my life without him. But that's what I want, that's the life I want to live, so why am I struggling to do this?

My phone comes to life, and it pings, telling me I have two voice messages. I put my earphones in and dial the voice inbox. My stomach drops at the sound of his voice. He's coming here. He's on his way right now to stop me. My eyes widen in shock and a tear escapes. He wants me to stay...

Then the second messages plays ... '*Be happy...*' '*I'm proud of you....*' '*I love you...*' now tears fall freely as I'm unable to stop them. My heart aches... no, it burns in agony... he truly wants what's best for me.

I see it now.

But we're a history now. My life is not in London anymore and I have to finish what I have now started. I can only hope he'll understand. I open the music app on my phone and put a playlist on, If Only by Dove Cameron plays. After setting the phone down, I take another sip of my hot chocolate. Miss. Brown's words sing in my head, '*it's lonely.*' '*no one to share your day with.*' '*coming to an empty house.*'

My heart pounds against my chest as I try to stop the tears. I finally decided on something by myself, so why suddenly the decision feels wrong? Right now I wish someone could tell me what to do, but knowing myself id still argue. I'm struggling to understand what's the right thing to do is right now, knowing I'm a step away from having my dream come true but also Gabriel is on his way to me... he's not turning around, that was clear from his message. But I'm not calling him ... I wouldn't know what to say to him...

Let me go.

Find me.

Take me home.

Forget I ever existed.

So many thoughts are going through my mind right now, I feel dizzy. Of course, I return his feelings; it was known to me for a long time, but what if it doesn't work out, what if one day I wake up and regret choosing him… do I even have to choose? I have another deal here but I chose the one on another continent … And why? To run away from him. To run away from someone who only wants to see me happy.

I push myself off the seat and race to the window. Maybe if I see the plane, I'll know. I'll know this is the right thing to do. There'll be no going back from it once I step on the plane. My gaze lowers to a line of airplanes and I stare and stare at them… feeling nothing but dread. Can I have both? Can I have my dream and him? I've never wished more than now to have my dad with me to tell me what to do. Tears start spilling again as I rest my forehead on the window. A sound of an engine vibrates through the air and when I look up, I see a plane take off in the air and on it, as clear as the sky says 'for the purest of loves' with a dandelion around it. I gasp and throw my hand over my mouth.

A dandelion.

'Don't live your life where one day you'll wonder what if.' It hits me right in the chest, words pouring into it, every word from my mum, Aaron, Tess and Gabriel hit me at once.

I know what I need to do.

CHAPTER FORTY-ONE

PART 2

Gabriel

Thanks to the bloody traffic, it took me way too long to get here. Even a fast car can't overtake the queues of cars ahead, so I was stuck. I was stuck with thoughts of her leaving. The sun is hidden behind thick, grey clouds when I jump out of the car and notice it's starting to snow.

'Oi, you can't park here!' someone calls out, but I ignore them as I race inside. I run to the check-in desk.

'Flight to New York.' I place my hands on my knees as I try to catch my breath.

'Excuse me?' A woman struggles to understand.

'New York flight.' I manage to choke out.

'Yes?'

'Can I have a ticket, please?' She looks into her computer and I realise one thing i didn't think about. I don't have my fucking passport…

'I'm sorry.' I walk away before she can speak.

My gaze travels to the security.

Should I?

No. It's stupid.

But I'm also stupidly in love with her.

I make my way to the security guard.

'I need to see someone.' I demand.

'Yes?'

'Yes. And I'll be happy to pay for you to allow me through.'

He snorts, 'Can't do that. Sorry, mate.'

Think, man. Think.

'How much?' He just stands there with his hands behind him.

'£1000.' I see his eye twitch. I'm going to win.

'£2000.' His mouth opens slightly.

'£5000.' His gaze meets mine.

I've got you.

'You got anything banned on you?' He asks quietly.

I put my hands up in defence. 'Just my phone and car keys, I swear.' He looks me up and down and then he opens the barrier. I pull out a business card from my wallet and pass it to him. 'Call me and I'll get you the money.' He nods and takes it.

'Thank you.' I murmur before racing away from him.

I'm now stuck in the queue to the security. An older lady is next to the front of the line, so I push myself through to her.

'Hello.' I offer her a warm smile.

'Oh, hello.' She replies, smiling back.

'I know this might sound crazy, but out there....' I point to past the security, '...is a woman who I love very much and if I don't make it to her in time, I'm going to lose her forever.'

'Oh.' Her eyes widen. 'Like in a movie?'

I chuckle. 'Yes, like in a movie. Now, can I ask you if you'd be kind enough to let me through?' I put my hands together in a prayer position.

'Anything for real love, right?' She winks at me and gestures for me to go in front of her.

'Thank you.' I choke out and go straight through. Luck is

with me when I don't buzz and can carry on. My heart races as I get nearer.

'Which gate for New York flight?' I ask one of the security guys.

'11'

I run without saying thank you. I run and run, my whole body burning, longing to see her. My throat is dry and I don't even notice the cold, considering I'm wearing gym shorts and a vest. My focus is on her and her only. I bump into a group of people and apologise as I carry on running.

Be there. Please be there.

I reach the gate 11 but there's no one there. A woman stands by the door, so I rush to her.

'New York flight?!' I shout louder than necessary, which makes her jump.

'I'm sorry.'

'It's ok.' She chuckles. 'I didn't see you there, sir.'

'New York flight?'

She looks to the right through the window.

'That's it.' She points to the plane that is taking off into the air, flying far, far away, along with my whole heart on board.

A stab of agony hits me as I walk up slowly to the window, my gaze following the plane and I slam my fists into it.

'Fuck!'

I missed her. I'm too late and she's gone. My eyes are burning like fire, so I allow the tears to escape. All the fighting was a waste. I've lost her and there is no coming back now. She's on her way to a life without me and maybe I need to be ok with it. Is that how my mother felt, giving me away, knowing I'll be better off somewhere else? Shit, this is harder than I ever expected.

I leave the airport and see a parking fine on my car.

Awesome.

It's now snowing heavily, but my head doesn't register the cold. People stare at me as my gaze lifts to the sky. It's dark, but snow lights up the surroundings. It's quiet – Too quiet. You know the quiet when it snows, and it blocks any background noises? Yes. That quiet. I thought I was empty before but it doesn't compare to how I feel now. Everything I worked for feels... pointless now. Nothing is worth doing if she's not here. I swallow a hard lump in my throat and I see a man in his 40s, having a cigarette in a smoking area.

'Excuse me?' I come up to him, and he looks me up and down and frowns.

'Bloody hell, man. Aren't you freezing?'

'I'm ok. Can I... maybe...' my gaze lowers to his hand.

'You want a cigarette?' I nod in response. He pulls out a pack and lets me pull one out. I use his lighter, thank him, and make my way to the car.

My body shakes and I don't know if it's because of the cold or at the loss of her. I cough a few times, but I force myself to finish it.

Smoking is meant to help with stress, but I find no relief from it. I throw the bud to the ground and step on it. When I get in the car, I quickly put the heating on, rubbing my hands together to warm them up. I set my phone on the stand again. I feel... I can't even decide on what I feel... sadness and anger are two main things. I rest my head on the headrest and stare straight ahead. My whole chest aches, wanting me to allow the pain to explode. My head throbs. A painful 'Fuck!' leaves my mouth when I slam my hand onto the steering wheel multiple times.

Once I calm down, I find myself breathless. I look at my phone and dial Max.

'Did you make it?!' I can tell I'm on the speaker.

'No.' I choke out.

There's a long pause.

'The plane took off by the time I got there.'

'Gabe...' I hear Tess sobbing in the background.

'I'm going to...' I stop what I'm saying, because I can't believe my own eyes. I lean forward to see better and my whole body comes to life, burning, making me want to throw up when I see Brooke standing now outside the entrance, with her suitcase behind her. She seems to be looking for a taxi.

'Gabe? You there, mate?' I don't respond. Like a robot, I open the door and step out of the car, not taking my gaze off her the whole time, in case I'm hallucinating. She then looks in my direction and almost takes a step back, surprised to see me. She looks me up and down, and frowns. Her beautiful brown hair is covered in snow as she makes her way toward me. I take steps forward too. And before I know it, we're standing right in front of each other.

'You didn't...' I start, but struggle to speak. She gives me a nod.

'I didn't get on.' Her chin shakes just slightly and I touch her hair to make sure she's real.

'Why...?' A tear escapes and falls down my cheek when I see a matching tear on her face.

'I don't want to wonder what if one day...'

'But... but your deal.'

'I have another deal here in UK I told no one about.'

I let out a small chuckle.

'So...'

She lets go of the suitcase, allowing it to drop to the ground, and cups my face in her hands. My whole body coming to life at her touch, forgetting about the temperature surrounding us.

'So...' A wide grin appears on her face. 'I love you, Gabriel.' And just like that, with these three words, I'm put together.

'And you'll never leave me again?'

She shakes her head. 'Never again.'

I pull her into my arms, holding her tight as the sound of her beautiful laughter reaches my ears.

'I can't breathe.' She chuckles out.
'I don't care.' I put my head on hers, breathing her in.
She's mine.
'I love you.'
'I love you too.' She finally answers.

EPILOGUE

Brooke
2 years later

The scent of the cinnamon jerks me awake. I turn to see a plate filled with churros and a chocolate dip next to it.

'Mmm, morning.' I murmur as I stretch arms and legs.

'Morning, baby.' Gabriel replies, placing a kiss on my forehead. He sits down next to me, stroking the hair off my face.

'Are churros even appropriate in the middle of July?' I chuckle as I prop myself up on my elbow.

'If it means you'll moan in your sexual, cute way as you do when you eat them, then I'll make them every day.'

I take a bite of the churro and a moan escapes my mouth involuntarily.

'That's it.' He shoves the covers off me, making me laugh while trying to swallow. His hands grip at the hem of my pj's bottoms and he pulls them off me.

'That's rather early.' I choke out, placing one arm behind my head.

'You eat your food and I'll eat what's mine.' My heart

flutters as he lowers himself between my legs. His fingers stroke against my pussy through the fabric of my thong.

'That's my girl. Always ready for me.' His cheerful voice reaches me.

'Let the feast begin.' He announces, before taking my clit into his mouth. I try to laugh, but the arousal takes over as he sucks hard. I grip onto the sheet with both hands and moan loudly. He slips his finger inside me, groaning in pleasure himself.

'Should... we... get... ready?' I manage to ask between my moans but he ignores it and adds in a second finger, rubbing my g spot aggressively. This man doesn't need to do much to make me come, and of course, within the next few pushes, I shatter as the orgasm explodes through my core, making my toes curl.

As I catch my breath, Gabriel sits up again with a wide grin on his face.

'Now we can get ready.' I laugh as he gets up and takes his clothes off seductively.

'I'm now getting a pole dance?'

He stops and looks around. 'Yeah, I think we need a pole in here.' A laugh bursts out of me.

'I'm first.' A quick kiss is placed on my lips before he disappears into the bathroom. I sit up in bed and take another bite of my hot churros.

I don't think I could ever get sick of them.

I get up, throw a dressing gown on, and make my way downstairs. Heading to the kitchen, I put the mug down on the coffee machine and turn it on. The sounds of it pouring liquid fill the room. Once done, I take it and go to my study. Placing the mug on the desk, I power up the laptop. Seeing the screen comes to life, I log into my email and see no new messages.

While sipping on my coffee, I glance at the photos on my desk.

1. Me and Gabriel on our wedding day, only last month.
2. Me and Gabriel in front of our built house.
3. Me with my book on the publication day
4. Me and Nala.

After I called Mr. Maxwell and told him I decided to go with the English publisher, he was happy to inform me their offer has gone up because they wanted my book so badly. Miss. Brown wasn't even upset when I told her about the change of plans and she said she was happy to see a woman deciding to have it all.

Yes, I do have it all now.

I couldn't believe when I saw this room, and he did it all for me.

So far, I've written two more books in here and both hit bestsellers. Gabriel comes with me to all my singings and is probably my biggest fan when it comes to my writing. He also reads all of them before they get published, which then leads to hours long sex. But I'm not complaining... at least not for 90% of the time. Gabriel also finished his apartment building project, where he renovated all the flats, to make them liveable for its residents and I even met Theo, who is superb at football as we learnt when we went to see one of his matches. We get often invited to dinners, which is lovely as we get to see their lives changing, and becoming better, thanks to my amazing husband. As for Nala, unfortunately she passed away about two months after me and Gabriel got back together. I spent a whole week in bed and he was there for me, allowing me to mourn in any way I needed. I miss her every day and I still think if it wasn't for her, I probably wouldn't even consider the fling with Gabriel. Now, Bruno is still with us, but he's an oldie. We had since adopted two more dogs named Tia and Nessa, the twin Westies. I love them to bits, but they're much younger, which means they often get up to no good.

'Whatcha doing?' Gabriel pops his head through the door, which makes me jump.

'Just... thinking...'

'About how good my hard cock feels inside you?' Heat reaches my cheeks.

'It's ok, you can feel it again tonight.' I chuckle and get up. As passing him in the door, I give him my mug, 'Going for a shower.' And rush upstairs.

Knock knock.

'I've got it!' All dressed in my flowery mid-thigh sundress, I run to the door. I squeal like a little girl when I open it and see Aaron, holding a baby carrier with Dean behind him.

'Come in. Come in. Come in.' I call out, opening the door wider. We all say our hellos and head to the living room. It's probably one of my favourite rooms in this house, with its floor to ceiling windows, allowing so much sunlight in, the warm brown and crème colours, giving a proper country living vibe. It's so big, yet the colour makes it so warm.

'I wanna see her!' I rush to Aaron's side when he sets the carrier on our large coffee table and Gabriel shoos the excited dogs away. Taking a peek inside, I see a beautiful baby girl, fast asleep.

'Ohhhhhh....' Aaron chuckles and my amazing husband brings over a tray with four coffees.

'How was the flight?' I ask as we all take our seats, me and Gabriel on the sofa and Aaron with Dean on a big snuggler. 'It was good. She slept the whole way.' Dean speaks up and I can't take stop looking at her beautiful almond-shaped eyes and her black hair.

'It still doesn't feel real.' Aaron adds as Dean takes his hand and squeezes it.

'I bet.' Gabriel chimes in now. 'So, is everything completed?' They both nod in response.

'We couldn't thank you enough, Gabriel. We owe you our lives for paying for the flights.' Aaron's eyes glisten and my heart melts for them. My gorgeous husband just waves it away.

'Not a problem. You gave her an amazing, loving home, so that's what matters.' I squeeze his thigh and smile at him.

'So, what's her name?' I turn back to Aaron and Dean and they're both grinning widely now.

'Say hello to Nicole Brooke Marshall.'

Tears immediately spill from my eyes and Aaron rushes to pull me into his arms. Gabriel just chuckles.

'I love it.' He comments as he glances at little Nicole.

'It wouldn't be possible if it wasn't for you two.' Dean now speaks. Me and Gabriel both snort at the same time. 'Don't worry about it.'

'Now, maybe auntie Brooke can give her a little cousin.' Aaron says, and my eyes widen in horror. I snap my gaze to Gabriel, but he only shrugs with a cheeky smirk on his face.

'I think I'm happy with auntie title for now.' I explain. 'I mean, we're busy now, ain't we?' I look back at Gabriel and he nods in confirmation. 'But maybe one day, who knows?' I smile and Aaron sighs.

'Yes, auntie Brooke Gertrude Alstons.' Gabriel tells everyone and Aaron gasps in shock.

'Gertrude?! You told me you didn't have a middle name!' He laughs so hard, a tear rolls down his cheek.

'You'll pay for this.' I mutter to Gabriel, whose smirk remains.

'Anyone know where Tess is now?' I ask to quickly change the subject, but Gabriel shrugs again.

'Last I heard... they've gone to Cuba,' Aaron says, holding onto his stomach and now calming down.

'Still can't believe she got Max wrapped around her little finger.' Gabriel snorts out and takes another sip of his coffee.

'She's worth it thou.' I elbow him in the side.

'He's planning on proposing.' He adds blankly, as if it wasn't news of the year. Me and Aaron gasp at the same time.

'Do not...' He points his finger at me, then at Aaron, '...say anything to her!'

'Yes, sir.' We shout out in sync.

'Anyway, how was your honeymoon?' Dean asks us and my lips pull into a grin as I lean back into the cushion. 'Amazing. No one tells you how friendly Greek people are! And the weather and food ... Oh, we're definitely going back.' I nod.

'I still can't believe your whole contract thing.' Aaron snorts out.

'What?' My brow arches.

'You know, the rules so you don't catch feelings...'

'Oh.' I cringe at the memory, and Gabriel laughs.

'It was such a love me not thing to do. But then you scratched the not off.' He shakes his head.

I only shrug in response. 'I told him to not love me, but he couldn't help himself.'

'That's correct...' Gabriel replies. Our eyes lock and my heart bursts with the love I have for this man and our love me not story.

Once Aaron and Dean put Nicole in the car and say their byes, Gabriel turns to me in the door.

'You don't want a baby?' He asks.

'I mean... I'm ok as we are now, but maybe one day... You?' He smiles widely at me.

'As long as I've got you, I'm more than happy.' My heart flutters at his declaration. His hands travel to the hem of my dress, but I slap them away.

'They haven't left yet.' I murmur out, and we both turn and wave to them as they drive away.

'Now?' He asks, and a laugh escapes my mouth.

'Sure.'

He lifts up the hem of my dress and strokes the fabric against my pussy. I immediately notice the bulge in his jeans.

'My dick has been very lonely today.' He murmurs.

'Are you sure, ***sir***?'

'Oh yes.' He nods, smirking at me in that dark way that makes me clench my legs. 'So lonely.' Another laughter escapes me as he leans in and rests his forehead on mine.

'Mine.' He whispers.

'Yours.'

The End

AUTHOR'S NOTE

What can I say other than a massive thank you for choosing my book as your next read! I've spent days and sometimes nights, writing, proof reading and editing, hoping to one day be able to publish this story. I hope Brooke taught you that risks are sometimes worth taking and sometimes, things we try to avoid, find their way back to us because it is exactly what we needed. I met my husband when I was ready to give up on love and now I've been happily married for 9 years.

So know this... Life is full of surprises.

I'd like to thank my husband Andy and my friends Sophie and Gemma for being my supporters throughout the process and kicking me in the ass when I was ready to give up.... on multiple occasions. You know the days where you feel like you're not good enough? Yeah, they did not allow me to have them.

I also want to say big thank you to my BETA readers: Sophie, Jess, Gemma, Shannon and Natalie. (I really hope I didn't forget anyone?). You all helped me believe in myself and I love you for it.

And big thanks to my husband who would much rather paint his Warhammer figures than read, yet he proof-read my book to check for any last mistakes because he knew I was sick of staring at my draft. ***You're my hero, baby.***

You can find me on Instagram and Tiktok under the name paulinabaker_author

P.S I'm already plotting my second book which I'm very excited for. ;)

instagram.com/paulinabaker_author
tiktok.com/@paulinabaker_author

Printed in Great Britain
by Amazon

14367053R00200